THEY
ALL
FALL
DOWN

ALSO BY TAMMY COHEN

DYING FOR CHRISTMAS

THEY ALL FALL DOWN

TAMMY COHEN

PEGASUS CRIME
NEW YORK LONDON

THEY ALL FALL DOWN

Pegasus Books Ltd
148 West 37th Street, 13th Fl.
New York, NY 10018

First Pegasus Books hardcover edition March 2018

ISBN: 978-1-68177-647-7

10 9 8 7 6 5 4 3 2 1

Printed in the United States of America
Distributed by W. W. Norton & Company, Inc.

For the Tuesday Club – Ed, Steve and Jo.
Because every day should be a Tuesday.

1

Hannah

Charlie cut her wrists last week with a shard of caramelized sugar.

We'd made the sugar sheets together in the clinic's kitchen earlier in the day, under Joni's beady-eyed supervision.

'Yours are thick enough to do yourself an injury,' I'd said to Charlie, as a joke.

'I wonder if that's what gave her the idea,' Odelle commented afterwards, pointedly.

After Charlie died, *Bake Off* went on the banned-programmes list.

I don't feel guilty, though, because I don't think Charlie killed herself. Just as I don't think poor Sofia killed herself. In a high-suicide-risk psych clinic like this, people die all the time. It's one of the clinic's USPs. That's what makes it so easy for a killer to hide here, in plain sight. That and the fact that the only witnesses are us, and no one believes a word we say.

You don't have to be mad to live here but . . . oh, hang on, yes, you do.

I'm frightened. I'm frightened that I'm right and I'll be next. I'm even more frightened that I'm wrong, in

1

which case I'm as crazy as they all think I am. Shut away in here, the only escape is in my own head. But what if my own head's the most dangerous place to be?

Stella comes into my room and lies across the end of my bed without speaking. Her skin is stretched tight over the sharp points of her cheeks and I can't look at it for fear it might tear.

'It's not true,' I tell her.

My room is at the side of the building. I am sitting by the window in the beige armchair, looking out across the rose garden to where a half-hearted rain is drip, drip, dripping from the flat roof of the dance studio and running down the wall of folding glass doors. All the furniture in my room is a variation on beige. Ecru. Biscuit. Stone. The whole of the upstairs is the colour of a surgical bandage. To avoid us getting over-stimulated, I imagine. Not much chance of that in here.

Stella turns her head so her wide blue eyes are fixed on mine. The necklace she always wears has fallen to the side so that the tiny silver cat seems to be nestling into the duvet.

'How do you know?' she says at last, in her soft, smoker's voice.

I frown at her.

'Come on,' I say. 'It's Charlie.'

'Was,' she says. And starts to cry.

The Meadows is an old Georgian-style country house, complete with ivy growing across the front and elegant floor-to-ceiling sash windows. From the semicircular gravel drive at the front you might imagine yourself on

2

the set of a Jane Austen adaptation where at any moment the grand front door will burst open to disgorge a gaggle of giggling young women in bonnets. But drive around to the car park behind the house and the impression is ruined by a large modern extension stuck on to the back, giving the overall effect of a stylish man with a bad toupee.

All the consulting rooms and the day room and admin and therapy rooms are in the old part, while the cafeteria and the bedrooms are in the new bit. Sofia told me once the old part was haunted, but I've never sensed anything weird. Mind you, I was so numb when I first arrived a ghost could have climbed right on to my lap and I wouldn't have registered it. The thing about staying in a place like this, where we have group therapy twice a day and keep journals detailing our every thought, is that we're so busy gazing inwards we're blind to what's going on all around us.

Which might explain how two women have been killed and nobody seems to have noticed but me.

The art therapy room is at the back of the old house with two huge windows giving out on to the car park and beyond to the flower garden and then the vegetable plot. The jewel in the Meadows' crown – the manicured lawn leading down to a lake that is disproportionately large and deep, a legacy of an earlier, grander incarnation of the house – is hidden from view by the ugly jut of the new extension on the left.

It is ten o'clock on Wednesday morning and we are at art therapy. Laura gets out the poster paints and asks us to do a self-portrait. The last time we did this exercise she gave us mirrors made of plastic instead of glass, so our reflections were smudgy, like we were looking at ourselves through smoke. 'Sorry,' she said when we complained. 'Regulations. You know how it is.' But today is different.

'I want you to paint yourselves the way you see yourselves when you close your eyes,' she says. 'Where are you? What are you doing? What are you wearing? Don't overthink it. And don't pay any heed to the camera. Just forget it's there.'

The film crew – which most of the time consists only of director/presenter Justin Carter and his cameraman Drew Abbott – have been installed at the clinic for the last seven weeks, just one week less than me. I arrived on the third Monday in January, auspiciously known as Blue Monday, which is officially the most depressing day of the year, although, as you can imagine, competition for that title is fierce in here. Justin and Drew turned up the following week in an SUV loaded with equipment which they carted through from the rain-soaked car park, propping the door to reception open so an icy draught swept through the building and Bridget Ashworth, the clinic's frowning admin manager, bustled about adjusting thermostats and ordering cleaning staff to mop up muddy footprints.

They're calling it a fly-on-the-wall documentary. But Dr Roberts spun it differently: 'An important film in breaking down the taboos surrounding mental illness,' he said. 'Of course, you are all perfectly entitled to opt out of the filming and at any stage you can be retrospectively edited out. But just think what your example could mean to a young woman going through what you've been through, feeling there's nobody out there who could possibly understand.'

4

On the first day, Justin said, 'Just imagine we're not really here.'

'That's how most of us ended up in this place,' Charlie told him. 'For seeing things that aren't there, or not seeing things that are there. You could seriously set back our recovery.'

Justin had smiled without committing himself to laughing, just in case it wasn't appropriate, not understanding that appropriateness is something you leave at the door in here.

Today, in my painting, I am sitting in the low blue velvet chair in Emily's room. Through the sash window behind me the sky is navy and I put in a perfectly round yellowy-white moon so it's obvious it's night-time. I am looking at something over to the right, out of sight. I'm wearing my pale blue dressing gown. My face is a pink blur, streaked with black because I didn't wait long enough for the paint to dry before trying to do the eyes.

'Nice dress,' Laura says when she comes round to look. 'Is that in your house? Your bedroom, maybe?'

I nod. I don't want to tell her the truth because when I talk about Emily it gets noted down in a book and then I have to talk about it at Group. And then Dr Roberts will cock his head to one side and write something in his notebook and I might have to stay here longer. So I don't tell her that the me in the picture is looking at the right-hand corner of Emily's room, where her cot used to be.

Stella's painting is all black, except for a tiny figure at the bottom, naked apart from her long, yellow hair, which reaches almost to the floor. Laura looks at it for a long time and then puts her hand on Stella's narrow shoulder and squeezes before moving on to someone else.

Since Charlie died, all Stella's paintings have been black.

As usual, Odelle has painted herself hugely fat. She's wearing the same black top and skinny jeans the real Odelle has on today and is looking into a mirror in which a slimline version of herself is reflected back. Or maybe it's the other way around and the slim Odelle is the real one and the fat one the reflection. Either way, it's just another variation of Odelle's sole enduring theme. Herself and her body.

'It's very . . . narrative, Odelle,' says Laura. Odelle glances towards the camera at the back of the room, wanting to be sure they are capturing this. 'But just once, I'd love to see you really let rip. This exercise is about here' – Laura taps her chest lightly – 'not about here,' tapping her head.

The mild rebuke sets Odelle's bottom lip trembling. Odelle tends to fixate on people. That's one of the reasons she's in here. That and the fact she weighs around eighty-five pounds. When Charlie first arrived, Odelle apparently fixated on her too for a short while, following her around, sitting too close to her at dinner and on the sofa in the lounge. But mostly it's authority figures she goes for. Roberts is basically God as far as Odelle is concerned, and Laura comes a close second. Odelle's always loitering in the art room after class, offering to help clear away or asking for extra, one-to-one help.

The Meadows believes in niche therapy. We have people who come in to cure us through horticulture, music, baking and movement. Last week, Grace, the aptly named movement therapist, had us fling ourselves around the dance studio pretending to be leaves blown about by the wind and Odelle actually cried. 'I feel so insignificant,' she said. Judith said the reason Odelle got upset was probably because she really did get blown about by the wind, on account of weighing so little.

Basically, nothing happens in here that can't be turned into some kind of therapy. There's even recreational therapy, which really means watching TV. Charlie and I had a running joke about that. Instead of asking if I was going to dinner, she'd say, 'Are you coming to eating therapy?' One time, when I was late down to breakfast, I said I'd been doing some 'pooing therapy' and we laughed for about ten minutes, until Odelle told us we were being childish and also 'insensitive' to all the people in here who 'can't find much to laugh about'.

But Laura is the therapist people get closest to. She used to be a nurse in her younger days, and she still emits that I-can-make-you-better aura. She has her own little office at the back of the art room, with a fan heater and a kettle and several different types of tea, and you can pop in there and curl up on the armchair and wrap yourself up in the soft woollen tartan throw for a chat without feeling like what you say will be noted down in your file somewhere. Laura can be a little bit new-agey. For those who are into that sort of thing, she offers informal meditation or relaxation therapy, which is basically hypnosis. Charlie used to love it in there. 'It's the only part of the clinic where I can be myself,' she told me once. Odelle nips in there at any opportunity. She installs herself in the armchair, with the tartan blanket wrapped around all those other layers she habitually wears, and discusses her favourite subject. Namely, herself.

Laura spends a few moments murmuring something to Nina, who is slumped in front of a piece of paper which is blank apart from a faintly drawn oval. Last week in art she produced seven paintings in one class, her brush flying over the paper, colours bleeding into one another, but today she can hardly summon the energy to lift her stick of charcoal.

Frannie is crying again, tears tracking slowly down her cheeks, and she brushes them away as if she hardly notices them. Her painting has two figures in it, which, strictly speaking, is cheating, but no one is judging. Firstly, there's a huge face with a long, fine nose and a small, full mouth and massive green eyes. The face is Frannie's, and in one of the eyes is another face. It's too small for the features to be identifiable but the black curls mark it out as Charlie.

'Because she's in your thoughts?' asks Laura.

My chest feels tight when I look at the straight brown bob Frannie has given herself in her portrait, hanging just below her chin. The real Frannie is wearing a blue-and-white striped beanie hat, but underneath it her hair is sparse and thin with bald patches that break your heart, vulnerable as the soft part on a newborn baby's head.

My baby was called Emily.

And now I don't want to paint any more.

Later on, in Evening Group, we start, as always, by going round each one of us in the circle, reporting back on whether we've achieved the two goals we each set ourselves this morning. Mine were to start reading a proper book, as opposed to the celebrity magazines which are all I've read for the last two months, and to wash my hair. I failed at the first, the letters moving across the page like lines of tiny ants. But in the second goal I can claim some success, having dragged myself, finally, into the shower, so that my hair, while still a tangled mess, is at least clean for the first time in days. I hate myself for the glow of pleasure I feel when Dr Roberts says 'Well *done*, Hannah,' and everyone gives me a round of applause, as if I've climbed Mount Kilimanjaro or something.

After about half an hour we go back to talking about Charlie. Odelle shares a story about when she first arrived here and was missing her family and had just gone through her first meal with someone sitting next to her monitoring everything that went into her mouth and was curled up on her bed, crying into her pillow – Odelle holds a hand to her face to demonstrate, visibly moved by her own story – and Charlie knocked on her door and sat on the end of the bed and chatted to her, and even made her laugh. That was the thing about Charlie. She could say things to make you laugh so hard your tea came out of your nose. Then she'd go back to her room and make bite marks on her own arm. Of all the people I've met in my life, she was the one who was most forgiving of others – and the least forgiving of herself.

'But she didn't kill herself,' I say, when it's my turn to speak.

Dr Roberts sits back in his seat with one leg crossed over the other at the knee and one elbow hooked over the back of the chair. He has a pen in his hand and he clicks the end in and out as he listens, and nods. His eyes are narrowed so I can't see them, but I know they are blue in some lights and green in others. His hair, brown but liberally threaded with silver, is swept back from his face, although a lock often falls over his left eye when he gets animated. His close-cropped beard is equal measures of silver and brown, and when he smiles, two dimples appear in his cheeks and the lines around his eyes concertina into folds a person could get lost in.

The transference rate – that thing where patients end up in love with their shrinks – is pretty high in our clinic.

'It's a very interesting theory, Hannah.' His voice is warm and honey-coated. 'But you know – we all knew – that Charlie was deeply, chronically depressed. Just because we loved her doesn't mean we could help her. It's inevitable that we all feel some sense of failure that we couldn't do more, and failure is a damned uncomfortable feeling. It's far preferable to imagine she was done away with against her will, because that's not anything we could have prevented or seen coming. But the fact is, we weren't responsible. There's nothing anyone could have done.'

'Yes, we have to forgive ourselves,' adds Odelle.

I look around the circle, where twelve women sit on chairs, one leg twisted around the other, heads bowed, hands fidgeting. I see Frannie plucking at her almost non-existent eyelashes. She studies a hair and then pops it into her mouth. I see Stella staring impassively ahead through her widely stretched eyes. She's wearing a powder-blue dress today that has a tight bodice and a flared skirt. I try not to look at the waist, made artificially

10

tiny by the removal of a rib, nor at the painful swell of her surgically enhanced breasts. I see Odelle, who layers clothes on to her body like she is making papier mâché, leaning forward earnestly, sniffing for approval like a blind laboratory rat. I see Judith and Nina and the eight other inmates – service users, as we're officially known – and Justin and Drew, shadowing our every move with the camera. And though my back is towards the door, in my head I see, through the safety-glass panel behind me, across the hallway and up the sweeping wooden stair-case that leads to the plush consulting rooms, to where Dr Chakraborty, the clinic's deputy director, sits in his office, reading through notes with his sad, brown eyes, while downstairs in the therapy rooms I see Laura and Grace and the other part-time therapists. At the back of the staircase, through the door that leads to the new build-ing, and the cafeteria and kitchen and the Mindfulness Area and the tiny staffroom where the medicines are kept, I see Joni and Darren, the psychiatric nurses, clutching their notebooks, and Bridget Ashworth, the clinic's brisk admin manager, and the well-meaning volunteers and the kitchen staff and the orderlies. All the people charged with keeping us safe. And then my gaze is pulled back here again and I see Dr Oliver Roberts, guru, Svengali, saint, sage, saviour.

Murderer?

It could be him. It could be any of them.

But it definitely happened.

I'd have to be crazy to make a thing like that up.

Towards the end of our session, at about seven thirty, I slip away while the others are still stacking up the chairs.

After eight weeks here, the grandeur of the hallway, with its glass chandelier and vast oil painting of the earl whose home this once was, no longer comes as a surprise. No one uses the front entrance anyway, unless they're an important dignitary or there's a fundraising event going on. The main entrance is round the back in the new wing, where a receptionist checks in visitors and politely searches their bags under the gaze of a smiling Oliver Roberts clad in a formal academic gown in the act of being awarded some honour or other.

But when I go through the door that divides the old building from the new, I don't go straight ahead, past the Mindfulness Area and the blond wood of the cafeteria, to where the vibrant orange reception sofa calls a cheerful greeting, as if to reassure visitors this is not a place conducive to dark thoughts. Instead, I take the first door on the left, which leads to the stairwell, with its muted oatmeal walls, and hurry on up to the bedrooms.

My room is the first on the left, but I walk straight past it and continue down the corridor, with its framed photographs of nature – a close-up of dew on a blade of grass, a feather floating in a muddy puddle, sunlight glittering through a canopy of green leaves. The photographs are caulked to the walls so that we can't take them off and use them against ourselves, or each other. The very last room is Charlie's room.

How many times have I made this journey between my room and hers over the last eight weeks? I'm surprised my feet haven't made indentations in the strip wood flooring. Yet now I feel strange and unease prickles at the back of my neck. I glance up into the eye of a CCTV camera. The camera has always been there, but it is the first time I've really noticed it. Its unblinking stare makes me anxious.

Our doors don't have locks. For obvious reasons. Even so, I'm surprised when Charlie's handle turns. I hesitate before stepping inside.

I've been steeling myself to find her room cleared and emptied of all the things that made it Charlie's. But it's all still there – the blown-up photograph of her and her little nieces in her parents' garden, their three heads dark against an explosion of yellow hibiscus, the lifesize cardboard cutout of Ryan Gosling given to her by an ex-workmate, the old-fashioned patchwork quilt on the bed, a riot of colour amidst the oppressive beigeness.

Yet whereas Charlie was notoriously untidy, with paperbacks piled precariously on the floor next to her bed, and jeans and sweaters strewn over the chair or heaped on the floor, the room has been meticulously tidied. The desk has been cleared of old newspapers and magazines and empty crisp packets, its white surface bland and clean. The bed, which was always messy, as if someone had just that minute got out of it, is now perfectly made, the quilt pulled taut.

I put a hand on the pillow and it feels smooth and unnaturally cold to the touch, like a bar of soap, and I snatch it back. I slide open a desk drawer. Empty, apart from a few pens and a pad of paper. The wardrobe has no door, its edges rounded in case anyone should decide to string themselves up from a sharp corner. I almost cry out when I see her fuchsia cashmere cardigan hanging on one of the weirdly shaped cardboard hangers, suspended from a rail designed to break under 'undue

13

weight'. How she loved that cardigan. She'd told me about a decluttering handbook her mother had given her in a not-so-subtle hint. Charlie had refused to read it on principle but had grudgingly flicked through, taking away from it just one thing – that you should only hang on to things that spark joy. 'This here is my joy-sparking cardigan,' she said to me.

Now it hangs on the clothes hanger, its empty arms drooping.

The absence of joy is palpable. Rather, again, I have that sense of unease, of being watched.

Charlie has a corner room, and I cross to the window on the back wall that looks out over the sloping lawn and, at the very bottom, the dark smudge of the lake. There are days when the sun is reflected on the surface of the water, making the lake appear to be lit up from within. But not today.

A radiator runs underneath the window. On especially cold days Charlie would throw a cushion down on the floor and sit cross-legged on the carpet with her back to the radiator. 'I can never get warm enough,' she once told me. 'I'm like a chicken breast that hasn't quite thawed out, with a hard, frozen bit in the middle that refuses to defrost.'

I drop to the floor and assume her position, trying to inhabit her skin, to feel what she felt. Did she really sit here that last day with the heat against her back and think about how best to slice into her wrist, the right angle, the right point? Is it possible I could have got it – got her – so wrong?

There was a time I was sure of my own judgement, trusted in myself. But that was before.

I hug my knees into my chest and rock gently for a while. Sometimes this soothes me, but there is something about this room without Charlie in it that makes me anxious.

I hear the soft thud of footsteps outside, and voices drawing closer.

'We've cleared as much as we could, and I don't mind telling you the place was a pigsty. But there's a limit to how much we can do before the relatives turn up.'

The woman says 'relatives' as though it's something not quite nice. I stop rocking abruptly, putting my hand down to steady me. My fingers brush against a piece of paper tucked away behind the pipe of the radiator which the cleaners must have missed. The footsteps stop outside the door and my mouth goes dry as I recognize Dr Roberts' familiar baritone, sounding unusually clipped and impatient.

'With any luck, they won't stay long. Quick in–out, then we can get all her stuff bagged up. We've a new one arriving a week on Monday.'

The door handle turns and I've just time to snatch up the scrap of paper and stuff it up the sleeve of my sweatshirt before the door bursts open.

I scramble to my feet, my heart hammering.

'Right. Let's have a quick check over . . . Hannah! What are you doing in here?'

Instantly, Dr Roberts reverts to his usual slow drawl and I wonder if the woman with him, who I now recognize as Bridget Ashworth, has also clocked the change in his voice.

Bridget Ashworth has a severe brown bob with a grey re-growth line along the parting and glasses with purple frames and a dark wool jacket with what appears to be a single thick white cat hair on the shoulder. She clutches her lanyard and blinks behind her lenses as if she has surprised a wild fox rifling through her kitchen bin, while I shift from foot to foot.

Who would believe I used to give presentations to roomfuls of people, scanning the crowd and making deliberate eye contact with random strangers?

Now I keep my eyes on the carpet, but still, as I mumble some story about needing to feel close to Charlie, I sense Bridget Ashworth's disapproving gaze crawl over me.

Even when I get back to the safety of my own room, I'm still scratching, trying to get it off.

2
Corinne

'I thought she looked very well. Didn't you think she looked well?'

'I guess.'

Corinne decided to take that as a yes.

'Definitely better, I thought. Didn't you?'

'Hmmm.'

Corinne knew she should stop talking. Danny never liked to chat straight after a visit. But still the words kept coming, almost as if she had no control over them.

As they waited at the roundabout, he put the hand-brake on. Under cover of darkness, Corinne studied his profile. He'd lost weight. He'd always been a handsome man. When Hannah had first brought him home Corinne had worried privately that perhaps he was *too* good-looking. She would have struggled with a man who attracted so much attention. But Hannah had always been sure of herself. Very much her own person. Which made everything that had happened doubly shocking.

'What's happening to her?'

Danny's question came out of the blue, freezing

17

Corinne's throat as if she'd swallowed an ice cube.

'She's just tired. Emotionally overwrought. The baby . . .'

'This is nothing to do with the baby. This fixation on murder.'

'Well, naturally, she would take it hard. These were her friends.'

'They were women who were known to be high suicide risk who'd attempted suicide before and who very sadly killed themselves. Of course she's upset, but this point-blank refusal to listen to reason is something else.'

Corinne didn't want to hear what the something else could be.

'It's normal, Danny. These were women she saw every day. She doesn't want to think of them hurting themselves. I'd be exactly the same.'

'No, you wouldn't. Not that same blanket denial. Not when the facts were staring you in the face. We have to look out for symptoms of paranoia. Isn't that what Dr Roberts told us?'

'Yes, but this isn't paranoia, is it? It's real.'

'Is it?'

They were driving past Alexandra Palace, the great Victorian landmark strung out across one of the highest peaks in north London. To their left, the vast building loomed against the murky sky, while to the right the Palace's parkland sloped down the hill into darkness, the distant lights of the city sprawled at its feet.

When Danny dropped her off outside her house Corinne gave him a dry kiss on the cheek.

'I can't wait for her to get out of that place,' she told him. 'Then everything can get back to normal.'

18

Danny didn't reply. Didn't ask her to define normal. Corinne longed to say something cheering to jolt him out of this stilted, distant mood. He was finding it hard to forgive Hannah. She could understand that. For a few months he'd been a father, and now, here he was, back to being a non-father again. How could he not feel diminished, as if something had been taken from him? Wasn't she struggling enough herself with not being a grandmother? But Hannah hadn't been in her right mind. The doctors had explained all that. 'Dissociative,' they'd said. Corinne still had the original notebook where she'd scribbled it down, underlining it and adding an exclamation mark after it.

Half in, half out of the car, she hesitated, searching for the right words to lighten the atmosphere, but nothing came. Danny could be intimidating in that way overly handsome men sometimes are.

As always, before she let herself into her little cottage at the base of the Palace grounds, Corinne had a moment of straining to hear Madge's excited squeals before remembering, with a cold thud, that the little Jack Russell they'd rescued from the pound as a puppy and who'd been her companion for nearly seventeen years, was no longer there. It had been nearly three months since Madge's heart finally gave up, but still Corinne kept expecting to be greeted at the door by a blur of black-and-white fur, usually with a shoe in her mouth as a gift, as if Corinne had been gone for weeks, rather than hours.

That evening, Corinne couldn't settle. She paced through the cottage's few small rooms, picking up objects – a

book here, a photograph there – and setting them back
down again. She grabbed the house phone from its
cradle and stared at it for a long time. Who would she
call? What would she say?

I'm worried my daughter is going crazy.
I'm worried my daughter has gone crazy.
Those were the words she couldn't say out loud.

Sinking down into her ancient, saggy velvet sofa, still
furred with the odd white dog hair that she couldn't
bear to vacuum up, she pulled out her laptop, thinking
perhaps she could Skype Megs, but just as she was about
to press the green phone icon she remembered the time
lag. If it was 9.15 p.m. in London, it'd be 5.15 p.m.
in New York. Megs would still be at work, holed up in
that funny little office, surrounded by men. Her younger
daughter had always been so quirky Corinne had
struggled to imagine what career path she might follow
but, of all the outcomes she'd envisaged over the years,
writing scripts for phone app games on the other side of
the Atlantic had not even crossed her radar.

She knew Megs would drop everything to talk to her,
but she was forcing herself to ration her calls. When the
whole awful business with the baby first happened,
Megs had wanted to jump on the first plane home, and
Corinne had been sure the awful rift between her
daughters would be forgotten, but Hannah was in no
state for visitors. And by the time she'd come back to
some semblance of herself, she'd decided she still wasn't
ready to see her younger sister.

Instead, Megan did her best to support Corinne from
the States, but she had a busy life there, a job Corinne
didn't fully understand, a boyfriend they'd yet to meet.

Her mobile rang, startling in the silence, and Corinne snatched it up from the coffee table, hoping to hear Megs's voice. Instead, Duncan's name flashed up on her screen. There was a time when he had been stored under the moniker 'Git' in her contacts list, but that was years ago, when the betrayal was still fresh. Nowadays, she had other things on her mind.

'How is she?'

There was no preamble, no niceties. But really, what would be the point?

'She's good. She's great, in fact.'

Corinne knew she didn't have to talk Hannah up to her own father, but still she couldn't bring herself to mention this new business with the suicides. Since Duncan had had his second family when already well into his fifties – his second wife, Gigi, producing two babies in indecently rapid succession – she'd felt even more protective of her own two daughters, as if they were in some unspoken competition with their infant half-siblings.

Corinne had come to terms with the fact that her husband had left her after thirty years for a woman he'd met at an Arsenal match of all things. What choice did she have after Gigi got pregnant and it was a fait accompli? But what she found much harder to accept was being the only one who now put Hannah and Megs at the centre of the universe. Duncan's love for his daughters, hitherto unconditional, had now become qualified by having these other, needier drains on his emotional resources.

Corinne always wondered if it was latent guilt that had led him to create a job for his son-in-law, helping to establish the company's fledgling office in Edinburgh. Hannah hadn't been happy about her husband being away three days a week, but decent jobs in architecture were rare.

'Have you asked her?' Duncan wanted to know now. 'About the baby? Have you talked to her? Have you tried to get to the bottom of it?'

So typical of Duncan. So sure that there would turn out to be a reason, a rationale. That there would be an explanation with a top and a bottom.

'It's too soon. We can't push her.'

'Too soon? She's been in there eight weeks, Corinne. It's not about the money—'

'I should think not, when the insurance is footing most of the bill!'

Corinne was glad to find a peg for her anger.

'That's not the point. Christ, Cor, I'd pay whatever it took to see Hannah through this, but surely she ought to be making more progress by now.'

'She *is* making progress. Baby steps, Dr Roberts says.'

Duncan made a noise like he was snorting something through his nose.

'Maybe if Dr Roberts spent more time at the clinic and less time throwing lavish fundraisers, she'd be doing a lot better.'

'He has to keep a high public profile so that they continue to get finance for the clinic. Otherwise, the insurance company would have to be paying out even *more*.' Pointed. So he'd get the message. 'They're lucky to have him. Dr Chakraborty says he's the reason they manage to recruit such high-quality staff.'

'I'm starting without you,' came a woman's voice in the background at Duncan's end.

He sighed.

'I've got to go. We're watching a box set.'

A box set? Corinne felt every muscle inside her tense up. She closed her eyes, sucked air in deep through her nose, waiting for the moment to pass.

'OK,' she said, preparing to ring off.

'Cor?'

'Yes?'

'You're not in this alone. I want you to know that. I care about Hannah as much as you do. I'm right here.'

Corinne was embarrassed to find that his clumsy attempt at comforting her had brought tears to her eyes.

'OK, then.'

She pressed end call before her trembling voice could give her away.

Angrily, she pointed the remote at the TV. It came booming into life with a cookery programme in which harried contestants were trying to cope with the pressure of a professional restaurant kitchen. *Yes, chef! No, chef!* She turned it off. There was so much work she ought to be getting on with. Thirty-six mid-term papers to be marked. Five or six years ago, Corinne's students on her pop-culture social anthropology course would all have been UK-born, with shared cultural reference points and similar backgrounds, but now eighty-nine per cent of them were from abroad. China, mostly. She was having to find a whole new way of teaching, a new focus to the syllabus, at the same time as having to fulfil all the research and publishing requirements the university bureaucrats had imposed on them to justify their students' tuition fees.

Corinne sighed and picked up her laptop.

The screensaver was a photograph of her and Hannah and Megan on holiday in Crete ten months before. They'd gone out of season, in mid-May, on a girls' holiday, a last trip, just the three of them, before Megs started her job in New York the following September.

They had been happy that holiday, she was certain of it. Not happy in the way one is always happy on holidays in hindsight, but really happy. This was before Hannah and Megs had their falling-out, and for once the two of them had managed to put aside long-standing niggles and patterns of behaviour that had been set in child-hood – Megs inclined to be spiky and defensive; Hannah sometimes taking teasing too far. And Corinne had felt truly herself for the first time since she had found a strange text on Duncan's phone and he'd admitted that not only was he seeing someone else but she was pregnant.

Hannah had seemed content that holiday, at peace. She'd stopped crying at odd moments about the mis-carriage she'd suffered three years before and the unsuccessful attempt at IVF that had followed. She'd seemed relaxed, said she and Danny were getting on so much better since they'd agreed to stop talking about babies.

The men had flocked around them. Hannah had always attracted attention, not because she was beauti-ful, although she was, but because she was so at home within her own skin. Megan's beauty was less obvious. Corinne had seen people's eyes skim over her younger daughter, with her serious mud-brown eyes and her angular features, but then something would make them look again. That fierce intelligence you could sense even from a distance.

She'd come back from that holiday feeling a new optimism. For the first time in years, she felt excited about the future, rather than feeling as if her best years were all in the past. She had already been planning to visit Megan in New York the following spring and had even agreed to try out internet dating, if only to have a fertile fund of new anecdotes to trot out at dinner parties. She'd looked in the mirror of her tiny bathroom that first evening back, at her lightly tanned face, sprinkled with freckles, and the faint white lines at the corners of her eyes where she'd been laughing too much and too often for the sun to reach, and for once she'd liked what she'd seen. Life had seemed full of possibilities.

And then Hannah had got pregnant.

3

Hannah

Charlie was the first person I met in here. Or the first I remember meeting. The initial twenty-four hours were a black hole of numbness where new people merged together into one faceless blur, and even after that I remained in shock, my brain dull with disbelief. I wasn't looking to make friends because I was so convinced I wouldn't be staying. As soon as they realized there was nothing wrong with me, I'd be off.

I didn't let myself think about Emily, or what had happened. Instead I focused on Danny and how he'd looked in the registry office when he'd said that line about sickness and health and held my hands in his and I could feel his whole body shaking.

I didn't – wouldn't – think about my sister Megan and the things she'd said about him. Some things are too hard to forgive.

Danny has wavy brown hair. He likes to keep it close cropped, says it's easier to manage, but I prefer it when it's longer and falls across his eyes. He's broad across the shoulders and when I clasp my hands around the tops of his arms they don't reach. But his mouth is full and soft, and his chin has a slight dent that fits perfectly when he rests it on the top of my head.

Danny would get me out of here.

I had no idea then that it was Danny who'd wanted me in.

So when Charlie came over and introduced herself on the first full day, I wasn't forthcoming.

'Your first time?' she asked. No need to ask how she guessed.

'Uh-huh.' Nodding. Wanting her gone so I could be alone to unpack the fog in my head and understand what had happened.

'It's really not so bad.'

She had a lovely soft, lilting voice with a laugh bubbling away there under the surface of it, like she was thinking of something amusing that at any moment she might share with you. Curls the colour of freshly turned soil, green eyes, high cheekbones that shone where they caught the light.

I made one of those 'yeah, right' faces. That first day, I couldn't see past the locks on the doors and the rounded corners on the furniture and the fact the laces had been taken out of my Converse shoes so I had to shuffle about to keep them on my feet, and the way my jeans wouldn't stay up because I wasn't allowed a belt, and the skeletal girl reading a book in the corner while a machine fed her through a tube in her nose.

My body was in mourning for the baby that was gone, breasts achy, hormones ricocheting around inside me, so that one minute I was buzzing with nerves sharpened into points, the next slumped over with grief, oblivious to the tears running down my face.

Once I'd had a chance to view the clinic with

dispassionate eyes, I could see that she was right. There are far worse places to be. This is a private clinic and everything about it reflects the price we pay to be here. The old building is tastefully decorated, the wide oak floorboards scattered with muted rugs and there are comfortable sofas in the TV lounge where we sit and watch movies on Friday nights. We each have our own beige bedroom with en suite bathroom. We bring photographs from home, and jolly prints to brighten up the walls, although the glass in the frames isn't really glass so it smudges easily.

But I couldn't see any of that when Joni brought me downstairs, even though I'd begged to stay in my room.

'No one is going to force you,' she'd said. 'But I should point out that non-compliance *may* be flagged up as something requiring further exploration, which *may* mean you end up spending longer in here than otherwise.'

'I'm not staying in this place,' I told her. 'There's been a mistake.'

But when she led the way into the cafeteria I followed her.

Though I was dismissive of her attempts to be friendly, Charlie didn't turn away from me. She'd seen it before and, anyway, she never judged people. That's why everyone liked her. When I started to get better I'd joke that I was jealous of her popularity. 'Good job you're suicidal, otherwise I'd have to kill you,' I told her once. We laughed a lot about that.

It doesn't seem so funny now.

*

Odelle was the next one to approach me. In a place like this there are some people, like Charlie, whose wounds are all internal, buried so deep no one would ever guess that there were deformed places hidden there, lumpy with scar tissue. Then there are others, like Stella, whose damage is on the surface. Unmissable. Odelle was one of those. A long-time anorexic, her head, with its thinning mousy-brown hair, was balanced on her neck like the top of a lollipop. Her body was swathed in outsized clothes – T-shirts, jumpers – that revealed themselves like layers of old wallpaper through the gap at the front of her zip-up hoody (cordless, of course). Her face, close up, was covered in a soft, apricot fuzz of downy hairs, soft as suede.

'You mustn't be scared,' she said. And though I hadn't felt any fear up till then, being too mired in self-pity, now, all of a sudden, my skin began to prickle.

'We're all friendly here,' she went on. 'Stick with me, and I'll look after you.'

As Odelle was talking, a memory was pricking at the back of my mind of the time we moved to London from Cambridge because Dad had changed job and I had to start a new school and was allocated a girl to show me around on the first day. I could still recall the showy-off way in which she paraded me around the corridors like a new pet. 'This is Hannah. She's new,' she'd declare, and people would shoot me looks of sympathy.

At twenty-five, Odelle is seven years younger than me, so I try to make allowances but, sometimes, being with her feels like someone scraping sandpaper over every one of my nerve endings.

Odelle is an habituée of psychiatric institutions. If

29

mental clinics gave loyalty points, she'd have the free drink, the coffee maker *and* the spa weekend. 'There isn't anything I don't know,' she announced as she shepherded me from room to room. Psychiatric patients tend to form different tribes, Odelle told me. The Emos, like Charlie, for whom life is a deep, dark void; EDies, like Odelle, battling eating disorders, swapping tips on how to bulk up on water to cheat the scales, vying with each other over concave stomachs and thigh gaps; addicts of all persuasions; OCDs, like Sofia, with their habits and their tics and their obsessive thoughts running on a loop; bipolars, like Nina, veering from comatose to manic, on a perpetual emotional bungee jump. And then there are the rest. All damaged in our own way.

'Where do you fit?' Odelle wanted to know.

I thought of telling her about Emily, but the words built up, unsaid, in my mouth until I feared I would choke.

'It's complicated.'

Sofia was crying, big sobs that tore from her lungs.

Odelle had introduced me to her earlier that first evening, explaining that she had the room next to mine. That night, I lay in my bed listening to her and wishing I was back in my own bed in our first-floor flat in Haringey, north London, with Danny's arm around me, my face buried in his chest.

On the days we both worked in London, I used to get up earlier than him to catch a train to my job as a publicist for a children's book publisher. Danny would still be in bed when I left for work. Lying awake in my room at The Meadows, listening to Sofia through the wall, I remembered how he used to look so alone in that big bed, his arm flung out, reaching for a me who was no longer there.

Now when he comes to visit it's as if he's a stranger.

The next morning, when I went into the cafeteria for breakfast, Sofia was already there at the buffet table, her eyes puffy. After piling food on to her tray (not one of the EDies, then), she started making her way towards one of the three round pine tables, all perfectly laid, as if in a top-class hotel. Halfway there, she stopped, still, for a few seconds. Then, with a resigned air, she retraced her steps to the buffet station, replaced her yogurt pot and the banana, scraped the cereal into the bin, stacked up her plates next to the rest of the dirty dishes, and began making her selection again, choosing exactly the same items.

'She had a bad thought,' said Charlie, reading the question in my face. 'Probably about something horrible happening to one of her children. It usually is. So then she has to get rid of everything infected with that bad thought. Sometimes it's the clothes she's wearing. This time it looks like it's the food she's carrying.'

I opened my mouth to say, 'But that's crazy,' then closed it again.

When I had come to know her better, Sofia told me, I'd be disgusted by her if I knew the things that went through her head, the thoughts she had about strangers, friends and family. Not fantasies. The opposite of those. Nauseating sexual thoughts that came unbidden into her head. I told her that nothing disgusted me any more. But that's not what I meant. What I meant was that nothing surprised me any more.

At least, not until my friends started dying.

Sofia was in her late thirties, but time hadn't been kind to her and at first I put her at a decade older. Capillaries had burst like fireworks under the pale skin of her face, so her cheeks had a rough, ruddy edge to them, and her shoulder-length frizzy hair, which she wore pushed back from her face with a velvet band, was the faded orange of a canvas deckchair at the end of a long, hot summer. She was large-boned and wide-shouldered and wore baggy cardigans and shapeless mid-calf skirts.

She had two children – a son of nine and a daughter of twelve – who dutifully trooped in to see her on Sunday afternoons, ushered in by Sofia's husband, Rob, a short, slight man with a perpetual air of having boarded the wrong bus. On those occasions, Sofia would make a Herculean effort to curb her behaviours – the repetitions, the doubling back, the constant changing of clothes. But the effort of holding herself in would show and, after a few hours, she'd be leaning forward rigidly in her chair, her lips moving as she counted the taps of her hand against the side of the chair.

After they'd left, Charlie or I would hold her while she sobbed until our T-shirts were soaked through.

I know what you're thinking, but you're wrong. She didn't want to kill herself.

She wanted to get better. For them.

4
Laura

The flower was quite lovely. Fat yolk-yellow petals reaching up from the soil like an open hand. Winter aconite. A sign that spring was not far off.

Thank God for that.

Laura stepped over the flower bed that bordered the car park and inhaled deeply, welcoming the cold air that made her breath cloud around her mouth, the scent of this morning's rain on the damp gravel mixing with the odour of boiled vegetables that wafted over from the vents. In her experience, no matter how expensive or exclusive a place was, the kitchens always had that institutional smell.

Flicking the switch on her key fob, she felt the usual lift at the sight of her bubblegum-pink VW Beetle, winking its lights as if in greeting. In her job, you often needed all the cheering up you could get, and her car never let her down, giving her a warm jolt when she saw it waiting patiently for her at the end of another emotionally draining day.

Laura was worried about Hannah.

She'd thought it would be Stella who took Charlie's death hardest, but Hannah seemed unable to process it.

Today in class, she'd asked them all to incorporate their names into a design on separate sheets of paper that she intended to bind together and turn into a book for Charlie's parents. She'd thought it would be a thoughtful gesture instead of everyone giving a shop-bought card. And most of them had thrown themselves into it. Odelle had come up with an intricate, lace-like pattern into which she'd woven the letters of her name. Frannie's card was like the cover of a fantasy novel, the 'F' a tower with castellated top, the 'N's a mountain range, topped with snow and cloud.

Only Hannah had struggled to come up with anything. She had half-heartedly doodled the first three letters of her name, tried out different effects – swirls and flowers, a leafy vine that wound itself around the 'H' – only to rub them all out. In the end, her page was just those three letters, grey and blurred.

'Don't worry, you can finish it next time,' Laura told her. But after they all left the art room, she had paused for several minutes, gazing at those three letters: 'HAN'. Roberts would relish the opportunity to ponder the meaning of Hannah leaving herself half formed.

Her core muscles tightened at the thought of Roberts, his maple-syrup voice and hard blue eyes, and her fingers clenched around the pink leather steering wheel. Deliberately, she forced her thoughts along a different channel. She had taught herself how to do it. You had to imagine you were herding sheep and corralling them into changing course. Thought visualization. It was a useful technique.

*

Despite having been here so many times over the years, Laura was struck afresh by the disconnect between the kind of place she'd have imagined Annabel living in and the reality. There was nothing *wrong* with the small, neat modern house on the executive housing estate, and it was certainly convenient that it was in a part of outer north-west London where one could still park immediately outside. It was just that Annabel was so smart, so educated. If you'd only just met her, you'd picture her in a rambling old house in the countryside with piles of books on every surface and a row of wellies by the front door.

Laura was surprised by the intensity of her relief on seeing Annabel's curiously flat, square face, with its wide-apart hazel eyes and the snub nose that was almost recessed so that, in profile, everything was in unbroken alignment from forehead to chin.

'You have no idea how glad I am to see you,' she said, flinging her arms around Annabel's neck.

Annabel smiled and gently detached herself.

'Drink?' Annabel called, leading the way through the narrow hallway, where a single hook held just one coat and one scarf.

'Water's fine,' she said, as she always did.

While Annabel was in the kitchen, Laura walked through to the lounge and threw herself down on to the pale blue sofa, dropping her keys on the wooden table next to her. She rested her head back and allowed the peace to settle over her.

'You look tired,' said Annabel, studying her from the armchair opposite, and a lump formed in Laura's throat. Recently, she'd worried that Annabel wasn't quite as attentive to her feelings as she'd always been in the past, so today's welcome solicitousness caught her by surprise.

'Do you think you're getting too involved again?'

'No. Yes. Oh, you know what I'm like. I try to keep up barriers but a few always get past.'

'We've talked about this.'

'I know. I know. And I'm working on it. It's just that things have been so strange there since Charlie's . . . passing . . . There's a heavy, thick atmosphere, and if you stay there too long it feels like it might choke you. And of course *he's* using it as an excuse to play the strong leader calm in the face of adversity.'

She glanced over at Annabel to see how this new conversational tack had gone down, but the older woman's expression remained blank. As usual, the lack of response just made her talk more.

'It's not doing his reputation much good. Two deaths in as many months. One set of parents have already withdrawn their daughter because they don't think it's safe. And loss of revenue is something Dr Roberts takes extremely seriously.'

She shot Annabel a sly smile that wasn't recipro-cated.

'Maybe it's time to remind yourself exactly what you're doing there, Laura. Remember all those con-versations back when you decided to become a therapist? What made you take that leap from nursing? What made you decide to help people suffering mental rather than physical illness?'

Laura sat back and ran both hands through her spiky black hair, as she'd done since childhood when faced with difficult questions. Annabel always had this effect on her, turning her back into the anxious child she'd once been, desperate for love and approval.

'Because they need me,' she replied eventually.

Annabel sat back. Blinked. Said nothing, in that way she had.

5

Corinne

Hannah's first pregnancy had been an accident. She and Danny had only been together a year and were still in that magical period of finding things out about each other. It had been a shock, but Danny had said he'd go along with whatever Hannah wanted. And once she'd decided to go ahead, they'd both thrown themselves into it. 'I know I'm supposed to be feeling sick and tired and ill, but I bloody love being pregnant,' Hannah had told Corinne after her twelve-week scan. Less than a fortnight later, she started bleeding heavily and another scan revealed the baby had been dead for several days.

It had hit everyone hard, including Corinne. Though it wasn't something she'd planned for so soon, for a few weeks she'd imagined herself as a grandmother, glimpsing a future of babysitting weekends and finger-painting, her kitchen table splattered with colour, her little cottage alive with noise. After the miscarriage, she'd folded that new self away and crammed her into the very back of a drawer.

Her focus had been on Hannah, who seemed shrunken following her return from hospital, as if the machine that had sucked out what that doctor referred to as the 'aftermath of pregnancy' had removed some essential part of her as well.

Corinne had assumed that Hannah would dust herself off after a period of grieving and conceive again. It was common enough, she knew, for first pregnancies to end suddenly. She herself had suffered a miscarriage before Hannah came along, so she understood all too well that particular agony, the grief over the little being that no longer was. But Hannah's relatively late miscarriage, which involved delivering the tiny foetus herself, left her bludgeoned by grief. Doctors had failed to offer a satisfactory explanation, telling her only that there was no reason for her not to go on to have a healthy child.

Having stumbled into her first pregnancy by accident, Hannah became fixated upon a second. But the much longed for second baby had never arrived. And over the following three years Hannah's wild grief had transmuted into a quiet, persistent sorrow which an unsuccessful attempt at IVF had served only to deepen.

'You know, I've never really failed at anything, Mum,' Hannah told Corinne. 'I did well in my exams, passed my driving test first time. Do you remember? I ended up with Danny, even though people thought he was out of my league. And now to fail at something most women do without even thinking about it . . . It feels like some kind of cosmic practical joke.'

Comments like these broke Corinne's heart, so she was both encouraged and relieved when Hannah finally stopped talking about babies and gradually became once more the outgoing young woman she'd been before. Their regular phone calls were again full of parties she'd

·been at, book signings she'd organized, movies she'd seen.

As she parked her Fiat in the car park of The Meadows two days after her previous visit with Danny, Corinne found herself hoping her son-in-law wouldn't be there. They had always got on in the past, Corinne refusing to take sides during his and Hannah's frequent rows. Just as well, given what had happened the one time Megs spoke out.

But since Hannah's breakdown she'd found Danny's presence intimidating. He rarely volunteered any conversation and she couldn't help noticing that his visits to his wife were becoming increasingly sporadic. On one hand, she was relieved to be spared his taciturn awkwardness but, on the other, she felt worried his absence might set back Hannah's progress.

You can't hold what happened against her, she wanted to say to him. *She wasn't well. Think of it like a fever.*

Except it wasn't a fever.

As she signed the visitors' book, Corinne scanned the other signatures. No Danny Lovell. Hannah would be upset that he hadn't come.

Corinne frowned when she saw the names Justin Carter and Drew Abbott. When Hannah had first told her the clinic was being filmed for a documentary, Corinne had been horrified and tried to insist that her daughter be left out of the filming, but she had reckoned without Dr Roberts' persuasiveness and Hannah's boredom. 'At least it's something to do,' Hannah had snapped, as if it were Corinne's fault that she was there in the first place. 'And we can always say no afterwards if we don't like it.' Even Duncan had overcome his initial misgivings once he found out Roberts was offering a discount in the fees to cover the 'inconvenience'.

The young woman on reception told Corinne that Hannah was outside, and she made her way around the back of the building, stopping to admire the velvet lawn leading down to the vast lake, which, legend had it, contained the rusting wreck of a motor car driven into it by a drunken party guest back in the days when it was still a private house.

Though it was a chilly day, with pewter clouds gathering ominously in the sky, Corinne found Hannah sitting beside Stella on the bench just inside the rose garden. Corinne frowned when she saw the cigarette in her daughter's hand. Hannah hadn't been a smoker before she came here, but now she spent hours outside, shoulders hunched against the cold, sharing cigarettes with the others.

'Everyone does it here, Mum,' she'd said the first time Corinne brought it up. 'It's the one vice we're allowed. I'd be a fool not to make use of it.'

'Hi, Hannah! Hi, Stella!' she called out as she made her way towards them.

Hannah got up to give her a kiss, but Stella, who'd been sitting with her back to the arm of the bench, drew her knees up and hugged them tightly to her chest.

'Hello, Corinne,' she said, in that strange, breathy voice of hers.

She had on a tight red knee-length dress that emphasized her tiny waist, and high red platformed shoes which glittered as she rocked back and forth. Her long blonde hair was tied up in a high ponytail.

Looking at her beautiful face, with the skin stretched

41

tight over exaggerated cheekbones, that rosebud mouth, that tiny, pointed chin, those outsized blue eyes, Corinne felt the usual conflicting sensations Stella induced: appalled fascination coupled with a fierce desire to protect her.

The first time they had come to the clinic, that awful first week when Hannah sat and wept and repeated, 'I'm sorry, I'm sorry,' over and over, until Danny had got up and left, Corinne later finding him in the car with his forehead resting on the steering wheel, she hadn't been able to stop staring at Stella. So pretty, but something not quite right. The eyes just a little too wide. The features just a little too symmetrical.

Later, Corinne risked asking about the disturbing blonde girl and had been taken aback by the offhand way in which Hannah replied: 'Oh, Stella. She's addicted to plastic surgery.' As though it was nothing unusual, just another interest, like training for a marathon or studying Mandarin. Still later on, she learned that Stella's wealthy mother in America had had her referred to The Meadows after medical experts warned that additional surgery could kill her.

Corinne had felt suddenly totally out of her depth. This kind of thing didn't happen to people like her. Or families like theirs.

Or women like Hannah.

'She didn't do it.'

Corinne could understand why Hannah didn't want to believe that Charlie had killed herself. Death is always brutal, but some deaths startle more than others. Charlie's had been one of those.

'I know it seems impossible to take in. But Charlie had her demons, just like the rest of us.'

'You.'

Corinne didn't understand.

'That's what you really want to say. She had her demons, like the rest of *you.*'

Corinne hated it when Hannah got like this. Playing the mental-illness card. Making it us against them.

'I don't think your mama meant anything by that,' said Stella mildly, and Corinne felt a warm rush of gratitude towards her. As far as she could tell, Stella's family was as remote emotionally as they were geographically, preferring to shower her with money rather than affection.

Corinne tried to make her tone conciliatory. 'Why?' she asked her daughter. 'Why would anyone want to hurt Charlie?'

She couldn't say *kill.* The preposterousness of it made the word stick in her throat.

Hannah shrugged. 'Maybe she upset someone. People in here take offence easily. We're all hiding things. Every one of us. Charlie told me that.'

Hannah was sounding paranoid and Corinne felt a tug of nausea. Every time she convinced herself her daughter was getting better, something would happen to make her realize just how far there still was to go.

'Look.' Hannah reached into her jeans pocket and pressed a piece of paper into Corinne's hand.

Corinne gazed at it blankly.

1. *Switch phone provider*
2. *Write up journal notes for Dr Chakraborty*

43

3. Google WK
4. Book flights for Croatia(!)

'I don't understand. It looks like someone's to-do list.'

'Exactly. It's Charlie's to-do list. From the day she died. I found it in her room.'

Now Corinne got it.

'But sweetheart, this doesn't prove anything. Maybe she wrote this in an attempt to force herself to look ahead. Maybe she was trying to convince herself that if she kept things normal she could make herself feel normal. What's that phrase – "fake it to make it"?'

Corinne watched the skin on the bridge of her daughter's nose concertina like a paper fan and knew she'd said the wrong thing.

'Croatia, Mum!' Hannah exclaimed. 'Next summer. Why would she spend hundreds of pounds on flights if she knew she wouldn't be going?'

Corinne knew she should back down now. But old habits are hard to break.

'If she was feeling desperate, she might have booked flights as a way of tethering herself to life. Surely you can see that, Hannah?'

But Hannah had closed herself off, drawing a curtain across her face.

'The day I first tried to kill myself, I ordered a new dress from ASOS,' said Stella in her dreamy way, as if she were spinning a story from the ether, rather than relating something that actually happened.

'I was looking for a sign, I think,' she went on. 'If they have my exact size, or if they offer free next-day delivery, then I won't do it. But, you know, I still went ahead.

Now I think the only sign that would have made a difference is if I'd been able to unzip my skin and find a whole new different person underneath. And that didn't happen.'

Stella said things like that all the time. As if it were normal to talk about unzipping your own skin.

'You see?' Corinne turned to Hannah, over-eager to make her point. 'Charlie was testing herself. Looking for signs. You can't read too much into this note.'

Hannah gazed back at her, blank-faced, and Corinne saw that she had lost her. Regret flooded through her.

After Hannah was first admitted to The Meadows and Corinne was having to face up to the awful truth about what her daughter had done, she'd almost snapped under the weight of her own self-reproach. What kind of mother was she, not to notice what was going on? If only she could have another chance, she'd do everything differently.

Yet here she was, and Hannah was once again slipping through her fingers and she had learned nothing.

6

Hannah

3. Google WK

The more I stare at the third entry on Charlie's to-do list, the more convinced I am that it holds the key to what happened to my friend. Mum has left, and I'm curled up in a padded, egg-shaped chair in the Mindfulness Area, which is a little room tucked just inside the entrance to the new building. I recall Charlie's face after she'd told me how people in here are always hiding something. And how when I tried to push her for information, she just shook her head, with that look in her eye. That infuriating it's-best-you-don't-know look.

I hold the paper in my hand and close my eyes, as if I can absorb Charlie's thoughts through her spiky handwriting on the scrap of paper.

Some days I don't recognize myself.

I try to think back five days to the day Charlie died. I used to have a great memory. Pin sharp, past events lit up in high definition. But trauma, plus my nightly sleeping pill, have blunted my mind. Now when I try to summon up a memory it's like trying to catch a dust mote, grabbing at the air and finding my hands always empty.

I know I saw her at breakfast and she was just as she normally was. Her hair matted on one side where she'd slept on it and hadn't yet brushed it out. Wearing tartan slippers and blue sweatpants and a blue jumper. Not the joy-sparking cardigan. Not that day. I wonder, would that have made a difference?

We sat together, but Charlie rarely spoke much at breakfast. It took her a while to get going in the morning. Most of us are like that. We eat our toast and croissants (or just push them around the plate, in Odelle's case) in silence while we wait to surface from our Diazepam fug.

We would have set our goals for the day during Morning Group, as we always do. I strain to remember what Charlie's goals were, but my mind is blank. Probably something about calling her mother. Most of hers involved calling her mother.

I remember Nina was flying that day and kept shouting over everybody, rocking her chair backwards until it seemed impossible the legs wouldn't break. Roberts has taken her off all her meds so they can observe how she is untreated, and we're all counting the days until she gets back under the chemical cosh and the rapid mood cycling stops. Her goal was to finish writing her book, which she said had kept her up all night and was a guaranteed bestseller. 'It's my entire philosophy on life,' she said. 'It'll change lives.'

Afterwards, Charlie and I went to the kitchen for a cooking therapy session, which is basically just cooking, but as I said before everything gets called therapy in this place. That's where Charlie and I made the caramelized sugar and hers was thick and hard and I told her how it could do someone damage and we both laughed. Joni was on supervising duty that day. The nurses aren't allowed to have their phones with them, but Joni always looks as if she's composing texts and Facebook updates in her head. She's never quite present. But when Charlie quizzed her about her new boyfriend, she came alive and told us they'd booked a summer holiday in Majorca. All inclusive, premium brands, she told us. 'Gotta have something to look forward to, dontchya?' I remember Charlie smiled and said, 'That's exactly right.' Maybe that's what prompted her to book the Croatia tickets.

People who are planning to kill themselves don't look forward. Do they?

We made a chocolate cake and decorated it with the caramelized sugar. Did Charlie really break off a shard and slip it into her sock or the waistband of her trousers while my attention was elsewhere, thinking about other kitchens, other cakes, other lives?

This is where my mind goes hazy, the memories flabby around the edges.

I know at one point I looked at the finished cake and felt a sense of achievement, verging on contentment. And when I recognized that feeling I thought for a second that I might be sick. Because I'd almost let myself be happy. Even after everything I'd done. Then I wanted to punish myself, and Charlie must have seen that in my face, because she put a hand on my arm and said, 'It's only a cake, Hannah.' And Joni looked up at us, sharply, not understanding what was going on, and she didn't like it.

''Course it's cake,' she said. 'What else would it be?'

And after cooking we had individual therapy. I was with Dr Chakraborty and Charlie would have been with Dr Roberts. Unless he was off somewhere – at a fundraising lunch in Mayfair, or giving a talk to health-care chiefs at a convention in Palm Springs. I like Dr Chakraborty. He has a way of steepling his fingers and gazing at me from his sad brown eyes.

'Hannah, Hannah, Hannah,' he says. 'How are your sisters?' And we both smile. Neither of us finds his lame reference to the old Woody Allen movie amusing any more; still, it has become a form of greeting. A short-hand for *Ah, so here we are again, we two, and nothing much can be done about it.*

Then there was lunch. We always ate at the same table – Charlie and me and Stella and Sofia, back when she was still alive. Since Charlie died, Stella and I spread our plates out over the table and put jumpers on the spare chairs so no one else comes to join us. But it's a small clinic and there's a new person arriving every week, so we know it's just a matter of time.

I try to think back to what we talked about that day, but the intervening hours and days have cocooned them-selves around the memory, cutting it off from view. It's a fair guess that, afterwards, when we'd drained the last trickle of lukewarm decaffeinated coffee, we'd have gone back to our rooms, as we often do. Until I arrived here, I'd never been able to sleep during the day, but now I take any opportunity I can get to lie down. The sleep-ing pills most of us take sacredly every evening like the holy wafer leave us hungover the next day, our mouths furred, our minds always half submerged.

Was that when Charlie sat on the floor with her back

to the radiator and wrote her list? Even while the shard of sharpened sugar was digging into her calf?

The chair I am sitting in is organically shaped, the back curving overhead, a squishy cushion nestled into the half-moon base. It feels protected. Private. Besides, no one really uses the Mindfulness Area. It's more of a status symbol for Dr Roberts. It's one of his favourite stop-offs when he's taking groups of private investors, or foreign dignitaries, or representatives of the media on one of his regular tours of the building: 'This is where our residents can be alone for a little contemplative time. At the clinic, we're great believers in the benefits of mindfulness, and the residents can come here to have a safe, quiet, comfortable space to empty their minds of everything except the here and now. Which is so important for all of us.'

Charlie's to-do list is crumpled now from being folded and unfolded so many times.

Even so, I read it again, and that old Einstein saying pops into my head about the definition of insanity: doing the same thing over and over again and expecting different results. It strikes me as ironically funny. Seeing where I am and everything.

Google WK.

I've gone through all Charlie's friends and acquaintances – the ones I know of, anyway – but none of them fits the initials. I've even tried combinations of words beginning with W and K, but still drawn a blank. Yet I can't shake off the conviction that those two letters hold the key to her state of mind that last day, and how and why she died.

Then it comes to me. Sitting in that padded egg-chair

that's like a flesh-coloured womb. Charlie's laptop. If I go on to her search history, I'll be able to find out exactly what she was googling that last day. The clinic doesn't have WiFi in the rooms, probably to stop the EDies poring over the pro-anorexia websites and the rest of us taking notes from www.101waystotopyourself.com. And we're not allowed our own phones either, for the same reason. 'The screen can become its own addiction,' is one of Dr Roberts' favourite lines. So when we want to talk to anyone, we all have to queue up for one of the landlines in the admin office and everyone pretends not to be listening to what you're saying, but you know they are really.

So Charlie would have had to wait for one of the supervised WiFi sessions in the day room. We're supposed to stay away from social media. The pressure to appear 'normal' or compare ourselves to our ever-achieving friends is not healthy, Roberts says. We are considered insufficiently robust to see past the shiny, shellacked selves most people hide behind on social media and too sensitive to deal with the endless charity requests, the kids with cancer, the abandoned puppies, the tug, tug, tug of the heartstrings. But she would have had no trouble logging on to Google.

Charlie had a Macbook. One of those lightweight ones that seem like they could snap in half when you pick them up. I don't remember seeing it when I was in her room three days ago, but I'm sure it must be there somewhere. Tucked away in a desk drawer, perhaps.

I get to my feet, suddenly heady with resolve, and try not to think about the last time I was in her room, my heart hammering as Bridget Ashworth's cool gaze slipped over me like a net. I remind myself that Charlie issued me an open invitation to visit her room any time, and ignore the little voice that adds, *But Charlie's dead*.

I make my way past my own door to the end of the corridor, steeling myself against the treacherous lurch of hope that I might hear Charlie's voice call 'Come in!' and enter to find her flung out across her bed or sitting against the radiator, her black-framed glasses resting halfway down her nose.

I glance up at the CCTV camera, its one-eyed stare trained upon me from the ceiling. My mouth is sand-dry and when I swallow the sound seems deafening.

I go straight to the desk. I'm doing it for her, I tell myself.

The top drawer is empty apart from a pack of coloured pens and a pad of paper. Stationery is a strange commodity in a place like this. Scissors are out, as are paperclips. Even pencils were banned after one woman, many months before I arrived, sharpened her 5H to a point and stabbed herself in the neck, narrowly missing an artery. When Mum brought me in a ring-bound notebook to keep my journal in, it was confiscated at reception. 'A patient could take out the wire and hurt themselves with it, d'ya get me?' said Joni.

The second drawer contains a stack of photographs in a clear plastic folder, and I am very nearly derailed by the picture on the top of the pile, which shows a young Charlie, maybe thirteen or fourteen, smiling up at the camera from a striped deckchair in a nicely kept English garden. She's wearing jeans and a pale blue vest, and her eyes are so full of the life that lies ahead of her that I almost cannot bear it. She told me she was sixteen when she suffered her first major bout of depression, and after that everything changed, her horizons narrowing as the bouts became more intense and protracted, medication piled on medication, expert upon expert, her eyes gradually dulling.

Without stopping to think, I slip the photo out from the pile and tuck it into the back pocket of my jeans.

I hear a noise from the corridor and my heart jolts inside my chest. The noise stops when a door opens and closes again further down the corridor, and I sag with relief. The bottom drawer of the desk is stiff and I have to tug at it several times until, finally, it gives. And there's Charlie's laptop, scratched and pockmarked with dents. She was always so careless with her things. Sofia used to look as if she was about to cry when Charlie flung her computer down on the dining table as if it were made of rubber. 'It's just *stuff*,' Charlie would say.

As I pull it out on to the desk top, the memories come thick and fast. Charlie and I downstairs in the day room watching *Orange Is the New Black* on her laptop, until Odelle spotted us and alerted Darren, who was on supervising duty. 'I'm only thinking of Charlie and Hannah's wellbeing. It's so important that we make healthy choices,' she told him. Charlie hunched over her computer, struggling to compose an email to her mum. 'I want to be upbeat, but I don't want to lie to her. I've got as far as "hello".'

When the screen flickers into life I'm faced with the password request, something I'd deliberately put out of my mind. I try a couple of random guesses. Her middle name, Theresa? LeicesterCity, the name of her favourite football team? Still no luck. Panic is bubbling inside me. Concentrate. *Concentrate.*

Out of nowhere, another memory comes into my head. We are in Group and joking about our guilty pleasures. Frannie has admitted shyly that she used to be addicted to *Made in Chelsea* and even had a calendar of the cast on her bedroom wall. Nina has a crush on Paul Hollywood and Charlie says when she's stressed she plays Taylor Swift at full blast. 'What can I say? She cheers me up.' And when someone else scoffs, she insists, 'It's true. I love her. I've even used her as my password before.'

My fingers are shaking as I type the letters. This is my third attempt. I won't get another. It works. Hallelujah. I experience a burst of jubilation as the dark blue screen of the home page gives way to Charlie's screensaver, a photograph of a beach in Thailand she visited in another life.

There's another noise from outside – the sound of voices in the stairwell – and I freeze until a door clangs downstairs and it's silent once more.

I click on Chrome and there's an agonizing wait while the multicoloured icon bounces up and down, until, at last, it opens. There is of course no wireless signal, so I can't call up any websites, but to my relief I can access the history bar. A quick look at the dates of the top entries shows they are all from five days ago – the day Charlie died. The first entries are all about Croatia. Loads of holiday sites and flight-comparison sites. Briefly, I feel a glow of triumph. *See, Mum*, I want to say. All this research proves she wasn't just trying to make herself feel better. She really did intend to go.

I carry on searching her history, my finger freezing when I see she has googled 'combatting loneliness'. Lonely? Charlie? Why couldn't she have come to me? I am about to scroll on when I hear the lift doors opening back down the corridor. No one ever uses the lift. It's small and claustrophobic and takes twice as long as climbing the two short flights of stairs. It'll be one of the cleaners, I tell myself, not wanting to lug a heavy vacuum cleaner up the stairs. Still, as I carry on scanning the list, there's a fizz of panic starting inside me. I hear footsteps further along the corridor. They grow louder. *Breathe. Breathe.*

My finger is hovering over the screen as I work down the list, and it's shaking so much that at first I almost go past it, then I backtrack. Yes. There. *William Kingsley.* *WK.*

But now, unmistakeably, there's a noise outside Charlie's door.

Heart thudding, I scroll to 'shut down' and icons start disappearing from the screen with terrible slowness. As I click again – *why won't you shut down?* – the handle turns on the door and Bridget Ashworth comes in, accompanied by an older couple I immediately recognize as Charlie's parents from the photograph she used to keep by her bed. I snap shut the lid of the laptop.

'Sorry,' I say. 'I was just borrowing Charlie's computer. Mine's playing up.'

Bridget Ashworth frowns, and a deep purple stain creeps over her sallow face.

'I don't think that's really appropriate, Hannah, given the circumstances. Do you? Now, if you'll excuse us, I'm sure Charlie's parents would appreciate being left in peace to sort through her things.'

'Yes, of course.'

I head for the door, but Charlie's father steps forward to block the way. He's a tall, broad man with close-cropped grey hair and dark-framed glasses behind which his brown eyes are magnified. He is wearing a dark navy suit and tie and I remember how Charlie said her dad had no idea how to be himself and could only be the person other people thought him to be, the person who went out to work in a suit and made decisions and gave orders. It was exhausting, she said, this colossal effort to be somebody else.

'You're Hannah.'

It's a statement, not a question, so I don't bother replying. Or smiling. Seeing as his face is set like concrete.

'I'm Trevor Chadwick. This is my wife, Sandra. Charlotte mentioned you. She said you were a friend.'

I nod, glancing over at Charlie's mum, who has her daughter's face, except that its features are faded and grey, like a photo left on a windowsill. She puts a hand on her husband's arm as if to restrain him, but he jerks it off like it's a fly or a wasp.

'So, as her *friend*' – he over-pronounces the word as if the very notion is somehow ridiculous – 'why couldn't you have stopped her from doing this? You must have known her state of mind. Why didn't you tell someone? Or is that how it works with you people? You all egg each other on?'

You people. The words feel shameful.

'Trevor. Please!' Charlie's mum's eyes, which are

Charlie's eyes, except older and sadder, are swimming with tears.

Her husband steps back and flicks his hand as if he wants no more to do with it all, and I tell them for a third time how sorry I am and hurry from the room.

7

Corinne

Corinne was sitting down in the low blue velvet chair with her head bent, holding a tiny white romper suit stamped all over with pale blue rabbits pressed to her nose. Inhaling. But there was nothing there, of course. No milky, talcy baby smell.

She laid it down carefully on her lap and smoothed it out, folding it neatly in at both sides and then over in thirds. Then she added it to the pile on the floor.

She had already been there over an hour and, so far, she had taken out just seven little outfits from the white wooden chest of drawers. The trouble is that they each had a story, each caused her heart to grow heavier and the memories to catch in her throat like toast crumbs.

Hannah's face when she first told her about the pregnancy, a smile stretching her cheeks out till they seemed like they would burst. 'I've even bought something for it, Mum. For her. I'm sure it's a her.' Corinne's own misgivings at celebrating too soon had melted in the face of her daughter's obscene happiness. And then Hannah had produced a velvet tiger-print babygro with a hood with little ears on it and held it up. 'How could I resist?'

So much happiness, now folded up and neatly stacked

on the floor ready to be put away in the two big plastic carriers. For a moment, Corinne surveyed the pile with all its memories and thought that she could not bear it.

Danny hadn't been able to face packing it all up himself. He'd rung Corinne the night before and she'd been surprised at her own slight thud of dismay when she'd seen his name flash up on her screen.

Recently, things had been strained between them. Even if he understood in theory why Hannah had done what she did, he couldn't entirely forgive it. And that bothered Corinne. That lack of unconditionality.

Corinne stood up and pulled on the lowest animal on the pastel-coloured mobile that had belonged to Danny as a baby and now hung over the empty space where the cot used to be. She watched as it swung into motion, twirling round and round with a momentum of its own, the sheep and cow and horse and pig shapes swinging gracefully from their different-length cords.

Danny had been so childishly excited when he'd brought it home from his parents' house in St Albans and hung it proudly in the nursery. 'You know, I'm sure I even remember this,' he'd said, and Hannah had told him not to be such a knob, but he'd insisted. 'No, really, I have a subconscious memory of these shapes.'

Corinne had been amazed at how Danny's mum had managed to hang on to it for all those years, and in such perfect condition as well.

She gazed at the mobile and sighed. That would have to come down next, she supposed.

All of a sudden, the realization hit her again of what she was doing and what it meant. Packing up every trace of Emily. Folding away all Hannah's dreams.

59

And her own.

She stood up abruptly and went to the window. Danny and Hannah had the top-floor flat in a neat little Victorian terraced house on a quiet road which was part of a grid of streets known as the Ladder because they were abutted at each end by main roads, along which the traffic inched painfully at all times of day. It was rented, of course. The ridiculous cost of living in London meant they'd never managed to put by enough for a deposit for a place of their own, and Hannah's insistence on saving to have more IVF at a private clinic hadn't helped.

It had been such a relief when Hannah announced they were giving up on the whole idea. And then she'd got pregnant naturally. It had seemed like a miracle.

The door to Hannah and Danny's bedroom was open, and Corinne wandered in. The room was painted white, with high ceilings and two sash windows looking out on to the garden. One wall was crowded with blown-up photographs of Hannah and Danny's wedding. A black-and-white montage of friends and confetti and smiles.

Happy.

The bed was vast with plump white bedding, the pillow closest to her still bearing the imprint of Danny's head. The bedside table on this side, a low, wooden chest of drawers with peeling white paint, more shabby than chic, was piled with various objects, marking it out as definitely Danny's. A fat book claiming to be a social history of the entire human race, lying page-down and open so the spine was cracked, a beer bottle, still with a couple of inches of amber liquid inside, a scattering of loose change, as if he'd just emptied his pockets straight on to the surface, a phone charger, its white cable looping over the other items.

Corinne wandered around the foot of the bed to Hannah's side, which was neatly made up, the duvet cover smoothed down over the pillow, suggesting that Danny still clung to his own side, despite his wife's lengthy absence. Hannah's bedside table was no neater than her husband's. Assorted make-up, two hair elastics (Corinne's heart constricted when she saw the long fair hairs caught up in one of them), a novel that Corinne immediately recognized to be one she herself had lent her. They often swapped books, texting each other to find out which bit the other had got to.

She sank down on to the white expanse of duvet and picked the book up, opening it on the page that had its top-right-hand corner folded down, remembering how cross she used to get when Hannah would return a book she'd borrowed and the pages bulged with tell-tale creases. How petty that seemed now.

Corinne snapped the book shut and was surprised to see a white corner poking out from between two pages.

She took hold of the edge and pulled out a photograph.

'Oh!'

The sound of her own exclamation, tearing through the silent flat, shocked her. But her attention was fixed on the picture of a young woman Corinne had never seen before, looking up from a sofa as if someone had just called her name, half surprised, half smiling, so that one cheek only was sporting a dimple as large as a ten-pence piece. She had wild, dark curls tucked behind her ears and was wearing a white vest and faded cut-off denim shorts, with her bare feet resting on the coffee table in front of her.

But it was her eyes that had caught Corinne's attention, her eyes that had made Corinne cry out in surprise. Or rather, the absence of them. Because just above the woman's nose, in the space where her eyes should have been, someone had taken a red pen and drawn a line through from side to side over and over again, hard enough to gouge a hole in the middle.

The violence of it shocked Corinne and she turned over the picture with a sense of deep unease. There was just one word, written in the same red pen, the letters gone over several times, leaving an indentation in the paper.

BITCH.

8

Transcript

Filming. Day Thirty-eight. Interview with Dr Oliver Roberts, Director of The Meadows, a small, women-only private psychiatric clinic. Shot: outside in the grounds of the clinic. Dr Roberts is sitting at a picnic table.

JUSTIN (out of shot): Dr Roberts, you've had two suicides in six weeks in a clinic of just fifteen women. That doesn't reflect too well on the clinic, does it?
ROBERTS: Obviously, all deaths in the clinic affect us very deeply. As you say, we're a small clinic, which means we become almost like family, and to lose two of our members is a tremendous blow for us all. But you know, Justin, this is a high-risk clinic. Most of the women who come here have either attempted suicide or threatened it, so unfortunately the chances of this kind of thing happening are always going to be high. And if you look at our long-term record you can see we hadn't had any casualties at all for the four years before these two recent deaths. Of course, even one death is too many, but it's important to put this into perspective.
JUSTIN: Isn't it worrying that, after so long without a

single incident, two vulnerable women in your care have taken their own lives within six weeks of each other?

ROBERTS: Naturally, that's of concern, and we're in the process of investigating very thoroughly the circumstances surrounding these two tragic incidents. But I would say that copycat behaviour is not uncommon in clinics such as ours, where some of the residents are highly suggestible and the bonds built between them can be very strong.

JUSTIN: You think Charlotte Chadwick took her own life to copy Sofia Redding?

ROBERTS: I'm only saying that's one of the lines of enquiry we are pursuing, but as I say, we are carrying out a very thorough investigation into the circumstances that led up to both deaths. And of course, we will be reporting back to the Mental Health NHS Trust.

JUSTIN: So what would you say to reassure the families of other residents in the clinic who might now be anxious about whether their loved ones are safe here?

ROBERTS: While we understand the concerns of the families, there is absolutely no indication that these were anything more than two tragic, but unconnected, incidents. Both the women involved had histories of self-harm and suicide attempts so, while their deaths are deeply regrettable, sadly they tie into a pattern of behaviour that was already in place long before they arrived here.

JUSTIN: But surely the very function of a clinic such as this one is to supervise these vulnerable patients to protect them from themselves? And yet you've managed to take your eye off the ball twice in less than two months.

ROBERTS: If I could just correct you there, Justin. While it's true that Charlotte Chadwick's death took place at the clinic itself, we mustn't forget that Sofia Redding was on day leave when she took her own life. We had reached the decision, after lengthy consultations with Sofia and her family, that she was stable enough for occasional day visits home or out shopping as part of the gradual process of phasing her back into normal life. She'd already been on several such visits without incident. It was unfortunate that, on this occasion, her husband had to take one of their children to a dentist's appointment, so he couldn't drive her back to the clinic and he accepted her assurances that she'd be fine catching the train, a decision he, of course, now bitterly regrets.

JUSTIN: For anyone not familiar with the case, Sofia Redding was dropped off in the centre of Watford to catch a train back to the clinic, but she never arrived. She was found some hours later in scrubland behind a multi-storey car park near the station. She'd thrown herself off the fifth floor.

ROBERTS: Sofia had made a very strong recovery during her time here. She had convinced everyone, including her own family, that she no longer presented a risk to herself. We were talking about fixing a release date in the not too distant future. This seems to have been an opportunistic decision on her part, something that no one could reasonably have foreseen. This is an issue I go into in some detail in my book *Women on the Edge of a Nervous Breakdown*. I'm afraid that, when you enter the world of the suicidal mindset the only golden rule is that there are no rules.

JUSTIN: Is that a quote?

ROBERTS: I'm sorry?

JUSTIN: From your book?

ROBERTS: I do say something of the kind, but I really can't remember the exact wording. Anyway, do you think you have enough now? I have a very hectic schedule today.

JUSTIN: Oh, but I had some more—

ROBERTS: We'll have to schedule in another time. Sort it out with Bridget, would you?

9

Hannah

If I see another adult colouring book, I think I might explode. You'll find bits of me all over the day room – tucked behind sofa cushions, trapped in the windows that only open three inches so that on sunny days you feel as if you're proving like dough in the oven. Before I came here, I knew they were a thing. I work in publishing, and they basically kept us all going for a couple of years. But I'd never really given them a second thought, let alone used one.

The first day, Mum came in with a towering pile of novels and stacked them up next to my bed, but I never even opened them. It was as if my mind had literally broken and there was nothing there any more. And then Becs at work sent over a package containing three adult colouring books.

'Thought you might appreciate something mindless,' she wrote. Which was apt on many levels.

Suffering from mental illness is like suddenly becoming a foreigner in your own country. Close friends and relatives start talking very loudly and very slowly in the belief that you might understand them better. They don't realize it's not the understanding that's the problem, it's the application. When everything that made you *you* has disintegrated, it's possible to make abstract sense of things without having the first clue how they might be relevant to you.

The first three days in here passed in a black fug and I still remember very little, apart from odd moments that flicker in and out of my head like subliminal images in a film. Danny sitting on a chair in the day room with his head in his hands, his fingers wound up in his hair and me focusing only on how split the ends were. Mum talking too brightly, enthusing over my bedroom like it was the presidential suite at The Ritz or something – 'Look, what a state-of-the-art shower, darling!' – and her face when she realized that the unusual recessed nozzle wasn't an avant-garde design feature but to prevent someone from hanging themselves from the showerhead.

But on day four, one of the nurses – Darren, probably, as he's the only one who really notices anything – picked up one of the colouring books Becs had sent over, plonked it on the table in the day room and me in the chair next to it with a box of felt-tip pens. Whether it was because I was institutionalized sufficiently by then to follow any line of action suggested to me, or because I genuinely thought colouring in between lines might be a cool way to spend some time, I picked up a felt-tip pen and started.

And I've discovered that, even if it's not cool, it is at least a pleasant way to spend time. Since then, I've lost count of the number of books I've filled in, painstakingly colouring the tiniest of areas, making sure I don't go over the lines. I know it winds Danny up. 'She used to read Hilary Mantel and watch films in French without subtitles, and now she's fucking *crayoning*!' I heard him say to Mum once, when they were outside the day room and thought I couldn't hear.

But still I can't quite kick the habit. Becs gets her assistant to send them to me. Brown envelopes arrive every few days, even though it now makes me feel a bit ashamed.

When the door of the day room bursts open and Trevor and Sandra Chadwick walk in, I shut the book so violently that Stella, who has been sitting opposite me at the oval wooden table writing her journal for Dr Chakraborty, looks up, startled.

Charlie's dad comes right over to me so he is blocking out the light from the window.

'I want to know what she told you,' he says, and his voice is not kind. 'She didn't leave a note. She must have talked to someone. Confided in someone. What did she say?'

Sandra Chadwick hovers behind her husband. 'What Trevor means is—'

'What I mean is, she seemed to be so much better. So why do this now? Someone must know.'

'I don't think she did,' I say, before I can stop myself. 'Do it, I mean.'

Stella makes the noise she always makes when she gets anxious. A kind of excited squeak in the back of her mouth like when you accidentally tread on a dog's paw. I watch Trevor Chadwick's reaction as he notices Stella for the first time. There's a moment of shock in those magnified eyes, followed by a kind of knowing look that upsets me a lot more than the shock. I want to step in front of her. To shield her from him. Instead, I say:

'This is Stella. She was also a friend of Charlie's.'

'Oh yes,' says Charlie's dad. And he's not smiling. 'We've heard *all* about Stella.' Then he switches his attention back to me. 'What do you mean, you don't think Charlie did it? Are you saying you don't think she killed herself?'

'No, I don't. I was with her that day. She was fine. She didn't give any indication—'

'You don't have a clue.'

Sandra Chadwick's voice – suddenly loud and cold – seems to belong to someone else, and I freeze. She continues, moderating her tone only slightly. Her neck is thin and taut like a steel cable, and her eyes pop as if they're too big for her face.

'Did you know Charlotte and I share a birthday?'

I shake my head.

'No? Well, there's a lot you didn't know about my daughter. A lot she didn't want people to know. When it was her thirtieth birthday and my fifty-fifth, we went away to Cornwall together, as a family, and stayed in a gorgeous hotel overlooking the sea. And on the day itself, the sun shone like it had been ordered specially and we had lunch in a restaurant on the beach – chilled champagne and grilled fish – and Charlotte said she couldn't think of a better way of spending her birthday. Then we went back to the hotel to get ready for the party we were having that evening with friends who'd come down specially – hers and mine – and when I went through the interconnecting door to see what she was wearing, I found her with a plastic bag over her head,

70

opening a canister of camping gas she'd bought from the outdoors shop in the town.'

'Exit bag,' says Stella, in that breathy voice of hers.

'What?'

'That's what they're called. When you put a plastic bag over your head and let off some gas inside.'

Trevor Chadwick glares at her.

'I really don't think we need a how-to guide, thank you very much. What my wife is trying to tell you is that it's impossible to judge Charlotte's state of mind. All that day, she gave the appearance of being perfectly at peace, and yet she walked to the camping store and bought the gas. She planned it.'

'But I still think—'

Whatever I'm about to say is drowned out by the arrival of Bridget Ashworth, looking pink and out of breath, her lanyard hooked around her left shoulder. And just behind her, the blue chips of Dr Roberts' eyes.

'There you are. I've been searching all over.'

Bridget stops short, as if she's just remembered she's talking to grieving parents rather than obstinate patients. Then a thin smile spreads on her face, as though she's scraped the bottom of the smile jar and that's all that's left.

'How lovely that you've managed to find two of Charlotte's closest friends to reminisce with. I do hope they've been sharing some of the many special moments we enjoyed with Charlie during her time with us.'

Trevor Chadwick turns his magnified eyes to me and I'm shocked to see how much he resents me. It's there in his wife's face too, the face that is so much like Charlie's.

71

The question they don't bother to disguise: *Why couldn't it have been you, and not her?*

'I'm so glad I caught you before you left,' Roberts tells them. 'I wanted to bring you up to date on the steps we are taking to investigate what happened. Shall we go into my office for a few minutes?'

The Chadwicks turn as one towards the clinic's director, but they make no move to accept the invitation in his outstretched arm.

'I hold you personally responsible.'

Trevor doesn't raise his voice, just says the words in a dead tone, as if he's remarking on the weather.

Bridget Ashworth makes a little gasping sound and immediately starts speaking.

'It's natural for families in your position to look around for someone to blame but—'

'She was here to be protected from herself. You were supposed to protect her.'

Trevor is directing his comments solely at Dr Roberts, as if Bridget Ashworth and the rest of us don't exist.

'God knows you charge enough. I wonder whether the families of the rest of your patients—'

'We prefer to use the term "clients",' murmurs Bridget.

But Charlie's father continues right over the top of her: '. . . will want to go on paying the exorbitant fees, knowing that you and your staff are incapable of keeping the women in your charge safe.'

Dr Roberts adopts the face I recognize from his fund-raising events and media appearances. Polite, interested, sympathetic. But only skin deep.

'Mr and Mrs Chadwick, I completely understand your concern and I want to reassure you that everything humanly possible is done here to look after our residents. But part of the process of being here is to prepare our clients to go back into the wider world, which entails a certain amount of trust. We cannot, and should not, watch them twenty-four seven.'

'But that's exactly why she was here,' says Sandra Chadwick. 'So you could watch her.'

Dr Roberts closes his eyes briefly and nods in that way of his that means he's about to disagree with whatever it is you've just said, but before he can reply Trevor Chadwick grabs his wife's elbow and steers her towards the door, passing inches from Roberts in his sharp, grey designer suit, and brushing past Bridget Ashworth as if she is part of the furnishings.

'We're going now. We have a funeral to plan. But let me assure you, Dr Roberts, you haven't heard the last from us. We will be making some very unfortunate publicity for you and for this clinic. You'd better start making contingency plans, because there are going to be some lean times ahead once it gets out how you let two women die on your watch. We intend to make sure this never happens to anyone else.'

In the doorway, Sandra Chadwick stops. Turns back towards Roberts. Her face – Charlie's face – is a mask of pain.

'Do you have children?' she asks him.

He blinks, and Bridget Ashworth steps forward as if to protect him. The light coming in through the large sash window glints off the lenses of her glasses so it's impossible to see her eyes.

'I really don't think . . .' she says. But Mrs Chadwick has already gone.

73

Roberts and Bridget Ashworth exchange a long look, and for a moment I see a twinge of something like fear in his expression. Then he looks over at me and Stella with a small, sad smile.

'The Chadwicks are hurting,' he says to us. 'And as we all know, hurt people hurt people.'

It's one of his favourite mantras.

After Bridget and Roberts have left, Stella and I gaze at each other dumbly. I see that her hands are shaking, so I take one of them in mine and squeeze. The unpleasant confrontation between Roberts and the Chadwicks has left me knotted up inside, but when the adrenaline has died down I return to the scene that preceded it, with Sandra Chadwick telling me about Charlie's suicide attempt, and I feel as if someone is steadily letting the air out of me.

What a fool I have been. Charlie was a high suicide risk. That's why she was here. And despite the face she wore to protect everyone around her, she must have been planning this, or something like this, all along, just waiting for the right moment. And that moment came five days ago.

As so often, Stella's thoughts seem to be running along a parallel track to my own, because she says:

'She didn't do it. Right, Hannah?'

Though I feel her blue eyes fixed on me, expectant, I cannot force my own to meet them.

10

Corinne

'You don't think I should ask Danny?'

'No, Corinne. He'll think you've been snooping around their bedroom. What am I saying? You *were* snooping around their bedroom.'

'I wasn't snooping. I was just . . .'

But what was she just? Now, when Corinne tried to remember how she'd ended up in Danny and Hannah's bedroom two days before, her reasons seemed woolly and ill formed.

She put down the phone to Duncan, and picked up the photograph on the coffee table in front of her.

The woman's angry red gaze glared back at her and, though she'd now examined it over and over, looking for clues, Corinne still flinched from the violence of those deep, red lines.

How angry would a person have to be to do that?

What else was a person that angry capable of?

Hurriedly, she turned the photograph over. The word BITCH slapped her in the face. Who was the woman with the dark curls and the dimple like a wink in the middle of her cheek?

And who on earth was her daughter?

*

Sitting on the charcoal-grey sofa in the lobby of the publisher where Hannah used to work – no, *still* works, she reminded herself – Corinne felt a tug of pure grief for the Hannah who used to be at home here in this bustling office, with the male receptionist who was always climbing mountains or running marathons for charity dressed up as a chicken or a giant burger, and the young girls with high ponytails sweeping in and out with piles of books and soft, pink cheeks.

How many times over the years had Corinne sat here on this same bloody uncomfortable sofa, leaning back against the orange cushions, leafing through one of the titles artfully laid out on the coffee table – many of which Hannah had fallen in love with and developed clever campaigns around and cried proud tears over when they made bestseller lists or were awarded prizes – waiting for Hannah to finish work so they could go to a movie or to dinner or to some publishing event? With Danny working away so much, Corinne had been glad to stand in as her daughter's date.

'Corinne. How lovely to see you again.'

Hannah's friend, Becs, swooped in and wrapped Corinne in a tight hug before she had a chance to react. She smelled of handwash and cinnamon-flavoured nicotine gum.

'I think coffee is called for. Don't you think? Or gin, perhaps? Let's get out of here.'

In the lift mirror, Corinne had a chance to study Becs' outfit, a voluminous black affair. Becs only ever wore black. 'Not because it's slimming, because it bloody well isn't,' she once told her. 'I go around perpetually looking like a fat person at a funeral. But it saves all that faffing about trying to match your clothes to each other.'

Today, she had on a long black velvet tunic over a long black skirt, with biker boots and a chunky silver necklace of mayoral chain proportions. Her frizzy brown hair stood out around her round face like the coir of a coconut, and her washed-out blue eyes gazed out serenely from behind a pair of severe, black-framed glasses, at exactly the height of Corinne's shoulder.

They went to the coffee shop next door to the office building, where they were served by a man with a complicated top knot.

Corinne took the photograph out of her bag and lay it on the distressed-wood table between them. In the two days since she had found it in Hannah's room, she'd handled it so much it was going soft at the edges. The dark-haired woman smiled up at them over the top of one bare, shiny, tanned knee.

Becs made a sucking-in-air-between-teeth noise at the sight of the furious red pen marks.

'I'm getting the message this woman isn't very popular in some quarters.'

Wordlessly, Corinne turned the photograph over. The word BITCH was shocking in this cool coffee shop, with the weak March sun slanting in through the window.

'Do you know who she is?' But she could see from Becs' face the answer was no.

'Never seen her before. And I'd recognize those eyes anywhere.'

Corinne remembered now how Hannah used to complain that Becs used humour as a defence mechanism to deflect any intensity of emotion. *Probably why she's*

never had a relationship that lasted longer than a year.
Wasn't there something about a narcissistic, controlling
mother lurking in Becs' past?

But then, didn't mothers always get the blame?

'Ah, well. I knew it was a long shot.' Corinne could
hear her own voice leaden in her ears.

'I might be able to take a guess, though, but it would
only be a guess.'

Becs looked uncomfortable, like she was talking out
of turn.

'The thing is, I don't like to comment on other
people's relationships. It's not something I'm exactly
qualified to do.'

'But?'

Corinne could feel impatience bubbling up inside her,
coming out through her pores. So it took a while for her
brain to catch up with what Becs had just said.
Relationships? So this was to do with Danny? The
possibility had crossed her mind, of course, but she'd
quashed it instantly, mindful of the rift that had sprung
up between Hannah and her sister when Megan had
gone down that route.

It had been two or three months after they got back
from Crete. Hannah and Danny had a huge row –
Corinne had never found out why – and Hannah had
thrown him out for a couple of weeks. But then she'd let
him back, and Megan had made no secret of what a bad
idea she thought it was. And that had been that. After
Corinne saw the damage that had been done to her
daughters' relationship, she'd never dared probe into
what was going on with Hannah and Danny. And if
she'd had doubts, she'd kept them tightly enough

wrapped to be able to pretend they weren't there.

'Hannah thought Danny had someone else, in Edinburgh,' Becs admitted now.

'Why? Why did she think that?'

Becs was looking uncomfortable, playing with her necklace so that the heavy chain links clunked clumsily together. She unwrapped another piece of gum and stuffed it into her mouth. The scent of cinnamon wafted across the table.

'Corinne, I'm just speculating. I don't know who the woman in that photograph is. All I know is that Hannah went through a phase of suspecting Danny had someone else.'

Becs took off her glasses and wiped them on the hem of her tunic. When she looked up at Corinne without them, her pale eyes looked naked and exposed.

Corinne knew how irrational Hannah had been when they were trying the IVF. All those drugs. All those injections. It wouldn't surprise her if her daughter had accused her husband of all sorts of things that weren't real. But when they'd decided to stop trying for a baby, she'd seemed so much more relaxed. Could she really have been covering up something as big as this?

'It was little things, like he always seemed to have his phone turned off; and he came back from Edinburgh one time with a new shirt. She said he never would have bought himself new clothes – she usually bought his clothes for him; otherwise, he'd wear the same thing until it literally fell apart. Anyway, I know they rowed about it. Remember how she kicked him out that one time? But then she got pregnant and everything seemed back to normal . . .'

Corinne picked up the photo and turned it over and then over again, as if she might see something different. But no. Same girl. Same dimple. Same gouged-out eyes. Could her son-in-law really have been having an affair? Could he have chosen this woman with her skinny, bare legs over Hannah? The bolt of anger took her by surprise.

'But surely she'd have told you if he'd admitted it? She'd have shown you this photograph?'

Becs shrugged unhappily. 'Hannah shut herself off from us all a bit after she got pregnant.' Her face fell. 'What I mean is . . .'

All of a sudden, Becs screwed up her features and brought her fist down on the table. 'Do you know, I still can't believe she did it. I've been over it a hundred times, and I just don't understand. I mean, how could she have . . . ?'

Corinne hurriedly snatched up the photograph and stuffed it back into her bag, then she got to her feet, pushing her chair back so violently it fell backwards into a young woman with dyed silver hair.

'I really should be getting back. Hannah will be expecting me to visit her.'

Becs blinked at her.

'I didn't mean . . .'

'I know.'

Now Becs nodded and stood up, then insisted on giving Corinne another hug.

'Please tell her I miss her,' she said. 'I miss the old Hannah.'

A voice inside Corinne that she couldn't quite control whispered, 'I miss her too.'

11

Hannah

Last night I dreamt of Emily. First she was sitting in her cot at home, the one I picked out with Danny on the Saturday after the twenty-week scan. He'd been reluctant to buy it so early. 'There's still plenty of time,' he'd said. But I'd insisted.

In the dream, Emily was crying and looking out from between the bars, her dear little face screwed up. 'I'm coming,' I said, but even though I was running towards her, I wasn't getting any closer. No matter how fast I ran, she was always the same distance away, looking at me reproachfully. *Why don't you come?*

And then, suddenly, we were here in the clinic, and now Charlie was holding Emily and walking across the lawn towards the lake, and I was thinking, *Oh, good, now she's safe.* But then I saw Charlie's wrists were bleeding and there was a trail of blood on the grass where she'd walked and Emily's white Babygro was becoming redder and redder. I wanted to make her stop, but I couldn't move or speak, and Charlie's parents were with me, getting ready to go out for dinner. *You can never tell what's going on in someone's head.*

I woke up just now, my heart racing and my face wet with tears.

I lie in bed, not wanting to get up. Joni comes in to find out why I haven't appeared at breakfast.

'Not being funny, but if you want to get out of here you've got to play the game. Know what I mean? You don't show up to breakfast, that's not going to look good for you. They'll be thinking, *Well, how's she going to cope with going back to normal life when she can't even get out of bed?*'

I turn over and lie facing the wall until the creaking of the door and an audible huff that tails off down the corridor tells me Joni has left. Then Stella comes in and lies in her usual position across the foot of my bed. I know it's her because Stella has a smell that's all her own – a mixture of cigarette smoke and the coconut shampoo she uses.

'What about Judith?' she says after a while.

That's what Stella does sometimes – throws out a random statement.

'What about Judith?'

'She has Munchausen's, doesn't she? Trying to make herself sick so she can be the centre of attention. Remember when she ate that wax crayon? What if she's moved on from doing it to herself? What if she did something to Sofia, and then Charlie, because she thinks life should always be like *Casualty*? That could have happened.'

I turn around then. It isn't like Stella to have thought something through so thoroughly, or to pass judgement. There's something different about her these days, though I can't pinpoint what.

82

'Don't be daft,' I say, more sharply than I intend. 'Sofia and Charlie are *dead*. That's a whole lot different to nibbling a crayon to make yourself throw up.'

Stella shrugs. She's wearing a soft, form-fitting, leopard-print jumper and her narrow shoulders move up and down like animal haunches.

'Well, Odelle thinks she had something to do with it.'

'Odelle is an idiot.'

Still, now she's planted the idea in my mind I can't get rid of it. A week on from Charlie's death, and it's still all I think about. That afternoon in art therapy I find myself staring at the back of Judith's head. How would you know if someone was dangerous? In a place like this, where we're all a bit dangerous, how could you tell if someone was a threat to the rest? *Could you have done that? What are you capable of?*

I look at Odelle and Frannie, and Nina, whose shoulders sag as if unable to bear the weight of her own head.

I can't believe it. Not of any of them. But then look at me. Look what I was capable of.

Today Laura is making us draw with sticks of charcoal. My fingers are already black with the stuff. My drawing is mostly black too. I can't shake off last night's dream and everything is smudged with grief.

We're supposed to be drawing Frannie, who is sitting in the centre of the room staring rigidly ahead. Every now and then she raises a hand towards her hair, then slams it back down again when she realizes what she's doing. Her face is stiff with anxiety and I feel an answering ache of sympathy.

'Don't get hung up on the individual features,' says Laura. 'Concentrate on the lines – the curve of her cheek, the lovely shape of her neck.'

Laura runs her fingertip over Frannie's throat to demonstrate and Frannie erupts into a furious pink blush.

'Try to capture the essence of Frannie. The thing that makes her special. Is it the way she hunches her shoulders because she's nervous, or her tiny, delicate hands?'

'Or the bald patches on her head?' mutters Judith.

Frannie doesn't indicate that she's heard, but I see tears beading in the corners of her eyes.

'Be kind, ladies. Never forget how blessed we all are just to be here in this amazing world,' says Laura, without looking at anyone in particular, and for a moment I think I can see tears in her eyes too, but then she's chatting to Odelle about perspective and I guess I'm mistaken.

At six o'clock, we have Evening Group, and I have that familiar feeling like I'm swimming in oil and every direction I look is black. I felt like this a lot when I first came here, and it scares me to think that nine weeks have gone by and I'm going backwards rather than forwards. It's a combination of last night's dream, and Sandra Chadwick's description of how Charlie had a lovely lunch and then went back to her hotel room and tried to gas herself in a plastic bag. I feel like I don't know anything and everything I think I know is wrong.

Yet, though the encounter with Charlie's parents has taken away the incentive to dig deeper into the meaning of her to-do list and that name William Kingsley, I still I can't fully shake off my misgivings. There's a stubborn part of me that remains convinced I'd have known if she'd been planning to kill herself, though I also hear her voice in my ear, gently mocking: *It's not all about you, you know, Hannah.*

The film crew are with us in Group. Despite their assurances that we can vet the documentary footage before the final edit, their presence makes me nervous. They're proof of the line that exists between us and the rest of the world. We're oddities. Freaks. Specimens in jars.

Justin, the director, is all right, I suppose, even though his hairstyle, foppishly long and messily swept over to the side, is far too young for a man in his late thirties and he is doused in self-absorption like cheap cologne. But Drew, the cameraman, gives me the creeps. Always watching with those dark eyes, so close together they're almost touching in his yellow, potato-ish face. Never saying anything, just staring or following you with his camera lens.

The day room is divided into two areas. At the back, nearest the window, is the oval table where we write our journals or go online during our WiFi sessions, while the area nearer the door contains a sofa and a smattering of low, cushioned chairs. When we have Group, we push the sofa back and bring the chairs into a circle, together with some of the white folding seats that are stacked against the far wall next to the shelving unit where we keep our books and pens in cubbyholes labelled with our names. This evening, Roberts is leading the session, and he has the look of someone with other places he'd rather be.

Judith has her hand up. She's a large-framed, lumpy woman with long, wild hair and a habit of folding her arms right across her body as if giving herself a hug.

'People are saying things,' she says flatly.

Roberts stifles a sigh, then glances at the camera and rearranges his face into an expression of encouragement.

'Such as?'

'They're saying I had something to do with Sofia and Charlie topping themselves. I didn't, and it's very hurtful.'

Judith's voice quivers with outrage, yet she can't help casting a look around to make sure everyone is watching her.

'Why do you suppose they're singling you out, Judith?'

'Because of my history.'

She sounds quite proud, and I'm sure I see her eyes flick towards the camera, as if checking to see how her performance is going down.

'Can you elaborate, Judith?'

'Because of times in the past where I've done things to myself deliberately so they would have to give me treatment.'

'Medical treatment, you mean?'

'Yes. But I never did anything to anyone else. I wouldn't.'

'Would anyone else like to contribute here? Anyone heard these rumours, or been passing them on?'

Everyone looks at the floor, or up at the ceiling. From the corner of my eye, I see Frannie's hand creep up to her hair and give a sharp tug. To my left, Nina slides further down in her seat, as if the effort of staying upright is too great.

Up until now, Dr Roberts has been sitting back in his chair with his left leg bent out to the side, ankle resting on his right thigh. Now, abruptly, he changes position, leaning forward over his steepled hands, taking a deep breath in.

'Right. I'm glad you brought the subject up, Judith.'

Judith flushes with pleasure.

'It gives me a chance to address this whole issue head on. Look, I know we're all still grieving. We will be for a long time. And grieving people look for answers, even when, sometimes, there are none. We all wish we could rewind the clock. But the fact is, there's nothing any of us could have done.'

He slowly scans the circle, his eyes lingering on each of us in turn. When it comes to me, the hairs on my arm rise up and I look away, straight into the camera, which Drew has moved around towards the front. The lens is trained on my face, as if it's trying to drill a hole into me and suck my soul right out.

12

Corinne

Corinne didn't know what she was doing here. By 'here', she didn't mean in this particular pub. She'd been here several times before – it was one of those airy north London gastropubs with high ceilings and wooden floors and huge windows looking out on to the wide, leafy street, and a stack of brightly painted wooden high chairs in the corner. No, she didn't know what she was doing here *tonight*. With a load of Hannah's friends, celebrating Danny's birthday.

Without her daughter.

The invitation had come about by accident. She'd arrived at the clinic to visit Hannah and found Danny there. 'Isn't it your birthday soon?' she'd asked him, just for something to say. 'You should celebrate.' Which is when Danny admitted he'd already organized a drink in the pub in Chalk Farm. 'Just low key.' And here she was.

Danny sat at the head of the long rustic wooden table, looking relaxed and handsome and – she might as well say it – happy. Around him sat all Hannah and Danny's friends and some of Danny's colleagues from Duncan's company, and the gay couple who lived downstairs. Plus a smattering of people Corinne had never seen before.

But no sign of the woman in the photograph, thank God.

Corinne nursed her large Merlot and forced her features into a half-smile in order to look approachable. 'You're Hannah's mum, aren't you?' It was one of Hannah and Danny's downstairs neighbours. Marco. She'd met him one night when Danny was away and she and Hannah had enlisted his help in putting up a set of flat-pack Ikea drawers.

'I've been wanting to find out how Hannah is. We've been so worried about her.'

'Couldn't you just have asked Danny?'

She hadn't meant to sound ungracious, but the question had taken her by surprise. Sitting here with her polite smile on, she hadn't been prepared for intense conversation. Marco looked embarrassed. He was a short, squat man with bulging biceps that strained the fabric of his T-shirt. His closely shaved head might have made him look intimidating if it weren't for his large, expressive brown eyes. Eyes which were now liquid with sympathy.

'I have asked him, of course. But he's made it clear he doesn't want to talk about it. And the last thing we want to do is upset him. After everything else he's been through.'

What about what Hannah is going through? She bit the words back and nodded.

'Of course. You're right. Hannah is doing fine. Really well.'

'We felt so guilty afterwards. Thinking that we could have done more. There were all those signs we didn't act on.'

'Signs?'

Suddenly, the rest of the pub, with the loud conversations vying with the background music, faded away and all she could see was Marco. Looking at her.

'Yes. I think I first noticed after the twenty-week scan. Danny had been away so he missed it and, when he came back, Hannah made him this really funky card where she'd cut out the scan picture and stuck it on the front, surrounded by kitsch neon flowers, with "meet our girl" printed on the bottom. Cheesy, but in a cute way. Danny was dead chuffed and insisted on showing it to me and Phil when we went up for a drink, but then they got into an argument about Hannah not wanting to send a scan picture to Danny's parents. I guess it's no secret they've never been close. She kept saying it was a private thing. And, after we'd gone, they had a huge row about it.' He looked sheepish and added, by way of explanation: 'The sound travels through the floorboards.

'And then, another time, they were round at ours and Hannah suddenly shouted out "now, feel!", wanting him to put his hand on her belly, but he took too long to get to her and she went ballistic with him for missing the moment. She accused him of deliberately detaching himself from the pregnancy, saying that he didn't want the baby. It just came out of nowhere. All this rage. Afterwards, she couldn't stop apologizing. Sent us down a home-made chocolate cake. Said she was mortified. Blamed it on hormones.' Marco said the word *hormones* as if it were something unpleasant he'd found on the bottom of his shoe. 'We've been kicking ourselves for not noticing. I mean, the alarm bells were louder than Big Ben.'

Marco was summoned over to the other side of the table. Corinne's smile felt tight in her face. If anyone ought to have heard alarm bells, it was her.

'So happy you could make it.' Danny slipped into the seat just vacated by Marco. Corinne glanced over at him. He looked flushed and slightly drunk. Alive. So different to the strained look he habitually wore when he was visiting Hannah in the clinic.

'I like the jewellery,' she said, pointing to a slim silver band around his wrist.

Danny shook down the sleeve of his shirt to cover the bangle.

'Getting in touch with my feminine side,' he said, but the stiffness was back across his shoulders.

'I'm worried about Hannah,' Corinne said. 'She is still refusing to accept that the two deaths at the clinic were suicide. She now believes someone might be deliberately hurting the patients.'

'That's because she's crazy, Corinne.'

It was as if she'd been slapped.

Danny continued, in a more conciliatory tone. 'I'm sorry. I shouldn't have said that. But you must see she's not getting any better. The rubbish she comes out with. Not surprising, I guess, when you see the people she's mixing with in there, like that girl who can hardly move her face.'

'Stella. Her name is Stella.'

'Whatever. She's not normal, Corinne. And Hannah's head is being filled with all kinds of shit. She thinks she's getting out of there. She thinks she's coming home.'

'Well, she is. Just as soon as Dr Roberts gives her the all-clear.'

'Dream on, Corinne.'

'What?'

'I spoke to Roberts. He says he's still a very long way off knowing exactly what happened. And to be honest, I don't know if I want Hannah back.'

'At the moment, you mean?'

Danny looked at her. Looked away. His fingers closed absently around the silver bracelet and he turned it round and round on his wrist as though he were tightening a screw.

On her next visit to the clinic, the day after Danny's birthday bash, Corinne found Laura in the art room, collecting up what looked like a pile of scribbles such as one might find in an infants' class.

'I got them to draw with charcoal taped on to the end of a stick of bamboo,' Laura explained. 'It's a really useful exercise in intuition and interpretation, rather than skill. It's about relinquishing control.'

Laura was wearing a long electric-blue jersey tunic with matching wide-legged jersey trousers and a scarf looped loosely around her neck. Corinne found herself gazing covetously at the younger woman's cropped black hair. Like most women she knew, she toyed periodically with the idea of having a gamine cut, but she was well aware that you needed a gamine face like Laura's to go with it.

'I came to find you to talk about Hannah,' Corinne said. 'It's just, she seemed to be doing so well. But I'm worried that this thing with Charlie—'

'I understand.' To Corinne's embarrassment, Laura stepped forward and took her hand. 'I've been worried about her myself. Her previous work has been so neat, so mannered, but her drawings recently seem to indicate a turbulent mindset, and the last task I set them she failed to complete at all, which is very unlike her.'

Fear twisted Corinne's stomach into a knot.

'Have you spoken to Dr Roberts about your concerns?' Laura's voice was light and calm, but Corinne thought she detected an inflection as she said the doctor's name, an emphasis where there perhaps ought not to have been.

'No. I didn't want to . . . that is, Hannah is very anxious to be home as soon as possible. And, obviously, we're desperate to have her home, so I don't want to give Dr Roberts any reason to think she should stay here longer than necessary.'

'I understand.'

Corinne was relieved when Laura dropped her hand and started moving around the art room, closing up easels and stacking them against the back wall.

Corinne had never been very touchy-feely. Even with close friends, it was awkward. She'd had one friend who insisted on looping her arm through hers when they walked along, and Corinne had never been able to tell her how stressful she found it. She was the only woman she knew who tensed up during a massage. All that laying on of hands.

Corinne stepped forward to help Laura clear up and, for a few moments, they didn't speak, the silence punctuated only by the clack of the easels folding together.

'Does Hannah ever draw Danny?'

Laura looked puzzled by Corinne's sudden change of conversation.

'Her husband. Danny,' Corinne went on. 'I just wondered if she ever put him in her art?'

'I'm afraid I'm not comfortable with commenting on the content of Hannah's work,' said Laura. 'Art therapy is a therapy just like any other, and there needs to be absolute trust between me and my clients. I'm sure you understand.'

'Yes, of course. I'm sorry for asking.'

'Is Hannah's relationship with her husband something that's causing you concern?' Laura asked.

Now it was Corinne's turn to feel as if the other woman had overstepped the mark. 'No! Hannah and Danny are tight as a drum!'

After she'd left the room she kept hearing her own voice in her ear. *Tight as a drum.* Where had that stupid expression even come from?

On her way into the day room she was accosted by the two men who were making the documentary about the clinic. Immediately, Corinne's hackles rose. The documentary had been sold to them all on the basis that mental illness needed to be destigmatized and that being able to see how 'ordinary' all the residents were would go some way towards removing the 'them and us' misconceptions that still abounded, and might encourage those currently suffering in silence to seek help. Plus, Roberts had offered a considerable discount in fees while filming was taking place: 'To compensate for the inconvenience,' he'd said.

Hannah had been happy to take part, but now Corinne wished she'd done more to dissuade her. With all the drama surrounding Charlie's death and Sofia's before, it sometimes seemed the film-makers were recording a soap opera rather than a serious documentary.

'Would you mind if we asked you a few questions? It's Corinne, isn't it?'

This man with the microphone was Justin. It was the cameraman with the dead, dark gaze whose name she'd completely forgotten.

'Not now,' she said brusquely, pushing past without meeting their eyes. It was the technique she used for street charity collectors.

'How are you feeling now about the tragic death of Charlie Chadwick?' Justin continued, as if she hadn't spoken. 'Has it made you more concerned about your own daughter's security?'

'My daughter is fine, thank you. We expect she'll be well enough to come home any day.' She paused. 'Can you stop pointing that thing at me?'

The cameraman put his camera down, but his impassive gaze was almost as intrusive as the lens had been.

Corinne pushed open the door of the day room, feeling flustered. Justin's words had hit a nerve. Just how safe *was* Hannah in this place? An image flashed into her head of the photograph of the woman with the dark curls, her eyes scored through with red pen, and she stopped still.

Maybe Hannah wasn't safe here. But what if home wasn't any safer?

13

Laura

The talk with Hannah's mum had upset Laura.

At home that evening, she moved from room to room in her garden flat, unable to settle to anything. Normally, the flat soothed her. Her sanctuary. She'd lived there for six years now and, even though it was only rented, the first thing she'd done when she moved in was paint it from top to bottom. Your home was your refuge. It was so important to imprint oneself on every surface of it so you maintained a sense of yourself and your place in the world.

Laura knew what it was like to feel you had no place.

The galley kitchen was a warm yellow, her bedroom a cool, soothing green, while the living room, with its high ceilings and French doors leading out on to the garden, was a deep red, so that sometimes Laura felt as if she was walking right into a pulsating heart.

She unrolled her yoga mat and laid it out on the floorboards in front of the black cast-iron fireplace and sat cross-legged with her head tipped to one side, trying to empty her mind. Then she tipped her head the other way and did the same thing.

She knew why the chat with Corinne had bothered her so much.

It was the look on Corinne's face when she'd talked about her daughter. That naked, almost greedy, need to see Hannah protected. Kept safe.

Laura remembered how she had found herself on the verge of tears and had had to bustle about the room snapping shut easels while she composed herself. But Laura was still learning to accept herself and that meant understanding what lay behind some of her behaviours and not giving herself a hard time about them. You'd have thought she'd know everything there was to know about herself by now. Converting from nursing to occupational therapy and then specializing in art therapy and even, recently, a bit of hypnotherapy, had involved a fair amount of mandatory self-analysis, laying bare her innermost thoughts and motivations. But she'd realized long ago that the human spirit is a work in progress, a pot that spins endlessly on the wheel, changing shape but never finished. One could never fully know oneself. The most one could hope for was to accept oneself.

She picked up her phone and dialled, growing impatient when the ringing went on and on. Annabel's voice on her voicemail was calm as always. Soothing. It was six fifteen and Laura imagined her standing in her little box-like kitchen cooking herself something. Or perhaps she'd have her grandchild to visit. The tiny, framed baby picture on Annabel's mantelpiece flashed into Laura's mind and she felt a brief, sharp pang at the thought of Annabel sitting on the living-room carpet surrounded by brightly coloured children's toys. She launched into a long message describing Corinne's visit and the feelings it had stirred up. Embarrassingly, she found herself tearing up all over again, just describing it. Nevertheless, by the time she had finished, she was surprised to find herself feeling much better.

Kneeling back down on the mat, she went into child's pose, bent double over her knees, her arms stretched out straight in front of her. She luxuriated into the stretch, envisaging the tension seeping slowly out of her like someone opening a valve in a radiator.

Still in child's pose, she turned her face to the side. A movement caught her eye. Something black scuttling across the floorboards. Laura sat up. Watched the spider's progress with interest. What was it even doing here, when the weather was still so cold?

She went into her kitchen to fetch a glass and then looked around for something to scoop the spider up with, eventually settling on a postcard of a Georgia O'Keefe flower painting she'd brought back from the Tate last year. Such a joyous picture.

The spider was still there, just where she'd left it.

Laura carefully held the glass over the insect, pausing to admire its legs, black and spiky, like the stitches in a wound. But hold on a moment. Now she was so close, Laura could see that one of the creature's legs was damaged, strung out behind it like a tow rope. Such a terrible pity. For a moment, all was suspended, the rim of the glass hovering over the crouched insect, the tip of Laura's tongue protruding slightly from her mouth in concentration. Then down came the glass. The spider trapped.

Carefully, she slid the postcard under the glass, making sure not to let up on the pressure with the other hand. Getting slowly to her feet, she made her way across the room, holding the glass with the injured spider outstretched. She noticed with a swell of pity that the end of the broken leg was showing on the outside of the glass.

Crossing the hall, she passed the front door. This being the garden flat, Laura had her own entrance. But instead of heading outside, she went straight into the kitchen. At the sink, she hesitated, watching the spider, which seemed now to have concertinaed itself so that it was half the size it had appeared before. Then, in a deft movement, she turned the glass upside down, dislodging the spider so it fell to the bottom.

Laura slowly slid the flower postcard from the top of the glass and then, being careful not to make any sudden movements, she positioned the glass under the tap and used her free hand to turn on the cold water, stopping only when the glass was completely full.

Satisfied that the spider had drowned, she put the glass down next to the sink and headed back into the living room to complete her salutations.

14

Hannah

'How are relations with your husband, Hannah?'

Relations? Ugh. Was ever a word more imbued with double meaning? Still, sitting in the padded chair opposite Dr Roberts, facing him across his impressive desk, I press my nails into my leg and try not to react.

'They're great. Danny's great. Really supportive.'

Roberts leans back in his chair and, using his right foot for ballast, swivels slowly from side to side until I want to kick his leg right out from under him, sending him sprawling on to the thick carpet of his corner office on the first floor of the old building.

'Did he tell you he came to see me?'

Now I'm the one feeling as if I've been kicked. Why would Danny go to see Roberts? I've hardly seen my husband recently. He claims to be working. *'You've been with her. Admit it!'* I screamed at him the last time he was here. I'd told myself I wouldn't go there. But the words were out before I could stop them. 'There's no reasoning with you,' he said, getting to his feet.

After he'd gone, it occurred to me that he'd been looking for an excuse to leave since he'd arrived.

Roberts is gazing at me with those blue eyes which,

apparently, make a certain type of television viewer weak at the knees. Charlie and I did a Twitter search on him once, after he'd appeared in a documentary about treating eating disorders.

I know it's inappropriate when it's such a tragic subject, but Dr Roberts? I totally would. #CantEatWontEat

Are all shrinks that hot? Where do I sign up to get myself committed. LOL. #DrRoberts #CantEatWontEat

We'd laughed about some of the things people had said, but at the same time the whole thing had left me feeling unsettled, as if I were out of sync with the world.

'What did he want to talk to you about?'

Roberts is still leaning back in his chair. He has a pen in his hand and is running it gently and deliberately across his lower lip.

'What do *you* think he might have wanted to see me about?'

Mouth firmly closed, I grit my teeth and focus on the pen. Back and forth. Back and forth. Then, when I can't bear to watch it any more, I turn my head to my left to look through the large sash window, following the slope of the lawn down to the murky grey sweep of the lake.

Finally, I shrug. 'No idea,' I say. 'Progress report, perhaps?'

'That was some of it, certainly. Danny wanted to know how you were getting on. He said you'd been talking to him about leaving us.'

The jolt of betrayal is sharp and surprisingly painful.

'It's just I'm feeling so much better,' I lie. 'I think being home would speed up my recovery.'

'Danny doesn't agree. And I'm afraid I don't either. Hannah, we've done a lot of work trying to figure out the background to what happened. But until you're willing to confront things head on, I'm afraid we're only just scratching the surface.'

'Confront what head on?'

'Your behaviour. Your thinking. The underlying causes.'

I have a flashback to making a card, sticking the scan photo down on to the card. Tracing my fingertip along the contours of Emily's head.

'I know what I did wasn't rational. I understand that now. There was a lot of stress in my life at the time. I let it get out of hand.'

I am conscious of the back of my mouth feeling dry and furry like felt. I don't want to talk about Emily. Don't make me talk about Emily.

'What did you let get out of hand, Hannah?'

'Everything.'

I remember myself lying in the bath, stroking my rounded tummy, talking to her. Telling her about her Grandma Corinne and her Grandpa Duncan. Looking up and seeing Danny standing in the doorway, an unreadable expression on his face. 'Come in and say hello,' I'd told him.

'I will. Just as soon as I've sent this one email.'

'Always in a rush, your daddy,' I whispered after he'd gone, dripping warm water on to the mound of my belly.

A savage twist of grief.

'You see, the thing that worries me, Hannah, is whether this is a pattern of behaviour, this unwillingness to challenge your own role in determining what happens to you, to take responsibility for your own agency. Take, for instance, your conversation with Mr and Mrs Chadwick, Charlie's parents. These are grieving parents who've just lost their daughter, and rather than offer them sympathy you insist on trying to impose upon them your own version of events – that someone deliberately harmed Charlie – despite knowing that it doesn't align with the facts, and despite the upset you could guess it would cause.'

'I wanted them to be aware, that's all.'

'Aware of what?'

'Aware that not everyone believes Charlie killed herself.'

'And you thought that might be reassuring to them?'

'Not reassuring. But truthful.'

'Hannah, you're an intelligent woman. You have a loving family, a supportive husband, a good job. You have everything to get back to. But there is only so much we can do here. You have to start trying to help yourself. Focus on the issues that affect you and your life. On what led you here. This is about your life. Your family. Your future. Your choice.'

Only after I've left his office and am heading back to the day room does it occur to me that this sounds like a threat.

All day I am haunted by the knowledge that Danny has gone behind my back to tell Roberts he doesn't want me home. At first I am only hurt, but later, upset turns to anger.

It's Danny's fault. All his fault.

If he'd just been more focused. More present. All those appointments he missed. All those scans. Happy to get the news second-hand. Another kind of husband would have been able to see I wasn't myself. Even Marco, our downstairs neighbour, had an inkling. I saw it in the way he watched me. His voice when he asked, 'Is everything OK?'

But Danny's attention had been elsewhere.

On her.

Not on his wife and daughter.

And now he's having private meetings with Roberts.

My anger is powerful, and I start to enjoy it. Such a welcome change from the guilt I've been drowning in. I'm angry with everyone. My mum for not being able to stop it all from happening, Roberts for thinking he knows me when he doesn't know the first thing about me, Charlie for leaving me.

'You have to let it go,' Mum said when she visited yesterday. 'This anger with Charlie. She was ill. Just like you were ill. That's why you're here. To get better.'

But that's not why I'm angry. I'm angry because, despite what Roberts says, I still can't make myself believe she killed herself.

You know, there was a time I couldn't think even a day ahead. Not even an hour. The future was so terrifying I had to exist from moment to moment. But now I'm booking a summer holiday. That's progress, right? That's what Charlie told me the morning she died.

But by not believing she did it, I've set myself apart

from everyone else. Once, that wouldn't have bothered me. But now I know that being apart, out of sync, is dangerous. The gap between your own self and the prevailing wisdom is a hole which a person can fall into and drown in without even making a splash.

Later that afternoon Darren is monitoring the internet session around the oval table in the day room. Most days we have two half-hour supervised internet sessions, one in the morning and one at this time of day, right before dinner and Evening Group. We tease him a bit about his purple jumper. Normally, Darren is the most conservative dresser – all checked shirts under navy or brown V-necks and corduroy trousers. But since he got a new girlfriend he's been dressing more daringly. Last week he sported a pair of black skinny jeans, which he wore with self-conscious stiffness. And now a purple jumper.

'I just fancied a change, that's all. It's nothing to do with Jolene.'

He pronounces it Joe-lin, heavy on the first syllable. But there's no disguising a name like that.

When the teasing dies down, I open up my laptop. There are internet sites that are discouraged in here. Facebook. Twitter. All the places that remind us of our other lives. The lives that drove us here. It's a relief, really. I don't want to know how smoothly the office is running without me, or how much fun my friends are having – all the parties and the holidays and the long Sunday pub lunches. I don't want to see the pictures of their weddings and their cats.

And their babies.

TAMMY COHEN

I go on to Google and type in 'William Kingsley'. There are over three million entries, including a chain of estate agents in Missouri (*'your home is where our heart is'*) and a nineteenth-century politician. I am on page four when I become conscious of someone behind me. A waft of coconut shampoo. The hairs on the back of my neck prickle.

I click off Google and turn my head so quickly I get one of those screaming muscle pains that come out of nowhere.

'What you doing?'

Stella is standing against the light so that her face is in darkness, and there's a weird halo effect around her head.

'Oh, nothing. Just killing time.'

I hold my head in both hands and gently move it from side to side, trying to uncrick my neck.

Stella pulls up a chair next to me and sits down. She is dressed down for her, in a black velvet top and black leggings. Darren looks over, blushes and looks away again.

Stella is such an enigma. So childlike sometimes, and other times seeming like she knows so much more than she's saying. So full of secrets. She's been in the clinic for five months already and still nobody is completely sure where she comes from, who she is. She has told me her stepfather was in the military and that he and her mother lived all over the world before ending up, finally, in Washington, where he now does something in intelligence. Stella went to boarding school in Devon and Northumberland and Sussex. There is family money. A wealthy grandfather on her mother's side. And new

106

half-siblings who have inherited her stepfather's red hair. A pattern of alcoholism runs through the generations.

Stella rarely has visitors. Her mother pays the fees and calls on the clinic's phone once a fortnight. I can always tell it's her because Stella sits in virtual silence, holding the phone and rocking backwards and forwards. As she's Dr Chakraborty's patient, he sends a regular progress email to her mother detailing her treatment and how she's responding to it.

'Our optimum outcome would be for Stella to reach a state of self-acceptance,' one of the emails read. Stella knows this because her mother quoted it back to her on the phone. We had a running joke about that for a while. 'My optimum outcome from this boiling kettle would be a cup of tea.'

Though Stella's family is rich, they stopped supporting her when they realized surgery had become an addiction rather than a one-off fix and when the surgeons in the States and the UK started refusing to treat her, so she'd go to Brazil or South Korea, not caring about the credentials of the doctors who sliced her open. When she was forty-nine thousand pounds in debt she had to have emergency surgery to remove a fat clot that had formed in her lung after a bungled liposuction procedure in Turkey, and when she came out of hospital she was jobless and homeless and broke enough to accept her parents' ultimatum. They'd pay off her debts if she got treatment.

So here she is.

I know Stella makes some people uneasy. The way her wide blue eyes never seem to blink. The sharp points of her cheekbones. The exaggerated curves and plastic smoothness. The way you never seem to be able to grab a hold of who she is.

Danny can't cope with her at all. 'Don't you find her freaky?' he asked after the first time they met. He doesn't see what I see. The child entombed inside the stretched skin like a sausage in its casing.

After dinner we are back in our safe circle in the front section of the day room while Dr. Chakraborty chairs Evening Group. He always looks so hunched and apologetic when he chairs, as though he's embarrassed to be here.

He's not the only one.

I used to make presentations to my entire company. I'd accompany important authors on grand book tours around England, organize parties where I'd dress up in my fanciest clothes and spend the evening introducing people to each other and engaging total strangers in conversation.

And now I sit in a circle with hair that needs a wash and bitten nails and sweatpants that I wear day in, day out because – well, why not? – and I don't recognize myself, I really don't.

Dr Chakraborty has skin the colour of poured honey and brown eyes that are like small pools of sadness in his face. His luxuriant white hair makes his smooth face appear almost boyish. He has a way of looking at you that's complicit, as if you're both in the same rather surprising boat. *Isn't this a turn-up?* his expression seems to say. *You and me. Here. Who would have thought it?*

Charlie told me he's divorced and that that, too, came as a surprise to him. 'His wife gave him no warning, apparently. He got home from work and she was gone.' I didn't ask her how she knew. She was just that kind of person. You wanted to tell her things.

He turns to me. 'Hannah, we were talking last time about the background to your admission here.'

When he says 'admission', he really means 'breakdown', and I think I might love him for his delicacy and the way he dips his eyes momentarily, as if in deference to my feelings – as opposed to Roberts, whose glacial blue eyes are like scalpels cutting you open, laying bare the pulpy, beating mess of you.

Dr Chakraborty checks through his notes.

'If you remember, you talked us through the miscarriage, the IVF, how it felt when, all around you, friends were getting pregnant, some seemingly by accident, and how every month when your period came it was like a bereavement.'

Everyone is looking at me, and I swallow, feeling like there is a golf ball stuck in my throat.

'Can you bring us up to date now? Can we talk about' – there's a momentary pause as Dr Chakraborty glances again at the notepad that is open on his lap – 'Steffie. Can you tell us something about Steffie?'

It's a name I never say out loud. I even avoid sounding it out in my head, as if just the sound of those two syllables linked together has magical powers. So to hear it spoken twice in the same breath is like a physical shock. I'm aware of my heart pounding, a tinny taste in my mouth.

'I don't like to talk about her.'

109

When I speak, it's as if my words are sandpapering my tongue.

Dr Chakraborty nods approvingly. 'Of course. Why would you? And yet.'

And yet, here we are. And I am here to get better. Getting better means talking about it. And it starts with her.

Steffie.

Curls, fat like squid tentacles and blackly glossy. A bare brown knee poking through her jeans like a knuckle. A smile that wrapped itself around my neck and pulled itself tighter and tighter until I couldn't breathe. Dark eyes that danced with the camera lens. It was only a photograph. It fell out from the pages of a novel Danny had been reading on the plane, and had stashed in the hidden inside pocket of the case he always takes to Edinburgh. I never touched that case. Except that Mum had to go away for work and the strap on her weekend bag was broken so she needed to borrow one, and I couldn't be bothered to go up to the loft to find mine. The case was dark blue, made of some kind of shiny nylon stuff. I can still remember the sound of the zipper of the pocket opening, my curiosity about the novel, whether it was the same copy Megan gave me ages ago which I thought I'd lost. The white flash of the back of the photo as it fluttered to the carpet. Turning it over and seeing those black curls. That smile. And I knew.

'Danny spends a lot of time in Edinburgh,' I tell the Group. 'We always knew that was part of the job. He used to hate it, and the night before he left he'd be in a foul temper because he didn't want to go. Then, all of a sudden, everything went back to front. He was moody when he came home, but as it got nearer the time to go back to Scotland he perked right up. I knew something was going on. Then, when I found the photograph . . .'

I stop. Swallow. There is nothing more to add.

'Men are pigs,' says Judith, to no one in particular.

'Hope you gave him a hard time,' ventures Frannie.

'At first, he claimed he hardly knew her. Then, after I went on and on, he admitted she freelanced at the same company. Dad's company. And finally, at around four in the morning, he admitted they'd kissed on a night out. "But that was it."'

Dr Chakraborty raises his liquid eyes to mine and sighs, and I wonder if he's thinking of his wife and hope he isn't feeling too shit. Then I wonder why I'm worrying about him when my own stomach is churning and I've an ache in my side just under my heart.

'And what happened then, Hannah?'

I don't want to tell him. I don't want to think about it. Don't want to remember how Danny had fallen asleep and I watched his face and he looked like someone I didn't know. Or how I got up out of bed and dug the photograph out of my knicker drawer, where I'd hidden it to stop Danny ripping it up, as he was threatening to do. Then I fetched a red pen from the kitchen drawer and I scored it through those dancing eyes again and again until I'd almost gone through the paper. BITCH, I scrawled on the back.

'Then things went back to normal.'

Except they weren't normal. It was as though

111

someone had taken our life before and rotated it a couple of degrees so that everything looked almost the same and yet nothing felt quite right.

'What's normal? Who decides?' asks Odelle. And she glances behind her towards Drew's ever-seeing camera, as if to make sure he got that.

'I thought Steffie was gone.' I almost choke on the word. 'Danny said she had left the company. He even agreed to consider another round of IVF, which he'd always maintained he would never do, going private this time to avoid the waiting list.'

'And then?' prompts Dr Chakraborty.

'And then,' I say, nodding, as if he has made a statement, rather than asked a question.

We'd agreed to put the whole thing behind us. We'd been getting on better than we had done in a while. I had the passcode to his phone and his emails. Danny has a tendency to dominate a conversation, talking over you in his determination to get his point across. But now he was taking time to listen. Deliberately leaving spaces for me to say what I needed to say. We agreed not to mention the 'B' word for three months, and that proved liberating. Knowing we could chat freely without ending up in a loaded baby discussion changed our dynamic. One Saturday morning, we were in the car going somewhere. Tesco, probably. And I remember looking at Danny and thinking how different he seemed. Wondering if he had changed his hair or was wearing something different or had just got older without me noticing. But then I realized it was because he was laughing. I hadn't seen him laugh for a long time.

'And then, Hannah?' Dr Chakraborty has fixed me

with his sad 'what can one do?' expression, and Frannie smiles at me from the seat next to him, a nervous smile that darts off her face and is gone, as if something has frightened it away. And I know I must go there. Because I must get better. I must get home.

'It was the weekend, and Danny was stressed because he'd lost something. A business card from a potential client, I think. I was helping him look for it. I was in our bedroom going through his jacket pockets. And I found this phone.'

A tiny, black plasticky thing. Pay as you go. And, me being so thick, it didn't sink in at first. I turned it over in my hand, almost laughing. It was practically a museum piece. I turned it on, puzzled, but not worried. Went to contacts. Just one number.

Just one.

Standing there in our room, listening to Danny in the kitchen crashing around and complaining under his breath. 'I know it was here. Why do you always have to move everything? Why can't you leave things where they were?' Kids' voices from the garden. Marco must have had his nephews over again. A smell of charcoal burning. Barbecue season starting early. And me in the middle of our bedroom, staring at a number in a contacts folder on a crappy phone.

I knew then. But still I put myself through it, as if I deserved the pain. I pressed call. It rang three times. Her voice was husky, with a laugh bubbling under the surface.

'Babe! What a lovely surprise! Don't tell me you've nipped out for milk *again*. You must have the biggest fridge in the world.'

'Babe?' I say now to the Group. 'What grown woman says that?'

I went into the kitchen with the black plastic mobile in my outstretched hand. 'Did you find . . . ?' Danny's voice tailed off as he saw what I was carrying.

Babe, I thought, looking at him.

Then came the terrible time. Tears and accusations and justifications and denials. Ultimatums followed by shameless begging. I wanted him out. No, I couldn't live without him. I hated him. I loved him. I was crazy. Crazy. Crazy. And, all the time, Danny wavered between her and me. 'You're my rock,' he told me. 'But she's my beating heart.'

'She was his beating heart,' I tell the Group. Nina, who has been sitting in silence up to now, lifts her head and Frannie gasps. Dr Chakraborty looks away, out of delicacy.

Finally, Danny decided. It was me he wanted. He would do anything to win me back. He gave me promises. IVF. Adoption. He offered to resign. He gave me every single email and internet password. Rang me five, seven, ten times a day.

I gave in. I loved him. Megan thought I was an idiot. But what did she know about love? He couldn't resign, though, because we needed the money, especially now we were saving for more IVF. Also, I didn't want Dad to know anything was wrong. But when Danny was away he called me in the mornings, afternoons, nights, and we had a rule: if I called him, he would always pick up, even in the middle of a meeting.

Rules. We thought we could govern jealousy and love

with rules. And grief. Because Danny was grieving.

The loss of his 'beating heart'.

We got back on track.

'You must have pretty low self-esteem,' says Judith.

I catch Stella's eye and we exchange a smile. Low self-esteem. Isn't that why we're all here?

Once again, Danny and I reconstructed 'normal' out of the debris of our former life. And if it had a few holes in it where some tiny pieces had rolled away or crumbled to dust we just politely ignored them.

I went on holiday to Crete with my mum and my sister. I thought myself happy.

Then came the knock on the door.

'Why a knock? Don't you have a bell?'

The question comes from a young woman who has only been here since yesterday and whose name I keep forgetting. Caroline? Catherine? Caitlin? She has OCD, I'm guessing. It's a safe bet in these parts.

'She'd been outside,' I say, 'and one of the guys from the downstairs flat had let her in. She said she was a friend of Danny's. She'd come to surprise him.'

It was a Friday evening. We were getting ready to go out. I had a new top. I can still remember the joy of getting it out of the bag. The rustle of tissue paper. The whisper of oyster-coloured silk. I had on my favourite black jeans and was planning to finish off the outfit with a pair of black suede wedge boots, but I hadn't quite got there yet when the knock on the door came. So I went to open it in my bare feet, the silver varnish on my toe nails chipped and peeling. Afterwards, that stuck in my mind, that she hadn't given me a chance to put on my shoes.

115

When I opened the door I was expecting Marco or Phil from downstairs.

I saw black curls under a white bobble hat. Leggings. Biker boots. A leather jacket with the zip undone to accommodate her stomach.

Pregnant.

I sit back in my chair. 'I don't want to talk any more.'

15

Corinne

Six thirty in the evening in London, which meant it was just after lunchtime in New York when Corinne Skyped her, but already Megan looked tired. That's the first thing Corinne noticed. As her younger daughter talked in that jerky way she had, lurching from one topic to another without the connecting bits in between so you felt like a passenger on a particularly bumpy plane journey, Corinne studied her face on the computer screen. Megan had always been gaunt, but now dark shadows striped her cheeks and the dome of her pale forehead was like the shell of an egg that could shatter in an instant.

Corinne wished she could step through the screen into her daughter's tiny Brooklyn living room with its wooden floor piled high with books and video games and coats and shoes, as if she'd just moved in, although she'd been living there at least six months. She'd sit down next to her on the shabby couch and put her arms around her bony shoulders and tell her to be calm.

Breathe, she'd say. *Don't take everything so much to heart.*

'I don't understand why she's still in there,' Megan was saying. And because the connection wasn't brilliant, and because Megan was a bit like that anyway, her words were erratic and staccato, shooting out of her mouth as though someone were typing them on an old-fashioned typewriter.

'She wants to get better, darling. She wants to be as well as she can be before she goes home to Danny.'

Megan put a hand to her mouth and started tugging at the skin around her thumb with her teeth. Corinne bit back the urge to tell her to stop. Megan mumbled something but, because her thumb was still in her mouth, Corinne couldn't understand it.

'I said, I don't know why she's even going back to him. He's no good for her.'

'Megan!'

Corinne's voice was heavy with warning. When Hannah and Megan had fallen out about Hannah's relationship with Danny just before Megs left for New York, the rift had cast a long shadow over Corinne's life. She'd always thought they were such a strong little unit, and the distance between her daughters, still ongoing despite everything, caused her acute emotional distress.

On the screen Megan was fiddling with her hair, twiddling it round and round her finger, as she used to as a child, and Corinne began to feel a chill trickling like icy water down her back.

'You know something, don't you?' Corinne said.

'What? I don't know anything. What are you talking about?'

'You know something about Hannah and Danny and you haven't told me.'

Megan's eyes flicked up to the side and then down again, looking anywhere but at her mother's face.

'Wait there.' Something sewed itself tightly across Corinne's chest as she crossed the room to riffle through her bag. Got it. 'Who's this?'

She held the photograph up to the computer camera so it blocked her screen. BITCH, said the angry red letters on the back, and even though Corinne knew Hannah had written them, it still felt as if the woman in the photograph were talking directly to her.

'Well?'

One thing about Megan. She was incapable of lying.

'I promised her I wouldn't tell you.'

'Tell me what, Megs? This is something to do with Danny, isn't it? Was he having an affair with this woman?'

Megan glanced up. Glanced down again. Nodded.

Though it was only confirmation of what she'd already suspected, the revelation left Corinne winded and breathless.

'Don't take it personally, Mum.' Megan guessed what was going through her mother's head. 'She didn't want you to judge Danny, that's all. She wanted you to carry on liking him. That's why she got the hump so badly with me. Because I couldn't go on pretending Danny was some kind of perfect man.'

'But it must have been so devastating. She loves him so much. When did it happen?'

Shrug. 'Last year, I guess.' Megan was still not looking at her.

'There's something else, isn't there? What aren't you saying, Megan?'

The tugging on her thumb became more frantic, drawing a small bulb of blood. Corinne tried to focus on something else. The window behind Megan through which she could see a grey smudge of daylight, reminding her of the five hours' distance between them. Her own curtains were already drawn against the cheerless London night. There was a cold cramp in her stomach caused by the things she didn't know. The things she hadn't been told. But she was certain there was more to come, and she needed to hear it.

'She was pregnant, Mum.'

For a moment, shock made Corinne stupid, and she said, 'Hannah? Well, I know—' and Megan snorted, looked annoyed.

'*She* was pregnant. Her. Steffie Garitson.'

Corinne's stomach spasmed. The fact that this woman had a name, and that Megan knew it, seemed to her obscene.

'Why didn't I know?' she wailed. 'I could have helped.'

'Oh yeah, and how could you have done that? Could you maybe have made the foetal cells join back up again? Sent the sperm back from whence it came?'

'You don't need to be facetious, Megan.'

'Sorry.'

It all made sense now. All of it. All those unexplained incidents that had kept her awake night after night, wondering. All those *why*s. The time Hannah had thrown Danny out. The bust-up with Megan. There was an anger building inside her stronger than anything she'd felt in a long time, and Corinne realized how much she'd been holding her feelings in check since the thing that had happened to Hannah, because she didn't dare let them go. She was afraid of how deep her feelings went.

Danny. How she'd tried to support him since Hannah had been ill. How sorry she'd felt for what Hannah had done. How she'd apologized over and over. Justified her daughter to him. And all the time . . .

And now she remembered something else.

'I was just there,' she spluttered. 'A few days ago. Clearing out Emily's room. So he didn't have to do it himself.'

Now it was Megan's turn to look angry.

'What the fuck, Mum? How's Hannah ever going to get well if you do that?'

'Do what?'

'You know perfectly well what! Listen to yourself, would you? *Emily's room?*'

Corinne closed her eyes, felt the world lurch horribly around her, as her own words repeated in her ears.

16

Hannah

'I understand this is painful for you, Hannah. But you're doing so well. I'd like you to carry on, if you can.'

When Dr Chakraborty raises his hand in a gesture of encouragement, his jacket sleeve rides up, revealing a silver watch setting off a smooth, brown wrist. I concentrate on the watch to take my mind off the things he is making me remember.

Emily calls to me from a far-off room. I try to fix the sound in my mind but it keeps fading in and out of range.

'Yes, you're doing brilliantly, Hannah,' says Odelle, once again flicking a glance to the camera.

The movement incenses me.

'Can you get them to turn that fucking thing off!' I snap.

Dr Chakraborty raises his eyes to the back of the room. 'If you gentlemen wouldn't mind?'

'No problemo,' says Justin.

Drew puts down the camera and stares until Justin says sharply, 'Come on, mate. Let's go!'

Once the door closes behind them, there is nowhere else for me to aim my anxiety but at myself. I hear it in my ear, like the high-pitched whine of a mosquito.

'So you were saying, Hannah?' Dr Chakraborty's calm, slow voice.

I try to tune him out so I can find Emily again, but she's not there.

'This woman – Danny's "girlfriend" —' Dr Chakraborty makes quote marks in the air with his fingers, but still the word hangs there. 'She turns up at your door. Pregnant. That must have been a terrible shock.'

Not just for me either. Danny's face when he saw her. The colour draining, like it was being bleached out by the sun. I was hyperventilating. I thought I would be sick. My hands on my knees.

'I didn't know,' he kept saying. 'I didn't know she was coming.'

And there she was, standing in my living room with her cute white hat and her curls and her mouth, saying sorry, but her eyes were dancing on my grave. And her stomach. Not huge. But big enough.

'It was the way she stroked it with her hand,' I say. 'Like she'd made it herself in a pottery class.'

The new girl – whose name I now remember is Katy – nods vigorously, as if to say she quite understands. I catch Stella's eye and she smiles. *The optimum outcome from this story would be . . . for it never to have happened.*

'How did you feel, Hannah? When you realized who she was, and her condition?'

By 'condition' Dr Chakraborty means 'pregnancy'.

I think I might love him.

'I felt . . . numb.'

But that's not exactly true. I felt all the emotions so

strongly they cancelled each other out, just as white isn't an absence of colour but all the colours blending together, giving the illusion of no colour at all.

'And after she'd told you that the affair had never stopped? How did you feel about her then?'

'She wasn't exactly high on my NBF list.'

I feel bad after I've said that, seeing Dr Chakraborty's sad, puzzled face.

'"NBF" means "New Best Friend",' Odelle translates for him.

'I hated her, obviously,' I say inadequately. 'There was something scary about her.'

'That's you superimposing your own fears on to her,' says Judith, who is on her fifth stay here and sees herself as something of an expert. 'She represented a threat to you, so you perceived her as threatening.'

It's a good theory. But it's not the truth. Despite the cute hat and the bouncing curls, I was sure there was a darkness under the surface of Steffie.

'Did you talk to her? Try to find out more details?'

'I didn't want details. I just wanted her out of my flat.'

Sitting on the sofa with my head bent and my hands over my ears like a child – *if I can't see or hear you, you aren't really there.* 'Get her out, get her out, get her out, get her out.' Repeat, repeat, repeat.

'And afterwards?'

'I kicked him out. And fell apart.'

Literally. Bits of me fell off. My hair came out. My skin turned dry and flaky. I left a trail of dust wherever I went. I made excuses to the office, to Mum. I drowned in shame. The woman who wasn't enough for her husband. The woman who couldn't make a baby.

Danny came over to the flat and wept when he saw me. He tried to explain. His life was with me but, paradoxically, she was the one who'd made him feel alive. *His beating heart.* I raged at him. Hated him. Begged him. And then fucked him. Wanting to reclaim every inch of him.

I had become the woman I'd always sworn I'd never be. The woman I'd always despised. Bending herself this way and that to fit the shape of a man, dissolving herself in him until there's nothing left, just a film of powder to show she ever was.

'Can you tell us about the pregnancy now, Hannah?' says Dr Chakraborty gently. 'Your pregnancy, I mean.'

I feel a terrible pain when he says that. Why does he have to say it? Why couldn't he have stuck with 'condition'? I close my eyes, straining to hear Emily, but she's not there. In her place is just a dark, shape-shifting grief. I force myself to remember how I began to feel poleaxed with tiredness, though at night sleep refused to come. I felt nauseous all the time. Becs was worried. She tried to make me see someone. She rang Megan, who threatened to call Mum.

I went to the doctor to get some pills. 'Could you be pregnant?' I laughed at that.

But afterwards I couldn't shake off the thought. It was possible. The doctors had always said there was no reason for me not to get pregnant again. The nausea got worse, especially in the mornings. My breasts were heavier. I did a pregnancy test. Nothing. But, by that stage, I was a world expert in margins of error, the percentages of tests that give a false result.

Every morning there were new changes to my body. A tugging low down in my abdomen, a feeling of things adjusting. A supernatural tiredness, a sudden and violent aversion to things that before I had tolerated perfectly well. Olives swimming around in orange oil; the smell of coffee, which I'd previously loved.

My belly started to swell. My breasts ached.

'When did you start telling people, Hannah?'

'I didn't need to. They noticed.'

When Megan came over just before we had that terrible row, I was still in my nightie – well, the thin T-shirt I wear to bed – and as soon as she saw me she said it. 'Oh my God, you're pregnant.' My belly, at just two months, already swollen. My boobs a whole cup size bigger. And once she'd pointed it out, Mum couldn't understand why she hadn't noticed it too.

'I bet Danny freaked,' says Judith, with some satisfaction. 'Two women pregnant by him at the same time. Doesn't look good, does it?'

'Oh, I don't know,' says Katy. 'Some men go in for that sort of thing. It makes them look virile.'

'He went white when I told him. The kind of white when you press on sunburn and it blanches out.'

I demonstrate on the skin on the top of one hand.

'And then?' prompts Dr Chakraborty.

'Then he moved back in.'

It hadn't been that simple. There was a lot of to-ing and fro-ing. Some days, I wanted him back. Other days, I couldn't stand the sight of him.

He went to see his parents for a few days. And when he came back he was different. Contrite. He'd made a mistake. He wanted to put things right. His mother had made him see that his life was with me. I never thought I'd be grateful to uptight Victoria Lovell, but the pregnancy finally brought her around to the idea of me and gave me hope of a more harmonious future.

She – beating-heart Steffie – had gone back to stay with her parents in Tunbridge Wells. Shortly afterwards, she told Danny she'd lost the baby. I felt for her then. Briefly. I knew what that particular pain was like.

I held out. At night in bed I stroked my growing belly and told it – told her, because I knew already that it was a girl – that we'd be fine on our own. Some nights I even believed it. But in the end I took him back. I loved him.

He moved back in and when I called him a shit, he agreed, and when I told him I hated him, he understood, and when I cried, he held me.

Meg told me I was an idiot. We had a hideous row the last time I saw her. Then she left for New York without us making it right. We haven't spoken since.

I miss my sister.

But I chose my husband.

I grew bigger. Things became calmer. The baby, Emily, made it possible for me and Danny to coat ourselves anew in a veneer of togetherness.

Some days we were even happy.

We painted the spare room, bought a cot and moved the low blue chair from the living room. Danny's parents gave him the ugly mobile he'd had when he was a baby with all the farmyard animal shapes and I didn't object when he insisted on putting it up.

Mum was uneasy. She thought we were tempting fate. But we needed to do it. She didn't know that, sometimes, we even spoke to each other through our unborn child. 'Tell Daddy he needs to brush his teeth. I can still smell last night's garlic chicken.' 'Try to sort it so that, when you arrive, Mummy still gets to keep those boobs, will you?'

Danny was still going to Edinburgh for work, but I knew through subtle enquiries at Dad's company that Steffie had left Scotland for good. And he rang me all the time and got the first flight home even if it meant travelling half the night.

'And all this time, the tests were still coming back negative?'

Katy has a face like a fifty-pence piece, very wide across with a shallow pointed chin. She is determined to get her facts straight.

'I stopped doing the tests. I'd read magazine features about women who'd gone out binge drinking because the test had been wrong and they'd believed they weren't pregnant.'

Listen to your body, those features said. I listened to my body. It told me I was pregnant.

I sit up suddenly, straining to hear Emily, but there is nothing.

'When was the first time someone mentioned the possibility of pseudocyesis, Hannah?' Dr Chakraborty asks.

Odelle leans towards Katy.

'That means phantom pregnancy.'

Everything goes dark.

17

Corinne

Megan was still glaring at her through the computer screen, and Corinne felt ashamed. After everything that had happened, here she was, saying 'Emily', as if she were real. A living creature, a cluster of reproducing cells growing fat in the shelter of Hannah's swelling belly.

A grandchild.

Even now, after all the psychiatrists' reports and the medical explanations and the sleepless nights lost to Google, Corinne still couldn't quite believe it had happened.

'Was it my fault?' she asked Megan now, even though they'd been over this so many times it was just picking at an old wound.

'Don't talk bollocks, Mum.'

'But why didn't I notice it was odd? That the doctor's appointments and scans all seemed to fall when Danny was away? That she cut out scan pictures and pasted them on to cards instead of showing us the whole printout?'

Hannah had printed them off the internet, it transpired. Cropping out the bit that said 'Baby Jenkins' or 'Baby Cooper'.

'All the signs were there,' said Megan. 'She looked pregnant. We saw her stomach, for fuck's sake. And her tits. We couldn't have known.'

The first psychiatrist they'd seen, a woman with blonde highlights and a sympathetic expression that made Corinne burst into tears within seconds of meeting her, had told them that some women's bodies literally fool them into believing they are pregnant, imitating the hormones of pregnancy. They'd probably be surprised how often it happened.

But the deliberate deceit, that's what Duncan had fixated on. The doctor's appointments that were never made, the scans Hannah never had. How could she explain that?

The doctor wasn't sure, but she would hazard a guess at some kind of dissociative disorder. Had Hannah had any major life crises recently? That kind of thing could make someone's behaviour erratic and cause her to distance herself from reality. So the rational part of Hannah could put the lies in a little box and shut it away somewhere so deep and dark she didn't even know it was there.

'If you hold this fervent, emotionally driven wish, it's possible you might disconnect yourself from the part of you that knows the wish is not reality,' the doctor said.

Corinne hadn't been able to think of any life crises at the time. Because Megan hadn't told her about Danny and this other woman.

'What else do you know about her, this – *Steffie*?' Corinne pronounced the word as if it were a lie, and they both knew it.

Her eyes travelled back to the photograph lying on

the sofa next to her. The bare brown legs in the cut-off shorts. The white vest over the perfectly flat stomach.

Megan shrugged. 'She had family in Tunbridge Wells,' Hannah said. Maybe she went back there to live. Maybe she is honing her husband-stealing skills on the unsuspecting men of Kent as we speak. Mum . . .'

There was a pause.

'Mum, I wish Hannah would let me come and see her. Have you talked to her?'

Corinne nodded. 'She's still hurt, Megs. About the things you said about Danny.'

'Someone had to tell her the truth.'

'Darling, I'm afraid you'll find out that, most of the time, the truth is the very last thing any of us want to hear. Hannah will come round. Just let her get out of the clinic and back home.'

Most of Corinne's other Skype calls ended awkwardly with no one wanting to be the first to cut the other off, but as always Megan cut out with a cursory 'Bye', so one minute Corinne was looking at her face and thinking again how tired she looked and the next there was just that wallpaper photo of the three of them in Crete.

A different lifetime, it felt like.

Without thinking about what she was doing, Corinne called up the Google home page and typed in 'Steffie Garitson, Tunbridge Wells'. Not much. A Facebook profile that led to a page with a picture showing the same photograph Corinne had already seen – only this time with eyes – and everything else set to private.

She tried 'Stephanie Garitson' and found a couple of entries. One was a 192 entry that kept the address hidden but listed the other occupants of the house.

Jeremy Garitson. Patricia Garitson. Jacob Garitson.

Corinne googled 'Jeremy Garitson, Tunbridge Wells'. She found a LinkedIn profile but couldn't access it. There followed a quote in a local newspaper piece canvassing opinion about Brexit, on why he'd voted Leave.

Nothing identifying.

Patricia Garitson, on the other hand, was more forthcoming. She ran her own catering company and the company address was listed, and it looked very much like a residential address. Bingo.

Corinne copied the information down carefully underneath the words 'Steffie Garitson', neatly underlined.

She closed down Google and gazed again at the smiling photograph of her and her daughters on the screensaver.

Then she looked at the name and address written on the piece of paper in her jagged, sloping hand.

There was a nugget of hatred inside her, dense and hard and solid as a bullet.

18

Hannah

After Group, I make my way back to my room, still shaken.

Dr Chakraborty said it was a breakthrough, because I've finally admitted there wasn't any baby; he said I'd done really well. But I feel drained and exposed.

Phantom pregnancy. The label shames me. I might as well have 'crazy' tattooed across my forehead.

And yet nothing about it had felt 'phantom'. And it certainly hadn't felt 'hysterical' – the other charming name given to what had happened to me.

Phantom. Hysterical.

Crazy.

Even now, I find it impossible to accept that my body could have so completely deceived me. The weight gain, the stomach cramps, the nausea. Could it really all have been my own biology's idea of a practical joke?

That bit I have to accept. But what I cannot accept is my own part in it. The way I colluded with my own lying body to fool myself and Danny and everyone else. The fake appointments I said I'd had. The scans I never went to. How could I have done it?

'Was this your idea of revenge?' he yelled at me that terrible night in the hospital.

The doctor had taken him aside then. Explained that, sometimes, if the mind wants something enough, it can trick the body into believing something that isn't true. That my uterus was enlarged, as if I were really pregnant. I was going through as real a bereavement as if there had been a baby, she told him, and after a while he'd calmed down.

I go through the door at the back of the hallway into the new building. It's always a shock stepping from dimly lit Georgian splendour into the bright low-ceilinged passageway, with its clean, symmetrical corners. Turning left into the stairwell, I climb the two short flights of stairs and come out on to the upstairs landing. I open the door of my room and turn on the light, which makes a kind of buzzing sound, which used to keep me awake but I now find almost comforting. I sit down in front of the dressing table. The photograph of the teenaged Charlie that I stole from her desk is tucked into the bottom of the mirror frame. She smiles up at me from her stripy deckchair with all of the older Charlie's goodness but none of her sorrow.

I look at my reflection in the shatterproof mirror and see that I look ten years older; there are dark smudges under my eyes. I pick up my hairbrush and start brushing my hair in long, rhythmic strokes. The repetitive movement calms me and for a moment I forget Group, forget how the words 'phantom pregnancy' felt like electric shocks in my brain, and how someone put their arm around me and for a moment I thought it was Charlie, but when I opened my eyes it was Stella, and

Dr Chakraborty was smiling at me like I'd just passed my chemistry GCSE.

I'm looking at my face in the mirror, and I'm not thinking of anything except how I need to brush my teeth and how much it pisses me off that we're not allowed floss in here, when my attention is caught by something on the bed behind me. It is small and pale blue. I peer more closely into the blurry mirror and my stomach twists into a hard knot of dread.

Then I scream.

19

Laura

In the narrow hallway outside her mum's flat, Laura took a deep breath, counting to four, then holding for seven and exhaling for a count of eight. While she was practising this controlled breathing, she tried to clear her mind, but still her thoughts snagged on things around her – the mat outside her mum's neighbour's flat, with its cheery 'Welcome', belying the fact that, as far as Laura knew, Mrs Papadakis never had any visitors; the flickering strip lighting that bathed everything in a sickly yellow light; the fading notices in the locked glass case: 'IN THE EVENT OF FIRE', 'COMMUNITY RULES', 'SITE MANAGER EMERGENCY DETAILS'. Nothing ever changed in this hallway. Not the blue vinyl floor tiles or the metal door numbers or the pervading smell of Cup-a-soup.

As soon as she let herself in through the door and heard the television blaring from the living room, Laura knew Katya was here. Sure enough, she found the young woman lying back in the leather easy chair, her feet in her bunny-ear slippers resting on the matching leather footstool in front of her. She was clutching a balled-up tissue to her face and her cheeks were tracked with tears.

'Is *Long Lost Family*,' Katya said, barely raising her eyes from the television. 'Davina just find this lady's mother. Thirty-five years searching. Is very sad.'

Laura glanced at the screen, where a heavy-set woman with dyed blonde hair and eyebrows halfway up her forehead like migrating birds was sobbing, as if in sympathy with Katya.

'I'll go and say hello,' she said. Katya nodded without looking up.

Her mother's room was directly across the hallway from the living room. Someone – Laura suspected it had been Femi – and once made a door plaque from a photograph of Laura's mother as a young woman stuck on to pink card surrounded by flowers cut out of magazines. The card and the photograph had since faded, and some of the flowers had dropped off, revealing the yellowing Sellotape underneath.

Something heavy descended inside Laura. Still, she arranged her features into the semblance of a smile as she went in.

'Only me! Just thought I'd pop in to see how you're doing today, Mummy. You look pretty! Has Katya been doing your hair again?'

Laura's mother was propped up in bed, wearing the orange pyjamas Laura had bought her to cheer her up. Her sparse brown hair had been pinned back with two pink plastic clips in the shape of bows. Her head lolled to one side and there was a thin string of drool coming out of the left corner of her mouth. Laura wiped it away with the cloth on the hospital tray over her mum's bed.

'That's better, isn't it?'

Laura perched on the bed and took her mum's hand,

which was as soft as cotton wool. It was impossible to believe there were bones in there. It felt like holding hands with one of those floury baps you find in old-fashioned bakeries.

'So, you remember the client I told you about? Hannah? Well, I'm still concerned. You know I said two of the girls had killed themselves. How tragic it was? Remember I said that? Well, Hannah can't accept it. Won't accept it. Total denial. And that's led to some worryingly obsessive behaviour.'

Her mother made a noise like a low moan and Laura leaned forward to dab at her mouth again with the cloth. Sitting back to survey the result, she sighed.

'You're right, Mummy. I have to step back and not get so involved. It's not healthy. I must accept the things I cannot change. Annabel always says that. But these poor girls in the clinic. They are so terribly lost. They find the world so frightening. At least I have you. And you have me. We are so blessed.'

20

Hannah

I am still screaming, looking at the reflection of the thing in the mirror. I recognize it immediately, of course.

I ought to. I bought it.

I'd run out at lunchtime for a sandwich. Five months not-pregnant. Can't eat Brie. Is there raw egg in the mayonnaise? No coffee for me. No alcohol.

Idiot.

It was in the window of a toy shop I'd walked past a million times and never really noticed. Pale blue velvet and black crinkly eyes that made it look like it was telling you a tremendous joke. And the longest, softest ears. I'd gone in and bought it, even though Danny had made me promise to stop buying baby things. 'It's tempting fate,' he'd said. But still I couldn't resist showing Danny the cuddly rabbit that evening. He raised his eyebrows and shook his head, but said nothing. Later, I saw him in Emily's room; he'd picked it up and stared at it for a good long time.

And now it's here on my bed, a reminder of all the things I'd once hoped for.

Except where the ears used to be there are now just

two little blue stumps through which the white stuffing shows obscenely.

I fall silent and turn around. My hand is trembling when I reach out to pick up the mutilated rabbit. I haven't touched any baby things since that night in hospital. Instantly I'm engulfed by a tidal wave of grief that seems to travel up from the toy through my fingers and into my bloodstream. I curl up on the bed, as if I can make myself small enough to disappear.

Darren arrives, alerted by my scream. He's on the late shift this week, the punishing hours coating his skin in a pasty, unhealthy-looking sheen.

'What happened?' he asks, out of breath.

Still keening, I hold up the soft toy by way of reply.

'It's a message,' I babble, incoherent. 'From her. My baby.'

When I've calmed down, I let Darren examine the rabbit. I search his face, looking for evidence that he's finding the whole thing funny, but I don't find any.

'Somebody left it here for me to find,' I say, calm at last. 'To upset me.'

Not a message then, from the baby I'd made up, as I'd originally decided.

'Could it just have been a present?' suggests Darren. 'Might someone have been wanting to cheer you up?'

'By chopping off its ears?'

Now I look at it closer, I can see it's not exactly the same one as was in the nursery at home. It's bigger, for a start, and not velvet at all but a kind of fluffy fake fur. Still, it's too similar to be a coincidence. I want to know how it got in my room. By now, one of the night orderlies is here too. Janice. An older woman with plump wrists and a kind face. They're supposed always to come in twos, but Janice is out of shape and arrives minutes after Darren, red-cheeked and breathing heavily.

'What happened to its ears?' she wants to know.

Janice has no idea how the earless rabbit came to be on my bed, but then she's only been on duty a couple of hours. She thinks it's a crying shame someone has done that to a brand-new toy. 'There's plenty of sick kiddies in hospital who would have loved that rabbit,' she says.

They leave, with Darren promising to make enquiries to find out how the toy got into my room as soon as the daytime staff arrive. He's respectful and reassuring. But I know what he's thinking. At the end of the day, it's just a toy, right?

They leave, taking the rabbit with them, Janice clutching it to her bosom as if it were a real pet.

I listen to the soft pad of their footsteps in the corridor. The clanging of the door to the stairwell. Then I lie down on the far edge of my bed, careful not to touch the bit in the middle where the rabbit was.

21

Corinne

Queueing in traffic along a narrow main road just outside Tunbridge Wells, Corinne was doubting the wisdom of her mission.

When she'd set out that morning, she'd been buzzing. After all these weeks of feeling helpless, it had felt good to be taking positive action. But with each passing minute spent parked up, watching the brake lights of the car in front, her sense of purpose was draining from her, until now she could hardly remember why this had ever seemed like a good idea.

She tried to focus on the town. Such beautiful buildings. So many antique shops and quirky little tea rooms.

So much traffic.

She got lost around a one-way system and pulled over to shout at Google Maps, to the amusement of a passing cyclist, but finally she turned into a wide road with houses set well back. She pulled up in front of a large semi-detached stucco Georgian villa with a neat front garden almost obscured by a giant sycamore tree which cast a dark shadow over the front of the house, in contrast with the neighbouring properties, which were bathed in weak sunshine. As she walked up the path, the single multi-paned window in the front elevation stared at her like a giant eye and Corinne felt her skin prickle.

She had been borne here by anger and by the knowledge of how Steffie Garitson's fat black curls and bare brown knees had destroyed her family. She'd pictured that smile turning to shock and then shame as Corinne spelled out to her the consequences of what she'd done. She'd imagined Steffie's mother, this Patricia Garitson, coming in from the kitchen, dusting off her floury caterer's hands on her apron. Her father, home from work for the weekend, would be sitting reading the paper. Probably, they had no idea what their daughter had done, the havoc she had wreaked. How readily Corinne would put them in the picture.

But now she was here, she was less certain. What if Steffie denied everything? Her parents would take her side, wouldn't they? She could imagine how tawdry it would get. How Jeremy Kyle.

As she approached the front door, along a path laid with square paving slabs set out in an oppressively regimented grid, her steps slowed. For a moment she considered turning back, or at least repairing to the car to phone ahead, but before she had a chance the large front door swung open, revealing a slight figure in a soft grey sweater dress with an arm full of cut red roses.

'Can I help you?' The smile was the same as the girl in the photograph's, but the brown eyes were wary.

Corinne took a deep breath.

'Is Stephanie . . . Steffie . . . here, please?'

The woman paused, shifting the bundle of flowers as if they were about to fall, and Corinne noticed for the

143

first time that she was carrying a large pair of stainless-steel scissors in the other hand.

'Sorry,' she said, waving them around. 'Just trimming these.' She had a dimple in her cheek like her daughter and something flashed gold in the back of her mouth as she spoke.

'Steffie isn't here, I'm afraid. She hasn't been for months.'

'Who is it?' A man's voice calling from inside the house.

'A friend of Steffie's.'

'No. Not a friend. Look, can I come in? I can see you need to get those in some water.'

The woman studied Corinne. But where Corinne might have expected suspicion or even hostility, following her denial of friendship with her daughter, Patricia Garitson displayed neither.

'I'd just really like to talk to you and your husband about Steffie,' she went on.

Corinne wasn't prepared to spill her family secrets on the doorstep. And if Jeremy Garitson was inside, she would rather speak to them both at once. Somewhere in the back of her mind lay the hope that by enlisting Steffie's parents' support she could ensure the girl stayed away from her daughter, and her daughter's husband, for good.

Patricia Garitson stared at her for a moment longer and then smiled again. 'Follow me.'

She turned and moved off down a hallway, the impressive proportions of which were accentuated by tasteful neutral paintwork and original ceiling mouldings. Up ahead, Corinne could see a large, white-framed

144

family photograph, clearly taken in an upmarket photography studio. Steffie was a teenager in the picture, wearing an old-fashioned choker around her slender neck, but even from a distance she was still instantly recognizable with those black curls. Corinne took a sharp intake of breath at the sight of her. All the Garitsons – a younger-looking Patricia, Steffie, a man Corinne assumed was Jeremy, and a young boy with dark hair and pale eyes – were dressed in white, as if they were members of the same band coordinating their clothes for a photoshoot. Though they were smiling, there was something staged about the picture, a certain stiffness. It was only as she got closer that Corinne realized that what she'd at first taken to be a choker was actually a faint silver line, but she didn't have time for closer inspection.

She followed her hostess past a formal living room on the right, done out in tones of ivory with two cream sofas facing each other on either side of a glass coffee table. How did people manage to maintain that kind of decor? she wondered. In her house, there'd be red-wine stains on the sofas and muddy footprints all over those white, deep-pile rugs.

The second door led into an expansive modern kitchen with banks of gleaming white cupboards unbroken by handles, and a white table with white leather chairs tucked neatly under it. There were four white moulded plastic-and-chrome stools lined up along the breakfast bar on the far side of the vast island. And on the stool on the far left was a man with a neatly trimmed white goatee that matched the decor and steel-framed glasses, jabbing at the keys on his phone with intense concentration.

'A friend of Steffie's?' he said, looking up. 'How novel!'

So Corinne was forced to repeat her denial of being Steffie's friend, although she modified her voice from the strident tone she'd used earlier with his wife.

The man jumped down from his stool, revealing himself to be shorter than he'd first appeared, and shook Corinne's hand, his eyes looking her up and down appreciatively. His grip was surprisingly firm and Corinne hoped she wasn't blushing.

'I'm Patricia,' said Steffie's mother, tossing the roses down on to the kitchen surface. A petal came loose and fluttered down, forming a red blot on the gleaming white floor. 'And this is my husband, Jeremy.'

Finally, Jeremy Garitson let go of her hand, though his eyes still lingered on her. Corinne's palm burned where he'd clasped it so tightly.

'Has Steffie been up to mischief?' asked Patricia, turning her attention to the roses.

Corinne was thrown. They seemed so unperturbed by her surprise visit. They hadn't looked once at each other. Not a raised eyebrow when she came in or a 'who is this strange woman?' glance.

'I'm sorry to have to tell you that your daughter – that is, I assume she's your daughter . . .'

Corinne looked from one to the other, seeking some kind of confirmation. None was forthcoming.

'She became involved with my son-in-law. That is to say, they had an affair. I'm afraid this distressed my daughter, Hannah, to the extent that she had a breakdown and is now undergoing psychiatric treatment.'

'Oh dear, I'm terribly sorry to hear that,' said Jeremy

Garitson, almost before Corinne had finished speaking. 'Steffie is a very passionate person. She tends to follow her heart. Not always advisably.'

He shrugged in a 'what can you do?' gesture, and Corinne bit down on her lip.

'It must be very worrying for you,' added his wife, studying Corinne more closely. She was standing under one of the downlighters, and its reflection flashed in her left eye.

Corinne had expected shock. Perhaps disbelief. Yet still the Garitsons didn't look at one another. Just at Corinne, who found herself growing increasingly uncomfortable under their scrutiny. Her mouth was as dry as dust and she made a noise in the back of her throat, as if to clear it.

'The thing is,' said Jeremy amiably, sitting himself back down on the stool and inviting Corinne to sit, 'Stephanie is an adult and she makes her own choices.'

He smiled, and she noticed how much longer his canines were than the teeth at the front.

'Selfish though those choices may be, there's not a lot we can do,' added his wife.

'Not selfish. High-spirited, maybe.' Jeremy Garitson was still smiling, but his voice was hard.

'I just thought you could . . . She was pregnant, you know,' Corinne blurted out.

She hadn't planned on saying this, knowing it to be a breach of confidentiality too far. But she needed to get through to this couple, to make them see exactly how much was at stake here.

'We're well aware of that,' said Mr Garitson. Now he'd stopped smiling it was like someone had snapped off a fluorescent light. His deep-set eyes were little pockets of grey.

Corinne felt herself faltering.

'I just thought it would be in all our best interests, especially Steffie's, if—'

'Most things Stephanie does are in Stephanie's best interests.'

Patricia Garitson's voice never varied from the pleasant, almost sing-song tone she'd used from the start, and Corinne found herself wrong-footed. She couldn't remember ever hearing a mother talk about her child in such a curiously dispassionate way.

'Look, maybe it's better if I talk to Steffie in person. Can you give me her email address or phone number?'

'I'm afraid I don't think that's a good idea,' said Jeremy Garitson. 'Whatever Steffie has or hasn't done, I'm sure you understand she's still our daughter and we love her.'

There was a loud snap as Patricia twisted her dark hair up high on her head with an elastic band she'd slipped from her wrist.

'Well, perhaps you could just pass on the message then – ask her to stay away from my son-in-law.'

'Of course,' said Jeremy, and smiled in that way that signifies an audience is over. 'Though I can't guarantee anything. My daughter has a mind of her own.'

There was something very like admiration in the way he said it.

Corinne headed for the hallway but, as she reached the kitchen door, Patricia Garitson called out to her. Turning around, she saw that the other woman was standing in the middle of the kitchen, still with the scissors in one hand and a rose, hanging by its stem, in the other, her head cocked slightly to one side.

'Look, you seem like a nice person. As a mother myself, I understand your need to protect your child. Steffie has *issues*, and that's why I should let you know – let *Hannah* know – that she's in London and—'

'Pat.' Jeremy Garitson's voice carried an unmistakeable note of warning.

Patricia Garitson pressed her lips together briefly. 'Anyway, we'll be sure to pass on your message,' she said. There was a flash of steel as the scissors snipped off the tip of the flower's stalk.

Hurrying down the path, hearing the door clang shut behind her, Corinne struggled to make sense of the Garitsons. That beautiful house, the attractive, friendly couple.

And yet.

Her eyes blurred with tears. The trip to Tunbridge Wells had been fuelled by her own sense of powerlessness. She'd hoped she might recruit Steffie's family to help keep her away from Danny. But she got the feeling she'd only made things worse.

Standing by her car, fumbling in her bag for the keys, Corinne heard footsteps behind her. She waited for them to go past, stiffening when they appeared to stop. There was the soft sound of someone breathing close to her neck.

She swung around, her heart thudding.

Standing just inches away was a heavy-set young man. His skin was pasty and puffy with a yellowish tinge, as if it had been a long time since he'd seen the sun. With a shock, she recognized him as the older version of the young boy in the framed photograph in the Garitsons' hallway.

'I'm Jacob Garitson, Steffie's brother.'

He was softly spoken, and Corinne had to lean so far forwards to catch what he was saying she could feel his breath on her face.

'I heard you downstairs. Heard who you are. What you want.'

'I shouldn't have come. It was stupid of me.'

'You don't know what she's like. She hurts people.'

Corinne felt a trickle of fear running down her back. 'Do you know where she is? Please, it's important. I just need to know she's not about to come back into my daughter's life. Hannah is so fragile still.'

Corinne put her hand on the boy's arm but instantly knew she'd made a mistake when he jumped backwards as if she'd burned him.

'I'm sorry. I didn't mean to—'

She was interrupted by the appearance of Patricia Garitson, materializing as if from nowhere at her son's shoulder.

'I think we should let the lady get home now, Jakey,' she said gently, putting her arm around him.

Jacob visibly slumped against her.

'He hasn't been well,' she told Corinne, and Corinne felt a sudden wave of sympathy for this woman, trying, just as she was, to keep her child safe.

But as she drove away, watching the Garitson house, with its single glass eye, recede in the distance, it was Jacob Garitson's soft voice that reverberated in her ear. *She hurts people.*

Corinne turned up the car heater to full but still she couldn't get warm.

Steffie Garitson was in London. And she was dangerous.

And Corinne would kill anyone who tried to hurt Hannah again.

22

Hannah

No one is completely sure how the rabbit got into my room. There was a temporary orderly on duty in the afternoon yesterday and there's a suggestion she might know something about it. Maybe it arrived by courier or was hand-delivered, and she brought it up to my room thinking it to be something sentimental with its missing ears. But the agency say she's working somewhere else now, and no one has followed it up.

In risk-management terms, cuddly toys don't come high up on the priority list.

'Is there a chance you might have put it there yourself, Hannah?' Dr Roberts asks me at our one-to-one this morning.

'Me? Why would I do that? Are you suggesting I'm deluded?'

He doesn't answer. Just gazes at me. And then I look around at where I am and who I'm with and realize that's exactly what he is saying. We're all deluded in here.

'What you have to remember, Hannah, is that you were able to compartmentalize yourself before, weren't you? The part of you that was lying about the doctor's appointments and the scans? You were able to detach that part off from the rest of you, to the extent that, even while all that intellectual subterfuge was going on, all those lies you made up to deceive the people around you, your body steadfastly believed itself to be pregnant.'

'And you think that means I'm capable of having a cuddly toy brought in, hacking off its ears for my own amusement, then laying it on my bed to freak myself out with it?'

He doesn't answer and I wonder if he's thinking that it sounds a lot more reasonable than inventing a baby that doesn't exist.

Afterwards, in art therapy, I can't concentrate. I keep wondering if it's possible that I could hide something like that from myself.

'Are you worried about something, Hannah?'

Laura is leaning against the table, where I'm painting an abstract impression of a bowl of fruit. 'Ignore the bananananess and lemonness of them, just concentrate on the colour and the texture and the light and shade,' she'd told us. 'You don't want someone to think, *That's a good likeness of a peach*, you want them to be able to taste it just by looking at it. To imagine biting through the flesh and that burst of juice in the mouth. You want to capture the essence, not the lines.'

I mix up a grape colour on my palette to avoid looking into her kind eyes because I know, if I do that, I'll be lost. I don't want to cry. Laura reaches out, nudges my chin gently so I have to look at her.

'Is it Charlie still?'

'No.'

But as soon as she's said it I realize that it is still Charlie. If Charlie was still here, I wouldn't have gone to pieces in Group when Odelle said 'phantom pregnancy', or lost the plot over a stupid toy. 'I miss her,' I say, painting a purply-red swirl on my paper.

'I know. We all miss her. She was the lifeblood of this place.'

All of a sudden, I have an urge to confide in someone.

'Charlie knew something about something,' I say incoherently. 'About someone. She was researching something on the internet. It was—'

A scream makes me drop my paintbrush so that a splodge of paint spreads out across the paper.

The new arrival, Katy, is standing up by her table with her hands over her ears.

'She shouldn't have done that,' she says, her words coming out ragged and uneven.

Next to her, Judith is concentrating on her painting, as if unaware of the commotion.

'Judith, did you do something to upset Katy?'

Laura's voice is as low and gentle as ever, but there is a catch in her throat and for the first time it occurs to me that the staff, too, have lost someone they liked. They, too, are grieving.

'It was an accident. My paintbrush just flicked some paint across her paper. I put too much on. It's only the tiniest spot.'

Laura puts her arm around Katy. Asks Odelle to clear away the spoiled paper and bring a fresh new sheet.

I look back at my own painting and the streak of

purple-red paint in the middle. Laura's voice echoes in my head.

Lifeblood.

23

Corinne

The first thing Corinne noticed when she went through the old box of family photographs was how happy they looked. When she thought back objectively to the early days of babies and toddlers, it seemed to her that she and Duncan were in a constant state of sleep-deprived shock, the girls perpetually in the midst of a tantrum or a fight. Yet the photos paint a different picture. Beaming, round baby faces and idyllic scenes – a rumpled, toy-strewn, Sunday-morning double bed with a blur of limbs and laughter, a beach with ice-cream mouths and plastic spades, a blow-up paddling pool in Duncan's parents' beautiful garden in Sussex.

There were no traces of the angst Corinne still remembered so well. The nights of Megan's colic, when she paced up and down their tiny flat, watching the clock ticking down to the time Hannah would be waking up, full of energy and ready to start the day; the chickenpox weeks cooped up inside with two bored, fretful children, watching life go on as normal through a pane of glass.

The second thing Corinne noticed was how few photographs she was actually in. While there were endless pictures of the girls, and many of Duncan, either on his own or with one or both daughters draped over him, Corinne herself was largely absent, except as a camera-wielding shadow on the lawn or a blurry reflection in a mirror behind the others.

Where had she been all that time?

And why hadn't Duncan picked up the camera more? She remembered being so swept away by love she'd wanted to capture him on film all the time. But clearly, he hadn't felt the same. Looking through the piles of photographs, Corinne felt like a ghost in her own family.

She'd been obsessing about families and the ways they can mess a person up since her visit to the Garitsons in Tunbridge Wells the day before. The parents had been perfectly civil, but she couldn't help remembering how they didn't look at each other, and how Jacob Garitson had jumped when Corinne touched him. The strain of having a daughter as disturbed as Steffie must have affected them all.

Corinne was looking for a family photograph to take into the clinic as a present for Hannah. She'd found a lovely antique silver frame in a charity shop and wanted to give Hannah something that reminded her of a less complicated time, reminded her of who she was.

Finally, she settled on a photograph of Megan and Hannah aged around five and seven with their arms around each other, huddling under a towel on a blustery-looking beach. Cornwall, she suspected. Though she couldn't be sure.

She wrapped the photo frame up in tissue paper but didn't tape it. She'd learned her lesson after the last present had had to be ripped open by the clinic's reception staff when she was searched going in. 'We do it to every-one, just in case there's anything they can use to harm themselves.' Corinne had been outraged. 'But Hannah isn't suicidal.' A look, that's all. But it said everything. *How do you know? You thought your daughter was six months pregnant. So what makes you an expert now?*

Corinne was meeting Duncan in the clinic car park for a rare joint visit to Hannah. Dr Roberts had suggested that Hannah might feel more supported if the people closest to her formed a united front with no gaps through which she might fall. Duncan had pronounced this theory 'bollocks' when Corinne first mentioned it but, in the end, had agreed with remarkably little argument.

He was standing by his car when she arrived, frowning at his phone. As always, that jolt of surprise that this man, this near-stranger, should be the father of her children, her husband of nearly three decades. He'd had his hair cut short, the way she'd never liked. He looked older.

Before she'd even got out of her car Corinne could sense his impatience.

'You're late.'

'Only five minutes.'

'Seven. I left work early for this.'

This was what she didn't miss. The inbuilt reproach in his voice when he spoke to her.

In reception, with bad grace Duncan surrendered his navy wool coat and leather satchel to be put away in the clinic's cloakroom. Corinne found herself over-compensating for her ex-husband's surliness by being too friendly, smiling as she gave the receptionist her fake-fur-lined parka and the enormous leather holdall she lugged everywhere, much to the amusement of her daughters. 'Oh, just a minute!' she said. She'd remembered the photo in its frame. The receptionist obligingly went back to retrieve it from her bag.

'Some things never change,' said Duncan, looking pointedly up at the clock.

Hannah was in the art room again. Corinne was glad she'd found an interest in here that was separate from the day-to-day business of the clinic, an escape from the endless analysing of feelings and behaviours, the why? why? why? that threaded itself through everything in this place.

'Oh my God,' Hannah said when she saw her parents walking in together. 'Two-pronged attack. This must be serious.'

Laura was in the far corner of the room, helping a woman Corinne didn't recognize make something out of a large mound of clay. 'It's supposed to be a bust of her own head,' whispered Hannah. 'But Katy is too scared to start it in case it goes wrong. She's been there for an hour and a half.'

'How are you, sweetie?' Duncan laid his hand over his daughter's, and Corinne had to look away.

'Fine,' the reply snapped out, and Corinne swung her attention back to Hannah.

'Are you sure? You seem—'

'I'm fine, Dad. Really. I just want to get out of here.'

'I know you do, sweetheart. But you made a promise to Danny.'

What about his *promises to* her? Corinne felt like saying, but she bit back the words.

'I just don't feel safe here.'

'Come on, sweetie. Here's probably the safest place for you.' Duncan had his Eminently Reasonable voice on, and it set Corinne's teeth on edge.

'Two women have died here, Dad.'

'Yes, but they were ill, Hannah. They'd already tried to kill themselves before. That's why they were in here.'

Duncan glanced over at Laura, and Corinne wondered if he was trying to impress the attractive art therapist with his air of calm authority.

'I just keep thinking, Mum, about that name Charlie was googling on the day she died. William Kingsley. That's what those initials WK stand for. It's got to be relevant somehow. I'm sure of it.'

'How are you getting on, Hannah? Hello, Hannah's mum and dad!'

Laura had come over and now stood behind Hannah with a hand on her shoulder so she could look at Hannah's latest artwork, a pastel picture of someone's Nike trainer, which stood on a stool in front of her easel. Corinne couldn't tear her eyes away from the other woman's hand on her daughter's shoulder, an unwelcome reminder that Hannah was becoming assimilated in here, forming bonds. Not just passing through.

'Aren't you cheating, though,' asked Duncan, 'taking out the laces so it's easier to draw?'

'Laces aren't allowed in here, if you remember, Mr Lovell,' said Laura.

'Lovell is my actually my daughter's married name,' said Duncan sharply, and Corinne could tell he was embarrassed by his faux pas about the laces. 'I'm Harris. As is my ex-wife here.'

160

Ex. It still hurt.

'Your daughter has real talent,' said Laura. 'You should be very proud of her.'

'Oh, we are,' Duncan replied. Corinne saw him squeeze Hannah's hand.

On the way back out to his car, however, Duncan was troubled. 'Didn't you think Hannah sounded a bit paranoid back there, rambling on about that random name? Remember when she first came in, Dr Roberts warned us to look out for signs of paranoia? Shit, Cor, I thought she was getting better.'

'She is getting better. I'm sure of it.'

But driving out of the main gates, Corinne couldn't stop thinking about the expression on Hannah's face as she'd told them she didn't feel safe.

There was no doubt her daughter was feeling genuinely threatened.

But what if the real threat was coming from inside her own head?

24

Hannah

I didn't tell Mum and Dad about the rabbit with the hacked-off ears. What would I have said? They already think I'm losing it. I could see it on Dad's face when I said I didn't feel safe. A cuddly toy would have been a step too far.

I can't resist asking Danny about it, though, when he comes to visit. We are in the rose garden. From the dance studio comes the sound of flamenco-style music and hands clapping and Grace's voice calling out, 'Stamp those feet! Harder, harder! Get it all out!'

'I haven't a clue where that bloody rabbit is,' Danny tells me. 'Your mum probably cleared it out, along with the rest of the stuff.'

'All of it?'

Mum said she'd been helping Danny 'sort out' our flat. I'd guessed she might have meant Em— the spare room, but it still hurts. I want to ask what they've done with the baby things, but I can't face hearing that they've gone to the charity shop. Someone else's baby wearing all those lovely clothes.

'So you couldn't clear out the nursery yourself?'

Danny looks at me coldly then from under his dark

lashes and I want to wind the words back in, like reeling in a fishing line.

'For fuck's sake, Hannah. What did you think? That I was going to kneel on the carpet in the middle of all her stuff and pick out little shoes and toys and have a little cry like she was a real baby? You made her up. That's the long and short of it. So what does it matter who clears out the baby things? I don't give a toss if it's your mum, or the fucking binmen. I just want them out of the house so I can breathe again.'

It's the longest speech Danny has made since I first came in here and, afterwards, we both look at each other in surprise. We are sitting outside on the bench and I am smoking a cigarette, even though I know Danny hates it.

Do I still love you?

The thought comes out of nowhere, sucking the air from my lungs.

For the last six years, loving Danny has been one of the defining characteristics of who I am. If a stranger had asked me, I'd have said, *I'm Hannah. I work in publishing. I'm married to Danny.* It's one of the pillars that has held the rest of my life up.

What would happen if someone took it away?

But now the world slides into focus again as Danny sits back and runs his long fingers through his hair and I recognize him. That is, I recognize him physically rather than intellectually, with my whole body, not just my mind or my eyes.

Of course I love him. I'd do anything for him.

Maybe he's having similar thoughts, because there's a softening in him when he looks at me now, a blurring of hard lines, that meets with a corresponding dissolving inside me.

'You know, Han, there isn't a day goes past that I don't feel guilty about what I did. The affair. That's what set this whole thing off. I know that, and I have to live with it. But we have to put this behind us now. Or there's no hope for us.'

The phrase 'no hope' shimmers between us like a heat haze.

'I *am* moving on,' I say. 'I feel like I've made a real breakthrough in the last couple of days. Ask Dr Chakraborty.'

'I've already talked to Dr Roberts.'

My heart plummets.

'And?'

'And he thinks there's still a lot more work to do.'

'Maybe I could come home and do the rest of the treatment as an outpatient.'

Danny has already started shaking his head, even before I've finished the sentence.

'We agreed, Han. You promised you'd stay in here until the doctors think you're well enough to come home.'

'Yes, but I don't think this is the best place for me, Danny. There's something off about it. People *die* in here.'

Danny throws his hands up and hurls himself backwards on the bench.

'Not this again. Please. Not the Charlie thing. Do you realize how crazy you sound? How paranoid?'

Desperation makes me angry.

'Yeah, well, maybe you'd be paranoid too if your

husband had screwed around behind your back and lied to you for months. You know there's nothing forcing me to stay here. The section has been lifted. I could check myself out and come home any time I like.'

'Just don't expect me to be there when you do.'

We glare at each other and I have the fleeting impression that he's no longer *my* Danny but just some random good-looking thirty-something man. Then his face crumples.

'I need to know you're better, Hannah. I can't go through that again. Do you have any idea what it was like? I thought I was about to be a dad.'

I think about reminding him that I thought I was about to be a mum, but the words stay stoppered in my throat like I am choking back a cough.

After he's gone, Stella joins me. It's a bright day but there's a biting wind that undercuts the clear, crisp air. Stella has on her coat with the fur collar that makes her look like Greta Garbo.

'Were you waiting for Danny to leave?'

She shrugs. It bothers me that there's no love lost between these two. They each seem to feel I've been taken in by the other. I hate it when the people I love don't love each other. It makes me question my own judgement.

'Why don't you like Danny?'

'He cheated on you. I don't like cheats.'

'But I've forgiven him. And if I can, surely everyone else can too. Besides, what I did to him was much worse.'

She flashes me a 'yeah, right' look and thrusts her

hands deep into the pockets of her coat. From the music therapy room behind us comes the sound of three notes of a piano being played over and over again, while in one of the bedrooms above someone is sobbing softly.

'How come you haven't got anybody?' I ask her. 'You're so lovely, Stella. Why isn't there a queue of men beating down the door? Or at least your family. Where's your mum? Your dad?'

'People aren't my thing,' says Stella.

She is smiling, but her cheeks are pink – although that could be from the cold wind – and her hand is at her throat, reaching through the fur collar to worry at her silver cat necklace.

'But haven't you ever had a long-term boyfriend?' I persist.

'I went out with someone for five years from when I was fifteen, but Mama and my stepdad didn't like him.'

'Why? Because he was a bad influence?'

'No. Because he was thirty-eight.'

'Thirty-eight! But that's not even legal.'

'He was a writer who came in to school to talk about his books. I emailed him afterwards, and that's how it started. He liked to call me in the evening and tell me what clothes to wear. I had one of those little Flip camcorders and I'd send him footage of me dressed in the clothes he'd chosen.'

Stella says all this in her everyday, breathy voice as if it were normal and somehow this is even more chilling than what she has just told me.

'But Stella, that's abuse. You know that, right?'

Stella smiles.

'Who was abusing who, though?' she says. 'I instigated it. And I kept it going even after he tried to finish it.'

'Why?'

She shrugs.

'If I knew that, I wouldn't be here, would I? Isn't that what we're all here for – to find out the why? Isn't that our optimum outcome from all of this?'

'But you've never talked about this in Group. Do you discuss it in your one-to-ones?'

'It's not relevant, Hannah. That girl isn't who I am any more. She's gone. I'm a different person now. I even have a different name.'

'Really? So what—'

'Aren't you two cold? It's freezing out here. What are you guys talking about?'

Odelle is shivering, despite the huge puffa coat that dwarfs her tiny frame and the outsize knitted woollen scarf from which her head emerges like a tortoise's.

'Oh, just boring stuff,' says Stella.

Odelle sniffs. Her nose is already bright red from the freezing wind.

'Fine. Whatever. Anyway, Dr See is looking for you, Stella.'

My startled brain grapples to work out which doctor could have earned that epithet, until I realize that of course she is saying 'Dr C'. Classic Odelle.

As Stella stands up to follow Odelle's hunched shoulders along the path that leads around the back of the clinic and in through the car park, I put a hand on her arm.

'What happened to him? The writer? Please tell me he got done for something.'

167

Stella giggles, showing all her small, perfect, white teeth.

'No. But I nearly did.'

'You? What on earth for?'

'Harassment. But like I say, I was a different person then.'

When I'm alone I find myself shivering. But I don't think it's the cold.

25

Corinne

Corinne loved her office.

It was in one of the university's cramped department buildings, a gloomy, red-brick, monolithic structure with creaking floors and an antiquated heating system that meant they all boiled through the summer because the radiators never quite turned off while, in winter, the cold wind came gusting through the cracks in the wooden window frames. But her room had a high ceiling and a huge window through which she could observe the goings-on in the swanky high-rise apartment block on the other side of the street. It was lined with shelves on which books, many of them by people Corinne knew well, were stacked two and sometimes three deep.

Corinne's name was on the door, and every time she came in, no matter how stressful the day – and university life was becoming increasingly so – she felt a sense of homecoming. Though she'd come to adore her little house, this was definitely the place she felt most convincingly herself.

Settling down in her padded desk chair, Corinne sighed at the chequerboard of pink and yellow Post-it notes all over her desk. They'd been put there by the new departmental secretary, who looked about twelve, had round writing like a child's and finished off each message and telephone number with a smiley face. It made Corinne feel old.

There was a 'stuff to be dealt with' pile in the middle of Corinne's desk that seemed to have doubled in size since she was last in. She pulled the top document off, a printout of a chapter she'd contributed to a book about whether the internet had destroyed pop culture, which had been sent to her for proofreading. She'd written it in that magical period after Hannah announced she was pregnant but before the first signs of odd behaviour, when the world had seemed absurdly benevolent and the future bursting with possibility.

Even re-reading the first paragraph, a typically dry academic introduction, Corinne was transported back to that time, when the most she had to worry about was getting this chapter written so she could put another tick in the box when it came to personal-assessment time. When she first started at the university, academia was all about the teaching, the interaction with students, the transfer of ideas. But nowadays you were too busy justifying your existence for any of that. Where was the passion? Where was that practically audible mental *click* when a student finally got it? It was all about value for money these days. Students liked to see exactly what they were paying for. Spreadsheet education, she called it.

A knock on the door halted Corinne's musings.

The man who came in was tall and broad with closely cropped salt-and-pepper hair and a smile that split his face.

'I'm Paddy?' he said, seeing her blank look. 'I'm doing an MA in sociology and anthropology. You've kindly agreed to be joint supervisor for my dissertation.'

'Oh God. It's today! I completely forgot. Of course. Come in.'

She glanced over to her academic flip calendar, and there he was: *Paddy Collins. Mature Student. 11.30 a.m.*

Corinne was so flustered that it took her a good ten minutes, until Paddy was well into his list of the research documents he intended to use, to realize how handsome he was. Not pretty-boy handsome like Danny, but the kind of handsome that crept up on you so you felt you'd discovered it for yourself, like treasure other people had overlooked, and doubly valuable for being hard to find.

'Tell me a bit about yourself,' she asked when he'd finished. 'You're slightly older than my usual students.'

'I've got a sourdough starter that's older than your usual students.'

Corinne must have looked confused, because he said, 'You're not a baker then? Starters are those natural leavening agents you use to make some types of bread. They can last for years. And now I've had to explain the hell out of that joke I feel like a right idiot.'

Paddy smiled and Corinne felt a curious sense of recognition, as if she knew him from somewhere. After they'd finished discussing his dissertation, Paddy seemed in no hurry to leave, happily answering her questions about his background. He'd been a firefighter until he was laid off five years earlier and since then he'd taken a degree and was now doing an MA. He wanted to write a book, make his children proud. Then they talked about children, and divorce. His children were teen-agers, still angry about their parents' split. 'They get over it,' she said. Then she wondered if, in fact, that was true.

They were talking so naturally that for a moment Corinne thought about telling him about Hannah. It was on the tip of her tongue, but then she swallowed it back down. *My daughter is in a psychiatric institution.* It wasn't the sort of thing you told strangers. Paddy was her student. She needed to keep a professional distance.

After he had gone, Corinne couldn't settle back into work. She gazed out of the window. The luxury flat directly opposite her office was occupied by a middle-aged couple. Sometimes, if Corinne stayed working late, the woman would be there, with her cloud of fair hair and dark, formal clothes, but mostly it was the man she saw. Clearly, he worked from home, because he spent many hours a day at a computer screen, which was framed against one of the windows of the flat. Over the years, Corinne had imagined many careers for him. He was a famous poet, tapping out his latest opus. Or he was a designer, someone creative. At one point, she'd even been convinced he was a politician, certain she recognized him from *Question Time*.

Today, he'd shifted his computer screen to the side and was sitting staring down at his desk top, reading something. Whatever it was, it wasn't holding his attention. He looked up frequently, gazing through the window as if searching for inspiration. Before she could duck, his eyes locked with Corinne's and, after a split-second delay, he raised his hand to wave. She lifted her own half-heartedly and then made a show of picking up her red pen and turning her attention back to the chapter printout on the desk in front of her.

But the words swam in front of her eyes.

Ever since she had got the call from Danny nearly ten weeks ago, his voice tight with all the things he wasn't saying, nothing in Corinne's world had made sense.

'Don't panic, but we're in the hospital. Hannah fell down the stairs at home. She's done something to her wrist.'

'And the baby?' Corinne had forced her voice to stay calm but she'd gripped the edge of the table so tightly that, afterwards, all the nails on her right hand were split.

'We're just waiting for an ultrasound. Hannah is hysterical. She's afraid something has happened.'

That was it. The thing he wasn't saying. The fear that pressed on his voice until it broke.

Then, 'I have to go. They're calling us. I'll phone you afterwards.'

Then the wait. Ten minutes. Twenty. Half an hour. All the different scenarios running through Corinne's fevered brain.

All except one.

As always, thinking about what had happened made Corinne feel useless. Desperate to do something – *anything* – she reached down and plucked a piece of blank paper from the tray in the printer by her feet.

'HANNAH', she wrote in capital letters across the top of the page in red pen, and then sat back, studying the word carefully. Then she added 'DANGERS' and underlined the two words.

Underneath that she divided the page into three

columns. At the top of the first one she wrote '1) Steffie Garitson' and underlined it. Number two was 'The Meadows'. That, too, she underlined. Then she stared at the paper for a long time before adding a third danger to the list: 'Hannah's own thoughts'.

Instantly, she wanted to erase the words, feeling as if she had betrayed her own daughter just by writing them.

Steffie Garitson was a little worm of fear wriggling in Corinne's stomach. The trip to Tunbridge Wells had been so strange, the brother's warning so ominous, Steffie felt like a malign black shadow over their lives. But aside from hoping that she'd cleared out for good, there was little Corinne could do about her. Instead, she concentrated on the middle column. The Meadows.

Objectively, Corinne knew The Meadows was the best place for Hannah. After the trauma of Hannah's admission to hospital and her subsequent breakdown, she and Duncan had researched Hannah's condition exhaustively, looking for places within easy driving distance that had a track record of dealing with delusions like their daughter's.

In the end, it was Corinne who had stumbled on The Meadows. As soon as she'd seen the well-appointed rooms and the beautifully kept gardens, she'd known Hannah could be all right there. It didn't look like a psychiatric clinic. It could easily pass as a small, select, five-star hotel discreetly tucked away in the Barnet green belt in the very outer reaches of north London. There was no stigma to being there.

'Stigma for who, Cor?' Duncan had asked, when she'd sent him the brochure. 'You or Hannah?'

But he hadn't quibbled about contributing to the astronomical fees, even though she was quite sure Gigi would have had plenty to say on the subject.

And she couldn't deny that Duncan had a point when he implied that one of the biggest selling points about The Meadows was its resemblance to the kind of place they were all familiar with – a hotel or a spa, somewhere that fitted within their sphere of reference. Hannah's mental illness had plunged them all into a completely unrecognizable world, so it wasn't surprising that Corinne clung to anything that reminded her of the people they used to be.

Corinne logged on to her office computer, ignoring the 234 unread emails that had appeared in her inbox.

When she typed 'The Meadows' into the search engine, she recognized the links as the same ones she'd checked before booking Hannah into the clinic. Care quality inspections passed with flying colours. Glowing testimonials from previous clients – not fully identified, but they had that ring of authenticity.

Then she tried typing in 'The Meadows danger', anxiety knotting itself in her stomach as she waited for the results to load, but in the event, there was nothing. Only a link to a speech Dr Chakraborty had made in which he'd talked about 'the danger of making assumptions about mental illness'.

Now she turned her attention to Dr Roberts. As figurehead of the clinic and its charismatic spokesperson, he was the one who shaped the ethos of the place.

Her search threw up page after page of references. Endless links to papers he'd written and speeches he'd given and celebrity-studded fundraisers he'd attended.

Gradually, she was able to piece together his career path over the previous fifteen years: he had moved from a mid-level post in an exclusive London clinic to set up his own successful private practice and then, five years ago, had opened The Meadows, answering a need for 'expert, highest-quality psychiatric care in a safe, discreet, luxurious, home-from-home environment'. But about his earliest beginnings, there was surprisingly little.

What had started out as a random exercise to make her feel as if she was doing something solidified into a real, burning need for information. This was the man in charge of Hannah's care. It seemed suddenly imperative that she know everything there was to know about him, from the very start of his career onwards, so she could be sure he was the best person for the job. How else could she persuade her daughter to stay where she was?

Link after link focused on the older, established Roberts. His first steps in psychiatry remained shrouded in mystery until, finally, she came across an article he'd written in an obscure medical journal on a controversial new approach to bulimia in which he referred to a case he'd observed while working in a small private clinic in the Oxfordshire countryside. The clinic wasn't named in the piece but he gave away sufficient details for Corinne to narrow it down to two options, both of which she found without difficulty on Google.

She picked up her phone but hesitated, then replaced it on the desk. Then she snatched it up again and punched in the first number. Listening to the ringtone, she had no idea what she was going to say, but as soon as the call was answered the lie popped into her head.

'I'm a journalist with the *British Medical Journal*. I'm

writing a profile piece on Dr Oliver Roberts and I believe he worked with you early in his career.' If Roberts was now in his late fifties, Corinne was guessing this would have been in the late 1980s.

It wasn't the greatest cover story. But it wasn't bad either. Especially not for Corinne, who, like her younger daughter, had been cursed from earliest childhood with an inbuilt inability to lie. Unfortunately, the first clinic drew a blank. 'We didn't open until 1998,' the receptionist told her in a clipped voice.

The phone at the second clinic, Westbridge House, was answered by a man with a strong Eastern European accent who seemed perplexed by her long-winded explanation. 'I fetch someone,' he said eventually.

The longer Corinne waited, the more she felt her sense of purpose dissolving away. She was about to hang up when a woman's voice came on the line.

'This is Christine Holmes, the administrative manager of Westbridge House. Can I help you?'

She took a deep breath. 'My name is Corinne Harris. My daughter Hannah is in a psychiatric clinic in Barnet and I'm so worried about her I can't breathe.'

Where had *that* come from? That unintentional splurge of honesty? No choice now but to plough on.

'One of her current . . . fixations, I think you'd call it, is that she has become convinced she's in danger, and I'm researching the staff whose care she's under so I can put her mind at rest.'

To her own ears, she sounded unhinged, but Christine Holmes proved surprisingly sympathetic. 'I do know what it's like,' she said. 'Wanting to help and not being able to.'

The problem was Dr Roberts' tenure would have been well before her day, she said. The clinic had had a total overhaul when it changed management thirteen years before with a complete change of personnel. There had been certain irregularities in the way it was previously run.

'Irregularities?'

'Oh, nothing illegal. I believe the original director favoured some more unorthodox theories that have since been discredited. But as I say, that was a long time ago, and there are no staff members still remaining from that period. We now have an exemplary assessment record.'

'There must be some records, though, relating to previous staff members. I'm just looking for basic biographical details I can relay back to my daughter, to reassure her.'

Christine Holmes made a noise that, if she hadn't been in the office of a medical clinic, Corinne would have sworn was someone taking a long drag on a cigarette; it was probably her sucking in air between her teeth.

'All the computer systems were replaced when the clinic changed management, I'm afraid.'

'There must be physical files, though.'

A hesitation. 'The truth is, all the files from before 2004 are missing. There was a disgruntled employee. My predecessor, in fact. It's a sad story. She'd been at the clinic since it opened in the mid-1980s but she had problems with alcohol and was dismissed after turning up one too many times half-cut. When she left, she apparently destroyed all the files out of spite, although that was never proven. As I said, a very sad case.'

'Do you happen to remember her name?'

Corinne was aiming at relaxed, but worry strained the fabric of her voice, and when Christine Holmes replied Corinne could tell that she had registered her desperation.

'I'm afraid I couldn't tell you that.' Her voice was once again detached and professional. 'Out of respect for the staff member concerned.'

Inwardly cursing, Corinne hung up. Sitting at her computer, she called up her search engine and typed in 'Westbridge House Clinic' and 'administrative manager', instantly generating a string of hits involving the name Christine Holmes.

She randomly added the year 2003 to the search box, remembering that Christine had told her she'd been there since 2004. This time there was a link to a one-day conference that had been run at the clinic in February 2003. There was a number to ring for more details and a contact name. Clinic manager, Geraldine Buckley.

It wasn't much. But it was all she had.

26

Hannah

Ever since Stella told me about the older boyfriend who used to choose her clothes for her, I've been feeling angry about the many ways it's possible for a man to fuck up your life.

I'm trying to keep focused on Stella, but my mind keeps drifting back to Danny and what he did with Steffie, and I can't go there, because that way madness lies.

'Why are you so concerned about what Stella told you?' asks Laura. It's mid-afternoon, and Charlie died more than two weeks ago, and I am hiding out in Laura's little office at the back of the art room while the others are in the dance studio doing some kind of exercise Grace has invented that mixes yoga with keep fit. She calls it Stretchercise. I call it a kind of torture.

To be accurate, Laura's office is actually more like a cupboard. There's a desk that's completely covered with paintings and drawings, and art books so well thumbed their pages curl up at the corners. There's one comfortable armchair, where I'm sitting, with a soft tartan woollen blanket covering my knees. And a swivel chair from which Laura is looking at me thoughtfully over the

180

top of her tortoiseshell glasses. The whirring of the fan heater blocks out any external noise, making our space feel even more intimate. No window, just the orange glow from a table lamp in the shape of a crystallized rock on Laura's desk. A lit, scented candle is releasing a heavenly smell of jasmine that feels heady in this enclosed space.

'Maybe because it just reminds me how little I really know anyone here. I mean, even though I've only been here two months, it still feels as though we're all like family, because we know each other's secrets. But really, we're only giving away what we want to give away.'

Laura nods, and the glasses slip back over her eyes so they appear magnified and blurry with understanding.

'I thought I knew Charlie,' I press on. Now that I've started picking at this scab I can't seem to stop. 'But I didn't know her. I saw her the morning she died and had no inkling what she was planning. None at all.'

'So you do accept she killed herself?'

I shrug.

'I swing from knowing that she did it to being utterly convinced that she couldn't have done it, all in the same minute. My thoughts are so disjointed at the moment. So all over the place.'

'Your mum says you feel like you could be next.'

I look at her, then back at the ground. It sounds ludicrous when she says it.

'I get paranoid, I guess. Isn't that why most of us are here?'

It comes out whiny and defensive. I don't mean it that way.

'Would hypnotherapy help? I can't promise to make

the paranoia disappear but I can certainly help you relax.'

I consider it. I know it has helped some of the others, but I worry about the lack of control.

I shake my head.

'Let me at least give you a massage then.'

Laura gets up and stands behind me with her hands on my shoulders, and the sudden physical intimacy is almost more than I can stand. It feels like it's been so long since I was properly touched. To my horror, tears start to pool in the corner of my eyes.

I'm relieved when Laura sits back down again, as if she has sensed the turmoil going on inside me.

'Your mum asked me if you ever paint your husband,' says Laura, and my stomach lurches in shock at her mentioning Danny like that, without warning.

'I don't need to paint him. He's never out of my mind.'

She looks at me, long and unflinching, until I look away.

'Do you want to tell me about that night? The night everyone found out there was no baby? Sometimes it helps to talk about the bad stuff and confront it head on. It lessens its power.'

I don't want to tell her. But once the memory is in my head it swells until it's all I can think of.

'I slipped on a Domino's Pizza flyer,' I tell her, as if it being Domino's might somehow change it to a funny story, easier to tell. 'I didn't want to go to the hospital, but Danny insisted. He was so protective of me and Em . . .'

I don't tell her how much I miss his protectiveness.

Because it makes me sound weak and pathetic, and that's not who I am. Was.

I don't tell her either about the row we'd had just before I fell. About *her* – who else? Though I'd banned Danny from mentioning her name, I exerted no such control over myself. Steffie was like a form of Tourette's for me. She came out of nowhere. We'd be eating dinner and chatting about something on the news, an election in Italy, for example, everything calm and civilized, and that would make me think of how much I'd love to visit Italy – Tuscany, Florence, all the places I've never been – and without warning an anger would sweep through me and out she'd come. 'I expect *Steffie* loves Italy.' Danny blinking at me in confusion.

The thing was, she was always in my head, skating across the surface of my thoughts. She was the shadow in front of my sun and, no matter where I moved and what I did to evade her, there she was, blocking the light. And because I never told Danny, because I didn't want to give her that victory, it was always a shock to him when I couldn't bear it any more and I'd lob her at him like a grenade, seemingly from nowhere.

We'd been watching something on telly. We used to love American box sets but now they were a minefield, with their casual infidelities and broken marriages, so we'd started choosing programmes purely on the basis that they were less likely to contain trigger elements, which basically ruled out most adult dramas. So we ended up slumped in front of anodyne shows that neither of us had much interest in. A lot of cookery programmes. That one about people building their own houses. But even then, Steffie managed to blow like dust into every

183

crack and crevice so there was a greasy film of her over everything we watched.

On this particular night, it was a programme about an unlikely choir of former prisoners. Danny claimed it was emotionally manipulative, but I saw him wipe a tear away when he thought I wasn't looking. One of the people taking part was a gruff, middle-aged man who'd never been able to form close relationships and wondered if it was because he'd been given away at birth. 'It stays with you. Rejection. It's like an invisible tattoo you don't know you're wearing.'

'Have I got one of those?' I turned to Danny, who hadn't made the connection and gazed at me blankly. 'An invisible tattoo? The rejection tattoo?'

Danny sighed his 'not this again' sigh, which just infuriated me more. 'I've told you,' he said. 'It wasn't a rejection of you. It wasn't about you.'

I've heard that's said quite a lot. It's in the Cheater's Manual, apparently. *It was nothing to do with you. It was about me, something I was going through.* As if it makes it better to know we didn't even feature in the decision that shattered our lives.

I stormed out of the flat, aiming at a dramatic exit but really intending to go down and visit Marco. Only, on the landing was a stack of flyers. Sometimes I pick up the mail near the front door and sort through it on my way upstairs, leaving the stuff I don't want outside on the landing, ready for recycling. The flyer on the top was a shiny Domino's Pizza one, and my foot, in its smooth-soled Moroccan slipper, went sliding over the top of it, and just like that I was falling.

Danny came flying out of our flat and practically beat

me to the bottom of the stairs. We both knew straight away that I'd done something to my wrist. It was badly swollen and I screamed when Danny tried to touch it.

'How did you feel on the way to the hospital?' Laura wants to know. 'Did you realize on any level that things were about to come crashing down around you?'

I try to think back to that car dash. Surely I must have had some clue that my fantasy world was about to implode? But the truth is I didn't see it as a fantasy. It was real. Emily was real. The rest of it – the appointments, the scans – they were compartmentalized. Hidden away in a pocket of my head where I couldn't find them. I remember feeling panic, sitting there in the front seat of the car. But the panic was for her. Not for me. For her safety, not mine.

'I had my wrist X-rayed first. Just a sprain. Then Danny insisted the doctor check over the baby. "Just to be sure."'

'And then?' asks Laura.

How to describe it? The doctor, a junior with purple rings around her eyes like cartoon glasses who told us she'd been on duty for thirteen hours straight, asking how pregnant I was and her face changing when Danny told her six months. Knowing it wasn't right. But she put her stethoscope in her ears anyway and placed the cold metal disc on my bump, and I made a joke about it being so cold and talked about when I'd gone for a smear test and how cold that had been and how the nurse told me to 'just relax' and every single muscle had instantly clenched. But then the doctor left the room abruptly and I knew I should warn Danny, although, even then, I couldn't have said what I needed to warn him about,

185

only instead I kept on about the smear test, and he must have thought I was getting hysterical. And now the junior doctor with the purple rings around her eyes was back with an older doctor who introduced herself and said she just needed to perform another check, and by now Danny was sensing something wasn't right and looking at me in confusion, and I felt it then, a sucking of energy from my centre, and I knew.

It came in stages. 'I'm afraid there is no baby.' Then, after another test: 'There never was any baby.'

Danny's grief turned to incomprehension as the ultrasound gel dripped down my belly, and I closed my eyes so I couldn't see him, or the lying monitor that said Emily was never there.

'You made it all up? The scans? The GP appointments?'

'I didn't need them,' I told him. 'I know what I felt. I know what my body told me.'

I look at Laura now and say, 'I had no idea then that my body was a big, fat liar.'

We both laugh, as if it is funny.

There's a knock and, before Laura has a chance to speak, Bridget Ashworth pokes her head around the door, bringing with her an icy draught. Her eyes behind her glasses flit around the room, as if taking account of the messy desk and the artwork on the walls and the two of us arranged in our chairs as if at confessional, and she frowns.

'I didn't realize you had company, Laura. Sorry to interrupt.' She doesn't sound sorry. 'Oliver . . . Dr Roberts . . . would like a quick word in his office.'

Laura's smile never leaves her face, but four deathly

white splodges of knuckle appear on the hand that grips her mug.

We follow Bridget out into the hallway. She's wearing the same black jacket as when she caught me in Charlie's room the first time, but I notice the white cat hair has gone.

'Everything's in chaos today,' she calls over her shoulder. 'The film crew are shooting in the admin office.' I can tell from how she says this how much she enjoys bandying around words like 'film crew' and 'shooting'. She likes how it makes her sound inside her own head, the kind of person it makes her. Stripped of the fan heater and the woollen blanket, I shiver.

While Laura follows Bridget Ashworth's clacking heels towards the main staircase that leads up to Dr Roberts' office and the smaller consulting rooms, I cross the hallway into the day room. The disruption of my session with Laura, just as I had forced myself to dredge up the most painful of memories, has left me feeling anxious, like there's a line of ants marching across my chest. I head for the shelving unit at the side of the room where we each have a cubbyhole labelled with our names, to store the things we can't be bothered to cart upstairs to our rooms. It's where I keep the colouring books that arrive in the post from work with gratifying regularity.

The one I'm working on at the moment contains intricate patterns of flowers and leaves that interweave and wind themselves over the pages. I take it from the top of the pile, together with my felt-tip pens, which I keep in a large, zipped pencil case, and sit down at the big oval table near the window. Inès, the French woman with the lazy eye who comes in twice a week to offer horticulture therapy, is pushing a wheelbarrow full of broken branches and twigs across the drive outside, with her ancient dog waddling behind. Her wellington boots make a soft crunching noise on the gravel. A puff of black smoke in the sky overhead tells me she has the incinerator going somewhere safely away from us residents.

Darren is sitting in an armchair at the front of the room with an open file balanced on his knee, and he looks over and smiles as he catches my eye. Gradually, I feel the tension easing.

I open the colouring book. It's a new one, with only one page filled in. The picture I did last bursts off the paper in blooms of vivid fuchsia and violet. *Crayoning*, echoes Danny's voice in my head. As I turn to the next page, a flash of colour further on in the book catches my attention. Curious, I flick through until I find a page around three-quarters of the way through that appears to have already been filled in.

'No!'

Darren looks up, startled to see me on my feet, my hand over my mouth. He crosses the room to see what I'm looking at.

'I don't understand,' he says. And he picks up the book to have a closer look at the page, where, in place of a design featuring plump camellias and sprays of delicate meadowsweet, someone has taken the colours that most resemble flesh tones and, painstakingly, with minute attention to detail, mapped out the softly rounded shape of a baby.

27

Corinne

Whenever Corinne thought of Oxford, she envisaged honey-coloured stone and rambling detached houses overrun with ivy, and bikes with wicker baskets leaning up against the walls.

The Oxford Geraldine Buckley lived in wasn't like that at all.

Around five miles from the city centre, it was in an area of housing estates and ring roads where the only greenery was on the hoarding of the local betting shop, and any bike leaning against a wall was unlikely to be there long, as the smattering of lone front wheels still locked to lamp posts attested.

If you'd asked Corinne what she was doing here, she wouldn't have been able to tell you. The fact was, as with the visit to the Garitsons in Tunbridge Wells, doing *something* felt better than nothing.

Hannah, having appeared to be getting better, now seemed to be regressing in her recovery, with Charlie's death triggering a deep-seated and worrying paranoia. When Corinne had visited the day before, Hannah had been barely coherent, rambling on about a toy rabbit with broken ears and something about her wretched

189

colouring book, and distrusting everyone from Dr Roberts down to the woman who cleaned her room (this last one linked to the sudden appearance of the rabbit). But when Corinne had said, 'So discharge yourself. We'll find somewhere else if this place upsets you,' Hannah had yelled at her, 'I can't. If I discharge myself, Danny will leave me. And I know that's what you want. You've never liked him. You don't want me to be happy. You want me to be single and miserable like you.'

Well. That had surprised them both.

Without mentioning Steffie, which would entail admitting she'd snooped in Hannah's room, there was little Corinne could say to explain her recent antipathy towards her son-in-law, which Hannah had clearly picked up on. Instead, she'd tried to reassure her by promising to investigate the background of the clinic and its staff, making doubly sure that this was the safest place for Hannah to be.

It wasn't until she'd come home from the clinic, called out a cheerful 'hello' to her next-door neighbour and let herself in through her front door that she'd allowed herself to slide down the wall of the hallway with her head in her hands.

The savagery of Corinne's despair had taken her by surprise. Even at the start, when she'd first found out about the pseudocyesis, she hadn't felt this level of bleakness. Then it had been about shock and the search for solutions and reasons; she'd been sure that, if she looked hard enough, researched thoroughly enough, she'd find the key that unlocked the door back into Hannah's old life. The diagnosis was traumatic, but at least it held within it the possibility of cure. If you knew what was wrong, you could find out how to fix it. But this new downturn, just as they'd seemed to be making progress, seemed so bitterly unfair.

Nevertheless, by the time she'd hauled herself to her feet off the hallway floor, weak from crying and something in her knee making an ominous clicking noise as she straightened it, Corinne was flooded with new resolve.

She hadn't managed to find a phone number for Geraldine Buckley, but she'd sent her a message on Facebook and, within two hours, she had a message back. And now here she was, on a dismal road on the outskirts of Oxford, piling coins into a parking meter and being shocked all over again at how much it was possible to be charged for the privilege of parking your car outside an off-licence and a kebab takeaway.

Geraldine Buckley's flat was in a modern block that was set back from the road through a metal gate next to a wall with a notice on it saying 'NO DUMPING' that someone had vandalized so it read 'NO HUMPING'.

Once the intercom had buzzed her in, Corinne was relieved to find the block was well maintained and smelled reassuringly of bleach.

Geraldine Buckley also wasn't as Corinne had imagined. She'd been expecting to find her wild-haired and drink-ravaged, with shaking hands and egg stains down her top, but instead, the former clinic manager was a neatly groomed woman in her late fifties with well-cut brown hair framing a pleasant, squarish face.

'Three years sober now,' Geraldine told her after she'd made them both tea and shown Corinne to a sofa in her small but bright open-plan living room. 'Well, three years, five months and two weeks, give or take a day or two.'

'Good for you.'

'Don't get too carried away. It's still a full-time job. Staying off the booze.'

'So you never went back to work after you left Westbridge House?'

'Oh yes, I had a couple of other jobs. One in a leisure centre, one in a dentist's surgery. But I lost those. It seems customers don't like being greeted by a receptionist who reeks of last night's vodka.'

In her Facebook message, Corinne had again fallen back on her bogus *British Medical Journal* profile story, reasoning that Geraldine Buckley would be more likely to share information with a journalist than a worry-stricken parent she'd never heard of. She'd been hoping for a few background details and had been taken aback when Geraldine suggested she drive over in person.

'I expect you're wondering why I asked you to come all this way,' said Geraldine, reading her thoughts. 'I wanted to be sure you were who you said you were. I could be in a very vulnerable position if certain things ever got out but, at the same time, I'm glad people are digging around into what went on at Westbridge House. Lives were destroyed and, so far, no one has had to pay for it.'

Corinne didn't know how to react to this inform-ation. It startled her. All she wanted was confirmation – that Dr Roberts was exactly as he represented himself, that Hannah was in the best hands. Cold needles of unease began to prick at her spine.

'I took the files.'

Corinne couldn't at first work out what it was Geraldine was saying.

'The filing cabinet that contained all the clinic's records – the staff details, the patient case notes. I took it.'

There was a flare of pink in each of Geraldine's cheeks, and Corinne formed the definite impression that this was the first time the former clinic manager had confessed to what she'd done.

'I was so furious when they sacked me. I hadn't even admitted to myself that I had a drink problem, so for them to imply I was an alcoholic was something I couldn't stomach. I'd already had two written warnings and I'd managed to come up with a rebuttal for both of them. I hadn't been drunk that afternoon, I'd been taking antidepressants that made me slur my words. I hadn't been drinking at breaktime – the smell of booze was because I'd been out at a friend's leaving do the night before. In my own head, I'd squared it all, so when they told me I had to leave I flipped. I had a spare set of office keys at home because I often came in at weekends, when there was just a skeleton staff.

'So I came back with my brother and we loaded the filing cabinet into the back of my Golf. Nearly broke my back into the bargain!'

Corinne was hearing the words but not following their meaning. Why would Geraldine Buckley steal a filing cabinet? 'I'm afraid I don't really understand,' she said.

'Sorry. I don't have a lot of company these days. I alienated a lot of friends during my drinking years. I'm a bit out of practice in holding a proper conversation.

'The filing cabinet was my insurance policy. I had some wild notion of claiming for unfair dismissal, so I wanted all the records. I thought I could make a case that they were getting rid of me because I knew too much about what had happened there. In the end, the lawyer I went to see took one look at me, smelled my breath and said there was nothing he could do. Uptight little sod he was. He said the disciplinary procedure had been followed to the letter. So the bloody filing cabinet has just festered here ever since.'

'You've still got it?'

'Of course. I'm too scared to try to get rid of it. This is all off the record, by the way, isn't it?'

For a moment, Corinne teetered on the edge of the truth. She found that she liked Geraldine Buckley, with her square chin and her tidy little flat. She was eternally thankful that she hadn't been born with the addiction gene, because she didn't know how she'd be able to resist the lure of the cold bottle of wine in the fridge on days when the world seemed out to get her. Recovering addicts had to do battle each and every day, and Geraldine's struggle was written into every fine line of her face.

But if she told her the truth, she might never find out what had happened at Westbridge House. If the Meadows' director had any secrets lurking in his past that made him unfit to care for her daughter, Corinne needed to know about them.

After hesitating, she said, 'Of course it's off the record. So what's the big secret?'

Geraldine bit down on her lower lip, as if debating a point inside her head. Then she began:

'The first director of Westbridge House was a very controlling individual called Professor Dunmore, who ran the place like a kind of Svengali. Incredibly smart and ambitious, but no room for dissent.'

'And Oliver Roberts? I'm assuming he did work there, right?'

Geraldine nodded.

'He was the professor's protégé. I think he was already in his mid-thirties when he worked with us.'

Mid-thirties? Corinne was thrown.

'So we're not talking about the late 1980s?'

Geraldine shook her head. 'Sorry. You're about a decade out. Dr Roberts had come to psychiatry late. I seem to remember something about him starting in a different branch of medicine but switching direction. Surely you'd know all about that, if you're writing a profile piece on him?'

Geraldine frowned, and Corinne quickly tried to move the subject on.

'Of course. So Professor Dunmore took a liking to Dr Roberts?'

'In as much as Dunmore ever really liked anyone. Roberts moulded himself into a mini version of the professor. And Professor Dunmore was arrogant enough to be flattered by that.'

'So what went wrong?'

'The time period we're talking about was just after the False Memory Syndrome scandal had erupted.'

'False Memory Syndrome?'

Corinne had heard the phrase, but her mind was frustratingly blank.

'It's when a therapist, all too often poorly qualified,

asks leading questions of a vulnerable patient so that he or she comes to believe their problems are down to abuse that happened in their past; abuse that is so traumatic their subconscious has buried it. The therapist will say something like "I've seen symptoms like yours before, always triggered by abuse. Could that have happened to you? Try to think who might have been in a position to do that to you." It's amazing how quickly repeated suggestion can become fact.'

Now it came back to her. An article she'd read somewhere years ago about a middle-aged woman who'd accused her elderly father of abusing her forty years before, after a therapist had 'unlocked' those memories. By the time the false memories had been debunked – using old diaries and photographs to prove that the events described could not possibly have taken place – the old man had died, distraught and estranged from his family.

'Professor Dunmore had treated a case of False Memory Syndrome in which a once close, loving family had been torn apart by an allegation that later proved to be false. The professor was hugely affected by it, becoming convinced that many of the cases we were seeing at the clinic where the patient was alleging childhood abuse could actually be cases of FMS, where the memories had been planted by a previous therapist. In the mid- to late 1990s, this was a really "sexy"' – here Geraldine made ironic quote marks in the air with her fingers – 'topic. There were lawsuits in which therapists were sued for implanting false memories of sexual or even satanic abuse. I think Dunmore, who like I say was quite a cold, ruthless person, saw it as a way of grabbing media exposure. And Roberts followed where his master led.'

'But some of the cases were genuine?'

'Of course. In fact, I'd say probably all of them were. Do you know how hard it is for someone to own up to something like this? Secrets they've been carrying around their whole lives? Secrets that make them feel grubby and unclean?'

There was something about Geraldine Buckley's intensity that set the cogs in Corinne's mind whirring and made her wonder about the demons in Geraldine's own past that had led her to seek obliteration at the bottom of a bottle.

'Professor Dunmore became something of an expert on the subject of FMS and how to treat it. So, not surprisingly, we started to see young women, and a couple of men too, persuaded into attending the clinic by relatives who wanted, for whatever reason, to be told that the abuse never happened, that it was just a fantasy that had been planted in the patient's head.'

'And they were all treated by Professor Dunmore?'

'Or Oliver Roberts.'

'And what happened?'

'One of the women killed herself, leaving a note explicitly blaming Dunmore for negating what had happened to her. It caused a big public scandal. Afterwards, some of the other women who'd been treated at the clinic threatened a class action, although that didn't come to anything. In the end, Dunmore had to resign and was later struck off. Roberts stayed on a few months after that, but he didn't get on with Dunmore's replacement and he got a job somewhere else. And a short while later I was dismissed.'

'So Roberts himself was never implicated?'

'No. The General Medical Council decided Dunmore was a domineering figure and the rest of the staff couldn't be blamed for following the ethos of the clinic. There was a rumour that Roberts turned on his mentor in interviews with the investigators and gave them the evidence they needed to force a resignation, in return for complete exoneration for himself, though he always vehemently denied it.'

'And you took the files because—'

'Because I was so angry and so screwed up I thought I could blackmail them into giving me my job back, or sue them for unfair dismissal and use the files to show what a shit company they were. And also . . .'

'Also?'

'I felt a responsibility to those women. The ones who'd had their stories disbelieved. There were still rumours of a class action and I wanted their case notes to be safe.'

Corinne was trying to work out what it all meant – whether, indeed, it meant anything. She couldn't see a connection between what had happened at Westbridge House and the deaths at The Meadows, but still those cold pricks of unease on her back told her there was something here worth pursuing. She took a deep breath.

'Is there any chance I could take a look at the files in the cabinet?'

Her eyes sought out Geraldine's and she held her gaze, hoping that the other woman would see that, even if she wasn't telling the truth about being a journalist, her motives were pure. 'Oliver Roberts currently heads up a psychiatric clinic where he has charge of fifteen vulnerable women. I need to make sure he is fit for the job.'

A shadow flitted across Geraldine's pale eyes that looked like they'd been washed and wrung out one too many times – and Corinne held her breath, half expecting a refusal.

'OK,' said Geraldine.

28

Laura

Annabel's head and upper body were framed in the little window on the first floor of her house. From her admittedly sketchy knowledge of the upstairs, Laura knew she'd be at the desk in her office, working. Her face was lit up from below by the glare of an Anglepoise lamp and Laura could just make out the top part of her open laptop screen.

It was cold outside and Laura shivered in her thin jumper. She'd abandoned her orange coat in the car, thinking it might stand out too much in the gathering dusk. But now she was regretting the lack of it.

She cast another longing look up at the cheerfully lit window. Would it be so awful if she just walked up and rang the doorbell? She could come up with an excuse. Her yoga class wasn't a million miles away from here. She could pretend she'd been driving back and decided to make a spur-of-the-moment detour. She rehearsed it in her head. *I was desperate for a wee and I just thought,* Why not call in at Annabel's? *You don't mind, do you?*

Breezy. Relaxed. Normal.

But on the road next to Annabel's, her courage had

failed her. She remembered the last time she'd done that, ringing on Annabel's neat white door one Sunday morning with a bag of freshly baked pastries she'd picked up from the chic bakery near her flat. 'Bought these to take to a friend's, but she cancelled at the last minute, so I thought I'd bring them round here and *force* you to share them with me,' she'd said. But Annabel hadn't even let her through the door. 'I'm afraid this isn't a good time,' she'd said, looking embarrassed and awkward. 'I have company.' But when Laura had looked in through the slatted blinds of Annabel's living-room window on her way back to the car, the room was empty.

Suddenly mindful of that, Laura had pulled up her VW before getting to Annabel's road and sat with the engine idling, trying to decide what to do, until a young woman with a buggy had tapped on her window and apologetically told her it wasn't really legal to do that any more. 'Bad for the environment. Urban pollution.'

So then she'd parked up properly and walked the rest of the way on foot: one of the disadvantages of having such an immediately identifiable car.

There was a house on the other side of the road from Annabel's and slightly further down that had a tree in the front garden with low branches that reached over the wall and overhung the pavement. Laura was hovering in the shadow of that tree, pretending to read something on her phone. But really she was watching Annabel's face as she concentrated on whatever she was writing.

She felt a stab of irrational jealousy towards whatever it was that was so holding Annabel's attention. There was so much Laura wanted to discuss with her. She wanted to tell her about Hannah and how she felt she was making real progress in gaining her trust. That last session, when Hannah had described her trip to A&E and the nightmare of her fantasy world ripping apart at the seams, had been a real breakthrough. Annabel would want to be told that, surely? And to hear all the rest of her news?

Still something held her back.

Laura's eyes filled with tears. It wasn't fair. She was so giving of herself. Never with any expectation of something in return. To her patients. To her mother. And yes, to Annabel too. She'd always gone along with everything Annabel suggested. Always accepted she knew best. So why must Laura find herself always on the outside looking in?

A siren sounded in the distance, and Annabel glanced up. For a moment, Laura held her breath as the older woman's widely spaced eyes seemed to look in her direction. *Here I am. Please see me.*

The siren grew fainter and Annabel turned back to her computer. Cold was causing a pain in Laura's lower back and one of her toes was cramping. Yet still she remained under the cover of the tree, gazing up at the yellow-lit rectangle across the street.

29

Hannah

I worry I am losing it.

The rabbit no one remembers delivering to my room, the baby no one admits to drawing in my colouring book. Dr Chakraborty made a point of asking everyone about it in Evening Group yesterday, but they all denied knowing anything. He tried pressing again, until Frannie burst into tears. 'You're making me feel guilty and I haven't done anything,' she said. So then he moved on to something else. But I spent the rest of the session looking from face to face, thinking, *Was it you?*

It's getting harder to remember the person I used to be.

Dr Roberts is taking Group this morning, and he wants me to carry on talking about Danny. He wants to dig him of me out like he is coring an apple.

'But it was Hannah's turn last time,' says Odelle.

Odelle is keen to talk more about her family. They're her favourite topic of conversation. Her mother used to be a professional violinist and, according to Odelle, was a renowned beauty. Her father is a scientist. She likes to list the various pressures they put her under, the different ways she felt she didn't match up. She catalogues her weight loss during her adolescent years with a connoisseur's lingering appreciation. We've heard it all before but still I prefer to hear about Odelle's high-achieving parents and the brother who rowed for Cambridge and who used to call her La Porchetta, meaning 'little pig', which was the name of the local Italian restaurant but which she now blames for kick-starting her body issues, than to have to dig away at the scab that is Danny. But Dr Roberts is adamant.

'You know the golden rule of Group, Odelle. That there are no rules. I feel Hannah is making progress and I think that progress might be held up if we break, so we're just going to push on through until it comes to a natural end. This is a safe space for her to talk around things, and you guys are a vital part in her recovery, just as she is in yours.'

He turns to me. His right ankle is hooked over his left knee so the hem of his grey wool suit trousers rides up, revealing a dashing scarlet sock and a glimpse of tanned calf. Where's he been to get that tan in March? I wonder. Behind my head, I hear a clicking noise and know that Drew and Justin have begun filming. I don't know why they're bothering. I've decided I'm not going to let them use any footage of me when they're done. I've told Justin that, and he just nodded. 'Absolutely,' he said, in that infuriating puppy-dog way of his. Joni thinks we're his last chance. She says his last project bombed and the BBC executive who commissioned this one said it has to come good or he'll find himself out in the boondocks. I didn't ask her how she knew this. Joni has a gold medal in eavesdropping.

'So Hannah, I'd like to talk a bit about how Danny

reacted when he found out about the pseudocyesis. You'd gone into the hospital after a fall and then the physician checking you said there was no baby. I imagine that was a shock for him, after all those weeks of doctor's appointments.'

How to describe it? That look in his eyes. Incomprehension that gave way to grief and then to a rage that took us both by surprise.

'I thought I was going to be a dad!' he yelled at me, his face so close to mine I could have reached out my tongue and licked it. I knew what he was thinking. He thought he'd made two women pregnant, and he'd chosen me over Steffie, my baby over hers. And ended up with nothing.

The senior doctor in the hospital had told him it wasn't my fault, that I was as much a victim of my own mendacious body as he was. She had a glossy black plait that hung over one shoulder like the fat strap of a bag. She was calm and kind and, afterwards, I was grateful for that, but she'd never seen a case like mine before and there was a wariness in her huge, dark eyes, as if she felt out of her depth.

'Once we were referred to the psychiatric ward, he calmed down. Probably only because I was so hysterical myself by then. It felt like a death, you see. It felt like my baby had died.'

I'm saying this for the benefit of the others, explaining myself to them.

'Even though you'd made her up?'

Judith, of course. She likes to imagine she has a reputation for straight speaking but, actually, she just enjoys the confrontation.

Roberts raises his eyebrows. 'We've been through this many times, Judith. The baby was as real to Hannah as if it had been actually there, growing inside her. That's how her body became convinced it was pregnant.'

'Her body wasn't the one that told lies about going for scans.'

'Judith!'

The warning is unmissable and Judith sits back in her seat. But her expression is that of someone who's just won a small victory. Next to Judith, directly facing me, Nina is drumming her fingers insistently against her chair leg, a sign she could be in the early stages of an upward swing.

'It's bollocks, though, isn't it?' she says to no one in particular. 'Bollocksy, bollocksy bollocks.'

She nods her head as she speaks and her dangly yellow earrings quiver like miniature suns.

'If you don't mind, Nina,' says Roberts.

She darts her eyes around the circle. 'That told me,' she says, and gives a short bark of laughter.

'Can you tell us a bit about what it was like in the psych ward on that first night, Hannah?' Roberts says, turning his attention back to me. 'What state were you in?'

'I was beside myself. I think I scared Danny to death. He kept looking at me as if he didn't recognize me. By then my mum was there and, even though she was scared too, she was doing that thing she always does of trying to talk through a bad situation, as if she can reason it into becoming something else. "OK, so Hannah has this condition, which I'm going to research when I get home, but in the meantime let's see if I've got this straight."'

I'm saying this in my mum's voice, and it's quite convincing, because Stella starts to giggle behind her hand.

'Did Danny's parents come to the hospital?'

I shake my head.

'He called them himself to tell them, later that night.'

I don't describe how, when he came back from making the call, he was so white he was almost translucent or how he told me his mother had howled like a fox in pain. Or how I haven't seen either of his parents since, although they did send a 'get well soon' card, written in his dad's neat, sloping hand.

'Hannah, do you feel you deserve Danny's forgiveness?'

The question is like a punch.

'I lied to him.'

'But the lies were buried in a part of your psyche so well hidden you didn't even know it was there.'

I stare at my feet in my tatty, laceless Converse shoes and wonder what happened to the woman I was when I bought them two years ago.

'Let me ask you another question,' says Dr Roberts, and I brace myself.

'Do you think Danny deserves your forgiveness?'

'For what?'

There is a silence as everyone holds their breath.

'For Steffie. For all the lies he told you.'

'The two things are not connected.'

Judith snorts with laughter.

'Get real,' she says.

After lunch, Stella and I walk the fifteen minutes to the local high street and sit in Costa Coffee and drink cappuccinos from cups bigger than my own head. Even though Dr Roberts still thinks I have a way to go, he has agreed that, after nearly eleven weeks in the clinic, I should start getting used to being in the real world again. So I am allowed out, as long as I sign myself back into the clinic after no more than an hour. Stella, on the other hand, isn't supposed to leave the clinic grounds and expose herself to such pernicious influences as the magazine rack in the local supermarket, with its row upon row of perfect, airbrushed bodies and faces. But Stella does what Stella wants. She is no longer sectioned. No one can stop her leaving.

'I just hate the way he keeps on making me relive it,' I say.

'Maybe he just gets a kick out of seeing you suffer.'

We all complain about Roberts from time to time, but Stella is extra critical.

We sit for a while in ill-tempered silence and I can feel the eyes of the other customers on us. Stella is wearing a soft cashmere jumper in baby yellow that clings to her body like a layer of fur. Her pale blonde hair is piled up on her head in a kind of beehive and her full lips are the colour of blood. In Barnet, north London, on a Tuesday afternoon she is as exotic as it gets.

'Tell me about what happened with the ex. The writer who was so much older than you. How come he ended up accusing you of harassment?'

If Stella is taken aback by my sudden change of subject, she doesn't show it.

'I think I freaked him out. I was only twenty, and I didn't want it to be over. I kind of stalked him.'

'Kind of?'

That breathy little-girl giggle.

'I did. Stalk him. And his wife.'

'Stella!'

'And his daughter.'

'Hang on. I thought he was only in his thirties, so his daughter—'

'Was still at primary school. I think that's what finally made him confess to his wife, when I turned up at his daughter's Nativity play. I waved to him across the hall.'

I'm hit by the dead weight of all the things I don't know.

'My stepfather sorted it out so I didn't have to go to court. That's when I did my first stint in a happy farm.'

'And after that, you had your first op?'

'Don't be silly, Hannah. I had my first op at fourteen in the States. My nose. My mum gave me the surgery as a birthday present. Afterwards, she sat on the edge of my bed and said, "Are you happy now?" Like that was all it took.'

Stella has froth all around her lips because of the cappuccino, and when she smiles her red, lipsticked mouth looks like a hole a person could fall into and never get out.

30

Corinne

The kitchen table was strewn with papers. Corinne hadn't taken all the files, of course, but even the relatively small number that Geraldine Buckley had grudgingly allowed her to borrow were enough to cover the entirety of the scratched wood surface.

And still she hadn't come up with anything that cast Dr Roberts in any substantially different light.

True, three of his female patients had threatened to join the class action against the clinic. But it was Professor Dunmore's philosophy and leadership that were in question. Roberts and the other junior psychiatrist who worked in the clinic were only following guidelines set by their boss. The official investigation, with which Roberts had fully cooperated, had wholly exonerated them.

Corinne had the files of the three patients concerned, all women ranging in age from twelve to twenty-three. She'd been through their case notes thoroughly, looking for evidence of malpractice, and had bristled at how, in the margin of a transcript of a young woman describing how her uncle used to call the abuse 'being nice to each other time', he'd written, 'Sounds rehearsed,' and on another one 'Therapy-speak?'. Her heart ached for these broken girls who'd already been through so much and then were disbelieved by the very person who was supposed to be helping put them back together.

There was a registration form for each patient on which Geraldine Buckley had carefully blacked out the address and phone number, together with a small photograph. Corinne studied the face of each girl, looking for anything that might be of help to Hannah, but there was nothing. When it came to the youngest patient, whose name was Catherine Pryor, there was a momentary flicker of something, but it disappeared on closer examination. Corinne found she could hardly look at Catherine's trusting grey eyes, in her plump, still-unformed face, without her own eyes filming over with tears.

There was a newspaper cutting in the files from 1998 in which Professor Dunmore talked about being on a mission to reconcile families ripped apart by the 'torpedo' of false memory. It was accompanied by an anonymous boxed-out account of a woman whose family had been destroyed when her adult daughter made false allegations of abuse against her husband after consulting a therapist for depression. The woman, who appeared in a photograph with her face pixellated, had been forced to choose between her husband and her daughter, and had been cut out of her daughter's life when she stood by her husband. She'd despaired of ever finding a way out of the nightmare they were plunged into, until her sister had read about Professor Dunmore and persuaded her niece to visit the clinic. 'It's no exaggeration to say that decision saved us,' the woman said.

Corinne was torn. This woman had clearly suffered terribly and, by debunking the false memory, Dunmore had transformed her family's life. Yet at what cost to the genuine survivors of abuse who came after?

For a brief moment, she felt a warm glow of gratitude that her own little family had emerged from the maelstrom of the girls' adolescence relatively unscathed.

Then she remembered where her older daughter was, and felt sick all over again.

31

Hannah

Now that I'm not far from the date I'd decided Emily would have been due, I think I might finally be ready to let her go.

We have the easels out today and we are painting a chair on which Laura has draped a piece of fabric with a beautiful blue-and-white fleur-de-lis print.

'Look at the way it hangs, the way the pattern changes around the folds in the material. Look at the contrast between the restrained colours of the chair itself and the vibrancy of the print. What about the textures? The hard, polished wood and the soft weave of the material. Switch on all your senses. This is the moment. Right here, right now. This glorious blue-and-white print. This earthy chair.'

Laura is in full flow this morning. It's something she talks about a lot, switching on our senses. It's a form of mindfulness. If we ground ourselves in the here and now and focus on what we can see, hear, smell, touch, all the blessings that surround us, there won't be room in our thoughts for the things that have brought us here, the dark shadows that lurk at the edges of us.

I find I enjoy the limitations of our still life. The world

213

honed to a point where only the chair and the fabric exist. I am so engrossed in my painting I don't notice Laura is behind me until I feel her warm breath on my neck, her hand on my shoulder.

'Well done, Hannah. Your work has come on so much since you arrived. You seem so much more alert to the world around you. Remember how dark your palette was when you first started? How everything ended up a mixture of brown?'

'That's because it took me ages to judge just how potent even a drop of black paint could be?'

She looks at me, and I pre-empt what she is about to say: 'Please don't tell me how that is a metaphor for the human condition.'

She smiles. 'You know me too well.'

'Laura, can you come here a sec? I'm having trouble with my perspective.'

That's Odelle, of course, needing attention. She's very possessive over people, but particularly Laura. The first time Laura invited me into her office for a chat, Charlie said, 'Odelle's not going to like that.' And she was right. Whenever she can, Odelle disrupts my time with Laura, suddenly requiring urgent help with a self-generated art project, one time bursting into Laura's office in tears because Joni had caught her guzzling water from the tap in the bathroom before her morning weigh-in.

I glance over to my left, where Katy is chewing anxiously on the wooden end of a paintbrush and staring down at her still-virginal paper, not daring to start in case with the very first brushstroke she commits some fatal error.

As this is a Strong Day, as opposed to one of the days

214

when I wake up to find I have deconstructed during the night and lie scattered in little pieces all over the mattress like toast crumbs, I allow myself to think of Charlie.

It's in the art room that I feel closest to her. She loved coming here, experimenting with chalky pastels and colour washes. One time I came in and found her bent over her paper, painting a self-portrait with the brush in her mouth.

'Why not?' she answered when I asked her the obvious question. 'If we don't try everything, what's even the point?'

She didn't kill herself.

The conviction is a weight I cannot shake off.

Sometimes I'd come here looking for Charlie and find her deep in conversation with Laura, talking about art or politics or just gossiping about Joni's latest faux pas or whether or not Dr Chakraborty was hot. Or they'd be in the back office and Charlie would be curled up in the armchair with her eyes closed and Laura would be talking to her in a low, rhythmic voice and I'd back out because Charlie only wanted hypnotherapy when she was feeling tense and needed talking down.

She still didn't kill herself, though.

After art I take my laptop to the day room. Darren glances up at the dinging sound when I turn it on. He's scribbling notes in an A4 notebook. I remember he has exams coming up but can't remember what they are. I wonder if his new girlfriend is distracting him from studying at home.

I check my emails, impatiently deleting all the junk. There is an email from Becs, filling me in on all the office gossip, and one from my mother telling me she's still 'running background checks' on the clinic and Dr Roberts to 'set my mind at rest'.

Out of habit, I look for Meg's name in my inbox, before remembering that we're all but estranged. She wanted to come and see me when it all first happened, but I told Mum she couldn't, not until she's ready to apologize for the things she said about Danny. But I know my sister. She won't apologize, because she still thinks she was right.

Maybe she was *right*, says a voice in my head.

Clicking abruptly off Hotmail, I consider for a moment logging in to Facebook, even though we're not supposed to. Darren is clearly preoccupied with his studying and I'd love to catch up with what my friends are getting up to. Then I remember the last time I did that, when I'd only been in here a few days, and the shock of realizing that other people's lives were going on just as before, even while my own was shredded beyond recognition. Instead, I call up Google. Charlie has been on my mind since I allowed myself to think about her in art earlier. I feel I've let her down by not taking any more steps towards finding out exactly what happened to her.

Taking her to-do list from my back pocket, where I always carry it, I smooth it out on the leg of my jeans. *Book flights to Croatia.*

This was not someone courting oblivion.

Then I gaze for a long time at that third entry. *Google WK.* The last time I'd tried to search for William Kingsley, it had thrown up so many returns I'd given up after page one, but now I resolve to persevere.

Checking to make sure Darren still has his nose buried in his notes, I put the name into the search engine. My spirits drop at the sight of the 3,750,000 results. Still, I begin to work my way through, skipping over the entries about the nineteenth-century politician and the estate agents in Missouri.

It's not until page five that I find an entry that piques my interest. It's a link to an article in the *Daily Mail* about medical misdiagnosis, highlighting various infamous cases where physicians have made catastrophic errors. And there at the bottom, almost in passing, is a line that reads, 'as was the case with the now largely discredited evidence given by Dr William Kingsley in two misdiagnosed cases of Shaken Baby Syndrome'.

Shaken Baby Syndrome? I dredge my Diazepam-dulled brain for the information I know is in there somewhere and come up with a memory of a blonde woman standing on courtroom steps, having been freed from prison after evidence proved her baby most likely died from natural causes, and not because she'd lost control and shaken him.

I add 'Shaken Baby Syndrome' to William Kingsley's name in the search box and instantly get pages of results. The first few are newspaper reports from the mid-1990s, all with one-word headings like 'FREED!' or 'INNOCENT!', with a photograph of one of two shell-shocked women, and a report of how their convictions for shaking their own babies to death had been overturned, casting doubt on the evidence of key medical experts such as neurologist Dr William Kingsley.

These are followed by earlier factual newspaper reports at the time of the original trials one or two years previously, and a long in-depth feature about one of the women, illustrated with a smiling family photograph of

Mum, Dad and baby, and headlined, 'SHE WAS THE PERFECT MUM – UNTIL SHE SNAPPED'. Towards the bottom of the feature there's a photograph of the same woman taken just after her conviction for her baby's murder, looking blank-eyed and slack-jawed.

Studying the photograph more closely, I give a start of recognition. There on the woman's face is the same look that greeted me in the mirror when I first arrived here. The shell-shocked stare of someone whose world has just given way under their feet.

The search engine throws up a couple of links to websites set up by the families of the women and others in the same position protesting their innocence, and also a site advocating the reintroduction of hanging for women who murder their own children as well as one that links to a blog called 'Baby-Killers'.

I still can't be sure that this William Kingsley is the one Charlie was researching on the morning she died, but he is the right era, the right country at least. I scroll impatiently through, looking for anything that seems like it might throw more light on Dr William Kingsley and find, tucked away at the bottom of page six, a link that looks promising – 'The Doctors Who Play God', but before I can click on it a hand lands on my shoulder, causing me to gasp out loud in shock.

'Why so jumpy?'

Stella has her head on one side, so her hair, which is swept up into a high ponytail, swings around her ears, and is regarding me quizzically.

'You startled me.'

I click the little red circle on the screen so that the Google page disappears, leaving just my screensaver, a picture of Danny and me on our honeymoon, sitting under a palm tree on a white sandy beach in Costa Rica. It was taken by one of the hotel staff who'd just brought us cocktails and we are smiling as if we can't believe our luck.

Or maybe that's just me. Maybe Danny's smile means something different. Maybe his smile just means 'This beats being at work.' Or 'This'll do nicely. For now.'

'What were you doing? You looked completely engrossed.'

'Just reading the papers.'

'Well, turn it off then and come and talk to me. I need saving. Judith says she's going to teach me to play chess. I don't want to play chess with Judith. She's too intense. Sometimes she stares at me as if she wants to turn me inside out to see how I work.'

Stella reaches across me and clicks the sleep option so that the screen goes dark, and I don't know why but I get the feeling she just doesn't want to look at Danny.

As we get up, I imitate Judith's death stare and Stella giggles but, inside, a question is troubling me.

Why don't I trust Stella?

32

Corinne

Corinne was in the shower in her little upstairs bathroom with the sloping ceiling when the doorbell went.

At first she ignored it, sure it would be a charity collector thrusting their lanyard in her face or a sombrely suited group determined to find out her feelings on the Second Coming.

But when it sounded a second time, she started to worry. She'd left her phone charging downstairs. What if the clinic had been trying to get hold of her? What if Oliver Roberts was even now standing on her doorstep because of some emergency with Hannah?

She stepped from the shower and wrapped herself in a towel. Her hair was dripping on to the wooden treads of the stairs as she hurried down and then on through her living room. But when she flung open the front door there was no one there.

She craned her head to the right, towards where the overhead wires of Alexandra Palace station traced a silver line through the watery blue sky. Nothing. To the left, her leafy street was empty of life.

'Bugger.'

She was about to close the door when a flash of red

caught her eye. Bending down to pick up the object that had been left on her step like an offering, she didn't at first realize what it was. When she did, her heart constricted with pain.

A tiny red knitted hat.

Just the right size for a newborn baby.

33

Hannah

'How do you think you're getting on, Hannah?'

Dr Roberts does this a lot. He tries to get me to rate my own progress. I think it's to do with trying to instil a sense of empowerment.

'How about you tell me. You're the expert.'

'I think you're getting stronger all the time. When you arrived here, almost twelve weeks ago, you were this shell of a person, and it's like restoring a painting: each day, I see a bit more of Hannah returning, which is wonderful news.'

'But?'

'Interesting that you should sense a but.' Roberts leans back in his chair. He has one leg crossed over the other in his usual fashion and he bounces gently on the ball of the foot which is in contact with the floor so his swept-back hair gently quivers.

'So there's no but?'

He smiles. But his ice-chip blue eyes don't look amused.

'No. You're right. There's a but. The thing is, I'm alarmed by certain reports that have reached me. I remember you were upset by a cuddly toy, and by a picture of a baby in your colouring book?'

The way he says it makes me sound mad.

'I think that was someone's idea of a sick joke.'

Not a joke. A message, a reminder of how messed up I am. And I know who from. Steffie. Who else? The colouring books come in plain envelopes from Becs' assistant. I don't even look at them. Steffie could have sent one with a page already filled in. I wouldn't have noticed it was any different from the rest. I don't have enemies. I'm not that sort of person. Steffie is the only one. It must have been her.

Dr Roberts gazes at me without speaking. The moment stretches between us, taut and strained. He strokes his beard with the fingers of his right hand. His nails, I notice now, are perfectly shaped. Finally, he speaks.

'It could be someone's poor idea of a joke,' he agrees. 'Or could it be that you've misconstrued the situation? The toy arrived unpackaged, didn't it? So the note had been lost. Couldn't it just have been a well-wisher, trying to cheer you up?'

'And the ears?'

'Damaged in transit? It happens.'

'And the colouring book?' I ask him. 'How can you explain that?'

He waves his hand, as if I'm splitting hairs.

'All I'm saying is that there are always other possibilities. And it might be healthier if you explored those first, before jumping to the very conclusion that is most harmful to you.'

'When can I go home?'

The question comes out in a rush, making me sound, to my own ears, like an anxious child on her first day of school.

'We're not your jailers, Hannah. There's nothing stopping you leaving, if that's what you really want.'

'So will you tell Danny I'm ready? I feel so much stronger.'

He bounces harder on his foot. It's starting to make me feel queasy.

'Tell you what,' he says, his foot coming to a sudden stop. 'I'll talk to your husband once you've had a couple of days in a row without *incident*.'

I don't ask him what he means. I don't need to.

As I get up to leave, he puts a hand on my arm to stop me. I look down at those perfect nails resting on my old jumper with the moth holes in the sleeve.

'I know you're in a rush to get back to your old life, but what you have to ask yourself, Hannah, is whether that old life really exists any more. And if it doesn't, what are you going to put in its place?'

After I finish my session with Dr Roberts and go downstairs, I don't head to the day room, which is where Stella will be waiting for me. I don't feel like being sociable. There's a heaviness to everything, my legs moving as if pushing against a weight of water, my thoughts slow and sluggish. I feel myself dipping backwards towards the person I was during my first few days here, when everything I looked at was tinged with black. The person Charlie helped to save.

The door to the music room is closed and I can hear Graham, the part-time music therapist, encouraging someone to play a minor scale on the piano. 'That's right,' he says. 'That's the sad note right there.' Sometimes Graham lays mats down on the wide oak floorboards and we all lie down and close our eyes while he plays us

Schumann or Handel, and when the music finishes almost all of us will be crying. We cry a lot in here. There are boxes of tissues everywhere.

I have an idea to go to the Mindfulness Area and curl up in the egg chair and be alone, but when I pass the door of the art room and glimpse Laura sitting on her own in her office at the far end, I change my mind.

'Cup of tea?' she asks. Clearly, my state of mind is written on my face.

'As long as it's not herbal. Or good for me in any way. And contains shedloads of caffeine.'

'I think we can manage that.'

Without even thinking about it, I settle into the comfortable armchair and wrap myself in the tartan throw. It's second nature now to sit here like this. It's the one place in the clinic where I don't feel like I'm being assessed.

'Tough day?'

Laura leans forward and puts a hand on my knee, looking up into my face with eyes so full of warmth I almost cannot bear it.

'No such thing as a tough day in The Meadows,' I joke. 'Every day's a holiday.'

'You know, you don't have to entertain all the time, Hannah.' Her hand still on my knee, brown eyes close to mine. 'You're allowed to be dull from time to time. Most of us are.' She sits back and a smile twitches her lips.

'I just . . .' I tail off. I just what? 'I just feel like my brain isn't making connections any more. Things happen and I jump to the wrong conclusion or else no conclusion at all. I'm so tired of feeling like this. I'm half drugged

225

with the sleeping pills, yet I don't sleep. I can't shake this awful dread that something terrible is about to happen.'

I catch up with my own words and let out a half-groan.

'What I mean is, something even more terrible than ending up in the nuthouse and having my closest friend here die on me.'

Laura keeps her clear gaze fixed on me.

'Will you let me try to help?'

She means the hypnosis, I'm guessing. I've always been resistant, but I've reached the stage where I'll try anything.

The strange thing is, I don't notice her doing it. We've talked before about places that mean things to us, and I told her about the walk I used to do with our dog Madge. So now she invites me to remember how Hampstead Heath looks in autumn with the leaves carpeting the ground, and how Madge loved to rustle through them, and the view of the London skyline from the outside pagoda near Kenwood House, and what it's like to come over the hill and see the ponds shimmering in the distance. As far as I can see, we're just sitting having a normal conversation, except I'm kind of zoning in and out of it in a very pleasant way and, all of a sudden, I notice that the lead weights that were attached to everything I say and do seem to have lifted. I'm in the room, but also outside of it looking down on myself and seeing how small I am in the scheme of the world, how little my problems really matter.

'Hannah?'

'Yes?'

I force myself to focus on Laura's face.

'It's just that I have a tutorial in a minute. Odelle wanted a little one-to-one time.'

I glance through the open doorway at the old-fashioned clock on the art-room wall and am taken aback to find I've been here for nearly half an hour.

'Thank you,' I say, standing up. Dazed.

I don't know whether it's just the power of suggestion but I do feel noticeably lighter.

'Just don't operate any heavy machinery for a while,' she says, smiling.

I find myself smiling back, though I can't help wondering just where the last thirty minutes have gone.

Odelle is waiting at one of the tables in the art room. Her eyes follow me across the room as if they would burn a hole clear through my skin, but her scrutiny doesn't bother me. I feel a sense, not of euphoria, that would be too strong, but certainly of peace. My new-found wellbeing stays with me as I walk out of the art room and up the stairs to my room, where I find someone has slipped my post – two letters – under the door.

One has been sent on from work; I recognize Becs' writing. My publishing office continue to send me catalogues and acquisitions bulletins. The second letter has a typed address and a central London postmark.

I tear the envelope open with the nail of my thumb and unfold the single sheet of paper inside.

The room spins.

34

Corinne

The coffee shop, down a side street near Charing Cross station, was dark and crowded and Corinne regretted picking it when she saw how Steffie's mother, Patricia Garitson, clutched the collar of her elegant, powder-blue wool coat tightly around her neck.

'Thank you for turning up. I was half expecting you not to,' said Corinne, setting her tray down on the table and pushing Patricia's green tea towards her. 'I got you something to eat.'

They both gazed at the slab of chocolate cake as if it were an art installation.

'I want to help if I can. I feel responsible.'

'Don't be silly. Your daughter's a grown woman, as are mine. We're not responsible for the choices they make.'

'Nevertheless, I can't help thinking I could have done more to protect Steffie – and, though I hate to say it, to protect other people from her.'

Fear snaked through Corinne's veins as she remembered Jacob Garitson saying, 'She hurts people.' Just what was Steffie capable of?

'The thing is, weird things have been going on at the

clinic where Hannah . . . where my daughter is staying.'

'Where she's being treated, you mean. When you say "staying", it makes it sound like she's having a few nights in a nice hotel.' Patricia threw back her head and laughed. That flash of gold in the back of her mouth.

Corinne was thrown.

'Right. Anyway, Hannah says things have been planted in her room specifically to remind her of what happened.'

'You mean the imaginary baby?'

Patricia Garitson was only stating fact, but still it felt like a sharp, painful jab, and Corinne decided not to mention the colouring book, or the tiny knitted hat left on her own doorstep. All evidence, she increasingly suspected, of a systematic campaign of harassment.

'I just want to know what we might be dealing with here. I know your husband was, understandably, not keen to discuss your daughter's past with a stranger.'

Patricia made a *pah* sound and gave a tiny flick of her wrist, as if shaking off a speck of dust.

'No use talking to *him* about Steffie. He thinks the sun shines out of her behind.'

Corinne swallowed. She sounded so bitter.

'I just need to know if Hannah is in any kind of danger.'

It sounded so melodramatic but, to Corinne's dismay, Patricia didn't try to brush it off. Instead, she picked up a mini-fork and began absently jabbing at the chocolate cake that sat on the table between them, its icing sweating under the café lights.

'Can I speak frankly?'

Corinne nodded.

'As a mother yourself, you must know that sometimes our children can be . . . *disappointing*.'

'But not dangerous?'

Jab, jab, jab.

'You know I am a caterer?'

Corinne blinked, caught out by this sudden conversational switch.

'Well, this one time, Stephanie was angry with me over something. Probably because I'd given her a curfew. She'd have been around fourteen, I suppose. Anyway, I was catering a small birthday dinner for a neighbour: six individual apple pies. The fancy kind, with leaf shapes on the top, each traced with a delicate pattern of veins. Only, one of them had a special ingredient.'

'I don't follow.'

'The needle I'd been using to decorate the leaves.'

Corinne put her hand to her mouth. 'You can't mean she did it on purpose?'

Patricia licked her finger and dabbed it on the table, where a crumb of cake had fallen.

'She denied it, obviously. But she wanted to get back at me. Any way she could.'

'So you're saying we should be worried?'

Patricia Garitson held her finger to her mouth and flicked out her tongue to lick the crumb off. 'Put it this way, when they were children, Jacob used to drag his chest of drawers against his bedroom door before he went to sleep.'

Corinne thought of the girl in the photo, her eyes an angry slash of red, and closed her own as a shiver of fear passed through her.

How can I keep Hannah safe?

When she opened them again, Patricia Garitson was leaning forward watching her face intently, as if anxious not to miss a thing.

Corinne was still feeling jittery about her meeting with Patricia Garitson hours later when she returned home from work. At least, that's what she told herself was behind her heightened anxiety. Certainly it had nothing to do with the fact that she'd spent the last hour of the day in conversation with her mature student, Paddy, about his dissertation.

Normally, she wouldn't have expected to see him again for a week or two, and she had been cross with herself for the treacherous flare of pleasure when she'd read his email requesting a quick chat. He was nine years younger than her. She'd looked up his details on the social sciences departmental system. Corinne had known more than one male colleague who'd fallen for a young undergraduate while in the grip of midlife madness. And even though Paddy was no callow nineteen-year-old school leaver, she refused to turn into the same tired cliché.

Still, she hadn't been able to completely stifle the way her stomach jumped when he'd walked into her office. Or the spark that flew between them as they talked, so that it was less a conversation than a game, with ideas the ball they batted between them. She'd thought she had successfully shelved her worries during their chat, had even congratulated herself on her professionalism, but when Paddy had finally got up to leave, nearly half an hour after she'd normally have left to come home, he'd hesitated in the doorway.

'I hope you don't mind me asking this, Corinne. I mean, I hardly know you, so it might sound presumptuous, but are you OK? You just seem – I don't know how to put this – but you seem like you're carrying quite a weight around with you.'

At first, she'd been affronted. 'I'm perfectly fine, thank you,' she'd said.

She'd regretted her snippiness as soon as the words were out, but it was too late.

'I'm sorry. I didn't mean to overstep the mark. Please excuse me.'

After he'd gone she felt bereft but, then again, she argued with herself, what could she have told him? That her daughter, Hannah, was in a psychiatric clinic and it seemed possible that her son-in-law's ex-lover could be stalking them both with mocking gifts of cuddly toys and baby hats? It sounded preposterous. Yet just for a moment, she indulged herself in the fantasy of unburdening herself to Paddy. Feeling those big arms around her, not having to be the strong one for once.

She allowed herself a moment of self-pity while she poured herself a glass of red wine, trying to remember when she'd opened the bottle and wincing at the first vinegary swallow until her palate got used to it. It had probably been sitting there slightly too long, but it was a decent bottle and she didn't have another.

Corinne couldn't remember when she'd last felt this tired. Tired to the very marrow of her bones. The files from Westbridge House she'd borrowed from Geraldine Buckley a week ago were still strewn over the table in front of her, and her eyes passed over the pictures of the three girls Dr Roberts had treated – and failed.

She wondered if he ever lost sleep over them, these young women who'd been entitled to be listened to without being judged, to be supported rather than disbelieved. She knew Roberts had been heavily influenced by Dunmore, and had not been found guilty of any wrongdoing, but surely he must feel some measure of remorse?

The last photograph was that of Catherine Pryor and Corinne felt another brief flicker of recognition. She studied the face, those grey eyes gazing out from cushions of puppy fat, the wide, strong nose. But nothing seemed familiar.

Taking another gulp of wine, she sat back, surveying the photograph from a distance.

Suddenly, her hand flew to her mouth.

'Oh my God,' she said out loud. And then, softly, leaning in again to take a closer look. 'Oh my God.'

35
Hannah

The paper lies on the table between us. I try not to look at it.

'And you have no idea who sent this?'

When Dr Roberts frowns, I realize how rarely he does it. He is all about show, it strikes me now. All teeth and good hair. He doesn't like to appear troubled or irritated and, when he does, he looks instantly five years older.

'I could take a guess,' I say, leaning away from the table so I don't have to see it. It's a photocopy of a scan photo. I think it's a generic one taken from the internet, although, of course, last night I'd convinced myself it was Emily. I can still taste the bile in my mouth.

'But why would this woman be doing this?' Roberts asks. 'What does she want from you?'

'Revenge? After Danny chose me over her, she had a miscarriage. At least no one can accuse me of making it all up now.'

I don't know what I'm looking for. An apology, maybe. Roberts fixes me with those cold blue eyes, saying nothing, until I say it for him.

'You are kidding me, aren't you? You really think I could have sent that to *myself*?'

Roberts holds up one of his perfectly manicured hands in an infuriating placatory gesture.

'I'm not saying for one minute that you did anything, Hannah. However, I should point out that it isn't unheard of for a patient to go to sometimes quite extreme lengths to establish evidence that corroborates her own version of reality. Tell me, Hannah, how secure do you feel now in your relationship with Danny?'

I stare at him while my drug-fuddled brain scrabbles to catch up with his sudden change of direction.

'Hold on. You think I'm making this up to win back my husband and turn him against his ex-tart?'

'And are you?'

'I don't need to win back my husband, Dr Roberts. He made a choice, and he chose me. And, actually, more to the point, I chose him. I chose to allow him a second chance, and he was bloody grateful.'

'It's only that he seems to be *uncomfortable* with the idea of you being here. I don't mean The Meadows specifically, but any place like this one. Would you say that was accurate?'

'Of course he's uncomfortable with it. Who wouldn't be? *How's your wife, Danny? Oh, she's in the nuthouse, thanks for asking.*'

'It seems clear, Hannah, that your pseudocyesis was triggered by the situation at home. You were struggling to conceive and then your husband got another woman pregnant. Until you're prepared to address the under-lying issues at the heart of your relationship, we're not going to be able to fully understand what happened to you and prevent it happening again.'

I'm angry now. I don't want to be told that we have

'issues' in our relationship. I don't want to be reminded that the marriage I believed inviolable turned out to be made of paper.

'Was there an autopsy?' I ask.

The question takes us both by surprise.

'What do you mean?'

'For Charlie? Surely there must have been some sort of inquest.'

Roberts sniffs. 'There was a post-mortem. And there is to be an inquest, although the date has not yet been set. However, judging by the results of the post-mortem, there will be no surprises. Charlie killed herself, Hannah. And I think we now need to start looking at why you're having so much difficulty coming to terms with that fact.

'I wonder if, perhaps, you identified so strongly with Charlie, to the extent that you now see her fate inextricably bound up with your own. When you arrived here, you were a mother-to-be who'd just had her baby snatched away from her. All those nurturing hormones were still racing around your system.

'It wouldn't be unreasonable to try to replicate the familial hierarchy you'd been expecting. That trinity with you at the apex and on the two other points the needs of a new baby and the maternal wisdom of your own mother.'

I shake my head, but he continues as if he hasn't seen, warming to his theory.

'Just think about it for a minute. Stella is the one you've given your nurturing to, and Charlie was your mother figure. You were very much emotionally invested in Charlie. Little wonder you can't accept what she did.'

'And Sofia? Was I emotionally invested in her as well?
I know Sofia didn't kill herself. She wouldn't have done
that to her children. I never saw anyone with so much
courage and determination to stick it out.'

'That's just it, Hannah. For people like Charlie and
Sofia, every day requires courage and determination. It's
like running a marathon that never ends. Depression is
a relentless enemy. Sometimes you just don't have the
energy to fight it any more.'

'Sofia wasn't depressed.'

'You're right. Sofia had other issues, which I can't go
into with you for confidentiality reasons. But still, it
wasn't easy for her. Life with long-term mental-health
issues is an endurance test. Not everyone makes it.'

Later, I'm furious with myself for letting Roberts off the
hook. Every time I try to challenge him he slips through
my fingers. I fold up the scan photo and stuff it into the
front pocket of my jeans.

Mum and Danny are supposed to be visiting, but
when I get to the day room only Mum is there, sitting on
the chair nearest the door. She sees my expression.

'Sorry, darling, Danny couldn't make it. Don't look
like that, because it's actually a good thing. There's
something I really need to talk to you about.'

Disappointment makes me sullen. 'So? Talk then.'

Mum looks around the day room. Joni is at the oval
table, filling out some of the interminable paperwork all
the nurses complain about. Judith and Frannie are on
the sofa, reading magazines. I once asked Frannie what
she wants to do when she gets out of here. She looked at
me, startled, like I'd asked her to strip naked and run

237

around the room. 'I don't know,' she said eventually. 'Be quiet somewhere?'

That was the height of her ambition. To be quiet.

'Could we go somewhere else? Your room maybe, or out for a walk?'

Now I look more closely, Mum looks weird. Her hair is tied back in a kind of knot at the back of her head with wispy bits escaping – and not in an artful, casual-not-casual way either – and her black jeans have toothpaste drips down one leg. Also, one of her eyes is doing this kind of flickering thing in the corner.

We put on our coats and go outside. Though it's mid-morning, the light is grey and soupy, with that kind of damp cold that seems to come from the inside out.

Mum digs her hands into her coat pocket and makes a short, sharp exhalation to watch the cloud of her breath. Normally, her skin is clear and relatively unlined, but today it's as grey as the day itself and there are two deep vertical scores in her cheeks. I've done this to her, I realize suddenly. Worrying about me has made her ten years older.

'I think you should discharge yourself,' she says at last.

'What?'

I must have misheard her. Or else my brain must have processed what she said the wrong way. I know Mum wants me home, but she also wants me well. I've lost count of the number of times she's assured me I'm in the best possible hands.

'Hear me out.'

She tells me a convoluted story involving a psychiatric clinic and a discredited professor and a younger version of Dr Roberts who was mentored badly and made terrible mistakes. She tells me about three women. Girls. Who suffered horribly and then were let down by the people who were supposed to help them. The threat of legal action that never happened. And the clinic manager who stole their files.

'Hang on, you drove to Oxford? To visit this alcoholic with a grudge? And to look at people's private records. Is that even legal?'

'Ex-alcoholic. And she blacked out the phone numbers and addresses.'

'Oh, so that makes it all right then.'

'I wanted to reassure myself that you're still safe here.'

'And now you don't think I am.'

She takes a long pause. 'There's something bizarre about the records, Hannah. Something that has really frightened me.'

Icy fingers tippy-tap on my spine. I hear her out.

'There were photographs of the girls attached to the files. I think Geraldine thought that seeing their faces would make their story more human for me, make me more inclined to dig deeper into what happened at Westbridge House.'

'For your fictitious journal article?'

Mum ignores my sarcasm.

'There was something about one of the girls, Hannah. The youngest one. I didn't recognize her but I kept going back to her picture. And then, last night, it hit me. I don't know why I hadn't spotted it before.'

'Spotted what?'

'The necklace. She was wearing a cat necklace. Hannah, the youngest girl was Stella.'

36

Corinne

As soon as she'd made the connection with the necklace, Corinne could see it was her. The individual features had been changed, skin stretched over newly implanted cheekbones, nose cracked and sawn and put back together, chin reshaped, weight loss, hair extensions, coloured contact lenses. There wasn't a single bit of Stella that was still Catherine Pryor and yet the essence of Stella was obvious in the angle of the head, the impassive expression in the eyes.

All night, Corinne had lain awake, trying to get to the kernel of truth she knew lay at the core of this mystery, but all night it had eluded her.

That Stella had changed her name was fair enough. Many survivors of unhappy childhoods choose to leave the trappings of their childhood selves behind when they grow up, and victims of abuse often reject their own names if they were given to them by their abusers. Corinne once had a friend who'd married to rid herself of her hated father's name, and then when the marriage went sour had randomly changed her surname to the name of the road she was living on.

That Stella had been so full of self-loathing that she'd

paid someone to take a scalpel to her face and her body again and again also made a kind of horrible sense. Corinne had had students who cut themselves compulsively when the pain of their lives got too much to cope with.

But the central mystery remained.

Why had Stella chosen to put herself back in the care of Oliver Roberts?

'I don't understand,' Hannah said, for the tenth time since Corinne had managed to make her believe she was serious. 'I mean, do you think Roberts knows who Stella really is?'

'I doubt it.'

'So why come here? You'd have thought she'd run a mile from anything to do with him. He thought she was making it up! Oh, poor Stella.' Hannah's voice broke on the last word and Corinne felt a sharp tug of worry.

Her daughter was so fragile at the moment. Could she really cope with this? Whatever *this* turned out to be.

'She could be seeking some sort of closure. She might see the whole episode at Westbridge House as unfinished business in her life that she needs to process before she can move on.'

Hannah groaned. 'God, you sound just like him.'

'Who?'

'Roberts.'

'Or there's another, less welcome, explanation. What if Stella is here seeking revenge?'

'Revenge? How?'

'This clinic is Roberts' baby, the showcase of his professional achievements to date. You said yourself that the deaths of Sofia and Charlie have hurt admissions, and investors are pulling out. What if that's the plan? To ruin him?'

Hannah was staring at her as if she'd grown another head.

'Mum, you can't be serious. This is Stella we're talking about. Dreamy, otherworldly Stella. Are you honestly suggesting she would murder two people – two people she liked very much – just to get her own back for something that happened fifteen years ago?'

'No. Of course not. Only . . . Oh, I don't know, Hannah! I don't know anything except that I no longer trust Dr Roberts and, until we understand Stella's motivation, we can't trust her either.'

'I'll talk to her. Ask her straight.'

'Don't!'

Corinne spat out the word so loudly it stopped both her and Hannah in their tracks.

'If you talk to Stella, it could put you in danger. Who knows what she might do if she thinks she's about to be exposed?'

Hannah looked sceptical.

'Also, I don't know what laws I might have broken taking those confidential records. And think of the trouble Geraldine would get into. I lied to her, Hannah. I told her I was writing a profile on Roberts. She thinks he's about to be discredited, finally.'

'Lying? Breaking laws? God, Mum. What's happened to you?'

Corinne couldn't answer that, because what could she have said except that it's surprising what you'd do to protect your children.

'That's why I want you to leave here now, Hannah. You can go to a different clinic to finish your treatment. As an outpatient.'

A strange expression crossed Hannah's face and Corinne had a sudden realization. She was scared. Her brave, headstrong elder daughter had become so institutionalized she was scared of leaving The Meadows.

'Hannah, I'll help you.' She took hold of Hannah's hand and pressed it, feeling how cold the fingers were, and how the skin was tight to the bone, like a latex glove. 'I'll take time off work. I'll look after you.'

'Mum. You can't shield me from everything. I've made a mess of things. No, don't argue, I have. I chose Danny, even though I knew, deep down, I loved him more than he loved me. There always has to be one person who loves more, right? That's what I told myself. And in our case it was me. And I chose to press on with plans for more IVF, even though it was destroying us.

'And on some level, I must have chosen to believe I was pregnant. One more test, one scan, could have proved I was deluded, and I chose not to have any. I'm not a victim, Mum. I need to take responsibility for the choices I've made. Even the shitty ones. Especially the shitty ones.'

'Darling, if it's about Danny, you don't owe that man anything—'

'It's not about Danny. I promised myself that I wouldn't leave here until I was better, and I have to follow through. And I need to find out what happened to Charlie.'

Corinne found herself flooded with so many conflicting emotions that, for a moment, she felt almost numb. She was still frightened for her daughter but, for the first time in months, Hannah was sounding like Hannah.

'You're sounding so much better,' she said, unable to help herself. 'So much more like your old self.'

'I've been having hypnosis from Laura. It's helping.'

Still, she didn't want Hannah to stay here.

'How can we entrust your recovery to Roberts, now that we know he's capable of such a serious breach of judgement?'

'That was a long time ago, Mum. How many patients do you think have passed through this clinic since it opened? Women who've suffered all kinds of abuse. What happened at that other place was awful, but he was just starting out then. He's clearly learned from it.'

'And Stella?'

'Mum, Stella is damaged. But she's not a murderer. She loved Charlie even more than I did.'

'So why come back here?'

'I don't know. The same as I don't know why my body decided to pump itself full of pregnancy hormones. You know, the more I learn about the human mind, the more I realize how clueless we really are about what goes on in our own heads.'

Corinne knew Hannah was right, and yet she couldn't shake off that unnerving sense of things not being as they should be. For a moment she thought about telling Hannah about the trip to Tunbridge Wells and about Patricia Garitson and her warnings about Steffie.

But even as she tried to formulate the words in her head, she knew she couldn't say them. She'd left it too late to explain to Hannah about finding the photograph of Steffie among her private things. Hannah would think it such a breach of trust. She remembered Jacob Garitson's pale, twitchy eyes, and how he'd said, 'She hurts people.'

Wasn't there a possibility, she thought, looking at her daughter, who seemed to be buzzing with renewed resolution, that Hannah was safer in here than outside?

37

Hannah

It's the day after Mum's visit and, in Morning Group, we are focusing on Stella.

Well, everyone else is focusing on Stella. I am focusing on Dr Roberts focusing on Stella.

He is leaning back in his chair with his legs straight out in front of him, imposing deep into the circle formed by our chairs. His hands are clasped behind his head, and he is half smiling, as if we are all in on the same joke.

What does it mean that they have this history together? And how can Roberts not know it? Is she really so unrecognizable from the Catherine Pryor of all those years ago?

Stella is wearing a soft black leather dress that appears seamless and stretches over her body like a second skin reaching to the knee. We're not allowed tights so her legs are bare, despite the cold outside, and on her feet is a pair of sparkling sequin platform shoes. Her blonde hair falls loosely around her shoulders. On her perfectly made-up face there is not a hint of fat. Just jutting bones over which the skin is stretched tight, like one of Laura's canvases.

How much pain has gone into making Stella look this way? How many hours, days, spent in consulting rooms and operating suites? How much blood has it taken to wash away every trace of her former self? How many stitches hold this new Stella together?

Stella is talking about her childhood, a time when her parents were still together and she and her mother and father went to the theatre and afterwards called in to a restaurant where the maître d' addressed her father by his first name and found them a table in the centre of the room, and the waitress fussed around them and her mother seemed actually to like the man she was married to. And both of them seemed actually to like Stella.

'I think it's really sad that being liked by your parents should be so unusual that it stands out in your mind like that,' says Odelle.

'My parents didn't like me much either,' says Katy. 'Don't think it did me much harm.'

'How do you work that one out? You're in the fucking loony bin,' says Judith.

Nina, who has been rocking backwards and forwards on her chair, shrieks with laughter, until Dr Roberts flaps his hand in a quiet-down gesture. Then he sits up straight and leans forward.

'Stella, we've talked a lot in these sessions about your early childhood. Do you feel able now to take us on a bit? To when you lived with your stepfather?'

In Group, Stella tends to circle around her stepfather like a suspect package. We know he was something high up in the military, which is why Stella's family moved around so much. Then, when he retired from the military, he became a high-level security adviser, first

247

working for an oil company in Iraq and later for the US government.

We know he has red hair.

We know that, whenever Stella refers to him, no matter how obliquely, her voice becomes higher pitched, like a child's.

'He didn't like me much. My stepfather. *Gordon*. My mother is very beautiful and my stepfather used to say, "Shame how looks always skip a generation, hey, Cat?"'

'Why did he call you Cat?' Frannie wants to know.

Stella's flush reaches her forehead so that even the areas of skin visible between the roots of her hair are shocking pink against the blonde.

'It was nothing. A stupid nickname my father gave me. Gordon used it sarcastically. He liked to rubbish anything to do with my real dad.'

Stella's hand worries at the necklace around her throat.

'And how did you feel about him?' Roberts asks her, tapping his fingers against his thigh.

'In the beginning, I hated him for stealing my mother from my father and making my father go away. It was my father who introduced Gordon to Mama and, after they got together, my father always referred to him as the Snake.'

'And afterwards?'

'After my father had disappeared from the scene and it was obvious Gordon was sticking around, I tried to win his approval by working really hard, getting top marks, but he wasn't interested in how I did at school. It was all about appearances for him. The smart car, the stylish home, the gorgeous woman on his arm. I was chubby and plain. I didn't fit at all. And he made that quite obvious.'

Odelle sits upright, bouncing in her seat with her arm up like we're at fucking kindergarten or something.

'Stella, do you think that could be why you put yourself through all that plastic surgery? Because you're still looking for his approval?'

Judith starts a sarcastic slow handclap but Roberts merely says, 'That's very perceptive, Odelle. Perhaps you'd like to respond, Stella?'

But Stella has had enough of talking now and is playing noughts and crosses on her leather dress with her finger. And I think:

I wish Gordon hadn't done whatever terrible thing he must have done to break you so completely. And:

I wonder if his name is even Gordon. And:

He can't really be an ex-military-turned-security-adviser, or Roberts would have recognized you for sure. And I think:

What else are you lying about, Stella?

Danny looks everywhere except at me. 'It's weird seeing you out of that place,' he says finally. 'I hardly recognize you.'

We are in a bistro on the high street later that afternoon, a few doors from the café Stella and I visited a few days ago. I am facing a huge canvas print of Audrey Hepburn with a long cigarette and I look at her face whenever I've had enough of the frown on Danny's. *What's a girl to do?* Audrey seems to say.

'Dr Roberts says I should take trips out now. To get

used to being away from the clinic. Ready for when I come home.'

When I say the word 'home', Danny does something weird with his mouth so that, just for a minute, he doesn't look handsome any more. A pebble drops down to the pit of my stomach and lodges there, hard and heavy.

I change the subject.

'Tell me again why you don't like Stella.'

He is so surprised by the question that he actually looks me in the eye before glancing swiftly away.

'Everything about Stella is too much. The looks, the clothes. The way she is with you, like she wants you to be her mummy or something. She's damaged, Hannah.'

'We're all damaged.'

It comes out sharper than I intended.

'Not like that, Hannah. Not like her. You know she came on to me?'

'I don't believe you.'

The pebble in my gut has grown spikes and is moving around inside me.

'It's true. I bumped into her in the corridor when I was coming in to visit you. I mean, literally, bumped into her. And she kind of rubbed herself against me.'

'You misread it, that's all.'

'For God's sake, Hannah. I know when a woman is coming on to me.'

'Oh yeah. Sorry. I forgot you've had recent experience of it. You've got a bloody A level in women coming on to you. You're a leading world expert in it.'

Danny throws down the fork he's been playing with so it clatters on to his plate. A woman at the next table looks up sharply. She has a tiny, flesh-coloured sticking plaster below one eye that looks like a wart.

'There's no point in talking to you when you're like this. I've said sorry a million times, but you have to understand that what happened, what I did, doesn't give you a lifetime's membership to the moral high ground. It doesn't make you right all the time. Or me wrong.

'Stella is damaged, and damaged people can be dangerous. Just be careful. That's all I'm saying.'

I go to bed early, the row with Danny still fresh in my mind. I brush my teeth in the en suite and try not to look at my pale, pasty face in the mirror. I am convinced I won't sleep, have a magazine ready beside my bed, but I drop off almost immediately. I dream Stella is chasing me, although she has Steffie's face. I know that she's carrying something that will hurt me, although I don't know what it is. All I know is that I must keep running. I must go faster, but my legs are made of lead.

I wake up panting, my muscles tensed with fear. For a moment I allow myself the delicious relief of knowing it was a dream, but then I realize it was a noise that woke me up. The noise of my bedroom door closing.

Someone is in the room.

I lie as if pinned to the pillow, unable to move or speak. The room is dark, but there's a crack in the curtains which allows a narrow slit of light to fall into the room. While I watch, paralysed, a dark shape moves across the foot of my bed. As it passes through the slit of light, there's a smell of coconut shampoo and a momentary glint of platinum-blonde hair.

38

Corinne

'Don't you ever get tired of waving that thing in people's faces?'

Rudeness didn't come naturally to Corinne, but she was so tired of seeing Justin and Drew hanging around with that intrusive camera and that rueful 'Don't you think it might help you to share?' smile sewn on to Justin's face.

'Sorry, Mum,' said Justin, which only infuriated her more. She was making her way out of the clinic after a spectacularly unsatisfying visit to Hannah. She ought to have let her know she was coming, but when her afternoon meeting had been cancelled, leaving her unexpectedly free, she had just got in the car and driven over unannounced. But Hannah had been morose and uncommunicative.

'I'm tired,' she'd said, when Corinne had probed about the tightness across her face and the deep, violet shadows under her eyes. 'Stella had a nightmare and woke me up.'

Corinne had been concerned then.

'She had no right to do that. And Hannah, she shouldn't be coming into your room. We have no idea what her agenda is in coming here. Or who she is.'

'She's a damaged girl who was treated abominably. That's who she is.'

It had taken a while for Corinne to get to the real root of Hannah's foul temper: the outing with Danny the day before and the row they'd had. 'I'll deal with it, Mum. It's my marriage. My issue.'

And then Hannah had cut the visit short anyway, saying she needed to finish her journal because later she was meeting Laura for relaxation therapy. By 'relaxation therapy', Corinne knew she really meant hypnosis.

'Are you sure she should be doing that?' Corinne asked. 'I mean, is she properly qualified? She's not doing it with the blessing of the management.'

'Would that be the same management that dismissed child-abuse claims as fantasy?'

She had a point.

Climbing into her car, Corinne buckled up her seat belt and then sat unmoving behind the wheel, feeling as if someone had taken a straw and sucked all the energy out of her. Every time she thought Hannah was making progress something set her back again. Some days, Corinne despaired of life ever getting back to normal, as if normal were a physical place to which the bus no longer ran.

From inside the car, Corinne observed the door to the clinic swing open. Laura walked out of the building, calling a farewell to whoever was hidden inside. Today she had on a burnt-orange coat that reached midway to her knees and there was a half-smile on her fine-boned face.

She lifted her hand and clicked and a bright pink VW Beetle winked its indicator lights.

Where was she going? Corinne wondered. She didn't have long if Hannah was going to see her in just over an hour. It occurred to Corinne she didn't know anything about Laura Whittaker. She'd investigated Oliver Roberts but, about this woman who had got so close to her daughter, she knew nothing. And now Hannah was unburdening herself to her, even taking hypnosis.

The pink car made its way to the exit and, without any clear intention, Corinne started up her own engine and began to follow. She couldn't do much for her daughter, but she could do this much.

The bubblegum-pink car was easy to keep tabs on. Corinne kept her distance as it made its way down the countrified roads surrounding The Meadows and then through increasingly suburban streets, before finally pulling up outside a modern low-rise block of flats in that red render favoured by developers of low-cost housing. Not that anything within spitting distance of London was low cost any more.

As Corinne watched Laura's orange coat disappear through the UPVC front door, she couldn't help wondering about the disconnect between the creative, cosmopolitan art therapist and this uninspiring block in a rundown suburban backwater.

Her curiosity piqued, and knowing that Laura was due to see Hannah back at the clinic in under an hour, Corinne decided to wait around for a while, perhaps find out something that would help put Laura into some sort of context. She was rewarded for her patience when Laura emerged just fifteen minutes later with a beatific smile on her face that Corinne found unnerving, and jumped back into her car.

Corinne switched on her engine, ready to follow, but then something caught her eye. At a first-floor window of the building from which Laura had just emerged, a woman was gazing out, her face a pale disc against the dimness of the room behind her.

Impulsively, Corinne switched off the engine and waited for Laura to drive off. Then she got out of her car and crossed the pavement to the red-rendered block, picking her way around a soiled mattress that had been dumped and was leaning up against the front wall of the house next door.

The front door of the flats was white and plasticky with a printed 'NO FLYERS & NO COLD CALLERS' notice taped above the letterbox and a grid of white plastic doorbells on the left, each accompanied by a hand-written name tag. On the first floor, where Corinne had just seen the woman's face, there were two bells. 1a bore the name WHITTAKER in careful blue ballpoint capital letters.

Corinne hesitated. Glancing upwards, she was startled to find herself locking eyes with the woman at the first-floor window, who she could now see was elderly, with long brown hair and greying skin. Her head was tilted to one side. Corinne smiled, but the woman didn't respond. Feeling self-conscious now and needing to justify her presence on the doorstep, she pressed the buzzer.

'Yes?'

The voice that came over the intercom was young and thickly accented.

'Hello? I'm here to see Mrs Whittaker.'

'OK. You come.'

The door buzzed and Corinne pushed it open, finding herself in a narrow, dark hallway smelling of fried mince. Pressing the light switch, she made her way along the passageway to the stairs on the right, which were covered in squeaky, dark blue lino. On the first-floor landing, the strip lighting flickered, bathing the narrow space in an intermittent greeny light.

There were two doors on this floor, one of which had a 'Welcome' mat outside it. The other was ajar, and from inside came the sound of a television playing full blast.

'Hello?' Corinne called.

'Yes. Yes. You come inside.'

Corinne made her way into a cramped hallway which sported a thick carpet that had once been peach coloured but was now faded and matted in places. In the room straight ahead she could see a pair of feet in outsized rabbit slippers resting on a leather footstool.

The feet were attached to a young, chubby woman dressed in grey sweatpants and a pink sweatshirt with the letters LOL spelled out in gold.

'You wait. I turn down sound. Is *Loose Women*. Is very funny show.' She cast Corinne a look of deep regret before pointing the remote at the television, plunging the room into a sudden and merciful silence.

'I am Katya. You are sherpodist.'

Corinne couldn't make out whether it was a statement or a question, and in any case had no clue what the woman was talking about.

'Sherpodist?'

'Sherpodist. You look at the feets.'

'No, I'm not a chiropodist, I . . .'

But Katya had already crossed the room and was leading the way across the hallway and through a door on which a photograph of a young woman in 1970s clothing had been stuck on pink card surrounded by flowers.

'Here Mrs Whittaker.'

The woman Corinne assumed to be Laura's mother was sitting upright in an armchair facing the window so Corinne could see only a side section of her face, though she could tell immediately it was the same person she'd seen from the street. But up close, it was obvious there was something very wrong with her. The way her head was angled to the side and one hand was curled up in her lap like a small pet, and the fact that she didn't turn around when they came in.

'You turn around now, OK? Your feets have visitor.'

Katya was heaving the armchair around so that its occupant was now facing into the room. Corinne's stomach muscles clenched with shock when she found the old woman's watery brown eyes fixed on her. There was a string of saliva trailing from the left-hand corner of her mouth that Katya did nothing to clear. Despite her lack of movement or response, there was an intensity about the old woman's gaze that gave Corinne the uncomfortable sense that she was trying to communicate something.

Katya knelt down and started easing Mrs Whittaker's right slipper off her swollen foot. Corinne found her voice.

'No, stop. You've made a mistake. I'm not the chiropodist.'

Katya froze, the slipper halfway off the foot.

'Well, who you are then?'

'I just wanted to have a quick chat. I'm a friend of Laura's.'

Mrs Whittaker made a moaning noise, and the hairs on Corinne's arm stood to attention.

Katya stood up, a frown concertinaing her soft, moon-like face.

'Why you not say?'

She wrestled the armchair back around so it was once again facing the other way with Mrs Whittaker all but hidden from view.

'You come. This way.'

Katya flounced out of the room, the ears on her rabbit slippers quivering in outrage. Corinne cast one final glance towards the back of the armchair then turned to follow. As she crossed into the hallway, the old woman moaned again, a sound like a heart breaking.

By the time Corinne got back into the living room, Katya seemed mollified.

'Is nice to meet friend of Laura. Is boring here by my own. Laura just here, in actual fact, but she don't stay long.'

'That's why I came,' Corinne said, improvising wildly. 'To meet Laura and give her something. I'm sorry to have missed her. Have you been here long, Katya, looking after Mrs Whittaker?'

'Ten month.'

Corinne noticed that Katya's eyes had been drawn back to the muted television, where four women on tall stools were talking animatedly to each other across a table.

'And does Laura come often?'

Katya briefly turned her attention back to Corinne.

'Oh, yes. Laura visit her mother all the time. She like a saint. You know who she like? She like Davina.'

Corinne must have looked blank because Katya's dull eyes widened.

'Davina from *Long Lost Family*. You know how she always cry with people. Always feeling what they feel. This is how is Laura.'

After that burst of speech, Katya seemed to lose interest in Corinne. Her fingers reached for the remote and began stealthily increasing the volume on the television.

'How long has she been like this? Laura's mother?'

Corinne found herself almost shouting over the laughter of the studio audience.

Katya shrugged, without bothering to look up.

'Is long time since she had stroke. Maybe twenty year.'

Twenty years. As she made her way back down the narrow stairs, Corinne tried to calculate how old Laura would have been when her mother became so catastrophically damaged. A child still, certainly. No wonder she'd thrown herself into a caring profession as an adult, trying to give to others the nurture she'd been robbed of herself.

Outside, she took a big gulp of fresh air. Crossing over to her car, she deliberately didn't look up to the first floor, but still she felt the force of Mrs Whittaker's fixed brown stare blazing into her back.

Once Corinne had had time to gather her thoughts, the visit to Laura's mother left her cheered. At least here was

259

one person she could be glad of being in Hannah's corner. Now Corinne knew Laura's personal tragedy she was better able to understand what lay behind the art therapist's brimming eyes and willingness to go above and beyond her professional role to help the women in her charge – in the way she wasn't able to help her own mother.

Pulling in to her own road forty minutes later, Corinne wasn't surprised to find there wasn't a parking space outside her cottage. Even though the council had long since brought in controlled parking, she lived near a railway station and her neighbours on both sides had two cars per household, so competition for spaces was keen. There was a time it used to infuriate her out of all proportion to the actual inconvenience caused, which was usually minimal. But these days she was more sanguine. Once you told yourself you weren't actually entitled to park outside your house, things became easier.

There was a space down at the end of the road which Corinne, · having a very small car, could just about squeeze into. She locked the door, feeling ridiculously uplifted, as if finding a place to park were an indicator of a change in fortune.

After a grey start, the sun had made an appearance for what seemed like the first time in days and Corinne noticed with a warm thrill of pleasure the green buds on the trees and bushes as she made her way from the car. Three doors down from her, a magnolia tree was already showing signs of flowering and Corinne stopped to admire it, drinking in the beauty of the blousy pink petals after the long barrenness of winter.

She came to her own cottage, which she'd bought in an emotionally charged rush after splitting up with Duncan but had, happily, grown to love. Pushing open the wooden gate, painted a defiant Mediterranean blue, she made her way down the path, with its uneven terracotta tiles, around which wildflowers grew during the summer months. Pausing on the doorstep, she rummaged in her silver leather tote bag for her keys.

Her head bent, she didn't see the shadow coming up behind. Until it was all too late.

39

Laura

'There's something a bit *off* about Stella.'

'Off? How do you mean, Laura?'

Annabel was wearing the green dress with the scoop neck that Laura liked so much. A childish part of her couldn't help wishing she'd worn it with the gold earrings Laura had bought her for her birthday. The two would go so well together. But Annabel was funny about gifts. She'd practically had to force her to accept them. It was tricky to know where one stood with Annabel.

'She's so damaged, you know. They all are. But with Stella it goes so deep she's like a stick of holiday rock – do you know what I mean? – where the writing goes all the way through?'

Annabel nods. Just the slightest of movements.

'I've been seeing her a lot one-to-one. Little bits of light hypnosis. Just on the quiet. Informally. It helps her sleep.'

Annabel smiled. 'You're so kind, Laura. How lucky they are to have you.'

Annabel's praise was hard to come by, and Laura found herself dangerously close to tears. What on earth was wrong with her at the moment? She was like a walking sac of saline, forever on the brink of springing a leak.

'Have things settled down at all?' Annabel asked. 'After the two deaths?'

Laura shot a sharp, questioning glance at her, then wrinkled her nose.

'Not really. Roberts is worried. One of the clinic's patrons just resigned. He said it was because of time commitments but Roberts is convinced it's because of Sofia and Charlie. New referrals are down and, obviously, the families of existing residents are nervous. I've had Hannah Lovell's mother in to see me a few times.'

Annabel frowned. She was one of those women who can look striking one minute and quite plain the next. But Laura loved that about her, that she was always unashamedly herself.

'No surnames, remember? You must be more careful, Laura. If anyone heard you talking about your clients out of the clinic you'd get into trouble, wouldn't you?'

'I only talk to you, Annabel. But you're right. I need to be more discreet.'

Laura held up her own hand with the fingers down and gave it a playful slap.

'It brings up such complicated emotions. Talking to mothers who are so protective about their daughters, like Corinne H—, like Hannah's mum. I can't help thinking of everything I missed out on.'

'That's only natural, Laura. What things in particular do you think about?'

'How it would be to have somebody fighting your corner. Instead of always feeling so alone.'

She wondered if Annabel would contradict her,

remind her that she wasn't alone, because she had her. Then she continued:

'I keep remembering those three years in the foster home. Liz did her best. She was kind enough. But she wasn't a mother. And we always knew her biological children came first. Then Gino, because she'd adopted him when he was still a baby. I remember when I had the lead part in the Christmas play at primary school. I was so proud. All the other kids had parents there for one or other performance, and loads of them came to both. I begged Liz to come, but it clashed with Gino's Nativity one day and her oldest son playing in the school concert the next. He only played recorder or something. There was no one there to take pictures or record me making a tit out of myself or cheer when I came on. My form teacher came to both performances and presented me with a bunch of flowers at the end because she felt so sorry for me.'

'That must have been tough. Do you feel that, maybe, you're still trying to plug that gap, all these years later? Still seeking that validation?'

'Isn't everyone?'

Laura liked these kinds of conversations. Annabel always helped her question her own motivations and actions. She eased off her suede boots and settled back into the blue sofa, tucking her feet under in their brightly coloured socks, and waited for Annabel's response.

Ber-ring.

The noise of the doorbell cut through Laura's good mood. Annabel's house was usually so quiet, but any disruptions were an unwelcome reminder that Annabel had a life outside of her. In the beginning, Laura regularly used to suggest they went out for coffee, so that they could give each other their undivided attention, but Annabel was never keen.

'Sorry, Laura.' Annabel stood up, smoothing down the creases in the green dress. 'I won't be a moment.'

Laura heard the door open and a woman's voice shout, 'Well, hello!' Then Annabel must have told her she had company because, after that, their voices were lowered to a mumble.

Laura crept to the doorway on her stockinged feet and peered out.

Annabel was standing in the hallway with a short, rotund woman dressed in a long raincoat, which emphasized her spherical shape, and brown hiking boots. They were so close together that some strands of Annabel's greying hair stood up where they were brushed by the edge of the raincoat's hood. The woman was pressing a card into Annabel's hand. It looked like an invitation. There was a dog, on the end of a red rope lead, a large Labrador covered in mud as if fresh from a long walk. The end of the animal's tail left a dirty mark on the wall. Laura saw Annabel glance at the mark then look away again. 'Thank you. I look forward to it. Look, I'd better go.' Annabel nodded her head in the direction of the sitting room, where Laura was.

The short woman leaned forward and gave Annabel a quick embrace, then opened the door and was gone.

Laura quickly ducked back inside and was installed on the sofa by the time Annabel reappeared.

'Now, where were we?'

The interruption couldn't have lasted over three minutes, but it seemed to Laura that the mood was broken. She couldn't recapture the intimacy she'd felt, that urge to probe further. Now all she could think about was the stiff card of the invitation. The knowledge of life being lived without her.

'I'd better be off now myself,' she told Annabel. 'You don't mind, do you?'

'No, but—'

'I'm looking after Mum tonight, as Katya has a family do.'

'OK. If you're sure.'

Laura was touched and gratified that Annabel looked genuinely taken aback to see her leave so abruptly.

It was raining again and puddles were forming on the neat, quiet road where Annabel's house was, gleaming in the gathering dusk. As Laura drove slowly out of the modern estate, her headlights picked up the woman who'd been at the door, walking along with her dog, her raincoat billowing behind her. There was a large puddle just ahead and, as the woman came level with it, Laura put on a burst of speed so that her tyres sent out a heavy spray of dirty water. When she looked in her rear mirror, the woman was standing still, her arms held out to her sides. Even through the dim, slate-grey light, Laura could tell that she was soaking wet. The woman gazed after the receding car with an expression of profound disbelief.

40

Hannah

'Why are you acting so weird with me?'

Stella and I are on the high street, at the pub rather than the coffee shop. The pub – which is modern but done up to look old-fashioned, a pub-themed pub, with carefully distressed wooden floors, faux-leather arm-chairs and little green shaded wall lights – is off limits, but I've decided to risk the 'setting back your own prog-ress' speech from Dr Roberts for the sake of a bottle of cold Peroni.

I didn't ask Stella to come. The shock of her creeping into my room last night still hasn't completely worn off, although it's not the first time she's done it after having a nightmare. Stella isn't supposed to leave the clinic grounds but when I said I was going for a walk earlier she just tagged along. And I obviously haven't done a very good job of disguising my dismay. I'm not frightened of Stella. It's just . . .

I *am* frightened of her.

I'm frightened of the history she has hidden from me.

And why she's hidden it.

'I'm not acting weird.'

Stella stares at me over the top of her beer. Now that I know the truth about her, I can see the joins. The almost imperceptible clear ring around her irises where the blue lenses end. The tell-tale dark strip at the roots of her blonde hair. So it turns out that Stella is not Stella but an imposter grafted on to the stalk of poor, broken Catherine. And the Charlie who baked with me and then booked her flight to Croatia and then slit her wrists is not the Charlie I thought I knew. And the Danny who can't look me in the eyes when he comes to visit is not the Danny who promised to love and cherish me in sickness and in health.

None of them are the people they first pretended to be. But which version is real?

'Hannah, you can't even look at me. What's going on?'

I try to look at Stella then, to meet her challenge, but my eyes slide off hers. *Who are you?* The question rebounds in my head. *Who are you? Who are you?*

'Who are you?'

I didn't mean to say it out loud but, suddenly, the words are there, suspended between us.

'What do you mean?'

'What I mean is, you're not who you say you are. What I mean is, everything you've told me is a lie. Your name is Catherine and you and Dr Roberts have history, and now I know that, I'm wondering why you're hiding it, and whether your history with Dr Roberts has anything to do with Charlie and Sofia dying.'

It's more than I thought I was going to say. More than I even let myself admit I was thinking. But now it's out and there's no stuffing the words back into my mouth so

I have to just sit here, with my heart hammering in my chest like a flamenco dancer's feet and my fingers clasped so tightly around my bottle that I wonder it doesn't shatter into a thousand little pieces. For a moment she is silent and I think she will refuse to reply. Then:

'I won't ask you how you found out. I've been waiting to be uncovered ever since I arrived. I think that might even have been what I wanted. But when Roberts didn't recognize me, and no one challenged me, I just thought, *Well, maybe I am Stella, after all.*

'Don't you think identity must be more fluid than we are always told? I mean, if this is all there is, this one life, wouldn't it make sense that we could be more than one person? Maybe all our different selves are inside us, one inside the other, like a Russian doll. So maybe Stella was inside Catherine all the time, or maybe Catherine is still tucked away inside Stella. And maybe there are others in there too. Don't you think that would make sense?'

Stella's breathy, beer-soaked voice has a dreamy quality and I find myself contemplating for a moment whether she has a point before remembering that she's a liar and quite possibly dangerous.

'And was it Stella or Catherine or one of your other Russian-doll selves who hacked off a toy rabbit's ears and left it on my bed and drew a newborn baby in my colouring book and sent me a printout of an antenatal scan?'

'No!'

Stella is looking as horrified as it's possible for someone to look when their skin has already been stretched into an expression of perpetual surprise.

'Hannah, no. I would never do anything to hurt you. You're my friend.'

'And Charlie and Sofia?'

'Of course not. I haven't hurt anyone. Not ever.'

'Only yourself.'

'Isn't that why we're here, all of us? Because of the damage we do to ourselves?'

And now I look at her, finally, at her eyes which appear blue but I now know to be grey, and her face which isn't her face but a mixture of features selected from a surgeon's catalogue, and I see suddenly that she is still who she was and that she is right and we are all too busy hurting ourselves to do harm to anyone else.

'So what then?' I ask her. And she hears the softening in my voice and leans back in her faux-vintage leather chair and she tells me her story.

'It was my stepfather, of course,' she starts. 'But then you knew that.'

The story is the one we've all heard before, featuring a critical stepfather and an eager-to-please girl desperate for approval. Pointed comments about her weight, her hair, the way she walked hunched over with her arms crossed over her chest. The visits to her room while her mother was in a Xanax coma. She'd started cutting herself.

'I was trying to slice off the weight,' Stella says. 'I wanted to slice off the skin his fingers had touched.'

As she speaks, she makes a blade of the side of her hand and slices at the air.

Stella's self-destruction repelled her stepfather, and the abuse stopped, though the cutting didn't. After two years of self-harm, her mother took her to see a therapist, to whom she gradually told her story. The therapist advised her to talk to her mother.

'Mama didn't – wouldn't – believe it. Her response was to find a different therapist and then a different one again. Looking for a different truth. What's that quote? "The definition of being crazy is to do the same thing and expect a different result?"' I'm not surprised to hear Stella repeat the Einstein quote. It's a favourite among residents of The Meadows. 'My mother thought she could change the therapist and get a different result. Even though it was the same old truth. And, of course, he denied it completely.'

'Didn't she have any doubts at all?'

'She couldn't. She needed to believe him. She needed to hold on to what she had.'

Finally, Stella's mother found what she was looking for. False memory. That was Roberts' diagnosis. The original therapist might have planted the seed of abuse, he suggested, and Stella's overactive imagination had allowed it to blossom.

'Gordon was vindicated,' says Stella.

'Tell me you didn't go back to living with him.'

'Where else would I go?'

'But surely your mother wouldn't have made you stay with him? Not when you were still accusing him of doing that?'

'Ah, but I'd retracted by then.'

Stella sees my face.

'What was I supposed to do, Hannah? I was twelve years old. I trusted Roberts. Wanted him to be pleased with me. And he told me the memories weren't real.

271

And all the other adults in my life – my mother, my stepfather himself – told me they weren't real.'

'And your father?'

'He'd remarried by then, to a younger woman who didn't much like kids. He wanted to believe Gordon hadn't done the things I'd said he'd done because the status quo suited him.'

She is playing with her necklace as she talks, twisting it around her finger.

'He gave you that?' I ask her. 'Your father?'

She nods. 'A cat for my Cat,' she said. 'Cat was his name for me.'

'So you went back?'

'I went back. And the abuse started again. Except, this time, I kept it to myself. And when I was fourteen they moved to the States, and I stayed behind at boarding school. That's the year my mother bought me a nose job as a birthday present. Guilt money, I guess.'

We fall silent and drink our drinks, and I think about little Catherine Pryor, whose sense of self was eroded so brutally and thoroughly by the adults in her life that the only way forward was to become someone else.

'What are you doing here, Stella?'

Stella has kicked off her shoes – the sparkly platforms again – and tucked her feet under her in the faux-leather chair, so she looks like a child. Her eyes when she raises them to me are varnished with tears.

'I want him to know me, Hannah. Can you believe it still matters so much, after all these years? I want him to recognize me and what he did to me. I want him to beg my forgiveness. But do you know what the worst thing is?'

I shake my head.

'The worst thing about the whole bloody messed-up situation is I still want him to be pleased with me.'

Emerging from the pub forty-five minutes later, I'm surprised to find it has been raining while we've been inside, and the air smells heavy and damp. There's a puddle by the kerb where we wait to cross the main road, and the car wheels send out a spray of rainwater over our legs. The sky is the colour of slate and the cars' headlights reflect yellow in the wet sheen of the tarmac.

The conversation with Stella has churned me up inside, forcing me to think of things I don't want to think about.

I'm beginning to feel breathless and panicky. Is this what I've done with Danny? By sweeping aside the reality of his affair with Steffie and focusing instead on what seemed to be the greater crime of my own false pregnancy, have I set myself up to be like Stella, losing sight of my own self in my determination to keep hold of him?

A huge lorry, its headlights like bright, staring eyes, approaches from the distance and I gaze at it, transfixed. Stella says something, but I do not hear her because my mind is taken up with the beams of light on the front of the lorry, which seem to be sucking me in towards them.

'Hannah?'

Stella's voice is coming from a different galaxy, light years away. The only real things are the lights on the lorry; they are like a rope of energy pulling me in. The lorry is nearly here now, and the reflections of its beams on the road are clouds of light that I want to lose myself in. *Go towards the light*, I tell myself. *Move towards the light*.

I step off the kerb, just as the first of the lorry's eighteen wheels hit the puddle to the right of us.

The squeal of brakes sounds like an animal dying.

41

Corinne

'Are you completely sure you're OK now? I didn't mean to creep up on you. I was sure you'd heard me coming through the gate after you.'

In the flesh, Steffie Garitson's eyes were a deep, warm brown, although ringed with purple, as if she hadn't slept in a long while. After so long knowing them only as a series of angry red pen marks, Corinne couldn't help staring.

'I'm fine. I feel like an idiot, screaming like that.'

'I have to say it's not the normal reaction I get from people I haven't met before.'

Steffie had a way of talking and smiling at the same time, as if the two things were actually one single smooth, effortless action. Corinne stopped herself just at the beginning of a reciprocal smile, reminding herself that this young woman standing in her hallway had all but destroyed her daughter.

'I was shocked to find you on my doorstep,' she said, keeping her voice cool. 'After everything you've put my family through.'

Steffie furrowed her brow, although her smile remained in place.

'You're talking about Danny. Let me explain—'

'Explain what? How you had an affair with my daughter's husband and got pregnant by him and turned up at their flat to taunt her with it, until she was driven crazy enough to imagine *herself* to be pregnant, because she couldn't bear not to be?'

Now Corinne remembered about the weird things that had been happening at the clinic.

'And what about the stuffed toy in Hannah's room? The rabbit with the missing ears? And the colouring book?'

The smile was gone, replaced by a look of – Corinne narrowed her eyes – could that be *fear?*

Steffie Garitson was afraid of *her.*

'I shouldn't have come. You're clearly distraught,' Steffie said, turning to leave in such a rush the bag she was carrying on her shoulder knocked over the vase of spring flowers on the little shelf by the door.

'Shit. I'm sorry. Have you got something I can clean it up with?'

Steffie dabbed at the pool of water with the tea-towel Corinne fetched for her, her bag still hooked over her back, a draught blowing in through the front door which had been left ajar.

'Danny told me they were separated.' *Dab, dab, dab.* 'He said they were only living together in the flat because they had such a massive mortgage. He said they were leading separate lives, but Hannah didn't want her dad to know so they were keeping it secret. I would never have given him the time of day if I'd known they were still a couple, let alone shown up on his doorstep. It makes me sick how gullible I was.' *Dab, dab, dab.* 'Do you know, I even bought him a present, a silver bangle? I used to imagine him wearing it in his London life and thinking of me.'

Corinne remembered the bangle Danny had been wearing in the pub, the way he'd kept touching it like a talisman, and a bit of her heart splintered.

'And you expect me to believe all that?' she asked, hardening herself.

'Believe what you want.'

Steffie tossed the tea-towel on the shelf and glared at Corinne.

'And as for the rest of it – cuddly toys and colouring books – have you any idea how totally crazy you sound?' Suddenly, she looked stricken. 'No offence,' she added.

Corinne found herself wavering. She was so convincing, this Steffie. No wonder she'd been able to cause so much devastation.

'So why are you here then, if it isn't you who's been tormenting Hannah? Why have you come to my home? This could constitute harassment, you know.'

'Oh, and you driving halfway across the country to turn up at my parents' house is perfectly fine, is it?'

'That's different. I was protecting my daughter. And after I'd had a chat with your mother, I realized I was absolutely right to think she needed protecting.'

Steffie's features sagged.

'That's why I came. My mother told me you'd been to see them. I don't generally keep in contact with my parents, but they have a number for emergencies and my mother called to say you'd been there. She took great pleasure in letting me know you'd had a "long chat".'

277

Steffie curled her fingers in the air to make speech marks.

'She warned me about you.' Corinne was scrabbling to hold on to the moral high ground, but it seemed to be crumbling beneath her feet. 'She told me about all the awful things you've done.'

'My mother is a narcissist and delights in causing me grief.' The words came out in a rush, and for a split second the two women stared at each other in surprise. Then Steffie took a deep breath and continued.

'Look, I don't know you, and I don't have to explain myself to you, but I want you to understand. Mine was not a happy childhood. When I was born, my mother couldn't stand the fact that my father loved anyone except her. She was jealous of her own baby. Can you imagine? My father had affairs because he couldn't stand my mother, and she took it out on us. We were terrified of her.'

'But your brother followed me to the car, specifically to warn me about you. "She hurts people." Those were his exact words.'

'He'd be talking about her. Our mother. Do you know he used to drag his chest of drawers against his bedroom door to stop her coming in?'

Corinne felt nauseous. Could she really have got this so wrong?

'My brother and I are really close. Look at my text messages.' Steffie waved her phone in front of Corinne's face. 'They're mostly from him. He's the only reason I ever go back there. He's not well.'

Corinne remembered Jacob Garitson's clammy yellow skin and the way he looked at her as if from the end of a long, dark tunnel.

'He has medication. Lithium. And when he's taking that he's like a different person, but my mother says it makes him like a zombie.'

Corinne warned herself not to be taken in. Steffie Garitson was dangerous, she reminded herself. And yet her words felt solid, as if studded with heavy rocks of truth.

'What about the needle in the pie?'

'Pardon?'

'Your mother told me she was doing a catering job for your neighbour's birthday dinner and you slipped a needle into one of the apple pies.'

'A needle? Are you serious? Don't you think I might be taking a long vacation at Her Majesty's pleasure somewhere if I'd done that? Shall I tell you what really happened? Mum agreed to do the catering job but then the client criticized the hors d'oeuvres, said they didn't taste of anything. So my darling mother crushed five laxatives in with the mixture in one of the pies and stuck a candle in the top to make sure the birthday girl got it. Ruined the evening, apparently, though no one else got ill, so they couldn't prove anything. And by the time the neighbour could tear herself away from the bathroom, all the evidence had been thoroughly cleared away. By the way, did you see that photograph?'

'What photograph?' Corinne's head was spinning.

'The one in the hallway, showing our perfect family? The one Mummy Dearest stage-managed to the nth degree, making us all wear white, like something out of a washing-powder advert?'

'Yes, I saw it. But what has that—'

'Did you notice there was a line across my neck?'

Corinne nodded slowly, remembering the faint silver line she'd at first mistaken for a choker.

'When I said I wanted to stay home to revise for exams instead of going out clothes shopping with her, she cut my head out of the photograph with a Stanley knife. I came downstairs and it was lying on the floor. Dad was the one who stuck it back in place.'

Corinne remembered Patricia Garitson standing in her sterile kitchen in Tunbridge Wells and describing her daughter as selfish, and how, when they'd met in the café in London, she'd said that thing about Jacob being scared of his sister and then stared so greedily at Corinne's shocked expression, as if she would gulp it down whole.

But from Steffie herself there was none of the same chill Corinne had felt with the rest of the Garitsons. And yet, if she accepted Steffie hadn't done those things in the clinic – the rabbit, the colouring book, the scan – the only other option was that Hannah had made them up, that they were a sign of a new delusion. The thought froze the breath inside her. Corinne's mind raced, trying to find an alternative explanation, one that pinned the blame on Steffie once and for all.

'You were here!' she blurted out suddenly. How could she have forgotten? 'You rang my doorbell and then ran away, leaving a baby's knitted hat on my doorstep for me to find.'

Relief flooded through her. Hannah hadn't made it up. Steffie had been taunting both of them, leaving reminders of the baby that never was. How unutterably cruel.

Yet instead of denying it, or crumpling into an abject

heap and confessing all, Steffie stared at Corinne with a strange half-smile.

'Was it red?' she asked at last.

'Was what red?'

'Never mind. Wait here.' Steffie stepped through the still-open front door.

'Hang on,' Corinne shouted after her. 'You can't just . . .'

There was the sound of the gate creaking and the bipping of a car electronically unlocking. Just as Corinne had convinced herself Steffie was planning to make a dash for it, there came the unmistakeable noise of a car door slamming shut and, seconds later, Steffie was walking back into the house.

'We've been looking for that hat everywhere,' she said. 'It was . . .' But Corinne didn't hear the rest of what she said because all her attention was focused on the thing Steffie was carrying in her arms. A thing that was wrapped in a red knitted blanket to match the hat Corinne had hidden away in her kitchen drawer and stretching its tiny arms as if freshly woken from sleep.

'Meet Eleanor,' said Steffie.

The baby started to cry.

42

Hannah

'I just wasn't thinking. That's all. I was in a world of my own and just didn't see the lorry.'

'How can you not have seen it? Stella says it was practically on top of you.'

'I was in a daze.'

'Because you were drunk.'

'I wasn't drunk. I'd had two bottles of beer.'

I glare at Dr Oliver Roberts across his desk, resenting being made to feel like a naughty schoolchild, although, the truth is, I do feel guilty. I can't explain that I did see the lorry but somehow didn't register it. I can still hear the screech of brakes and the sound of shattering glass as the car behind smashed into the lorry's tail-lights; still remember the painful jolt of my heart as Stella grabbed my shoulder, wrenching me backwards. The lorry driver was furious, but it could have been a lot worse. It was just bad luck that Joni was walking past at the time and saw the whole thing, including us coming out of the pub. And, of course, she couldn't wait to report back.

Dr Roberts leans back in his chair so that he's almost horizontal, never taking his cold eyes off me. But whereas a week ago I might have looked away, now I dig my fingernails into my thigh and hold his gaze, refusing him power over me. This is the man who sent Stella back to her abusive stepfather and then failed to recognize her when she presented herself again, seeking validation.

No, I will not be the first to break eye contact.

'What you need to remember, Hannah, is that my job is to keep you safe. I cannot recommend that you leave here until I believe you're not a danger to yourself.'

'It was an accident. I've told you. Anyway, you can't stop me leaving. It's up to me.'

'Unless I have reason to believe you pose a threat to your own safety, or the safety of other people. Remember how it was when you first arrived, Hannah? We wouldn't want to return to that, but we could if we had to.'

The inside of my mouth feels coated with dust as his threat sinks in. He could keep me in here against my will. There was a detention order on me when I was first admitted here. For my own safety. But then, I was in such a state the implications didn't even register. Now it would be different. Surely he'd need some kind of consent from my next of kin? Mum would never agree to it, I'm sure of it. To have my own agency taken away from me. And neither, surely, would Danny.

I picture Danny sitting opposite me in the bistro, unable even to look at me. When was the last time he held me, without me reaching for him first? When was the last time he called me on the office phone without wanting anything in particular, just to hear my voice? When was the last time I looked at him and thought, *My Danny?*

I can no longer be sure what Danny would say or do

in any given situation. I'm starting to wonder if he was ever 'my Danny'.

I find Laura in the art room, conferring with Odelle, who has a streak of orange paint across her downy face. They are both scrutinizing a selection of groceries – jam, margarine, a box of herbal tea-bags, a tin of beans, a bar of chocolate – that have been arranged on a tray. Laura steps forward to clasp one of my hands in both of hers.

'Hannah,' she says. 'You must remember, I am always here for you. Any time, day or night.'

'I didn't do it on purpose,' I say, feeling like I am stuck in some sort of groundhog day, doomed to justify for the rest of time that momentary impulse that led me to step off the kerb.

'Never apologize. Never explain,' says Laura, and smiles.

We remain there like that, hand in hand, for what seems like an age though is probably only a few seconds, until Odelle says, very pointedly, 'Laura, you said you'd help me with my still life.'

Laura winks at me and lets go of my hand, which suddenly feels very cold.

'Coming, poppet,' she says.

As I head for the door I glance at Odelle's painting, which features the tray of products on one side and on the other a woman who looks a lot like Odelle. Over the woman's mouth there's a pattern of small black lines, as if someone has sewn her lips together.

In the day room, Joni looks at me and shakes her head.

'I thought you were a goner then,' she says. She's talking about the lorry.

'Sorry to disappoint.'

'You should have asked me,' hisses Judith across the table. 'I can think of loads of better ways of doing it than that.'

I get out my laptop, angling the screen away from Joni, who is supervising the morning internet session, so that, if she wants to check what I'm doing, she has to stand up and move her lazy arse over here.

I'd almost forgotten about the list Charlie made on the morning she died and the mysterious WK she was researching. Now I'm determined to make amends.

I type 'William Kingsley' into the search box and scroll impatiently until I come to page five and the reports on the two mothers jailed for shaking their babies to death, largely on the evidence of neurologist Dr William Kingsley, only to be sensationally cleared when the evidence was found to be flawed.

Near the bottom of the next page is the link I was prevented from reading before by the untimely arrival of Stella. I click on the headline 'The Doctors Who Play God' and wait for the page to load.

Joni keeps glancing over at me, and I can tell she's been told to keep a careful watch and that makes my fingers tingle with rage, because there's no need for any of it. I made a mistake. (I saw the lorry yet didn't see it. Go figure.) On my computer screen, the infuriating circle keeps going round. The WiFi connection in here is pathetic. I'm sure they do that deliberately, to discourage us from spending too long online. Finally, a magazine spread appears on my screen, illustrated with snippets torn out of newspapers about cases where medical staff have been accused of overstepping their remit.

There's the private fertility expert struck off for removing all the male embryos from the sample of a mother of five sons who is desperate for a daughter. And the parents of a teenager left unable to walk or speak after falling from a balcony who are suing the doctors intent on keeping him alive at all costs. But I don't read the details of those, because my eye is drawn to a photograph in a newspaper cutting on the bottom-left corner of the page.

The cutting is about Dr William Kingsley, whose evidence helped send two women to jail for murdering their babies.

The photograph is of Oliver Roberts.

43

Corinne

As she queued at traffic lights to cross the North Circular Road, the afternoon after the encounter with Steffie Garitson, Corinne's thoughts were still racing.

It was so long since she'd held a baby. She'd forgotten just how small they were, and the funny little grunting noises they made, and how their whole faces scrunched up when they cried.

Eleanor had needed changing and feeding after her long nap in the car and, by the time that had been accomplished and Corinne had finished telling Steffie off for leaving her unattended, even if the car *was* directly outside and the front door open, the moment for anger seemed to have passed.

It wasn't until later that the inappropriateness of the whole situation had struck her. Her son-in-law had had a baby with another woman and then kept it secret from his wife. What was this news going to do to Hannah?

Steffie had apologized for shocking her. She'd assumed Corinne already knew about Eleanor. Though she admitted she'd at first told Danny she'd lost the baby, reeling from discovering he was still married, she'd relented and told him the truth once Eleanor was born, nearly a month ago. Even so, she hadn't given him the option of coming to visit, nor had he asked. She had considered herself completely done with the man who'd lied to her so blatantly. In fact, it was only Corinne's ill-fated trip to Tunbridge Wells that had brought Steffie back into their lives. 'I knew my mother would have been filling your ear with poison,' Steffie had said. 'I just wanted to see you, to give you some context.'

Corinne had looked at the dark rings around her eyes, and the practised way she paced and rocked her screaming daughter, as if they'd done this particular dance many times before, and she felt sorry for the girl. How could she not?

She'd tried to call on Corinne before, she said. Ringing the bell repeatedly before deciding no one was in and hurrying away, not realizing she'd dropped Eleanor's hat on the doorstep. Corinne remembered being in the shower. The insistent ringing of the bell. Her worry that it could be the clinic calling about some emergency.

After Steffie left, Corinne had tried to call Duncan, but his phone went straight to voicemail, and the idea that Gigi might have seen her name flashing up on his screen and ordered him not to answer made her hang up without leaving a message.

Then she'd FaceTimed Megan, who had only just got up and had seemed bewildered when Corinne mentioned Steffie, which then meant having to explain about going to the house in Tunbridge Wells, at which Megan's face sharpened to a point and she yelled at Corinne for having kept her in the dark about what was going on.

Perhaps not surprisingly, Megan had spared little sympathy for Steffie, no matter how many times Corinne tried to tell her that she hadn't known Danny was married. She saved most of her vitriol for her brother-in-law, and Corinne felt a creeping sense of dread as she realized how irreparable the rift would be between her daughters when Hannah finally moved back home.

If she moved back home.

Unsurprisingly, sleep had been hard to come by and, now, parking her car in the near-deserted car park of The Meadows, Corinne felt as if her brain had been scooped out and replaced by cotton wadding.

Her phone rang as she was waiting to be buzzed through the front door, and she answered, only registering too late that she didn't recognize the number.

'Yes.' It was her clipped 'don't you dare engage me in conversation' voice. Already she could feel fury bubbling inside her, looking for release. Whoever wanted to talk to her about PPI or that car accident she'd never had was going to get more than they bargained for.

By the time she'd belatedly recognized the voice on the line, the tone had been set.

'I can tell I've caught you at a bad time,' said Paddy, coming to the end of a rambling question about a text he couldn't decide whether or not to include.

'Yes, it is rather.'

Even as she was speaking, Corinne realized she was coming across as cold. Rude, even.

'I won't take up any more of your time then.'

And before she had a chance to explain herself, he'd hung up.

Afterwards, she couldn't help wondering how necessary it had really been for him to call her. Surely an email would have done? Might he actually have been trying to find an excuse to talk to her?

Well. He wouldn't make that mistake again.

'Mrs Harris?' Bridget Ashworth had a habit of materializing out of the blue. She hovered by the entrance to the old building, twiddling her lanyard and blocking Corinne's path to the day room.

'Dr Roberts was wondering if you could just pop in to his office. It won't take long.'

She was smiling, but it was that kind of default smile that could mean good news or 'sorry to tell you . . .' news.

Corinne's feet, as they followed Bridget's up the staircase, felt leaden.

'Ah, thank you for coming, Corinne.'

Dr Roberts got up from his chair as Corinne came in, and walked around his desk to clasp her hand in his, which immediately put her on her guard.

What now?

'I'll get straight to the point. I'm sorry to say that, after making great progress recently, there's been a slight glitch in Hannah's recovery.'

'Glitch?'

'Hannah went to the high street yesterday with Stella. To a pub.'

Corinne breathed again. A pub? She could deal with that.

'And when they came out of the pub, Hannah stepped off the kerb in front of a lorry. Don't be alarmed, Corinne – Stella managed to pull her back out of the way and she is completely unharmed. But, as you can imagine, we're rather concerned.'

'Surely you don't think she did it on purpose? Hannah would never—'

Roberts held up his hand.

'We are not jumping to any conclusions. Hannah insists it was an accident and she was just distracted. But either way, it's something we have to pay very close attention to. Let's not forget, Hannah is still a very vulnerable young woman. We know she has taken the death of Charlie Chadwick very hard. It's not unheard of in such cases for someone to display copycat behaviour.'

Now the shock was wearing off, Corinne was conscious of a dull pain under her ribs.

'I'm afraid this means she needs to be with us slightly longer than we initially thought,' Dr Roberts continued.

'But she thinks she's leaving this week.'

Roberts shook his head.

'That's not advisable. Not until we're sure she's not a danger to herself. I'm very much hoping she'll agree to stay a little while longer but, if not, I do have the authority, under the Mental Health Act, to seek a short-term compulsory order to keep her here, just while we reassure ourselves there won't be any repeat incidents.'

Corinne left Dr Roberts' office with that now all too familiar sense of being out of sync with the world.

'Mum! Where have you been? I saw you drive in ages ago.'

Hannah must have been sitting by the window in the day room watching for her. She looked flushed as she jumped up from the sofa to greet Corinne, as if it was too warm in the room. Corinne felt sick, thinking about

Hannah stepping off the kerb like that. There was no way she could tell her about the baby now.

'Dr Roberts wanted to talk to me. About the lorry. Darling, what happened? Are you OK?'

Hannah made a *pffff* noise, as if it was an irrelevance that didn't merit discussion.

Stella was sitting on the other end of the sofa, and her presence elicited conflicting emotions in Corinne. According to Roberts, she'd saved Hannah's life. Yet there was still no explanation for why she was here, with a new face and a new identity.

'I believe thanks are in order,' she said, groaning inwardly at the sound of her pompous voice.

Stella flapped her hand in a dismissive gesture.

'I need to talk to you, Mum. It's really important. Shall we go for a walk?'

Before Corinne could reply, Hannah had grabbed her arm and was bundling her into the hallway with that enormous crystal chandelier overhead.

'But it's cold,' Corinne protested feebly. Hannah ignored her, pressing the green release button so they could exit through the little-used front door, dragging her mother with her. To Corinne's surprise, Stella followed them out. She expected Hannah to make some sort of excuse to Stella, about needing to have a private chat, but her daughter seemed in no hurry to shake her off.

'I also have something I need to discuss with you, Hannah, but I'll save it for when you're stronger,' she said, when they'd followed the gravel path around the building to the smoking bench in the rose garden.

To her surprise, Hannah didn't pick her up on that

word 'stronger'; in fact, she hardly seemed to have registered anything Corinne had said.

'Mum,' she said, before they'd even sat down, 'you mustn't listen to Roberts. He's not what he seems.'

Hannah was gazing intently at Corinne, as if she was supposed to know what she was talking about.

'Is this to do with what we talked about *before*,' asked Corinne, with a subtle nod in Stella's direction.

'No. Not Westbridge House. Nothing to do with that.'

Immediately, Corinne felt wrong-footed. So Hannah had already confronted Stella about Westbridge House and her past dealings with Roberts. Then what was all this about?

'His name wasn't always Oliver Roberts.' Hannah was almost tripping over her own words in her hurry to get them out. 'It used to be William Kingsley. William *Robert* Kingsley. He was a neurologist who testified against two women accused of shaking their babies to death. Largely because of him, both of them were jailed, but they were released in the mid-1990s, when it was proved that the babies were far more likely to have died from complications resulting from illness or infection.'

Corinne was struggling to keep up.

'Are you saying he was struck off and then changed his name and continued practising medicine? Because surely that's illegal?'

Sitting on the bench, with her arms wrapped around her knees for warmth, Stella started giggling.

'I always think it's so funny when people say "practising medicine",' she said. 'As if it's a hobby.'

'He wasn't struck off, Mum,' said Hannah, impatiently.

'But he was publicly discredited. He must have thought it was easier to start again under a different name, in a different branch of medicine, without any question marks hanging over his reputation. You know how ambitious he is. That's probably what led him to volunteer himself as an expert in those cases in the first place. Wanting to make a name for himself as quickly as he could.'

Corinne could imagine it. The young Roberts. Handsome, charismatic and impatient to prove himself. Becoming known as an expert in a highly controversial, headline-making field would have seemed like an excellent shortcut to fame and glory.

'Oh, those poor women. Can you even imagine it – losing your baby, and then being accused of killing it yourself?'

As soon as she'd said it, Corinne wished it unsaid. Wasn't that just what had happened to Hannah? The baby had been real to her, and she'd lost her. Of course she could imagine it.

'Do you think the other patients ought to know his background?' asked Corinne. 'I mean, I thought full transparency was one of the cornerstones of public life these days.'

Hannah put a finger sideways into her mouth and sucked on the nail. It was a new gesture since her arrival at The Meadows, and it made the muscles in Corinne's chest constrict. She remembered how Roberts had called Hannah 'vulnerable' and she fought an urge to knock the finger out of her daughter's mouth, to force her back to the Hannah she used to be.

'I don't know,' said Hannah slowly, as if thinking

aloud. 'If there seems to be anything dodgy in Roberts' past, chances are the families will lose confidence. That means some of the parents, like Odelle's and Frannie's, will almost certainly pull them out of here.'

'Which is a good thing, isn't it?' Corinne persisted. 'You've always thought there was something not right about the way Sofia and Charlie died. Now here's a chance to raise the alarm and find out exactly what's been happening. I mean, it's not as if Roberts has an unblemished track record since switching to psychiatry. Look at what happened to Stella.'

It was the first time she'd alluded directly to the fact that she knew about Stella's past connection to Roberts, and for a moment she was worried she might have over-stepped the mark. But Stella merely fixed her with those stretched blue eyes and said nothing.

'I don't know, Mum, I feel really torn,' said Hannah. 'On the one hand, I do want everyone to know what kind of man Roberts really is – how ambitious and self-serving. But not until I know what's going to happen to the patients and staff here if he has to resign. People like Frannie and Odelle are so settled here. Everyone knows their stories. If the clinic closes down, it will be a huge wrench for them. And what about Dr Chakraborty, and Darren and Laura? I'd hate for them all to lose their jobs because of me.'

'You're not seriously suggesting we do nothing?'

'No. At the very least, the trustees of the clinic deserve to know about Roberts' background. But I'd prefer to hold off for a bit until we find out exactly what it's going to mean for everyone. I mean, it's not as if any of us in here are in any immediate danger from him. And the clinic does get results. You said so yourself. That's why you chose it.'

'Yes, but . . .'

Corinne stopped herself saying what she wanted to say, which was to ask where the results were for Hannah herself? Why her daughter, having seemed so much more herself, had stepped off a kerb in front of a lorry. Where was the quick fix she'd been so convinced they would find?

'I'm worried about you,' she said instead. 'I want to keep you safe, and I don't know if you are safe in here.'

She debated telling Hannah what Roberts had said about her being detained there against her will but, just as she was about to speak, the back door to the clinic was thrown open.

'There you are! I've been looking for you two everywhere. Why on earth are you standing out here in the cold?'

Laura was hopping from foot to foot in a blue-and-white stripy jumper, her short black hair spiky with rain.

'Hello, Hannah's mum!' she called out in a sing-song voice, before adding, 'Hannah, how about we go inside for our session now, hey? It's bloody well freezing out here.'

Corinne considered all the things she had still not told Hannah – about Steffie and the baby, and the secrets and lies with which her daughter's husband had coated his life.

'But Hannah, darling, I was hoping we'd be able to chat.'

'Later, Mum. I'll call you from the office phone.'

After they'd gone, Corinne and Stella gazed at one another. Stella had two spots of pink colour in her cheeks, like an old-fashioned doll.

'I expect you'll be taking Hannah away?' she said. 'The people I love always seem to be leaving me.'

'You need to get away from here too, Stella.'

Corinne waited for the inevitable question – 'But where would I go?' – and wondered how she would answer it.

So she was nonplussed when Stella raised those artificially blue eyes to her and asked something quite different.

'But who would I be?'

44

Hannah

'Smaller. Tighter. Tuck in those arms and heads.'

We are on mats in the dance studio, trying to make ourselves disappear.

'Now, slowly, slowly, start growing,' says Grace. 'First the tips of your fingers, then your wrists and elbows, your toes, the soles of your feet. Feel yourselves expanding. Stretch out your arms, your legs, unfurl every single vertebra in turn, make your necks as long as a giraffe's. Raise up the top of your heads as if someone is pulling on a string from above. Feel how tall you are. Give yourselves permission to get bigger, to take up more space. Take a deep breath and repeat after me, "I contain multitudes."'

'I contain multitudes,' we all mutter, our arms outstretched, necks craning.

I feel myself grow lighter. Since Mum's visit yesterday, when I told her about William Kingsley, my mind has been too churned up to relax. When I was with Laura afterwards she asked me to imagine I was on a riverbank in autumn with a gentle breeze blowing through the trees and causing coloured leaves to fall to the ground. 'Pick one up,' she told me. 'Feel its texture, stroke it against your cheek. Note how it's cool and damp against your skin. Now place it gently in the river and watch it float downstream. Pick up another one and put that too into the water. And another. Now imagine that each leaf contains a negative thought or memory. Watch them drift away.' Though I tried to focus on what she was saying, tried putting Oliver Roberts on a leaf and watching him drift away, I couldn't rid myself of the tight knot of dread in the pit of my stomach.

But today, standing on my mat, stretching every bit of me to accommodate my multitudes, I feel a sense of release. Normally, I run a mile from this sort of stuff. Megan once got dragged off to a breathing workshop by a new-agey friend of hers, and we laughed about it for days. 'I'm so much better at breathing than you,' she'd tell me. 'I'm a trained breather.' But I want to get better. I want to get out of here. I'll do as much growing and unfurling as it takes. When Danny comes tonight I'm going to tell him I'm coming home. I'm ready. And if he doesn't like it, that's too bad. I know he got hurt, and I'm truly sorry. But I don't think he was hurt as much as I was.

I know Stella will wait around for me after the class, but I want to be on my own. I want to make this sense of wellbeing last just a little bit longer. Not that I'm nervous of Stella any more. But I am sad for her. I don't know how she can be made whole again.

So I say I need the loo and dash out across the rose garden and round the back of the old building and in past the reception desk. I'm heading for the Mindfulness Area and the sanctuary of the egg chair but, through the glass window in the door that separates reception from the rest of the building, I see the route is blocked by Justin and Drew, who are talking to Dr Chakraborty. Justin has his back to me and doesn't notice me but, on the far side of him, Drew raises his head from his view-finder and stares at me through the glass. He is wearing a red jumper, against which his skin appears pale and grey. From this distance his eyes are like deep black holes, and I stop dead. Usually, Drew's face is an impassive blank, but now he twists his mouth into an expression I cannot read and which makes the skin on my arms break out in icy bumps, and I turn around and hurry back outside.

It's pleasant out here now there's a let-up in the rain, and the air has a freshness that I gulp down.

Conscious that the others will soon be spilling out from the dance studio, I head the other way, crunching over the gravel car park. There's a path that runs down from it, bordered by bushes, through which I get glimpses of the lawn on one side and the flower garden on the other. It leads to the vegetable plot, where, twice a week, Inès, the horticulture therapist with the lazy eye and the aged Jack Russell that always makes me think of Mum's dear departed Madge, comes to show us how to make mulch and check leaves for diseases.

I don't have much of a clue about gardening, but there is something therapeutic about getting your hands dirty and seeing things grow out of bare soil.

I go into the shed where we keep the tools. It's small, about two metres by three, and crammed with rakes and brushes and twine and shovels and things about whose function I have no clue. Selecting a small trowel and a pair of heavy-duty green gloves which are too big for my hands, I make my way back outside. Someone has left an empty sack by the door, and I grab it on the way out to preserve the knees of my jeans.

Most of the weeds come up easily, as if they weren't really growing at all, just passing the time. But some are really deeply entrenched and I have to dig my trowel into the earth underneath to loosen them.

While I'm doing this, I think of Danny. I have loved him since the moment I first saw him, and yet, can I say, hand on heart, that I have been happy with him? We have had moments of happiness, sure. Perfect days, like in that Lou Reed song. Perfect weeks even, staying in a beach bungalow in Thailand or holed up in a city neither of us knows, finding hidden treasure in the backstreet bars, staying up all night drinking unfamiliar drinks with strangers who become friends before the first glass is drained.

'But Hannah, if you can't be happy on holiday, God help you,' Becs said once, when I came back from a holiday in the early days of our relationship radiating contentment. 'It's how you are when you're home and arguing over who overfilled the food recycling bag that really counts.'

She was right. When the rows started, following the miscarriage and the IVF, we never addressed what was happening. We each hid more and more of ourselves from the other.

How else to explain *her*?

Steffie.

At the thought of her I start jabbing the sharp end of my trowel into the soil like I am prospecting for oil.

She came after him. It's what I always tell myself.

301

And yet women like Steffie don't do anything unless they're assured of success.

What do you expect? You lied to him. The accusatory voice in my head is never far away. But before I can crumble, another, unfamiliar voice pipes up.

He lied first.

I sit back abruptly on my heels contemplating this new voice and this new truth.

He lied first.

Three small words that change everything.

As I sit there pondering what it means, I become conscious of an uncomfortable prickling on my back. It's not warm here in the garden and I haven't got a coat, but this is different to feeling cold because I'm outside and underdressed.

This feels like being watched.

I whip my head around and scan past the flower garden to the car park and the back entrance of the clinic.

Nothing.

I turn back to my digging, but the feeling of being observed doesn't go away.

Once more, I turn around and, this time, I catch sight of a blur of movement behind the row of bushes that flank the path.

Red movement.

I scramble to my feet, my blood noisy in my ears. I don't know why I'm afraid of Drew, but I am. There is something about the cameraman loitering around our lives at the clinic, recording God knows what, that makes me feel as if a dampness has crept into my soul and is slowly spreading.

He is still shielded from sight by the bushes and I bolt for the shelter of the shed. Hidden behind it, I wait until he steps into the vegetable garden before dashing across the path and cutting diagonally across the lawn. The wet grass soon soaks my canvas shoes and I curse the lack of laces that makes running an impossibility. My breath is tearing from me in painful strips. When I get out of here, I will get fit. I will take up jogging. Join a gym. I will.

Glancing behind me, I see that Drew has spotted me and is coming up behind. I'm still anxious, but also embarrassed. He must know now that I am trying to avoid him. As I near the clinic, intending to go around the building and in through the front, I remember that the front door will be locked from the outside, so I change direction, cutting back through the car park towards the back entrance. Joni is on reception. 'Drew was looking for you,' she says, her strips of eyebrow travelling up her forehead when she sees the state of my shoes.

Inside, I think about going up to my room, but then imagine him coming up to find me and decide instead to go to the place I feel safest.

The art room is empty, save for the row of clay busts we've been working on. They're supposed to be representations of ourselves, and Stella has changed the nose on hers so many times that, yesterday, it fell off completely, which made us laugh a lot. Today, though, the busts are watching me steadily as I cross the room, towards Laura's little office at the back. The door is closed and I feel sure she's in there. Already, I anticipate the warmth from the fan heater, my fingers closing around the mug of tea she'll make me, the way we'll giggle when I ask her to hide me from Drew.

But before I've even fully opened the door I know the office is empty. There's no scent of jasmine, no waft of heat. I step inside, and close the door behind me.

'Hannah?'

The sound appears to be coming from only a few feet away, near the doorway of the art room. I don't think I have ever heard Drew speak, and his high-pitched, reedy voice comes as an unpleasant shock. I hold my breath, as if he might be able to hear me breathing through the wooden door of Laura's office.

For thirty seconds or more, I remain like that, not moving or breathing. When there is no further noise from outside I allow myself to exhale.

Then the door handle turns.

Before I have a chance to react, the door is flung open, light flooding in.

I close my eyes.

45

Laura

'I'm so happy Hannah has agreed to let me help her. She has such unhappiness stored up inside her. It's like a tumour. You know how you hear about cancer patients being cut open revealing tumours the size of a grapefruit or a football or a small child? Poor Hannah. There are some people who are too sensitive for this world.'

Her mother moaned and listed to the side and Laura leant forward across the bed to gently right her, feeling glad she'd made time for this rushed morning visit. She was due at Annabel's in twenty-five minutes and then The Meadows at one, but even the briefest chat was enough to brighten her mother's bleak life.

'It's all right, Mummy. I know you don't like to think about all the unhappy girls. But I'm looking after her now. Don't you fret. She already looked lighter when she walked out of my room yesterday. I won't leave her alone. You don't need to worry about that. I won't leave them to *him*.'

Outside in the lounge, Katya was eating a microwaved lasagne, still in its plastic tray. Her feet, still in the bunny slippers, were resting on the leather footstool. As ever, the television was blasting out.

'Is *Midsomer Murders*. Is about village where all the days people are dying. I would not like to live in this village.'

'Mummy seems more agitated than usual, Katya. Have you noticed anything?'

Katya shook her head, without taking her eyes off the screen.

'She just the same like always. District nurse come yesterday. She say your mother have red bottom. I explain her, your mother have red bottom because she have poo like yellow soup and is not possible to be all the time changing nappy.'

Katya had a round, doughy face framed by stringy brown hair, and a fleshy bottom lip that protruded when upset or affronted, as now.

'I am only one person, I say her. I have just two hands.'

Katya held up her pudgy palms in demonstration.

Driving to Annabel's through the cheerless hinterland of suburban north-west London, Laura was lost in thought about her mum.

She'd done what you were supposed to do. Left photographs prominently displayed around the flat showing her mother in her glorious youth, with her lovely dark hair curling around her shoulders and her wide, gap-toothed smile. And another with Laura as a baby, holding her up above her head and laughing, wearing paint-spattered shorts, her hair held back by a scarf and her bare feet planted firm and strong on the ground. It was supposed to help carers remember that there was a person there, who'd had a life, and laughed and loved, and held their baby up to a cloudless blue sky. There wasn't just this creature in the bed.

Yet sometimes she wondered if Katya, and Femi, who covered the night-time shifts three times a week, ever really believed her mother was human, like them. Because then they'd have to believe that what happened to her could happen to them, that they too could end up sitting in a nappy of yellow-soup poo. And that prospect was too terrifying to allow.

Normally, at this time of day, the roads near Annabel's house were relatively traffic free, but Laura noticed a queue of cars up ahead. As she drew closer, she realized she must have just missed an accident. A mangled bicycle was lying on the tarmac, one wheel completely buckled, and a white van was parked across the road, the front door hanging open. Laura turned off the ignition and hurried from her car. There were two men leaning against the back of the van and, as Laura came near, she heard one of them repeating, 'I didn't see him. I just didn't see him,' again and again.

Up ahead, she saw a small knot of people gathered round a shape on the ground and she gasped when she realized it was a young man, around sixteen, with an uncommonly beautiful face – on one side. The other side was pulverized, the skull above it caved in like the top of a boiled egg. Someone had placed a jacket over him like a blanket and Laura was astonished when she saw it move up and down. He was alive! And they were all just standing there, gawping.

She flung herself down next to him, seizing hold of his hand.

'You're all right,' she told him. 'You're going to be fine.'

She could see straight away that he wasn't all right at all.

Without thought to her clothes or to the watching spectators, who clapped their hands over their mouths in shock, she lifted his pulpy head on to her lap. 'You shouldn't move him,' someone said, but she ignored them. He was somebody's son. Somebody's baby. At least his mother would know he died knowing love and kindness and that he wasn't afraid.

'You rest now, lovely one,' she said to him, in a low, calm voice. 'There's nothing to be scared of. Everything is peaceful. Everything is love. You're going towards the light. You're going towards the love.'

It was just like hypnotherapy. Repeating key phrases and words. It was all about the voice, really. You wanted to make your voice into a warm bath they'd happily submerge themselves in.

It appeared to be working. The young man's breath was quieter and the half of his face that was capable of expression looked calmer.

She leaned further over him, so they were cocooned in their own world and he didn't have to see the rubber-necking onlookers who'd done so little to help, or the swollen, grey sky above them. Somewhere in her consciousness she registered the sound of a siren approaching, but she blocked it out, giving her whole attention to the broken boy in her lap.

'You're feeling so peaceful,' she told him. 'It's the most wonderful, blissful peace you've ever known. You feel calm and full of love and totally unafraid as you move towards the light, move towards the—'

'*Miss!*'

The man's voice was inches from her ear and, now, people were surrounding them, rough hands yanking her away.

'For God's sake, what were you playing at?'

The police officer who hauled her to her feet was overweight and flushed with anger.

'I was soothing him.'

'You were *suffocating* him!'

But as Laura got back in her car half an hour later to drive the rest of the way to Annabel's, having given her details and a witness statement to the police, she felt suffused in a warm glow of satisfaction. The police and paramedics didn't know anything. They hadn't seen the suffering on the boy's face.

She was the one who'd stepped in to help him.

And she'd do it again in a heartbeat.

46

Corinne

In her office at the university, Corinne gazed through her window at the man in the apartment facing her who appeared to be dancing. Raising one arm up in front of him and the opposite leg out behind. His bare foot was just visible over the top of the window frame, twitching like a tail.

He raised both arms up over his head and then bent over, disappearing from view. Not a dance then. Exercise. Suddenly, she was overwhelmed with tenderness for him, this middle-aged man trying to make the best of what he had.

On the desk in front of her was a thick volume called *Unpopular Culture: The Politics of Creativity in an Adversarial Society*, the latest academic tome from a visiting professor from University of California, Berkeley whom she'd invited to give a guest lecture.

She opened it determinedly and started reading. 'Aesthetic validation', 'urban ethnicity' – the phrases danced in front of her eyes, blurring into one incomprehensible line. She turned to the end of the book: 763 pages.

Concentration eluded her, thanks to a persistent tug

of anxiety, made worse by her being unable to pinpoint the cause.

The encounter with Steffie two days before had been unsettling. Not least because she'd found herself sympathizing with the woman who'd, knowingly or not, set off the chain of events that led to Hannah's breakdown. And Corinne dreaded having to tell her daughter about Eleanor's existence. But the sense of menace she'd felt after finding the baby hat on her doorstep had lifted now she knew that Steffie had dropped it by accident, the first time she'd tried to call on Corinne.

And although it was disturbing that Dr Roberts had started out practising medicine under a different name, he hadn't been struck off, so he wasn't breaking any law by continuing his medical career. And indeed, you couldn't argue with the results he got. She understood why Hannah wanted to delay the decision of what to do with the information they had. There would be time enough once she was well again.

But while there was an explanation or a resolution to each of Corinne's individual concerns, when you put them all together they formed a pattern of strange events that seemed too sinister to ignore.

And that was without Hannah's near-miss with the lorry. Though she seemed to be getting so much better, Corinne had to consider the possibility that her daughter might have stepped off that kerb on purpose.

Corinne had known enough friends and colleagues and students with depression to understand that mental health was not a linear construct. Mental health was like those crazy kaleidoscopic patterns that went round and round and folded in on themselves and then out again. And they were all just points of light in the pattern, coming in and out of focus, bigger, smaller, up, down. The lucky ones rode it out. The unlucky ones got sucked inside. There was no finish line with a big banner across it reading 'CURED'. There was just waking up one morning and realizing you didn't mind so much about having to get up.

But she still couldn't bring herself to believe Hannah had deliberately stepped in front of a lorry. *Not her daughter. Please, God. Not Hannah.*

The noise of an incoming email came as a welcome intrusion. In her inbox was a message from Paddy asking for a suggested reading list. It was polite and respectful, but distant, as if they'd never met in real life.

Awareness of having hurt his feelings was like a cheese wire around her heart. She thought about sending an explanation of what was going on, got as far as pressing reply but was stuck for the right words. Everything she wrote felt like a betrayal of her daughter. In the end, she deleted the draft and closed her inbox.

Through the window, the man in the opposite block was holding what looked to be a tin of beans in each hand and pumping each arm in turn into the air as if he were doing a routine to music that Corinne couldn't hear.

She thought again about Hannah, over there in The Meadows, under the care of Dr Roberts, who, it turned out, had not only returned a young girl to her abuser but also helped send two women to prison for crimes they did not commit, so shattering three families.

This was the man who got to decide whether to detain Hannah there against her will.

She called up her search engine.

What was the name Hannah had given her yesterday? William something. The surname was tantalizingly close – Corinne could almost taste it – yet every time she tried to pin it down, it moved out of reach at the last second. Had it always been like this, or was her memory getting worse? Like many of her peers, Corinne was always on the look-out for signs of a blunting of mental faculties, the dreaded flag staked into the top of the slippery slope.

She typed 'William neurologist shaken baby syndrome' into the search box and waited for the results to load.

Kingsley. That was it.

The links were mostly to newspaper reports and magazine features. Reading them tore at Corinne's heart. Grieving mothers, falsely imprisoned for killing their own babies. How would one survive such a thing?

Several of the reports carried photographs of Dr William Kingsley, the expert witness for the prosecution, arriving in court, and Corinne stared at these for a very long time. Even almost quarter of a century younger and clean-shaven, with short dark hair in place of his longer, white-streaked mane, Oliver Roberts was still just about recognizable if you knew what you were looking for, though Corinne suspected a person coming across his photograph randomly would be hard pressed to connect the two men.

Corinne skipped down the results, clicking on links that looked particularly informative. One of the two falsely accused women, Lucy McDermott, had a husband who'd stuck doggedly beside her after the arrest, spearheading the movement to get his wife's name cleared.

'I will never believe Lucy did anything to hurt our son,' he had told a tabloid paper, 'and I will never stop fighting for her release.'

The husband had thick fair hair that sprung up on one side but not the other, and his expression was a mixture of defiance and sadness that made Corinne's eyes blur with tears.

The second woman, Barbara Phillips, had been married just eight months at the time of her arrest. Her new husband was more non-committal than Lucy McDermott's and it didn't surprise Corinne to learn the marriage had ended while Phillips was still in prison. Phillips had an older daughter, then twelve years old, and one of the tabloids went to town on the circumstances surrounding the girl's conception. The father, it seemed, was a married man who'd begged his lover not to proceed with the pregnancy. 'Barbara is the most self-centred person I have ever met,' this man said when the media tracked him down. 'I actually think she got pregnant deliberately to try to force me to leave my wife.'

Talk about trial by media.

All the reports were dated 1994, when the women were first convicted, or 1996, when they were released, after it was proven the babies could have died from blood clots brought on by infection, but towards the middle of the third page there was a more recent link:

'The conviction was quashed but the nightmare never ends.'

She clicked and found herself looking at a feature from a Sunday-supplement magazine from 2009 investigating the human legacy of wrongful conviction. There was a case of a man who'd been falsely convicted of armed robbery until CCTV footage was tracked down showing him at a petrol station fifty-three miles away at the time the crime was committed. And another man who'd spent nineteen years behind bars for rape and murder before advances in technology showed the DNA found on the victim couldn't have come from him. Both were interviewed about the long-term psychological effects of being incarcerated for a crime they didn't commit.

Finally, there was an interview with Lucy McDermott, the first woman jailed for shaking her baby largely on the flawed evidence of Dr William Kingsley.

'I was grieving for my baby and I was in prison with women who believed I was a baby-killer. Even after I was completely exonerated, there were still people who believed there was no smoke without fire. That man destroyed my life.'

Corinne was so affected by Lucy McDermott's testimony and the raw pain in her words, even fifteen years after the event, and by the sheer devastation Dr Oliver Roberts had left in his wake, that it took her a few seconds to collect herself enough to read the next paragraph.

'Just how shattering the experience was can be gauged by the fate of Barbara Phillips, the second woman wrongly convicted on the evidence of Dr William Kingsley of shaking her own baby,' the newspaper feature continued. 'Following her release from prison, Phillips attempted to pick up the pieces, setting up home in a new town with her older daughter, who'd been taken into care while her mother was locked away, and reverting to her maiden name to disguise her past.

'However, she never completely recovered from her ordeal, suffering prolonged bouts of depression. In 1997, she attempted to take her own life by taking an overdose of the tablets prescribed for her depression. Though she survived, she suffered a devastating stroke which has left her unable to speak or care for herself.'

Instantly, Corinne was back in that poky flat, staring at the grubby pink ears of Katya's rabbit slippers as she shouted over the top of the television.

'Is long time since she had stroke. Maybe twenty year.'

Laura.

47

Laura

There was a gorgeous smell coming from Annabel's kitchen.

'Banana bread,' Annabel explained when Laura asked. 'I baked a quick batch just before you came.'

'Lovely,' said Laura, but the longed-for offer of a slice never arrived, not even after Laura told Annabel about the accident and how she'd nursed that poor broken boy. She could remember a time when Annabel used to bring her tea and home-made cakes and biscuits, but she'd been becoming increasingly distant recently, which only made Laura more needy. It sometimes seemed to her that, no matter what she did or how hard she tried, she would always be on the sidelines of other people's lives.

The smell of home baking was like a physical ache in Laura's stomach, a reminder of a life she'd never had.

'I used to bake with Mummy,' she said. 'She was the most wonderful cook.'

That was an exaggeration. Her mother had been a competent cook, nothing more. But Laura enjoyed the idealized version of her mum she'd created in her own head.

'And when I was still nursing and living in the shared

house with Tania and Nat and the other girls, we'd bake all the time.'

This was also a lie. It was true that Tania and Nat used to cook-together sometimes, sequestering themselves off in the kitchen with Amy Winehouse playing at full volume and erupting in peals of laughter that would tail off when Laura went in to see what was going on. But Laura had rarely made anything. So little point cooking for oneself.

'I'm thinking of going back to nursing, actually.'

There. That got Annabel's attention all right. Laura could tell by the way the other woman sat upright in her armchair and the new focus in her wide-set eyes. When Annabel spoke, however, it was in her usual measured tone.

'But what about your plans? You felt you were really making a difference at The Meadows. Remember we sat down together and made a list of all the people you felt you could help?'

That was better. Laura felt mollified. But then Annabel spoiled it by asking whether Laura felt she had a commitment problem. She reminded her of how, before she got so into yoga, she'd devoted her spare time to studying Eastern philosophy and before that meditation. And now the hypnotherapy as well.

'That was your idea!'

Laura was cross. She was sure the hypnotherapy had been Annabel's suggestion, and now she was being made to feel *flighty*. Anyway, what was wrong with diversifying? As far as Laura was concerned, life was like papier mâché: you layered it on, one piece over another, one experience over the next, blessing upon blessing, until you had something richly textured and vibrant.

'All I mean is that perhaps it's time to stick at something. Honour your commitments.'

She sounded so stern. It was all right for Annabel. She'd never be able to understand how people like Laura, who'd grown up the way she did, might feel they were incapable of stability, might even feel unworthy of it. But now Annabel surprised her by saying:

'Do you think there might be an element of self-sabotage? That when people start to like and appreciate you too much, you feel you don't deserve it?'

That was the thing about Annabel. You thought she didn't really get it, and then she said something so astute it took your breath away.

'Can I use your loo?'

Annabel hesitated for a moment before replying. 'Of course.'

Outside in the narrow hallway, the smell of cake was almost overpowering. There was a guest loo under the stairs, always spotlessly clean but so tiny one felt as if one was in a tiled coffin, so Laura ignored it and crept up the stairs instead, past a row of framed academic certificates. Upstairs, she padded along the landing, glad she'd removed her boots in the living room. The first doorway on the left was ajar and she peeped in. A pale green painted bedroom with a neatly made-up double bed. There was a cream duvet cover on the bed and a pair of tan sheepskin slippers tucked underneath it. Nothing to give anything away about the person who lived and slept here, whose head dreamed on that smoothly blank pillow.

Dissatisfied, she pushed open the door on the right of

the landing. Annabel's study. A bookcase running along the nearside wall was packed with well-thumbed academic books, while, directly opposite, a white desk sat underneath the single, mean window. Like everything else in this strange little house, the desk was clear of clutter, boasting only an open laptop, with a document up on the screen.

Well. No harm in looking, was there?

Treading as lightly as she could, Laura crossed the room to get a better look at what seemed to be a title page.

The Power of . . .

'What are you doing in here?'

Annabel snapped the laptop shut like a clam. She'd come up so silently Laura hadn't heard a thing. Why was she creeping around like that?

'I just thought I'd use the upstairs bathroom. More private.'

Annabel folded her arms. For a short person, she could look very forbidding.

'We've talked about this.'

Laura's mouth felt dry, but she made herself sound confident. 'Well. If it's that much of a problem for you, I'll use the one downstairs.'

She turned around and started down the stairs.

'Laura!'

Annabel's voice sounded loud and sharp. Laura stopped but didn't turn around.

'Laura,' Annabel resumed, moderating her voice so it more resembled her usual, measured tone. 'We've had this conversation before. Why do you find it so hard to respect boundaries. My house. My life. They're off limits.'

'I thought we were friends.'

Laura was aware of the whine in her voice but unable to stop it. Straight ahead of her, above the academic degrees, in her direct line of sight, was a small, framed photograph she'd missed before, of Annabel as a younger woman, holding hands with a small blonde girl with similar, flat features. A lump formed in Laura's throat so it hurt to swallow.

'That's just it, though, Laura, isn't it? I'm not your friend. Or your mother. I'm your psychotherapist.'

48

Hannah

'You're crazy.'

My heart has stopped its violent thudding, but I am still short of breath and wired up on adrenaline. My nerves feel like needles.

Drew is crazy.

Ever since he burst into Laura's office, where I'd been trying to hide from him, he's been telling me stuff. Crazy stuff. He says he knows everything there is to know about The Meadows. He says people don't notice him because he's unobtrusive and they say things they might not otherwise have said.

Also, he's set up tiny videocams in the communal rooms that film continuously, though, obviously, none of the footage can be used without permission. He started going through the film from the art room yesterday. And though you couldn't see into Laura's office, you could still pick up voices.

You could hear the things Laura said to Sofia, when she was still alive. And to Charlie.

And to me.

'It's the hypnosis. First she makes you feel calm and comfortable. Then she takes you deeper. Then she talks

322

about how there's a wonderful, peaceful place where all is light and love. You're all so special, she tells you. You deserve a safe place when the world gets too dark. Then, when you are completely relaxed and zoned out, she tells you how to get there.'

'Where?'

I am standing behind the armchair where I normally sit, putting it between me and Drew. My fingers pick at the tartan throw like they are tapping out a message in code.

'To the safe place. To the place you all want to be. To the light. With Charlie, it was by cutting herself. Except Laura didn't put it like that. She told her it was rubbing a massage point on her wrist, to release endorphins. Using something sharp. The sharper the better, she said. Charlie would know when she found something. Pain was release, she told her. She would find the most unimaginable peace, she said. With Sofia, it was different. She told Sofia she could fly.'

That's when I say it.

'You're crazy.'

But Drew acts as if I haven't spoken. 'She told Sofia she would find this beautiful place once she was weightless. That she only had to believe she could fly in order for it to be true. And with you, it was headlights. The lights would guide you home, she said. Follow the light.'

He is in front of the door, blocking my exit. The windowless room feels like it is closing in on me.

'She gave you triggers,' he continues. 'Certain things that would set you off in search of the safe place. A sense of being overwhelmed. Feeling claustrophobic or hemmed in. Too many demands being placed on you. Fear of the future. Dry mouth. Sweaty palms. Trigger, trigger, trigger.'

I have a flashback to standing on the side of the road in the drizzle with Stella. And that moment of painful clarity where I'd wondered for the first time how much it would end up costing me to stay with a husband who'd never fully acknowledged his own culpability. Right after that is when I'd looked at the lorry. *Follow the light.*

'Your visit to Laura yesterday was on the tape too,' Drew says.

There is not air enough in the room for the two of us. I feel light-headed, breathing in his exhaled breath. And violated. Drew is like a thief, rubbing grubby hands through things he has no right to. Those one-to-one sessions with Laura are where I have been most honest, laid myself most bare. And to know that Drew has listened to everything feels horribly exposing.

'She was talking to you about water, Hannah. Not like the first sessions, which were about traffic and how car headlights could guide you home. This time she told you your safe place was deep under the water. Deep. Deep. Deep. She must have said the word about a hundred times.'

Something darts like an eel through the murk of my mind, a memory that slips from my grasp as soon as I touch it. Drew sees something in my face.

'You remember, don't you? You know I'm telling the truth.'

But now the door opens, flooding the dimly lit room suddenly with light.

'Greetings,' says Laura.

She is smiling, but there is an alertness about her that makes me wonder just how long she has been standing behind the door and how much she has heard.

'Sorry.' Drew's voice is hardly more than a mutter. 'I'll be off now.'

He pushes past Laura without looking at either of us, and I should be relieved that he has gone, yet fear is tattooing itself in tiny pricks across my skin.

What is it I am not remembering? I curse last night's sleeping pill, with its morning-after fog.

'Is everything all right, Hannah?'

This is where I should tell her what Drew said, give her the chance to explain, to deny, to label him a fantasist.

'It's fine, Laura. We were just chatting. We came in here because it was quiet. You don't mind, do you?'

The words come from some part of me that seems separate from the rest. As I'm speaking, I'm edging round the chair towards the open door.

Suddenly, two things happen at once. Laura steps towards me just as Odelle appears in the doorway.

'Here you are, Laura. Did you forget you said you'd help me with my clay head? The mouth is all wrong.'

She glares at me as if I am intruding. Gratefully, I push past her. 'I'll leave you two to it.'

My heart feels as if it has come loose from its moorings and is ricocheting off the inside of my ribs, and my head is full of questions I can't answer.

In the hallway I hesitate for a moment under the shimmering glass chandelier. The earl eyes me coldly from the oil painting on the far wall. Then I press the exit button by the front entrance, yank open the door and begin to run.

49

Corinne

Pulling into the car park, with the gravel crunching under the wheels of her car, Corinne's chest was tight and painful, as if someone was sewing tiny stitches across the breadth of it.

As soon as she'd registered the import of what she'd discovered – namely that Laura Whittaker had a very good reason for wanting revenge on Dr Roberts – she'd tried to get hold of Hannah on The Meadows office phone, sitting rigid with tension while Bridget Ashworth went off to find her.

Please let her be safe. Please let her be safe.

But the longer the clinic manager was away from the phone, the more convinced Corinne became that something was wrong. And when Bridget did finally get back on the line to tell Corinne, in a tone soaked in disapproval, that Hannah seemed to have left the premises without letting anyone know or signing herself out in the 'special book', Corinne was already out of the door before she'd finished her sentence.

All the way there, she'd repeated her new mantra.

Please let her be safe. Please let her be safe.

Pulling into a space, Corinne cast her eye around the

327

car park, feeling a soft sag of relief at the sight of Laura's bubblegum-pink car. Wherever Hannah had disappeared to, at least she wasn't with *her*. Thank God.

Inside, she all but threw her bag at Joni, who was sitting on the reception desk.

'Someone's in a hurry,' said Joni, raising her already artificially arched eyebrows. She searched through the bag with what felt to Corinne like exaggerated thoroughness.

By the time Corinne reached the art room a balloon of tension had inflated inside her and was threatening to burst. Through the open doorway she saw that Laura was taking an art-therapy session. One of the patients, the woman who had only recently been admitted, was sitting on a striped deckchair, staring fixedly ahead as if in a dentist's waiting room, while the others worked on their drawings with sticks of charcoal.

Blindfold.

'Corinne! Do come in. I expect I'd better explain what we're doing. The ladies spent a good while studying Katy here before I put the blindfolds on, so they know roughly where the lines and curves should be. This exercise is about memory and interpretation and the things our minds hold on to.'

'Hannah?'

Corinne didn't trust herself to say more.

Laura frowned, wrinkling her nose and tilting her head to one side.

'I'm afraid Hannah isn't here, Corinne. She was here about half an hour ago, but she didn't come back, which is unusual. She normally never misses a class.'

Laura's brown eyes were melting chocolate pools

of empathy and, suddenly, Corinne found herself doubting everything she'd just learned. You could tell, couldn't you, if someone was pretending to be something they weren't? Once you knew what you were looking for, anyway. Yet everything about Laura screamed sincerity.

'Help!' The high-pitched cry caused Corinne's nerves, already stretched as tight as snare-drum skin, to snap.

Over on the far side of the room, near the window, Frannie was struggling with her blindfold, clearly in the grip of a sudden panic. As she stumbled, she knocked over her easel, sending it crashing to the ground.

'Oh my God!' cried Odelle, turning her face towards the source of the racket. 'What's happening?'

Laura hurried over to comfort the now semi-hysterical Frannie, and Corinne took the opportunity to slip out of the room. Every single cell and tissue fibre of her body strained to find her daughter and take her home.

She hurried up the stairs and along the corridor towards Dr Roberts' office.

'Excuse me! He's actually with someone at the moment,' Bridget Ashworth called out as Corinne passed the tiny admin office, but Corinne ignored her.

At Roberts' door, she knocked, and paused briefly before throwing it open and marching inside, only to stop short when she saw that Roberts was indeed not alone.

And the person with him was Danny.

'Corinne.' Danny was the first to recover. 'I'm just having a progress update from Oliver.'

Oliver?

'Oliver is strongly of the belief that Hannah is not yet

well enough to come home, and I have to tell you I agree.'

'Where is she? Where's Hannah?'

The two men exchanged a glance and an almost imperceptible shrug that ignited a spark of rage inside Corinne.

Dr Roberts spoke. 'Hannah seems to have taken herself off somewhere without notifying anyone or following procedures. Now, I appreciate she's a woman who knows her own mind and needs to assert her independence, but to me there are still question marks over this and some of her other recent behaviour.'

Question marks? The arrogance of him.

'I know who you are.'

'What?'

Roberts was caught off guard, his default smile frozen on to his face even while his eyes were clouding with confusion.

'How have you got away with it all this time? This criminal reinvention of yourself?'

'I'm afraid, Mrs Harris, I don't know what you're—'

'William Kingsley.'

The name was lobbed into the room like a live grenade and, for a split second, the three of them watched it in silence.

'Corinne, I really don't know what—' Danny began, but Roberts cut across him.

'I see you've been checking up on me.'

His voice was higher and tighter than normal, but still infuriatingly measured. He went on:

'Many professional people, medical staff included, change their names for one reason or another. I expect you changed your name when you were married. It's not unheard of.'

Danny turned his chair so he could see Corinne more easily and glanced from one to the other, his dark eyebrows furrowed.

'Are you honestly saying you didn't change your name and your medical specialty because two women wrongly went to jail on your account?'

Still Roberts remained calm, but at the top of his cheeks a network of burst capillaries burned a pattern of red lace into his skin.

'I still have faith I made the right judgement in those cases, Mrs Harris. And I had solid personal reasons for wanting to dissociate myself from my past. None of which have any bearing on my subsequent decision to retrain in psychiatry or my ability to do my job. I have an excellent reputation in this field, as you know, or you'd never have entrusted your daughter to us.'

'So it won't bother you to learn that the daughter of one of the women whose lives you destroyed is currently a paid member of your staff?'

Now she had him. Now he lost his loose-limbed, laid-back, stuck-on-smile demeanour and sat up straight, both his feet, in their leather brogues, flat on the floor.

Danny noticed the change, the question writing itself all over his face as he gazed at Roberts.

'Will someone please tell me what's going on?'

'Laura Whittaker,' Corinne said, still addressing herself directly to Roberts, 'is the daughter of Barbara Phillips, one of the women you helped put away for two years.'

She turned her eyes towards Danny.

331

'Barbara tried to kill herself a few years after she was released and hasn't been able to walk or talk or feed herself since. You could say Laura has grounds for bearing a grudge.'

'You can't seriously be saying . . .'

Roberts was on his feet. Now that the poise he wore like a Savile Row suit had been ripped away, he seemed sagging and older, his face collapsed, as if its customary smile was all that had been holding it up.

'You know she hypnotizes them?' said Danny, finally recovering himself.

'I know that's one of her areas, but I can assure you Laura Whittaker has never been given leave to practise hypnotherapy at The Meadows.'

'She might never have been given leave, but that hasn't stopped her bloody well doing it,' said Corinne. 'She's done them all. Charlie, Sofia, Hannah. Do you think that's a coincidence?'

'Are you suggesting she hypnotizes them to harm themselves? You know that would never work, don't you? Hypnosis can't persuade someone to do something against their will. That's not how the human psyche works.'

'Oh, and you'd know how the human psyche works, would you?' Corinne was furious. 'Even though you failed to spot that one of your patients here is someone you've treated before – and let down badly?'

'Now you've completely lost me, Mrs Harris. Laura Whittaker was never my patient, and neither was her mother.'

'No, but Catherine Pryor was.'

Roberts was still standing by his desk, as if caught on

the cusp of an exit he never quite managed to execute. His face betrayed a fleeting recognition, as if the name was familiar but too elusive to place.

'I can't discuss my patients with you, Mrs Harris.'

'I'll fill you in then. She was the twelve-year-old who confided in you about her abusive stepfather and who you chose not to believe, effectively sending her back into his care.'

Now, finally, Roberts became angry, the skin on his cheeks darkening.

'I imagine you are talking about a patient from Westbridge House. I don't need to tell you I was not implicated in any wrongdoing there. Whatever fault there was was deemed to lie with the clinic's director Professor Dunmore, who turned out to be quite a dangerous individual. I have to tell you, Mrs Harris, I do not appreciate the direction this meeting is going in. Your insinuations are beginning to border on the slanderous. I must ask you to leave and to put any issues you might have in writing, and I will do my best to address them – once the clinic's legal adviser has checked them over.'

'I'm not going anywhere without my daughter. And nobody here seems to know where she is.'

Danny sprang to his feet.

'If that woman has her somewhere—'

'She's not with Laura. I've already checked.'

'But what if she's told her to do something to herself? Got into her subconscious. I don't know how it works.'

'I've told you,' said Roberts, 'that's just not possible.'

Danny made a sudden movement towards Roberts,

and for a moment Corinne thought he was about to hit him, but instead he pushed past.

'I'm going to look for her,' he said, throwing open the door.

'I've done nothing wrong,' Roberts repeated after Danny's retreating back, his voice paper thin.

Nothing wrong? Corinne thought as she hurried after her son-in-law. All this damage?

Up ahead, she could see Danny striding towards the art room. She caught up with him just as he burst inside.

'Where is she?' he bellowed, advancing on Laura, who was in the far corner of the room, tightening Judith's blindfold.

'Oh God, Oh God, Oh God, Oh God.' By the window, Frannie rocked on her chair, plucking at her hair. 'Oh God, Oh God, Oh God.'

There was a clicking sound to Corinne's right. Justin Carter, switching on his microphone. 'Laura, we know who you are,' she called out. 'We know who your mother was . . . and what Roberts did. We know how awful it must have been for you, but you know Hannah had nothing to do with that. We just need her to be safe.'

Laura, still half bent behind Judith, seemed frozen into place, one hand still holding the end of the scarf she had tied around Judith's eyes.

Danny had crossed so he was just a couple of feet from Laura, with only Judith's easel standing between them, like a splattered wooden shield.

'Where is she? Where's my wife?'

'You're intruding into our safe space.' Odelle put down her brush and was standing by her workspace, her trembling fingers clutching on to the tray of her easel as if to stop her legs snapping under the weight of her upper half like two sticks of dried spaghetti.

'We have a right to feel protected in our safe space. Isn't that true, Laura?'

'Absolutely,' said Laura, recovering enough to step forward and fling an arm around Odelle's shoulders. 'I think Hannah's mum and husband have misunderstood something, but it's nothing for the rest of you to worry about.'

Nina, who'd been hopping from foot to foot throughout the entire confrontation, let out a bark of laughter. 'This is brilliant,' she said. 'This is effing brilliant.'

Corinne felt like the room was moving under her feet, the walls coming towards her.

'Corinne? What's going on? Is Hannah in trouble?' It was a measure of Corinne's distracted state of mind that she hadn't even noticed Stella standing off to the side, wearing her bright, blonde hair twisted up high on her head and secured with a red clip decorated with tiny, intricate fabric red roses.

'I don't know,' Corinne said. 'I think she might be. We need to find her.'

Laura stepped forward to stand in front of Corinne, so close Corinne found herself leaning back, just to put space between them.

'I have no idea where Hannah is,' said the art therapist in her most honeyed tone. 'As you can see, I'm in the middle of teaching a class. Like I told you, Hannah was here earlier and she seemed perfectly fine. I'm sure there's no need to worry.'

Laura's head was cocked to one side so her smile

appeared to slide down one side of her face. She took another step forwards and Corinne breathed in, shrinking back from the ruthless intensity of her.

She was quite mad. Why had no one noticed?

Corinne was conscious of a movement behind her right shoulder. She started when she realized Justin Carter, the documentary maker, was by her side, looking uncharacteristically flustered.

'Not now,' she snapped, turning on him. 'Have you people no shame?'

'Water,' he said, nonsensically.

'Oh, for fuck's sake,' said Danny. 'Now the fucking media are joining in. This place is a circus!'

'What do you mean "water"?' Desperation cracked in Corinne's voice.

'It's what Drew told me. Only now I can't find him to ask him to explain it to you.'

'Well, *you* explain then.'

'Apparently, *she*' – he flicked his head in Laura's direction – 'said it to Hannah. In hypnosis. She said that if she was stressed she should head for deep water. That would be her safe place. Look, I know this sounds crazy, but Drew said that was Hannah's trigger.'

'What the fuck?' The words exploded out of Danny, and Justin took a step backwards.

'Apparently, she uses triggers to make them do things. Look, I didn't really understand half of what he was saying. It was about half an hour ago and he was in a rush to go somewhere and he wasn't making sense. It didn't click until just this minute that there might be anything sinister about it.'

Corinne was floundering. She didn't understand.

'Oh my God!' The exclamation went up from the easel nearest to Laura's office, behind which the new patient, whose name once again escaped Corinne, had been sitting in silence this whole time.

'I saw her. Hannah. I saw her. Oh my God.'

'For fuck's sake, why didn't you say?' Danny was across the room in a fraction of a second, his six-foot-two frame looming over the woman's chair. She crossed her arms over her chest as if under attack, and Corinne rushed over to pull Danny aside.

'Where did you see Hannah? Please, try to remember. You could really help us.'

The woman seemed mollified and uncrossed her arms.

'I saw her about half an hour ago when I was on my way here. She was heading down to the lake.'

50

Hannah

It happens like a switch being thrown.

One minute I am stumbling through the trees with my breath being torn from my throat and my heart thudding in my ears like the bass from the house music we used to listen to at university a lifetime ago, and then I emerge on to the lawn and the lake is there, stretching away from me, flat and still, like a watery blanket I could wrap myself up in and, instantly, I am calm.

It's the strangest thing. All the stress of the last few weeks and months; the nights I'd lie in bed unable to sleep while Steffie's features painted themselves across my eyelids; the mornings I'd look at Danny's face on the pillow next to me and see a stranger lying there; those strange dreamlike months of the pregnancy-that-wasn't where I floated around as if on a cloud, ignoring the tiny worm of anxiety that was steadily eating its way through my gut. The cold-sweat agony of ending up in here and having to face up to what I'd done, the lies I'd told, the lies I'd allowed myself to believe. Losing Sofia, then Charlie. *Bish bosh.* All of that drains from me as I gaze out across the expanse of water.

In its place, I am filled with a warm rush of wellbeing.

It is as if all my life – the good, the bad, the heartwarming and heartbreaking – has been leading up to this one point. And here, by this lake, is exactly where I am supposed to be.

'Hannah!'

Someone is calling my name from a distance, and I peer out across the lake and suddenly, incredibly, Charlie is there, her dark head bobbing about in the middle of the water.

'Charlie?'

She waves.

'Come in. It's gorgeous. Sofia is here.'

I see now that there's another head just behind Charlie's, another hand waving.

I take five steps forward until I am on the very edge of the bank, where it tips down steeply. If I look ahead, the water looks black but, straight down below me, I can see dark fingers of weeds under the surface, waving at me through the murk.

'Hannah!' Charlie calls again. 'Stop being such a wuss and get in here.'

I look across to the middle of the lake, where she is splashing about with Sofia in their little pool of sunshine, and smile, and it feels like the first time I have smiled in months. And I feel a warmth spreading through me as if the smile has unblocked something that has been blocked for a long time.

'Coming,' I say.

And I jump.

51

Corinne

Corinne hated running, but here she was, flying across the hallway and pushing through the huge front door, and not understanding why it wouldn't open until Danny pressed the exit button to the right, and then they were outside and following the path around the side of the house past the dance studio to the back, where the lawn stretched away in front of them, the lake shimmering in the distance.

Now she was again running, running. And Danny was behind her, even though he was so much younger and ought to be faster, but there was no time to think about what that meant.

Please let her be safe. Please let her be safe.

The words kept pace with her feet pounding the wet grass.

Please let her be safe.

And now they were halfway down and . . . Yes. Yes. Something was moving in the water. Far, far, out in the middle, where it was deepest. Oh God.

She was too far out. Corinne could see that, even from here. The shape that was recognizably Hannah's head, with Hannah's streaming blonde hair, kept dipping under the surface. One minute there, the next gone, and Corinne, running, would not breathe until she saw it again. But the gaps between the reappearances were getting longer and longer and Corinne knew they would not reach her in time.

She turned her head. 'Run!' she screamed at Danny. And he went pelting down the slippery grass, just as Hannah's head slipped once more under the surface of the lake.

'Look!'

It was Stella shouting behind her, that husky voice unmistakeable, even now, when the effort of breathing was scraping her smoke-ravaged throat.

'There's someone there. To the left. See?'

Corinne slowed to look where Stella was pointing and, sure enough, there was someone else there. Already in the water. Heading out towards the middle. Towards Hannah. *Please hurry.*

In the middle of the lake, Hannah's head once again sank slowly under the water, just as Danny reached the water's edge and began taking off his shoes.

Behind him, Corinne held her breath, waiting for Hannah to reappear, but the surface of the water had closed over her as if she'd never been there.

'Hannah!'

Her scream tore a ragged hole through the air.

52

Hannah

'Hannah!'

Charlie's voice isn't calm any longer. Instead, there is an urgency to it that jars. I close my eyes and try to return to the peace I felt just a few moments ago, that comforting sense of safety and wellbeing. But though I try to relax, I cannot find again that feeling of grace I had when I started swimming across the lake.

'Hannah!'

The shriek goes right through me like an electric charge, jolting me into life, and now I am scared, feeling myself being sucked under the water. I open my eyes and everything is black around me. Holding my breath, I try to propel myself upwards, but my foot is caught on something deep down there in the darkness. I start to flail around with my arms, panicking, fighting against the lake and the blackness.

I struggle furiously, kicking out with my legs, trying to free my foot, but I cannot get loose. The pressure is building inside me from holding my breath.

Is this really how it ends?

I'm still fighting, but I can feel myself weakening.

There's a darkness on the perimeter of my thoughts that seems to be growing, pressing in on me.

An image of Mum comes into my mind, curled up on her old squishy sofa with her feet tucked under her and a glass of wine in her hand, smiling at me, with our sweet old dog Madge by her side, and I send a silent message to her. *I'm sorry. I love you.*

And now the pressure is becoming unbearable, causing a pain that mushrooms out from my chest until it fills every part of me, and I press my lips together, but the urge to breathe is too great to keep them pressed, and I can't help it. I open my mouth.

53

Corinne

Hannah had been under the water for too long. Though Danny was in the lake now, Corinne could already see he wouldn't make it in time.

All her attention was now fixed on the unknown person swimming out.

Come on, Corinne urged. *Please. Come on.*

Now that head too disappeared. But was that the exact place where Hannah had gone down? Corinne couldn't be sure. An image came into her mind of her daughter floating in dark water and she made a sound like a cat crying that shocked even her.

She was vaguely aware of others gathering beside her on the bank – the bright flash of Stella's hair, Roberts looking, for once, flustered, his tie flapping over one shoulder, his hair damp and dishevelled, as if he had just rubbed it with a towel.

The unknown rescuer's head reappeared and Corinne held her breath, watching for a break in the water that meant Hannah was coming up too, but there was nothing. Then, once again, the head dipped beneath the water, leaving the surface smooth.

Time stretched itself tight, the air pulsing with anticipation and dread.

Please please please please please.

Finally, a shape appeared. Corinne's heart sank when she recognized the dark hair of the stranger who was trying to save her daughter but who had now started swimming back towards them, as if giving up.

But no. Something else was in the water. A long, black shape being dragged behind the swimmer.

And there was Danny, finally arriving on the scene, taking over and pulling the shape to the shore. And, yes, Corinne could see now. It was a person. Hannah. Her Hannah.

Hope flared sharp inside her, replaced almost instantly by a gripping fear when she saw Hannah wasn't moving.

As the trio approached, Corinne's attention was fixed on Danny and his cargo. When they were just feet away from the bank, she stretched out her hand as far as it could go, not caring if she toppled into the water.

All around, the other onlookers were reaching out to help haul the unresponsive Hannah out of the water, and there was such frantic chaos that Corinne didn't immediately notice the person clambering out of the lake after Danny and sinking on to the ground at her feet until she felt a hand on her leg, a familiar voice.

'Mum? Is she OK? Is Hannah OK?'

She looked down at the slight, prone figure at her feet, dark hair plastered to her head, clothes dripping wet, shivering uncontrollably in the cold air.

Hannah's rescuer was Megan.

54

Hannah

The sky is the colour of the dirty water Danny used to leave in the sink after he'd finished washing up but forgotten to take the plug out. I can still remember the irrational surge of anger every time I came into the kitchen and saw those few inches of greasy, filthy water. I'd taken it as a swipe at me, a kick in the teeth, two fingers up at my bourgeois houseproudness. Now it occurs to me it was just, as he said at the time, dirty water. Nothing more.

I have allowed myself to be distracted by things that do not matter. I have allowed myself to be defined by what I do not have. I have lost sight of the beauty of this grey sky, of this damp air, of the faces of people gathered around me trying to keep me warm, of the sheer, vast, grubby, breathing, pulsing majesty of it all.

I choose life.

I choose my mother dancing around the kitchen to Beyoncé on a Saturday morning. I choose my sister raising her eyebrows in that arch 'Really?' expression that used to drive me mad. I choose my memories of Madge nudging her way under my duvet with her cold, wet nose, and of Danny, back in the days when we were invincible. I choose Becs and Stella and all the friends who raise me up and challenge me and tell me if I have spinach in my teeth or questionable taste in men and stop me falling.

I choose this. I choose life.

All of it.

55

Corinne

After Corinne's marriage ended, it was Sundays she minded most of all. As a child, Sunday had been the most boring day of the week, no television apart from sport and *Songs of Praise*, no shops open, just a yawning chasm of slowly ticking minutes. But when she and Duncan were together and the girls were young, Sunday became her favourite day. Duncan was no cook, but he prided himself on his roast and would spend the morning peeling and chopping while Corinne and Megan went to watch Hannah playing netball or football or whatever sport was flavour of the month at that time. Then the afternoon was family time, curled up together on the sofa watching a movie or playing a game, or testing whichever daughter was currently revising for an exam.

But the divorce had coincided with the girls going off to lead their own lives, with their own ideas of what the weekend should mean, and Corinne had found herself increasingly transported back to the stultifying Sundays of her childhood, eating baked beans on toast alone in front of the television, afraid to invade the sanctity of her coupled-up friends' weekends.

Which is why, as she stood at the cooker, making a last-minute bread sauce from a packet and listening to the chatter of voices from the living room, she was over-come by an enormous wave of gratitude. She'd come so close to losing everything and yet, here she was, about to serve an admittedly imperfect roast dinner to the people she loved most in the world.

'Is it ready yet, Mum? We're starving.'

Still such a jolt of pleasure from seeing her younger daughter here in her kitchen. Megan would be flying back to the States in a few days, but Corinne had seen a lot of her over the week she'd been here. And, after her original plan to visit Megan the previous spring had to be shelved when Hannah fell ill, she and Hannah now had Christmas in New York to look forward to.

When Corinne thought about how differently things could have turned out if Megan hadn't made that mad, spur-of-the-moment decision six months ago to fly back to confront Hannah at The Meadows and force her to see her . . . Well, Corinne tried not to think about that.

Finally, the food was ready and everyone was seated around the table.

'This is fantastic,' said Paddy, momentarily resting his big hand on her knee under the table.

'I wouldn't go that far,' laughed Corinne, brushing her hair out of her eyes and hoping she didn't look as hot and flustered as she felt. How strange it was having Paddy here with her and her daughters, and yet, at the same time, how very natural it felt. Especially now she was no longer his supervisor.

Early days, of course. But still.

Hannah was carving the chicken, still wearing the

baggy sweatshirt and leggings she'd put on earlier, straight from the shower. Corinne couldn't claim it had been plain sailing having her older daughter living here with her over the last six months, adjusting to each other's routines and idiosyncrasies, but overall, it had been rewarding on a level she'd never imagined. Hannah was moving out soon, which was only natural. When Becs' lodger had given notice, it was too good an opportunity to pass up. Corinne would miss her.

She glanced at Paddy, who was telling Megan about the summer he'd spent in New York as a nineteen-year-old, going door to door selling hideous artwork featuring the Statue of Liberty embroidered in neon thread on a black velvet background.

On the other hand, having her home to herself again would have some advantages.

Hannah's phone started ringing. Why on earth she'd decided to make her ringtone that Beyoncé song, Corinne would never know.

'Danny,' Hannah said, glancing at the screen. 'I'll call him back later.'

Corinne tensed but held her tongue. Though she still found it hard to forgive her soon-to-be-ex-son-in-law, she had to accept this was Hannah's life. Hannah's decision.

'Don't look like that, Mum. I'm not about to get back with him, if that's what you're worried about.'

This was a new thing. Hannah's uncanny ability to tell what she was thinking. Corinne supposed it had something to do with them living so much in each other's pockets these past months.

'I'm not worried.'

'Yeah, right. Look, Mum, I still care about him. Of course I do. You can't turn emotions off like a stopcock. But I don't love him. Not any more. I feel a bit sorry for him now, actually. I mean, what's he ended up with? No job since he had that showdown with Dad and stormed out, nowhere to live once the flat lease is up. And it's not as if he's going to be playing happy families any time soon.'

Corinne had dreaded telling Hannah about Steffie and Eleanor. After everything she'd gone through trying to have a baby with Danny, everything it had cost her, how would she cope with finding out another woman had had his child?

In the end, though, Danny had told her himself, blurting it out while Hannah was still in hospital, recovering from hypothermia. And though she had been devastated, she hadn't fallen apart. By then, she'd already decided to separate from him so, in a sense, she said later, his confession made that decision easier.

Corinne had never told either of her daughters about her first encounter with Steffie here in the hallway of her cottage, or how she'd held Eleanor while Steffie went to the loo, and how the tiny, snuffling creature had nuzzled into that hollow between collarbone and neck that always seems just made to fit a baby's head. Nor had she told them about meeting up with Steffie a second time, or about offering to give her a reference so that she could apply to university as a mature student. She liked her. That was the thing. Whenever Corinne thought back to that strange house in Tunbridge Wells, or to Patricia Garitson complaining that children could be disappointing, she felt a rush of pity for the young woman who'd believed Danny Lovell was her fresh start, her reward for surviving her past. 'In a way, I was as delusional as Hannah,' Steffie had told her. 'The truth was staring me in the face, blowing a bloody vuvuzela, but I didn't want to see it.'

If there was one thing Corinne had learned from the past year, it was how fine the line was that separated what was 'normal' from what was not, and how easy it was for a person to stray across it, reality unravelling until life itself was in freefall. She admired Steffie Garitson for trying to transcend the destructive pull of her family and for holding firm when a newly separated Danny came begging for a second chance, as Corinne had no doubt he had. She'd seen the way he played with that silver bangle Steffie had given him, as if it were a good-luck charm. If only he'd had the courage right from the start to tell Hannah he'd met someone else.

'He's not a bad person,' Hannah said, once again reading her thoughts. 'Just a bit weak. Like we all are.'

'Maybe he'll end up back with *her*. Serve them both right,' said Megan, prodding her stuffing with suspicion. 'I might be wrong, but isn't stuffing supposed to have a bit of give to it?'

'I may have left it in the oven slightly too long,' admitted Corinne. 'And if you're talking about Danny and Steffie, I'm quite sure she wouldn't go near him. She had no idea he was still married.'

'That's what they always say,' said Megan.

Later, while they were clearing up, Hannah lowered her voice to a theatrical whisper to say, 'I think Megan likes Paddy. That's like the papal seal of approval.'

Corinne felt herself glowing with pleasure.

'What time are you seeing Seema tomorrow?' she asked, changing the subject.

'I was going to talk to you about that,' said Hannah, turning away to put a saucepan into the cupboard. 'I've decided to cut my sessions down to once a fortnight rather than once a week. Seema agrees.'

Corinne bit back her first reaction, which was to say, *No. It's too soon.* When Hannah had been discharged from hospital following her near-drowning, she'd started off as an outpatient at their local hospital's psychiatric clinic, going in every day to talk through what had happened. Then, after a month, she'd gone down to twice-weekly sessions with Dr Seema Chauhan, and then once a week. Corinne worried she was leaving herself open to relapse, but she knew better than to argue with her headstrong daughter. 'You have to let her get back to herself,' Paddy had told her, just a few days before. 'And maybe part of that is letting her make her own mistakes.'

'If you're sure,' she said mildly.

'Mum. It's fine. I just want to get on with my life.'

'I know you do, sweetheart.'

Neither of them voiced what they were both thinking. That it was never going to be possible to leave Laura Whittaker and her legacy behind completely. Not just the two patients she'd induced to take their own lives, but also poor Drew Abbott. The cameraman's body had been found in the egg chair in the Mindfulness Area hours after the ambulances taking Hannah and Megan to hospital had departed. His phone was in his hand and the theory was he was about to phone the police when he was killed by a single blow to the skull from a baked clay head that was found at the scene.

By that time, Laura was long gone, having slipped away from the clinic while everyone was watching the drama unfolding down at the lake. The manhunt that followed was one of the biggest in recent history and had ended only when her pink Beetle was found parked by the cliffs at Beachy Head, her bag and phone still inside.

That didn't stop some speculating that she was still alive. There'd been a couple of unconfirmed sightings in France, and one in the Netherlands. But most people accepted she'd thrown herself into the sea rather than risk being confronted with the reality of her crimes.

Corinne had hoped that would be an end to it, but the media had latched on to Laura's case with barely disguised glee, combing through her life, interviewing old schoolmates and fellow nurses from the hospital where she used to work, who all professed themselves stunned. She was odd, they said, but harmless. The phrase 'she wouldn't hurt a fly' came up again and again. Several people brought up her first two victims' histories of suicide attempts and self-harm. 'Maybe she thought she was doing them a favour,' was one comment that had stuck in Corinne's mind.

The official line was that she'd engineered the deaths of the women at The Meadows to destroy Oliver Roberts' reputation and close down the clinic to which he'd dedicated his life. There was speculation that she'd stumbled on his new identity after seeing him interviewed on television, and that had prompted her to switch from nursing to occupational therapy, and then art therapy. Some had even suggested that she'd made a half-hearted attempt to confess after the death of Sofia Redding, which is why Charlie Chadwick was researching the initials WK on the morning she died. 'DID PSYCHO THERAPIST TIP OFF SECOND VICTIM?' screamed one tabloid headline.

Interest in the case had only intensified after Justin Carter's documentary had been aired the previous month, to furious interest. Hannah had refused to watch and Corinne had had to switch off after the message 'This film is dedicated to the memory of Drew Abbott' flashed up in the opening frame.

Just the day before, Corinne had come across a newspaper article written by an academic she'd met once at a university function asserting that Laura Whittaker had a God complex. 'When she saw people suffering, making multiple suicide attempts, she felt compelled to put them out of their misery, as she saw it, in a way she couldn't bring herself to do with her own mother,' he speculated.

Oliver Roberts had also gone to ground. 'On sabbatical' is what The Meadows' website had said before it was shut down. Corinne suspected he'd be back once he'd reinvented himself again. The clinic itself was closed while an investigation took place into what had gone wrong. The patients had dispersed, mostly to other psychiatric facilities. Odelle – who police now believed had been the original intended third victim before Hannah let slip the name William Kingsley in front of Laura and became the new focus of her attention – was, unexpectedly, back home. Her near-miss seemed to have reset something in her brain, prompting the realization that she really, really didn't want to die, and she'd begun eating again. She'd called Hannah a couple of months before to apologize for the things she'd done while they were all at The Meadows – putting the macabre toy in her room after Hannah had talked in Group about buying a cuddly rabbit for her unborn baby, sketching a baby into Hannah's colouring book, sending the scan picture. She'd been jealous, she admitted, that Laura was giving Hannah attention instead of her. Now she realized that had probably saved her life. 'I wasn't myself,' Odelle told her by way of explanation. Hannah could understand that.

Against all medical advice, Stella had insisted on moving back to the Notting Hill flat her mother had bought her when she left school. The last time Hannah had visited she'd found literature from a cosmetic surgery clinic in South Africa. 'I was only browsing,' she'd said.

Some scars run too deep to be healed.

In Corinne's kitchen, Hannah turned back to face her mother, leaning against the worktop with a tea-towel flung over one shoulder. Corinne recognized it as one Megan had brought back from the States that bore the Aristotle quote 'No great mind ever existed without a touch of madness.' 'It's post-ironic,' Megan had explained, and for a moment Corinne's heart had stopped, waiting for Hannah's reaction, to see how fragile was this newly born truce between her daughters. But Hannah had laughed.

'Mum, I just wanted to say, because I don't think I ever said it before, how grateful I am. If you hadn't believed me—'

'Don't be silly. Of course I believed you. You're my daughter.'

And yet there had been moments of doubt, and for that Corinne would always reproach herself.

They both knew it would never be completely behind them. But some truths were better left unspoken.

Now Corinne was aware of the knife edge on which all their lives balanced, there would always be a tiny knot of anxiety in the pit of her stomach. Still, she couldn't help feeling optimistic. They'd faced down the darkness once, she and her two daughters. And they could do it again, if they had to.

Reality was more fluid than she'd ever imagined. The human brain more fragile. And sometimes, love wasn't enough to win out. Yet it was all they had.

It was everything.

56

Annabel

At her neat, white desk in her neat, boxy house, Annabel was making some last-minute adjustments to her manuscript and feeling more energized than she had in the last fourteen years. This was it. She was sure of it. The book that was going to launch her back to the forefront of psychiatric research. She smoothed her hand across the title page.

The Power of Persuasion, by Professor Annabel Dunmore.

Oh, but it was beautiful. And bold. And brilliant. After nearly a decade and a half in the scientific wilderness, hiding away in this anonymous little house, listening to dull people talking about their dull problems for sixty-five pounds an hour, not even able to call herself a psychiatrist any more, just a wishy-washy, second-rate 'therapist', at last she was going to be back in the spotlight. Thanks to Laura Whittaker. Really, Annabel could kiss her.

If she wasn't dead.

Her triumph was all the sweeter for having been so long coming. Her years of patient planning had finally paid off.

When she'd been struck off following the debacle at Westbridge House, Annabel had been so utterly destroyed that it had taken a few months to realize that it was her own protégé, Oliver Roberts, whose evidence had formed the backbone of the case against her. By then she'd lost everything. The career she'd sacrificed everything for lay in tatters, her husband of fifteen years had filed for divorce and been awarded full custody of their daughter. She'd been labelled a neglectful mother. No one had even tried to understand how utterly devastated she was, how unable to focus on anything except the injustice that had been done to her.

When she'd finally hauled herself out of the dark pit of despair and moved into this house, which was all she could afford, since her husband and daughter got to stay in the family home, she'd started researching Dr Oliver Roberts with all the zeal she'd previously devoted to her work. She'd always known about his past and the flawed evidence he'd given in the trial of those two women. He'd had to admit all that when he first applied for the job at Westbridge House, but she hadn't let it influence her decision to hire him. Everyone deserves a second chance. And besides, she recognized that ambition to forge a name for oneself.

Which had made his betrayal all the harder to stomach.

After her very public disgrace, she'd read everything there was to read about Dr William Kingsley and the two women whose lives he'd helped destroy. And at the same time, she'd followed the career of Dr Oliver Roberts, keeping tabs on him.

Well, she had precious little else to do with her time.

When he'd opened The Meadows, she'd at first been full of such bitterness, she'd woken every morning feeling as if she were choking. But after a while, she'd realized that here might be an opportunity to settle some scores. When she read about him in the paper, mixing with celebrities at fundraisers or delivering a keynote speech to a rapt audience, she'd anticipate the pleasure she'd get from unmasking him to these acolytes as a twice-discredited opportunist.

But then, one morning, she'd woken to a Google alert saying there was a new link to Dr William Kingsley. And she'd clicked on it and found herself reading an interview with a nurse identified only as Laura whose mother had been sent to jail on Kingsley's evidence and who had been left totally dependent following a botched suicide attempt after her release. 'I try not to hate anyone,' the woman said. 'But if I could, I would make Dr Kingsley pay for what he did to my family.'

Annabel could still remember the thrill that had passed through her from the tips of her fingers and toes, rising up through her stomach, flooding her brain with excitement as she read. With the few biographical details the interview gave away, it wasn't hard to work out which hospital Laura worked at. And her old professor of psychiatry ID came in handy when asking around to find out which nurses called Laura matched the age and profile of the woman in the interview.

For the first time in years, Annabel had felt alive again.

She'd been able to tell right away from the newspaper interview that here was a desperately needy individual. Annabel had worked in the past with people whose relationships with parents had been severed suddenly in childhood, and they'd almost all remained stuck there, their emotions never fully maturing beyond that point of loss.

It hadn't been hard to befriend Laura. Her breaktimes were spent sitting alone at the cafeteria down by A&E, nursing a cup of tea and reading a novel or a self-help book she'd produce from her bag. Lonely. Desperate for love.

Laura had been impressed by Annabel's credentials. Flattered by her interest. Annabel told her she was attached to the hospital's psychiatry department, and Laura had never questioned it. They'd formed a relationship of sorts. At first, Annabel hadn't known what to do with it, just that she knew it was worth cultivating the one person whose hatred of Dr Oliver Roberts outstripped her own.

But as she listened to the younger woman and encouraged her to talk about her background and heard the high-pitched sharpness of her voice when she talked about Dr William Kingsley, and commiserated with her wish to move out of nursing and become an artist, something began to crystallize inside Annabel's mind, hard and bright as a diamond. A way to do him damage, and to relaunch her professional career in a spectacular fashion that would make all the doubters and haters sit up and take notice.

It hadn't been easy. There had been times she'd wanted to yell at Laura, with her fatuous new-ageisms, her blessings and her peace and lights. But she'd stuck at it, offering her services as a therapist for free, out of the goodness of her heart.

TAMMY COHEN

Laura had been so pathetically grateful for her attention, so eager to please, and Annabel knew exactly how to play it so that she always left her craving more. It hadn't been hard to persuade her that art therapy would be the perfect career for her, building on her nursing experience while also providing an outlet for her creativity. Getting her the post at The Meadows had been more difficult, but a phone call to Roberts with a personal recommendation had done the trick. She'd played on his guilt. He must have thought appointing this friend of his old mentor a small price to pay for appeasing his own conscience.

As if anything he could do would ever be enough to make up for what she'd lost.

He was leading the life she should have had. He had taken everything she valued and hadn't given her a second thought. Well, that was about to change.

Alone at her desk, Annabel leafed through the manuscript that would re-establish her as one of modern psychiatry's most glittering stars.

Everyone knew about Laura Whittaker. The public couldn't get enough of the art therapist turned murderer. Every day the papers raked up some tiny new detail about her life.

But no one knew her better than the woman who'd treated her for the best part of a decade.

Only Annabel Dunmore could tell the real story of what had motivated Laura to use hypnosis against two vulnerable patients in order to persuade them to kill themselves. Only Annabel Dunmore knew why she'd nearly killed Hannah Lovell.

Her book, all five hundred pages of it, was the

362

consummate study of a sociopathic mind, a masterclass in getting inside a killer's head.

Of course, she'd left out her own role in it all. The way she'd be encouraging one day and cold the next, leading Laura on until she would do anything to win her approval.

All Laura had ever really wanted was someone to mother her and, occasionally, Annabel had done that. Not often. Just enough to leave her craving more and distraught the next day, when Annabel would return to playing the detached psychotherapist.

She'd left out how she'd planted the seed in Laura's mind that helping Sofia and Charlie succeed at what they'd tried so many times before would be doing them a kindness, as well as destroying Oliver Roberts' reputation. She'd left out how she'd smoothed over Laura's doubts following Sofia's death, and then Charlie's, assuring her that they were in a better place and were grateful to her.

In the book, Annabel was a therapist, nothing more. And though she professed 'concern' about some of the things her patient had revealed in their confidential sessions, Laura Whittaker had never confessed to any criminal wrongdoing, so no finger of blame could be pointed her way.

It had crossed her mind to change her name, because of the link with Roberts during the Westbridge House days. But really, who would believe she could have had anything to do with the deaths of people she'd never met in a place she'd never been? She was planning to make a point of the connection and claim that Laura had sought her out specifically because of her past link with Roberts, though she'd hidden that from Annabel. And of course, she'd say that Laura had never used his full name in their sessions either. Revealing identities of patients or staff at the clinic would have been a serious breach of confidentiality. Annabel wouldn't have been able to continue to treat Laura if she'd known there was a personal past connection, no matter how tenuous, but as it was, she couldn't possibly be held responsible. The only person who could refute this version of events was Roberts himself, but she very much doubted he'd risk the publicity, particularly when he knew she'd just deny ever making that call to recommend Laura.

Who'd believe anything he said now?

Besides, changing her name would defeat the whole object. When this book was published the brightest luminaries in the field of academic psychiatric research would be talking about Professor Annabel Dunmore in hushed, reverential tones. It would be as if all these years in the wilderness were wiped out in one fell swoop.

At her desk, Annabel picked up the stack of pages and held them in her hands. So pleasantly weighty. She felt an immense swell of pride. And what made the feeling even sweeter was knowing there was no chance of Laura surfacing to give her side of the story.

It was always going to be a risk that, when Laura was finally caught – or rather, when Annabel, apparently fighting with her conscience, turned her in – she'd turn against her mentor, just as Roberts had done. Annabel had prepared for that, of course, made reams of notes showing Laura as a deluded fantasist, obsessed with her to the point that, if she thought she'd been rejected, she'd do anything to get back at Annabel. Even accuse her of murder.

Still it was a relief when Laura killed herself, rendering all of these contingency plans redundant. The most popular theory was that she couldn't live with herself after the third murder. While she'd been able to square the deaths of Sofia Redding and Charlie Chadwick as mercy killings, Drew Abbott had been nothing but a cold-blooded assault carried out in a panic to save her own skin when she realized he was about to call the police. Faced with the enormity of what she'd done, she had hurled herself off the cliff at Beachy Head.

Only Annabel knew that, before she got there, she had made a call from a phone box. To the pay-as-you-go phone Annabel kept only for Laura. Only Annabel knew just how devastated she'd been to be told they would not be able to see each other any more. Ever.

Poor Laura, dead. Oliver Roberts ruined. And her own career on the brink of an astonishing revival.

Really, it was hard to see how things could have worked out better.

57

Louise

Louise Bradford stepped off the bus and made her way slowly along the main road, largely abandoned at this time of night apart from a man, hood up against the rain, smoking by the pub door and a straggle of teenagers outside the fried-chicken shop. She was wearing a cheap, beige mackintosh which strained across her broad shoulders, and her swollen legs were crammed into flat, brown boots.

It was a dark night, and the street lights illuminated the damp, litter-strewn pavements. Louise frowned as a gust of wind blew an empty polystyrene burger box across the road. People had no respect.

As she turned left into a side road, a white van drove past, throwing up a spray which spattered over her mac, leaving dirty drip marks. She took a deep breath in. Counted to five. And then let it out, again for a count of five.

Coleridge Court was in the middle of a cul-de-sac two roads down to the right, a drab, grey building with rows of small, mean windows and a sign outside that was partly broken so it read 'IDGE COURT: RESIDENTIAL CARE HOME FOR THE ELDERLY'.

Louise made her way around the side of the building, entering a code into the keypad by the back door and letting herself in.

She advanced along the corridor to the staffroom. 'All right?' said Joy, the night manager of whom Louise often thought no one could less live up to their name. Joy was slumped on the boxy, brown two-seater sofa watching a reality-TV show on her laptop.

Louise opened her locker and folded up her mac and put it inside. Then she took a nylon pinafore from a hook and fastened it over her shapeless brown dress. The buttons strained across her chest.

'Diet not going too well then?' remarked Joy.

'Not really. No willpower,' said Louise.

'You don't want to put on any more. That's the largest size we can get.'

There was a note of disapproval in the night manager's voice, as if she regarded Louise's expanding girth as a mark of character weakness.

There was a small round mirror attached to the inside of the locker door and Louise caught a glimpse of herself in it, though normally she avoided her own reflection whenever possible. The soft, floury folds of cheek and chin seemed to belong to someone else, just like the badly permed hair. It had been a wrench letting the mousy brown grow back after all those years dyeing it lustrous black.

'You'll do the dining room first, yeah?' said Joy, eyes once more fixed on her computer screen. It wasn't really a question. 'And then the activities room. Mr Turner had an accident in there, just as the day shift was knocking off. They did what they could, but the carpet will need a thorough going-over.'

Louise went into the back hallway and opened up a full-length cupboard, extracting the vacuum cleaner and the trolley of cleaning products. She was already wheezing. She wasn't used to carrying around so much weight. She made her way first to the dining room, as instructed. It was a cheerless room, painted a drab institutional beige and lit by a sickly, greenish light. The only things on the wall were a laminated copy of the fire regulations and the stunted remains of a home-made paper chain left over from last Christmas and fixed to the wall with yellowing tape.

After she'd finished, Louise wheeled the trolley to the activities room, instantly spotting the site of Mr Turner's accident, a large, dark brown stain on the grey carpet. She sighed. But instead of getting to work, she went back to the doorway and looked up and down the corridor, even though she was sure she was safe. Joy never came out of the staffroom if she could help it. And the night carers weren't due to show up for another hour. It probably wasn't legal for only one permanent member of staff to be on the premises, but the care home's owners were cutting corners wherever they could. Slashing employee hours, turning a blind eye to cleaning staff who didn't exactly meet the requirements for the DBS check but were prepared to accept below minimum wage, cash in hand.

Sickening how little priority was given to the elderly.

Making her way along the corridor, Louise avoided the cramped lift, where she knew there was a CCTV camera trained on the doors, and slipped up the back stairs to the second floor.

There was a low groaning noise from behind the first door she passed, and she made. a mental note to look in on her way back. Mrs Goldstein was in constant discomfort now. It was nearly time.

Like all the rooms, the third door on the left had a laminated notice on it with the resident's name printed in heavy black type. **Mrs Barbara Whittaker.** In an instant, Louise had turned the handle silently and slid inside, quietly closing the door behind her.

'Hello, Mum,' she whispered to the twisted shape under the sheets.

'Did you think I wasn't coming?'

She lowered herself heavily into the armchair next to the bed and reached across to take hold of one of the tiny, clawed hands.

'You know I'll never leave you, don't you, Mum?'

Through the semi-darkness came a low moan, like an animal in distress.

'Don't be upset. There are a few little things I need to sort out, a few wrongs to be righted, but we'll be together soon and, wherever they move you, I'll find you.

'We'll always have each other. Aren't we blessed?'

Acknowledgements

They All Fall Down is my ninth novel, and the more books I write the more I realize how much publishing is a true team effort. What a stroke of luck, then, to have the best team in the business!

At Curtis Brown, I'd like to thank first and foremost my brilliant agent, Felicity Blunt, to whom I owe so much. And Melissa Pimentel, whose name in my inbox always means good news. Thanks also to Luke Speed, Jessica Whitlum-Cooper and Enrichetta Frezzato.

Transworld continues to be the most supportive publisher a writer could wish for. Thanks to my editor Jane Lawson for her insight and enthusiasm and for always being in my corner. And to Alison Barrow, Becky Hunter, Alice Murphy-Pyle, Richard Ogle, Larry Finlay and all the others who make it such a special place.

Writing about mental illness is a responsibility and I give heartfelt thanks to consultant psychiatrist Dr Mark Salter for taking time out from his busy schedule to answer my (occasionally ludicrous) questions. Thanks also to Dr Roma Cartwright for her valuable input. As always, any mistakes are completely down to me.

Thanks to all my writer and blogger friends who make this weird, wonderful job infinitely more weird and wonderful, including Amanda Jennings, Lisa Jewell,

Marnie Riches, all the Killer Women, the Prime Writers, Anne Cater and Tracy Fenton.

Finally, a huge thank-you to the readers who keep buying my books and writing reviews. None of this would be possible without you.

"A downright chilling psychological suspense novel. Perfect holiday reading."
—*The Globe and Mail*

"An exciting, chillingly complex psychological thriller."
—*Publishers Weekly*

"Satisfying twists and turns. Cohen's holiday-tinged psychological thriller is perfect for fans of Gillian Flynn's *Gone Girl*."
—*Library Journal*

A novel full of twists, surprising turns, and suspense, *Dying for Christmas* is Tammy Cohen's most disturbing psychological thriller yet.

Out Christmas shopping one December afternoon, Jessica Gould meets the charming Dominic Lacey and agrees to go home with him for a drink. What follows are Twelve Days of Christmas from hell, as Lacey holds Jessica captive. Each day he gifts her with one item from his twisted past—his dead sister's favorite toy, disturbing family photos, a box of teeth. As the days pass and the "gifts" become darker and darker, Jessica realizes that Lacey has a plan for her, and he never intends to let her go.

But Jessica has a secret of her own . . . a secret that may just mean she has a chance to make it out alive.

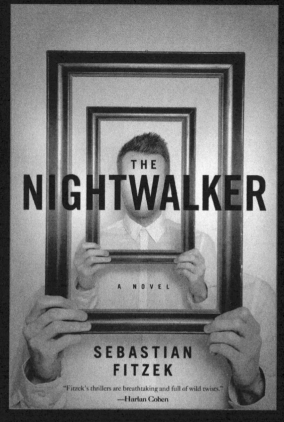

A psychological thrill-ride of a novel that finds an insomniac wondering if his nighttime excursions have turned into something beyond his imagination.

As a young man, Leon Nader suffered from insomnia. As a sleepwalker, he even turned to violence during his nocturnal excursions and had psychiatric treatment for his condition. Eventually, he was convinced he had been cured—but one day, years later, Leon's wife disappears from their apartment under mysterious circumstances. Could it be that his illness has broken out again?

In order to find out how he behaves in his sleep, Leon fits a movement-activated camera to his forehead. When he looks at the video the next morning, he makes a discovery that bursts the borders of his imagination. His nocturnal personality goes through a door that is totally unknown to him and descends into the darkness . . .

STEVE MOSBY

YOU CAN RUN

"THRILLER READERS WHO YEARN FOR INTRIGUE,
SWIFT PACING, AND SURREAL HAPPENINGS
WILL ENJOY EVERY WORD OF STEVE MOSBY."

-NEW YORK JOURNAL OF BOOKS

A NOVEL

A page-turning psychological thriller, the new novel from CWA Dagger
winner Steve Mosby explores the blurred lines between truth and fiction.

When a car crashes into a garage on an ordinary street, the attending officer is
shocked to look inside the damaged building and discover a woman imprisoned within. As the remains of several other victims are found in the attached
house, police believe they have finally identified the Red River Killer—a man who
has been abducting women for nearly twenty years and taunting the police with
notes about his crimes. But now the main suspect, John Blythe, is on the run.

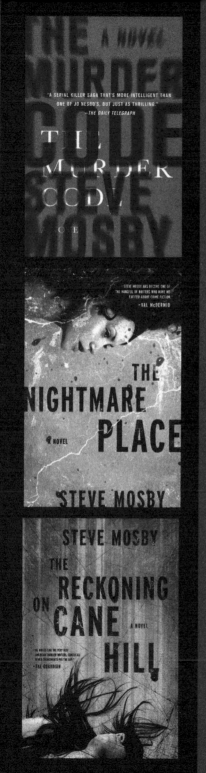

We hope that you enjoyed this book.

To share your thoughts, feel free to connect with us on social media:

 Twitter.com/Pegasus_Books

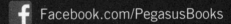 Facebook.com/PegasusBooks

 Instagram.com/Pegasus_Books

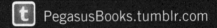 PegasusBooks.tumblr.com

To receive special offers and news about our latest titles, sign up for our newsletter at
www.pegasusbooks.com.